WHAT HAPPENS IN VEGAS, DIES IN VEGAS

Advance Praise for
What Happens in Vegas, Dies in Vegas

5 Stars: "*Things To Do In Denver When Your Un-Dead* was one of the most refreshing and original books I have read in a long time and the sequel is just as exciting as the first. In fact it may just be better than the first .... Exceptionally well-written and entertaining."

—Jerzri's Nightmares

"*Vegas* is non-stop action that will leave you with whiplash .... Stone leaves you gasping for breath by the end and of course, enjoys taunting the reader with the prospect of a third book in the series, which I will be waiting anxiously to read."

—Shay Fabbro, award-winning author of the *Portal of Destiny* series

5 Stars: "No reader could possibly feel slighted when all is read and done. It is a cracking good yarn from first to final page, no question .... Mark has cemented himself solidly into the position of Master in my self-created niche of Paranormal Suspense Thriller writing. His command of his art grows exponentially with each work of his that I read .... Two very enthusiastic thumbs up for a job well and properly done."

—Jeffrey Hollar, The Latinum Vault

"In a sequel guaranteed to please both new readers and fans of his unconventionally cool debut novel, *Things to Do In Denver When You're Undead*, Stone continues to develop the ultimate monster hunter, Kalevi Hakala, a flinty urban paladin of truth and champion of transmundane justice ... Don't expect a minute of down-time, for Stone is a zero tolerance taskmaster who brings a complicated plotline and well fleshed-out characters to heel and makes it look easy. What you *can* expect is for Stone to surprise you repeatedly, satisfy you completely and leave you wanting more."

—AJ Aalto, author of *Touched*

Praise for
Things to Do in Denver When You're Un-Dead

5 Stars: "If you crave a really enjoyable Paranormal Suspense Thriller to read, THIS is your book. It grabs you from the very first page and drags you along (snarling for you to keep up) and dumps you at the feet of one of THE most unexpected plot twists of an ending that I have ever read. While this novel is Mark's first, it reads as a cohesive, refined product that leaves me salivating for its forthcoming sequel. "

—Jeffrey Hollar, The Latinum Vault

"If you like quick wit, sadistic charm, and bad-ass gadgets, then you will enjoy the hell out of this book … no pun intended."

—Shay Fabbro, award-winning author of the *Portal of Destiny* series

Five stars: "This book was an absolute pleasure to read. It is witty, funny, dramatic and a well thought out paranormal with very fine storytelling. I couldn't put it down! That's a first for me in a long time …. I plan to be a loyal fan. Well done, Mark, and please, write me more?!"

—Clarrissa Lee Moon, author of the series, *The Nightwolves* and *Celeste Nites*

"I have really enjoyed reading this book…. The story could just be one of guns, blood and guts and magic, but … Mark Everett Stone has made these characters seem real."

—Michele Herbert, Fantasy Book Review

"This is not a story for the faint of heart or stomach, nor for those wanting a plot with any connection to reality. Personally, I'm really looking forward to the promised sequel."

—Gordon Long, TCM Reviews

"A fantastic read and very easy to follow. The way Mark combines magicians, zombies and super ghouls with a Bogart-style ultra sarcastic officer of the 'Bureau' makes you want to keep on reading. I highly recommend this for everyone—not just those into stories of the un-dead."

—G.R. Holton, author of Soleri, Guardian's Alliance and Deep Screams

"Five stars, two thumbs, fantastic! From the moment I began the first page to the final flip of the last, I was hooked .... The writing is sharp, fast and engaging. The characters are fun and/or not so fun in all the right places. Mark has captured the soul of his lead character so well that it's like the reader is sitting having a $300 bottle of vodka, chased with an aromatic and equally expensive cigar, while Kal spins tales of his heyday, punctuated by live action reenactments so real you wish you hadn't eaten dinner."

—Patti Larsen, author of *Fresco, Wasteland* (10/2011), *The Diamond City* (2012), and *The Ghost Boy of MacKenzie House* (2012)

"The blending of dark twisted humor in this chilling tale is utterly perfect, written with a sure hand. Comedic timing is everything, and author Stone has perfected the classic one-liner.... Make no mistake folks, this isn't for the faint hearted ... the sarcasm is used as a brief respite in the fastest paced action horror that I have read in a very long time."

—Suzannah Burke, aka Stacey Danson, Author of *Empty Chairs*

"In a first and quite brilliant novel, Stone proves himself equally adept at feverishly fast-paced action, edgy wit and banter, and the weaving of a richly satisfying and fresh world of mystery and intrigue. Write on, my friend."

—Michelle Izmaylov, author of *The Galacteran Legacy: Galaxy Watch*

WHAT HAPPENS IN VEGAS, DIES IN VEGAS

FROM THE FILES OF THE BSI

BOOK TWO

MARK EVERETT STONE

CAMEL PRESS

Seattle, WA

CAMEL PRESS

A Camel Press book published by Epicenter Press

For more information, contact www.camelpress.com
www.markeverettstone.camelpress.com

Cover design by Sabrina Sun

What Happens in Vegas, Dies in Vegas
Copyright © 2012 by Mark Everett Stone

ISBN (Paper): 978-1-60381-868-1
ISBN (eBook): 978-1-60381-869-8
Library of Congress Control Number: 2011942043

Printed in the United States of America

This one I dedicate to my sons, Aeden and Gabriel.
Hope I have made you proud.

Acknowledgments

First and foremost, I would like to thank my fellow writers:. Shay, Clarrissa, Bob H., Patti, CG, Elise, Lisa (the Queen of Horror), Jeffrey, Nicole, Michelle, Jenni, India, Alberta, Al, CP, Denise, Doug, Drew, Heikki, Charlotte, AJ, and all the rest. Thanks for all the support and interesting conversation. You help keep the juices flowing.

And of course, to my wife Brandie. She puts up with my BS and keeps me trucking down the road of righteousness.

Contents

Chapter One

Kal

The Apologetic Dead

Rock chips scored my cheek as a bullet smacked into the cave wall not more than three inches from my nose. A fragment of the shattered bullet creased my temple, stinging like a sonofagun. I knew, however, that once the adrenaline high wore off—assuming I survived the next few minutes—the real price of pain would have to be paid.

Head wounds are the worst, because they bleed something fierce and no matter what overly macho men might say, chicks do *not* dig scars.

"Dammit, Canton!" I roared into the green-lit tunnel as I scrambled backwards, blood running down my face. Bullets pocked the tunnel walls, following my hasty retreat. "Where are the grenades?"

Canton's deep voice boomed back. "Mouth has 'em! What's going on, white boy?"

"What's going on are dead guys with freaking guns!" Another bullet whizzed past my ear. I returned fire with the Lahti, then hightailed it down the tunnel as fast as I could, hoping that I wouldn't get shot in the ass.

The team and I, minus Winch—our sniper, who had stayed with the Jeep—had entered the labyrinthine tunnels deep in the guts of the Organ Mountains that morning. A couple hours later (after retracing our steps countless times) we reached our destination, the hiding place for Big Owl's Cloak of Feathers.

Big Owl was a boogeyman in Apache folklore, a giant human (something like an ogre) who took the form of a horned owl big enough to carry off children. Like most stories pertaining to the

1

World Under (that shadowy Other Place Supernaturals hail from), this one contained a grain of truth. Actually, a whole beach's worth. The reality was an artifact—a feathery cloak that allowed the wearer to shape-shift into a giant owl. Hence, Big Owl. What the Native Americans lacked in the colorful name category, they more than made up for in accurate oral history.

Canton Alsate, my Mescalero Apache friend and comrade-in-arms, managed to unearth the location of the Cloak's resting place, a place called Cave of the Foolish People, smack dab in the center of a mountain range. The Organs were a serrated, severe set of mountains that thrust up like knives from the desert between the cities of Las Cruces and Alamagordo in southern New Mexico.

I bumped hard into Mouth, our hand-to-hand expert, as she emerged from a side tunnel, nearly turning her into cave pizza. "What kind of dead guys?" she asked, her matte black Desert Eagle at the ready. "Ghouls again?" By the green chemical glare of the big glow stick Velcro-ed to my chest, she looked rather undead herself, her delicate china doll features a bilious olive.

"Ghouls?" I shuddered. Six months ago a seriously disturbed (by that I mean freaking psychopathically off-your-bloody-rocker nuts) magician and former Bureau of Supernatural Investigation teammate of mine, had tried to have me digested by a pack of super-steroid enhanced ghouls she'd created. Fortunately, I'd managed to avoid becoming an undead appetizer and eventually blew her head off with a shotgun. Considering it was either she or I, my choice was an obvious one. Kal: 1, Psychopathic Bitch: 0.

"No, not ghouls. Revenants," I panted. "At least four, all with antique Colt side arms."

She shuddered as Canton ran in from another side tunnel. I couldn't blame her. Revenants were the undead equivalent of unstoppable vengeance on a stick, spirits of the dead stuffed back into their own corpses and rendered virtually unkillable unless nuclear weapons were at your disposal. Think of Brandon Lee in *The Crow*, but smellier and a lot, LOT harder on the eyes.

Even Canton, who wasn't afraid of anything except losing to

an inside straight, looked concerned. "C'mon, Mouth!" he shot, sweat streaming down his swarthy face. "Hurry up and hand out the grenades."

"Damn!" she swore. "I left them with Winch!"

Canton cussed up a blue streak just as a voice slid down the tunnel toward us. *"Give it up, son. You can't stop us, sorry to say."* The words, carried on some other medium than air, slithered into our ears like skittering insects. The revenant, a man dressed in a U.S. Cavalry uniform circa 1870, stepped into the light of the glow stick, its green illumination doing nothing for his complexion. No amount of Proactiv could help *that* skin.

In life, judging by his saggy clothes, he might have been a big man, easily 6'3" or so, but time and mummification had shortened him up somewhat. Parchment thin skin covered his skull under a dusty, crumbling, navy blue cavalry hat that hung at what was once a jaunty angle, but looked rather obscene in light of circumstances. Stringy, colorless hair hung about his shoulders like dusty cobwebs. What really frosted my cake, though, were the two brown, very lifelike eyes that blazed wetly from his desiccated face.

I held up a hand. "Listen, fella, we don't want trouble. We'll be on our way."

His eyes met mine and the force of his regard turned my bowels to water. *"Sorry, son, but orders is orders. I gotta kill the lot of you for trespassin'."* That whispery, insect-like voice carried a wealth of regret and sorrow. Just what we needed—undead that were really, *really* sorry.

Interesting.

Without hesitation, all three of us fired, bullets pummeling the dead man. Bits and pieces of shrunken flesh spattered the tunnel walls. While Canton and Mouth unloaded into the revenant's skull, I aimed for his gun hand. After six rounds from the Lahti (a 9mm Finnish relic from my grandfather that resembled a German Luger), the revenant's hand decided to separate from the rest of him (I couldn't think of the poor guy as an 'it') and the Colt dropped to the tunnel floor.

"Stop!" I yelled and, like the highly trained professionals they were, my two companions ceased fire. Wasting no time, I ran forward and threw a kick at the undead that hurled him back almost clean out of his boots. He was a lot lighter than he looked, a corpse anchored to gravity by the thinnest of margins. I retrieved the Colt, the dead man's hand still gripping the ivory handle. His flesh felt like dried leaves and squirmed in the palm of my hand.

Gross.

"Let's boogie!"

We turned to leave just as the revenant's re-enforcements arrived.

Rounds streaked past as we beat feet, following the glowing telltales we'd left behind like breadcrumbs so we wouldn't wander those tunnels for ... well ... forever. A tearing pain scalded the fat of my left side and a sticky wetness began to ooze. A quick assessment showed me that the wound was merely a graze, but still painful. Without a magician for a healing, it was going to leave a mark, but it also ruined a perfectly good blue Ralph Lauren polo I'd just purchased the day before. If the previous revenant hadn't sounded so sorrowful, so regretful as it tried to kill us, I might have turned right then to open up a can of Finnish whoop-ass.

And probably would have been shot into itty-bitty bloody chunks, too.

Behind me I heard Canton grunt in pain and I knew he'd been hit as well. A few steps later we came to the safety of a left turn, out of the direct line of fire.

"You okay, Canton?" I panted, hand pressing against the sticky wetness in my side.

"Sonofabitch shot me in the butt!" he cried while attempting to stem the flow of blood from the affected area.

Sometimes the little editor in your head is asleep at the wheel and you say or do something stupid. In my defense, the little editor must have gone home for a nooner because I laughed hard enough to put as stitch in my already abused side. Beside me, Mouth did the same.

4

"Yeah, laugh it up, white boy," Canton groused, not once breaking stride. "Wait until we get outta here; then I'm shooting you in the keister. See how you like it!"

I was saved a sarky reply by revenants appearing from the cross tunnels in front of us, Colts raised, cutting off escape.

Before they could shred us into bite-sized morsels, we were among them. Too close for firearms, we drew blades. In my case, it was a fourteen inch Bowie custom made and given to me by my father. Its twin was wielded expertly by Canton, who was doing his best to fillet the revenant to my right while I grabbed the gun hand of the one on the left and pulled him off balance. I rammed the blade into a leathery neck and twisted, drawing back for another stab.

"*So, sorry, so sorry, so sorry,*" the dead man said in that annoying insect whisper that made me want to scrub my ears out with Comet. Mouth filled his undead jaws with eight inches of K-bar, muffling his apologies.

All too aware of the revenant coming up from behind, I chopped down with the Bowie and separated his gun hand from wrist. A trick worth repeating. If I kept it up, I'd have a very valuable collection of antique revolvers and enough disembodied hands for a host of *Addams Family* sequels.

Had the revenants been truly focused on taking us out instead of feeling sad and apologizing up a storm, things would have been much worse for mama Hakala's fair-haired son. As it was, all three of us had plenty of aches and pains to plague us over the next few days.

"Sorry, sorry. We're so sorry, son."

"What are they bitchin' about?" Mouth panted as she grabbed hold of Canton's arm and helped him shamble on.

"I think they're compelled to protect this place," I said, clutching at the burning pain in my side. Warm stickiness still flowed over and around my hand. "If they really wanted to kill us, we'd be dead already."

"Then who the hell sicced them on us?"

I pointed to Canton. "Talk to the guy with the hole in his butt."

She turned to the aforementioned perforated individual. "What?"

Canton winced with every step. "Makes sense. My ancestors were at war with the U.S. government, and I can tell you we fought dirty and hard." He bit his lip. "I reckon that Big Owl's Cloak was set in here and they turned those soldiers into watchdogs. Question is, where's the Cloak?"

"I don't know," came my reply. "The cave where it was supposed to be was empty except for four dead guys with guns."

Mouth gaped at me. "Four?"

I did the math just as we rounded the corner and saw daylight … as well as the fourth cavalryman silhouetted against the opening, twin guns in hand. "Oh, crap …"

"*Sorry, so sorry, I don't want to do this,*" he mourned right before he exploded with a deafening concussion. Pieces of shoe-leather-dry corpse pelted us the same moment the pressure wave knocked us ass over appetite. Our bodies became coated with bits of rock and we breathed in several lungfuls of dust.

Gagging and coughing, we picked ourselves off the ground and staggered toward the exit. A shadowy silhouette half-blocked the light.

"You guys look terrible," the figure said in a high-pitched voice.

I rubbed grit out of my eyes and spat it out of my teeth, along with revenant dust. Once again … gross. I really did *not* want to think about how much revenant I'd taken into my lungs. "What the hell did you use?"

"Just some dynamite. A couple of sticks."

A bit of shredded leather rolled over my boot and joined with other pieces that were doing their best to freak me out by moving. Pieces' parts shouldn't move, damnit! I knew it would be only a matter of minutes before the undead soldier put himself back together.

Crap … I hated undead. A lot. Even the apologetic ones.

Mouth and Winch turned a little green around the gills as they watched bits of revenant roll together and reassemble all in *Terminator 2* style. It took no effort to shoo the lot of us outside before the other unhappy undead made an appearance. Canton wore an amused smile, no doubt proud of his ancestors' handiwork. I resisted the urge to plant a boot on his leaking backside as we headed toward the Jeep.

By the time Winch had us on the road to Las Cruces, Canton's jeans were soaked in blood that was also staining the tan leather seats. I myself started to become dizzy with the loss of my own precious fluids.

"Why was the cave empty, kemosabe?" I asked, holding my wadded up shirt to the hole the Supernatural's bullet had put in my side. It was a clean graze, but it really started to sting like a bitch.

"Hell, white boy, I have no idea," he groused, sitting on his own wadded up t-shirt, his skin a burnished copper in the bright sunshine. "My old man said it would be there."

Canton had asked all the Mescalero tribal elders about the Cloak and they had all sung the same tune: 'It's in the Cave of the Foolish People, safe.'

Well, we'd found the tunnels to the Cave of the Foolish People only after trespassing onto government property (White Sands Missile Range). It took three days of searching to find those tunnels. Three days of baking in the winter sun of the deep Southwest (at least in Minnesota it was properly cold and snowy) to find the hidden tunnel entrance and two hours of exploring through the gut-rock of the mountains to find the Cave. That cave was big enough to park a semi in and I had found nada. Jack squat. Just some mummified remains and a few crude paintings on the rough walls.

It was only when I first heard a dry, papery voice say, *"Son, I wish you hadn't come here,"* that I knew we were screwed.

Mouth grinned at me, her overlarge teeth shining. "I reckon the Bureau found the Cloak first and left those revenants for the next party of idiots to find. That would be us, in case you hadn't noticed."

I raised an eyebrow. "Oh? You think?" My sarcasm was lost on her. No surprise there. Mouth was pretty much clueless to the whole damn planet except when it came to killing Supernaturals with her bare hands, and I loved her dearly for that.

Yeah, I know what you're thinking. How can I have such a vicious outlook on the Supernatural community? Easy ... go find the remains of unsuspecting Straights (i.e. regular humans) who have had run-ins with Supernaturals and, after you've wiped their guts off the draperies, come find me and try to be all touchy-feely. Don't believe me? Most people die in terror and unimaginable agony at the hands (or tentacles, whatever) of their Supernatural attackers, screaming until their throats collapse with the strain. It's how my sister died ... it's how they all die.

My former job at the Bureau of Supernatural Investigations was to kill them before they killed us and I did it for ten long years.

And I was very, *very* good at it.

Currently, I was using those skills to try to find an artifact. Most artifacts, however, were in the grasping hands of various world governments. There were a few—a precious few—that still remained unfound.

As far as the Bureau was concerned, I was a rotting lump of meat buried six feet under in a Minnesota graveyard, killed by a vampire at the same time I drove a stake through its putrid, black heart. I would have been worm food but for a magician who was good with stasis, healing, and soul-storing spells to bring me back to the land of the living. Thanks to my actually being dead, I no longer suffered Interdiction, the spell placed on everyone in the know about the Bureau's existence. It kept peoples' mouth shut, which was a good thing because if the Straights ever did find out about Supernaturals and the World Under, there would be mass panic and religious hysteria the likes of which the world has never seen.

No longer under the Bureau's employ, I had focused my energies on finding a way to kill the thing that had murdered my sister right in front of my eyes twenty years earlier. Thanks to the aforementioned psychopath who had tried to turn me into ghoul chow, I had the weapon. All I needed was the ammunition ... hence, my search for an artifact.

Chapter Two

Kal

A New Direction

A spike of nausea pierced my stomach as Winch administered a shot of morphine just before she stitched the hole in my side. Then a blessed lassitude settled over my brain and I didn't mind the large gauge needle punching through my skin. I didn't care. The motel bed was oddly soft and comfy enough for me to half-doze while she worked.

All of us had basic medical training, enough to qualify as EMTs. A 'patch 'em up and send 'em back out' kind of training. If we'd had access to a magician, we wouldn't even have needed a needle and thread. Hell, there wouldn't be any scars. Usually. I was one of the 'lucky' ones who had a few. Okay, a lot. My torso was covered in thin, ridged burn scars from silver wire that had absorbed enough magical energy to become red-hot, fusing the silver to my flesh. The damage had been so bad that not even magical healing could erase all the evidence. I don't recommend that as a party trick. I'd barely survived and, consequently, I wouldn't be posing for The Boys of the BSI calendars anytime soon. Some people think scars are cool, but not the kind that bring gorge to your throat.

Despite my disfigured torso, Winch worked impassively and with an economy of motion that most docs would envy. Pretty in a Betty Boop sort of way, she looked like a dizzy brunette without a care in the world, a look she cultivated to hide the razor-wire sharp mind housed in her skull. We were lucky to have her.

Three months earlier, Canton had asked me who we should recruit, who would be stupid enough to risk being caught by the BSI and magically lobotomized by government magicians. Naturally, I thought of Winch.

Last time I'd seen her was when she left my team, a two-year vet, no longer wet behind the ears and one of the ten best snipers in existence. I mean, she was a 'shoot the ass off a humming bird at a thousand yards with a single shot' kind of good. Her one flaw—and it was a doozy—was a penchant for using explosives without the know-how to handle them safely. To me, it was a miracle she had survived two years in the Bureau without blowing herself into strawberry jam. Not to mention anyone else.

After her stint, she'd bought a gym, the kind of trendy place where rich women and men go to work off the holiday season flab for a ridiculous amount of money. The cards and letters she'd sent me (all carefully screened by the BSI) had been cheery enough, but there was an undercurrent of unease that told me she missed the perilous life of an agent. Which put her in the 'crazy as a bedbug' category because the obscenely high mortality rate in the Bureau would have sent any sane person running for the hills.

Canton and I had walked into her fancy schmancy gym in Irvine, CA, and were immediately greeted by a bit of lycra-coated eye candy behind a granite-topped reception desk.

"Hello, welcome to La Petit. How may I be of assistance?" said the redhead, my favorite flavor, with a wide plastic smile. Briefly I wondered if she practiced that grin in front of a mirror.

I held up a finger to Canton, cutting off his standard "You can help me find my orgasm" line, and gave the woman my best hundred-watt smile. "Hello, we're here to see Diana."

Her smile faded a little around the edges. "I'm afraid she's rather busy, Mr.—?"

"Just tell her that the Finn and Injun Joe are here."

Apparently my non-PC reference to Canton as an Injun offended her sense of morality because she crossed her arms under her magnificent lycra-coated bosom and treated me to a "thou art beneath me" glare. Didn't really faze me … I'd been glared at by professionals.

Canton snorted, stepped into the door of the big mirrored

room, cupped his hands around his mouth and bellowed at the top of his very healthy lungs, "Winch! Get your lazy butt out here, woman!"

Tubby and thin people of all flavors stopped doing whatever torturous things they were doing with whatever machines they happened to be on and stared, disbelieving, at the two of us. I know what they saw. Me, a tall, blond, broad-shouldered, man in a blue Tommy Hilfiger polo and Wrangler jeans over black biker boots and Canton, a swarthy, snake-lean and muscled native American in jeans, cowboy boots, and a dark blue button down, his marine-style haircut razored to perfection.

"Gentlemen, please," said an equally lycra-covered male version of the receptionist, his muscles bulging under the tight outfit. Classically handsome, he had the look of someone who grazed rather than ate.

I bet if I waved a cheeseburger in his direction, he'd die of a heart attack.

"Easy, Tex," I soothed. "We're here to see the boss."

Lycra-boy was prevented from delivering a no doubt scathing reply by a squeal of pure feminine excitement. Winch hit Canton at Mach 3, wrapping her arms and legs around the delighted Apache.

"Ohmi*god!*" she enthused, peppering his face with machine-gun kisses. "I can't believe you're here! It's so good to see you! Oh, I've missed you so much, big boy!" Then the barrage of kisses stopped. She had seen me.

Her jaw dropped. I mean, really dropped. Not just an expression, but the real thing. I guess she didn't expect to see a dead man in her gym. At least one that wasn't undead.

"You sonofabitch," she said in a shocked whisper after untangling herself from Canton's iron embrace. Approaching slowly, she raised a hand to my cheek. "I don't believe it."

My smile could have lit Wrigley Field. "Reports of my death—"

Smack!

"Ow!"

11

I'd forgotten how *strong* she was. The red handprint on my cheek throbbed in time with my heartbeat and felt scorched onto my skin. "Damn, Winch, it's good to see you, too." At least she didn't hit as hard as Mouth. When I'd showed up at her place in Chicago, she'd dropped me to the ground with an overhand right.

Next thing I knew I was covered in 120 lbs of enthusiastic female as Winch covered me like a second skin, climbing high enough to whisper into my ear. "You jerkface! BB told me you were dead! I *mourned* you, you idiot!"

"When did you talk to BB?" I gasped as her strong arms almost crushed the breath from my lungs and bruised ribs.

Her breath tickled my neck. "Two months ago, moron." I could feel a salty wetness against my skin.

"Why?"

"I was thinking about re-upping. I'm bored here."

Perfect. "Well, I'm putting together a team …"

Her head jerked back and fawn brown eyes stared into mine. "A team?"

"Yeah," I said into her smile. "But not like you think. Outside the government."

"How dangerous?"

"We'll all probably die."

She kissed me soundly, her breath smelling of peppermint. "Sounds like fun!"

Which brings me back to the present, where a particularly hard jab with a needle had just pierced the morphine cotton that wrapped my brain. "Ouch!"

"Don't be a baby," muttered Winch, tongue between her teeth.

"You've never been shot, have you?"

"Nope. Never had that privilege."

"Then hush up."

Once again, the needle punched through my scarred flesh

harder than necessary and I cringed. Surely Winch wasn't suppressing a smile, was she?

"How's the side, white boy?" It was Mouth.

Damn, I hadn't heard the door to the adjoining room open. Growing old sucks.

"How's the butt?" I countered.

"Can't feel it, so okay, I guess."

"This big baby is going to be fine," Mouth said, following Canton into the room. "He has enough drugs pumped into his system to stun a mule. A big, ugly mule at that."

"C'mon, little girl," he said with an exaggerated drawl. "Ain't nothin' on me that's mule-like except for my—"

"Stop right there, Injun," I interrupted before he could hit me with a TMI overload. "If you finish that sentence, I'm going to puke on your cowboy boots."

Mouth laughed and switched on the TV while Canton grinned and pulled a beer from a Styrofoam cooler.

"You could've sprung for a nicer place," he said after a long drink and a belch. "Something with mini-bar."

"Not after that time in St. Louis," I muttered, a surge of fatigue forcing my mouth open in a bone-cracking yawn.

"Aww ... you still holding that against me?"

"Because of you, I can never look at a goat the same way again ..."

After Winch finished stitching my hide back together, she joined Canton and Mouth on the other queen-sized bed, and together they watched Optimus Prime kick some metallic ass. As for me, I lay on my bed and dozed, too high on opiates to dwell on the day's spectacular failure.

Next thing I knew Winch was shaking me awake, holding out my smart phone. "It's Ghost," she mouthed.

I took the phone and hit the SPEAKER button. "Yeah," I rasped, throat dry.

The tiny speakers emitted a very un-phone like *squawwwwwk* that turned into barely comprehensible words uttered in a gender-neutral sort of buzz. "Hello, Kal, how are you?"

"Still in one piece, Ghost." The ... being on the other end was just that, a ghost. A disembodied spirit trapped in cyberspace, a citizen of the information superhighway. Although *trapped* might be a less than accurate way to describe his condition; there was almost no server he couldn't penetrate, practically no data he couldn't retrieve. Thank God he was on our side.

"Any success? Did you get the Cloak?"

Once again I felt the crushing burden of failure. "No, Ghost, it wasn't there."

"What do you think happened to it?"

Canton fielded this one. "My guess is, the ancestors didn't put it in there but said they did. The caves were a blind."

"We're screwed, Ghost," I mumbled. "We have no artifact to power the coil." The psychotic bitch that had tried to have me killed had been a genius-level magician who had invented a magical Tesla coil, a device able to produce a large amount of magical energy from smaller sources, such as a spell gem. After I killed said psychotic bitch, I photographed the coil and my dad reproduced it; but no gem, not even a thousand of the most perfect diamonds, was able to produce the kind of power to kill a Class Five Supernatural—a being of mythic or god like proportions. However, an artifact, such as Big Owl's Cloak, could possibly generate the energy to wipe a Class Five from existence. Possibly. If there was a chance, I would take it.

That Class Five was something called Iku-Turso, a cross between sea-monster, a demi-god, and H.P. Lovecraft's worst nightmare. A creature so alien a mortal mind would refuse to grasp the reality of it. The Finns referred to it as The Thousand Horned, or Thousand Headed one as well as The Bringer of Disease. For me, he was the rat bastard who killed my little sister.

"Well, Kal, that is part of the reason I called." Ghost sounded smug. Think about it, a smug specter ... the mind wobbles.

"Go ahead."

"Recently information has been uncovered about a ... violent sporting event in Las Vegas."

Mouth's eyebrows nearly reached her hairline. "Sporting event?" she asked. Mouth liked nothing better than sanctioned violence. God help the idiot who turned the channel while she was watching UFC or the Steelers.

"Yes, Ms. McTavish, sporting event. Specifically an underground fight club that is more like pit-fighting than boxing."

I held the phone away before Mouth could drool all over it. Her short, auburn hair was practically standing on end in excitement. Canton and Winch shared a knowing look. "Okay, Ghost, what's the deal?"

"Well, Kal, I do not have much information, but it seems that the owner of the Desert Pride casino organizes the bouts and claims that the grand prize is given to the person who can defeat the current champion."

"Cool, but how did you find out about this little event and what is this grand prize? And who's the champion?"

"The data is available on an encrypted server disguised as a catering menu for the casino. All that was needed was the correct password to gain access to the site, which was child's play for me." For some reason, Ghost sounded a little … off, but I was still too high to probe as to why. "The grand prize, if the owner can be believed, is the actual Cestus of Spartacus."

"Is that a real artifact?" Canton piped up, rolling off the bed. "Sounds like BS to me."

"Mr. Alsate, I wondered the very same thing and did some digging on my own. It seems like the Cestus is a genuine artifact. Its last known location was the mansion of one William Randolph Hearst, who purchased the item in 1940. In a remnant of his diary, he refers to 'the Metal Glove,' which confers great power on its owner."

"So how did the owner of the Desert Pride get his hands on it?" I asked, manfully fighting the effects of the morphine and losing badly.

"That is unknown."

"So what do we do?" Mouth blurted. "We can't go up to the

owner—"

"Miles Cartwright," Ghost cut in.

"Really? Well, we can't go up to this yin-yang and demand the Cestus." She bit her lower lip, which she often did when frustrated.

"What about BB? Where does the Director fit into all this?" I slurred.

"I came upon this site by chance. The Director has no knowledge of the artifact."

"So, Ghost, is that it?" There had to be more. There was always more.

"Of course not. There is a Supernatural involved."

Okay, that cut through the drug haze right quick. "What?" The question was echoed less than a second later by the rest of the team.

"It seems that the reigning champion in this little fight club is a Supernatural of unknown origin."

That was it. All traces of morphine wooziness … gone. Canton and I shared a look. We both had our issues with the World Under.

"Let me get this straight," Mouth snarled, eyes narrowed. "In order to win the Cestus, one of us has to beat this Supernatural."

"I think so," Ghost said.

"Cool." She turned to me. "What's the play, boss?"

My smile would've given a shark the sweats. "Time to take a trip to Sin City."

Chapter Three

Kal

The Desert Pride

Considering that we were lugging a small arsenal around, it was a good thing Ghost was on our side. Infiltrating the computer systems at the El Paso airport allowed us to breeze right through security. Disabling the facial recognition programs also helped because the last thing I needed was for the Bureau to find out that I was still breathing. So no agents waited for us when we landed at McCarran in Vegas, no Homeland Security goons … no one. Instead we walked calmly though the terminal and flagged a couple of cabs to take us to the Desert Pride hotel & casino, just a few short blocks from the Rio. It was far enough from the Strip to be overlooked by tourists, but close enough to get some play.

Relatively small by Vegas standards, the casino/hotel boasted a modest five stories with the casino roughly half the standard size. This meant you could actually see all four walls from the center of the gaming floor.

The nighttime crowd was just starting to fill the casino when we checked in. Each couple had a suite, courtesy of Ghost. I shared mine with Winch and Mouth stayed with Canton. Separate beds, of course. Well, for Winch and me, at least. Canton and Mouth were horny enough to give a porn star pause. As for me, when on the hunt, no distractions were allowed. Not that I wasn't tempted. At 5'9", Winch was a whole lot of woman and sexy as hell to boot, with a black page-boy haircut and legs to drool for. However, I've found that sex has a tendency to complicate a mission.

Maybe, some day, I would rejoin humanity's ranks. After I'd killed Iku-Turso.

Maybe not. No one wants damaged goods.

Winch sat at the corner of her bed and threw me a long, level stare as I unpacked my bag.

After a few seconds, I broke down. "What?"

"You never told us the play, boss."

"It's complicated."

"You have no play."

"I have no play," I admitted and continued to unpack.

"Greeeaaaat. Wake me when you figure this thing out." With that she stripped to her undies and slipped into bed. It wasn't long before the suite echoed with the soft sounds of her snoring.

During the flight, I had racked my brains for ways to infiltrate the pit fights. We couldn't stroll up to the nearest casino boss and ask for a front-row seat at the local barbaric, bare knuckle brawl. I had a funny feeling that there was just one rule: Don't talk about ... well, you know.

Scouting the lay of land seemed to be the wisest course, so I hightailed it to the elevators and made for the casino floor. I hadn't quite made it to the slots when I felt a tap-tap-tapping on my shoulder. Of course, it was Mouth.

"Whatcha doin'?" she asked sweetly

"Looking around. What are you doing?"

Her muscular arm slipped through mine. She was wearing jean shorts and a tank top, showing plenty of bare bronzed skin and rippling muscle. In hand-to-hand combat, I'd stack Mouth up against anyone, myself included, and I'm pretty damn good. It figured that if I wanted to check the place out for a secret fight club, she'd want in on the deal. Feeling the wound in my side hitch and burn, I reckoned that wasn't such a bad idea.

"Can you behave?" I whispered.

Her smile showed a lot of very even, large teeth. The best money could buy. "Probably not."

I sighed. "Oh well, who wants to live forever?" Mouth and I had worked together when I first became a team leader. I'd had a hard time controlling her then, so why would I expect things to have changed?

God, I hoped she didn't get me killed.

So we strolled arm in arm through miles of jingling/jangling, rattling slots, past the Three Card Poker and Blackjack tables, trying to look like tourists who were overawed by the glitz and glamour of Vegas nightlife.

A pretty waitress wearing an outfit the size of a postage stamp took our orders and brought drinks, which we sipped slowly. My amaretto sour had very little sour and far too much amaretto. Mouth made a face at hers. "Way too strong."

"They want us drunk so we will relax and gamble away our next paychecks."

"Ugh. Too much whisky, though."

I gulped at my drink. "Free is free, kid." Despite her comment on the strength of the cocktail, she still drank. I hid a smile behind the glass.

My pocket buzzed. Ah, the call I'd been waiting for. "What do you have for me, Ghost?" I said, smiling at Mouth.

"I have your way in, Kal, but that is it."

"What do you mean?"

Ghost hesitated before answering. "There are ... protections in the casino mainframe I have not been able to penetrate. Protocols that protect what I can only suppose is the most sensitive data. The date and time of the fight, the artifact, and the methods of payment are all on the encrypted catering menu that lie on the ... periphery of the server, a less protected area, but the server core, that is something else."

My eyes widened. I knew he'd been cagey about something earlier. "Ghost, you can crash the NSA server. Hell, it was you who hacked into ASIO, Australia's National Security and Intelligence Service and made it look like the Chinese did it. So how the heck could you *not* hack a server in a *casino*?"

Ghost's eerie voice sounded contrite. "I am sorry, Kal, but I have never seen anything like it before, which makes it unique in the world of the electronic superhighway."

"Well, then, what is it?"

"If I were to hazard a guess, I would say it is … magical in nature."

Creepy crawly cold chills scampered up and down my back. "How … how …" was all I could say.

"I don't know, but whoever placed those protocols and defenses must be a magician and programmer of rare ability."

Interesting.

"Can you get Alex on it?" Alex Dumont was the Bureau's best and brightest magician as well as Ghost's good friend. A cross between Einstein, Hawking and Michael J. Fox, he was one of the last surviving magicians in the Bureau after Margaret Whitcombe (psychotic bitch, remember?) attacked and killed a majority of the Bureau agents and staff. The Director was still trying to pick up the pieces and recruit new personnel.

"Sorry, Kal, but Alex is off on assignment. There have been signs of magical activity in the Catskills." The Bureau had sensors on every cell tower that could pick up the release of magical energy in units called Merlins. That's how magicians are recruited and Supernaturals are eliminated. If Alex was on the case, then the case must involve a magician.

"Crap! What can you tell me?"

"I can tell you that you now have a reservation for the next pit fight. As a possible participant."

My smile was all teeth, and I was happy in a Hannibal Lecter sort of way. Killing Supernaturals and fighting were the things I did best. "And I didn't get you anything."

"At 5 p.m. Saturday, find the Pit Boss at the blackjack tables. Bald fellow named Jamison Sedge. Tell him you have an appointment with Dr. Reinhold. Your name is Wesley Steele."

"Wesley Steele? Really?"

"Yes, really. Wesley Steele is a real person who is currently being detained by Homeland Security because his name has cropped up on several terrorist Watch Lists. Your reservations and rooms are now under his name. You see, Kal, the only way to participate in this event is to be recommended. Millionaire industrialist Jason Armbrewster, whose name is in the database, has vouched for Mr. Steele. I merely substituted you for the actual Wesley Steele and included three friends to attend, all with suitable aliases, which I have downloaded into this cell. The name Dr. Reinhold is the current password and will allow you access. As a possible participant, your entry fee was only $1,000; however, for the rest of team it was $10,000."

Gulp. "Apiece?"

"Apiece."

"Good thing I'm rich." Not much longer at that rate, though.

"Once caveat, however, Kal. No guns."

Damn. That sucked, but wasn't unexpected. "Good job. Glad you're on our side, Ghost."

"Thank you, Kal."

"So the events are on Saturdays?"

"Every Saturday. That will give you four days to prepare."

"Thanks again, Ghost. One question though: All this information was on, what did you say, the periphery?"

"That is correct and I can anticipate your next question: why so much incriminating evidence on a less protected area of the server? Best guess: it is information that the casino does not think is vital or damning enough. Information the contestants and participants need."

Interesting-er.

"Okay, Ghost, that begs another question: what kind of information does Miles Cartwright think is vital or damning?"

"I wonder the same thing, Kal."

"Talk to you later, Ghost."

"I will call you the day of." *Click.* Gone.

Mouth smiled wide after I clued her in. "Goodie! Four days in Sin City! This is the kind of op I can get behind."

"Still have a hole in my side," I groused. "I'm going to head back up to the suite to catch some Zs."

Her strong hands grasp my forearm in a grip that felt welded on. "Why don't you give Winch and Alsate a little more private time?"

I'm slow, but I get there. "Canton and Winch? Really?" How come I didn't twig to that?

She snorted. "Men! Always the last to know. They've been hooking up for *years* now, you big dope."

"I guess that's why he was so eager for her to be part of this barbecue. But why keep it from me?"

A rock-hard finger jabbed me just under the bullet wound and the air left my lungs with a *whoosh!* Yeah, she knew exactly where to hit me. "Because, Kal, you are such a stick-in-the-mud when it comes to … fraternization. Remember Memphis?"

Yeah, I remembered Memphis. I remember a very warm, very naked Mouth creeping into my bead at 2 a.m. and nearly getting her damn fool head shot off by accident. Gunfire can cure a case of the hornies right quick.

"I apologized about Memphis at least a dozen times!" I whispered, trying not to attract too much attention.

"I know, slugger," she countered. "What I'm saying is that normal people still want to feel connected to something or someone … if only for a little while."

Grumble, grumble. I conceded the point, then led Mouth to the blackjack tables where we helped the casino pay its employees.

"You look fine," Winch said, adjusting my tie. "I swear, you're worse than a girl."

Four days in Vegas had felt like four years, I was so antsy. The artifact was so damn *close* I could practically taste it! Farting around in the nation's gambling capital really got on my nuts after a while. When Saturday finally arrived, I was more than a little excited. I'd purchased a new set of duds for each one of us. Winch was decked out in a strapless burgundy gown that complemented her olive skin and black hair.

"We're in Vegas and I want to make a good impression."

"Why? You're here to fight, right? You don't need to look good. By way, how's the side?"

"The local anesthetic you gave me is working fine." And it was. No pain, no feeling of stitches tugging my flesh. I adjusted my collar. "Gotta funny feeling, kid."

Her reply was cut off by the buzzing of my phone. "Ghost?" I said while posing in front of the mirror in my new gray suit.

"Yes, Kal. I have good news and bad news."

Of course. "Bad first." It was amazing what slipping a tailor an extra fifty bucks could do. The suit draped perfectly.

"I could not penetrate the server."

Heroically, I resisted a smart-ass remark about condoms. It seemed I was growing up.

Nah. "What's the good news?"

"I am reprogramming your phone as we speak, adding a small ... portion of myself. It won't have my full capabilities, but considering that I cannot enter the server, you can smuggle me in via your cell."

Interesting. "So you will be with us?"

"Think of it as a poor copy of me. Just keep your phone on you. It does not even have to be on. If you can manage physical access to the server, connect the phone to the computer via the USB cable. That might be the way to hack the system."

Interesting-er. "Doubt they'll let us sniff around one of their computers. This is a casino; there are cameras everywhere." I had a thought. "Unless you've penetrated far enough to disable them?"

"No, all the security protocols seem to be at the system core."

"Wonderful."

"Good luck, Kal. You too, Ms. Pennington."

Winch dimpled. "Thanks, Ghost." The phone clicked twice and made an unusual whining sound.

What was that? "Ghost?"

"Almost, Mr. Hakala." The voice that came from the cell kind of sounded like Ghost's buzz, only more ... robotic. "I will be available when you press the Ghost App button on the phone." Click. Gone.

I looked. Sure enough there was an app labeled GHOST. Proof enough of his sense of humor.

Canton came through the adjoining door to the other suite dressed to the nines in a black silk and linen suit with a purple silk shirt and black silk tie. His patent leather shoes gleamed. The outfit perfectly complemented his ruddy complexion. Like me, he'd taken a shot off local anesthetic so he could move without limping. I knew we would both pay the price of not babying our injuries. Nothing new there.

"Is this your idea of a joke, white boy?" he snarled. "I look like a hit man for the Native American Mafia!"

Winch smiled. Was there an extra little sparkle in her eyes? "You look so handsome, Canton."

I smiled inwardly as his scowl was replaced by an almost shy grin. Oh yeah, he had it bad. A second later I realized that I felt a kind of ... sadness.

What the hell was wrong with me?

"You look pretty snazzy yourself, boss," Mouth purred, swaying and sashaying into the room. Both Canton and I had to pick up our jaws from where they'd bounced off our toenails. Encased in a skin-tight black dress that barely came to the tops of her shapely, yet muscular legs, her ... endowments nearly spilled from a neckline that was almost a waistline. Hooker-red lipstick drew attention from her ample cleavage to her generous mouth and dimples.

"Holy crap," I breathed, tossing aside my rule about non-fraternization during a mission. Well, not so much a rule as a guideline. Heck, not even a good guideline at that.

Canton drooled while Winch raised an eyebrow.

"What?" Mouth said, executing a runway spin. "My nipples showing or something?"

"Uh-uh," I blathered intelligently.

Winch's glare contained the barest hint of amusement. "Prostitute much?"

Mouth tossed her a saccharine smile. "Jealous much?" Claws and teeth were evident.

"Let me guess," I said, unable to take my eyes from her ... you know. "You want everyone distracted by your charms while we carry out the mission."

"Good guess." She snapped her fingers at me. "My eyes are up here, Kal. "

"What eyes?" My brain told my head to lift, but it wasn't receiving any messages. The small head was completely in charge.

"Hmph. Men! Show some tit and you all turn into drooling idiots."

"Yeah," Canton breathed. "Ain't it great?" Winch slapped him on the butt. Later, when the painkillers wore off, he'd really feel that.

Tearing my eyes away from Mouth's scrumptious charms, I pulled a plastic bag from the sideboard and started handing out brand-new cell phones. "Considering they have security that Ghost can't hack, they'll probably ask for our phones. Give them these."

Winch smiled. "Sneaky, boss."

"Right. Put earwigs in, but don't activate them unless I tell you, I don't want them picking up our signal. Keep your microphones hidden until absolutely necessary." I mourned the loss of some of the tech from the Bureau, especially the subvocal throat mics that looked like little round Band-Aids. As it was, our tech was limited to what we could buy at Radio Shack. The mics we did have were disguised as wrist watches.

"You expecting trouble, white boy?"

"I always expect trouble." I checked my watch. "Okay, folks, ten minutes until show time. Let's go. And remember, we go in together, but once inside we split up. Tonight is only a recon to locate the Cestus, if possible. You've memorized your aliases?"

They nodded. "What about the Supernatural?" Mouth asked, checking her makeup in the mirror.

"We're not in the Bureau anymore. Not our problem." The three winced, their Interdictions tweaking their brains. Even mentioning the Bureau outside a sanctioned operation caused distress.

I cursed my slip. Thanks to my recent bout of death (I got better), I no longer had to worry about the Interdiction, but keeping my fat mouth shut was always a good policy and reduced the discomfort of my team members.

"Sorry guys."

Mouth wouldn't meet my eyes. "It's okay, boss."

Crap. I done gone and made them feel bad. They knew I was no longer under Interdiction and it chafed at them. In a very real sense, I was free while they labored under the only commandment that mattered to the Bureau: Thou Shalt Not Talk.

Saying anything else wouldn't help, so we exited the suite and headed to the casino floor where I spotted the Pit Boss Jamison Sedge right away. He stood out like a shark amongst minnows at the Blackjack tables. At least 6'5", shaved head, moustache and goatee dusted with gray, he carried himself with a sort of loose limbed but ready grace that told me he was a very dangerous man indeed.

Canton whispered, "Kal …"

"See it," I shot back. "Keep your eyes peeled, everyone." I pasted on what I hoped passed as a sincere smile and raised my voice along with a hand to get the Pit Boss's attention. "Sir?"

Sedge glanced over, eyes taking in the four of us in an instant, evaluating. "What can the Desert Pride do for you, sir?" he uttered in a smooth, velvety voice, his small smile coming nowhere near his cold, cold eyes … like chips of hazel glass.

"I have an appointment with Dr. Reinhold."

"One moment." Sedge removed a smart phone from his immaculately tailored black suit and punched an app. "Name?"

"Wesley Steele."

The voice became warmer, but the eyes remained icy. "Yes, Mr. Steele, you are expected, along with Mr. Red Horse, Ms. Cassiday and Ms. Bergstrom. Come this way." With that, he led us across the casino floor.

"Red horse?" Canton growled softly. "Really?"

"Shh …" It was not the time to be prickly.

One semi-hidden hallway later, Sedge stopped at a nondescript elevator where another big, dangerous looking man in yet another tailored black suit waited. I wondered if they all shopped at the same place. The 'Armani Henchmen Outlet Store,' perhaps?

"As this is your first time here, Mr. Steele," Sedge said with a frosty smile, "Charles will brief you on the protocols. Enjoy yourself, sir." He vanished down the hall back to the casino floor in a swish of barely disturbed air.

"Ladies and gentlemen," Charles began, small mouth barely moving, "please put these on." He extended one big hand that held four silver rings. "It does not matter which finger; just make sure these are on at all times during the elevator ride."

I took a largish ring and my blood temp plummeted to absolute zero. The ring was crafted of incredibly fine silver wire spiraling and flowing in a dizzying pattern that made my eyes water. We all exchanged looks because we knew exactly what they were.

Spell rings.

Oh, crap.

Chapter Four

Kal

Not in Kansas Anymore

"This is unusual," I remarked nonchalantly, holding the ring up to my baby blues. "What are they for?"

Charles stared unblinkingly. "For your protection, sir. Please hand over all phones and other electronic devices." From beneath his jacket he removed a small burgundy velvet bag.

Wordlessly, we gave him our dummy phones.

"Anything else?" Winch reluctantly removed an iPod Touch from her black sequin clutch purse. It was also brand-new. People always expect you to try something sneaky and it was good policy to be predictable in those kinds of circumstances.

Charles placed the device in the bag along with the cells. "You will receive these upon your return," he continued. "Since you were the first to arrive, you will be escorted to a waiting area where you may dine and drink until the rest of our guests join you. Do you have any weapons?"

I raised an eyebrow. "I have a knife."

The granite of his face softened. How cute, I had amused the goon. "You make keep it, sir. Do you have any real weapons?"

Real weapons? The knife strapped to my back was a 14-inch Bowie, and if he knew what I could do with it, I was sure he wouldn't have been so condescending. And Canton could easily have turned him into 'Filet of Charles.'

"No. No real weapons."

The goon pulled a smart phone from a belt holster and pressed a few buttons. "Mr. Steele, you have opted to be a participant in tonight's event; however, the roster is full. You will, of course, be added to the lists should there be a cancellation." He must have expected some sort of outraged reaction because my silent stare clearly puzzled him. "Very well, sir. When you arrive at the arena, two security personnel will meet you and will direct you to the waiting area. Please obey any and all instructions. Failure to do so will result in the ejection of your entire party. Is that understood, sir?"

I nodded.

"Very well." He touched the DOWN button and the elevator doors opened. "During the ride, you may experience a sense of dizziness. It will pass. Enjoy the event."

Without a word we entered. The doors closed and we felt a familiar, faint, falling sensation.

Canton nudged me in the ribs. "What do you—?" he began.

I held up a hand, eyes flickering to a small, smoky, plastic half-dome on the ceiling. He followed my gaze and nodded slightly. I had no doubt that the camera hidden in that dome came with a microphone. "Dunno, Red Horse. Interesting pattern on the floor, though, don't you think?"

All three looked down and paled. Running through the black marble tile was a line of gold wire that mirrored the pattern of our silver rings. Another spell Shape.

Interesting.

The pattern under our feet and in the rings was that of a Shape that defined a spell. The precious metal held the energy and gave it direction, a purpose cast in a pattern.

We were *standing* on a spell. We wore them on our fingers. Wherever we were going required us to wear spells and that thrust an icy hand of worry in my guts.

Not good, I mused and the thought was reflected in the faces of my team.

Then reality kicked us in the ass.

Charles mentioned dizziness. What we actually felt was the stomach-twisting sensation of free fall multiplied by a zillion. Before we knew it, all of us were on the floor of the elevator doing our damndest not puke up our shoes as stomach-tearing nausea tore through us.

Down and up were no longer directions I could identify. My eyes sent the signals, but my brain refused to process the information. Instead I saw a riot of colors that smelled like the wrong end of a dyspeptic mule and sounded as if the USC marching band had exploded.

Dimly, the rational part of my mind was aware that only a couple of seconds had passed, but the primitive, lizard hindbrain gibbered in fear like an Alzheimer's patient at a Lady Gaga concert, certain that hours had passed.

Then it stopped.

Interesting-er.

Thanks to years of training, the team and I rose unsteadily to our feet and shook off the after-effects of ... well, whatever the hell had just happened.

Stoically, we eyed each other and adjusted our clothes. Canton handed me a white silk hanky to mop my face with while the ladies removed compacts from their clutch purses and fixed their makeup. I heroically averted my eyes as Mouth stuffed herself back into her postage stamp-sized dress.

"Wesley," Mouth muttered softly as she dabbed at her smeared lipstick. "Do you feel that?"

"Feel wh— oh!"

Instead of the slight free fall feeling of a descending elevator, my bowels felt like they were being gently pushed down. We were rising.

What the hell?

It wasn't long after we sorted ourselves out that the elevator doors opened to reveal two men in fancy-schmancy tuxes that did nothing to hide their lack of necks, the width of their shoulders or the holsters underneath. Nodding slightly, they beckoned.

We traveled back in time. At first, that's what it felt like, stepping into a hallway straight out of a medieval castle, all rough cut, dark and poorly dressed stone. Then I noticed the well spaced bare 40-watt bulbs glowing softly on the ceiling. Cute ... King Arthur meets Thomas Alva Edison.

"Names?" said one of the men, a short guy sporting a black goatee.

"Wesley Steele." My eye caught the telltale bulge of an ankle holster. Talk about security, these guys also had creases of knife sheaths on the outside of their thighs. Canton flashed me a look that said he spied them as well while Winch and Mouth pretended to act like bored arm candy.

Short no-neck unholstered a phone and verified that we did indeed have reservations. "Sir, you and your party please head to the right until you come to a large wooden door. Enter and make yourselves comfortable," he said tonelessly with the dead, dead eyes of a man who has killed more than once. His partner sported the same kind of thousand-yard emotionless stare. Where had Cartwright hired these men, Sociopaths-R-Us?

Nodding, we did as instructed. The hall with its uneven stone floor made it difficult for Mouth and Winch to walk in stiletto heels, but they managed without breaking a toe or ankle. Soon we passed several more elevator doors on our right while the hall curved gently to the left. After maybe a couple hundred feet, the hall ended at a wooden door made of burgundy-stained oak and banded with iron. A shiny steel latch stuck out incongruously, a jarring modern touch.

"What the hell is going on here?" I growled. The stink of magic was all about the place along with a strange taint of rotting vegetation.

Canton shook his head. I could tell he really wanted to stab something, anything. "Dunno, white boy, but this is some freaky stuff."

"This is the damndest fight club I've ever been to," Mouth whispered. At our stares she said defensively, "What? A girl's gotta have fun sometimes."

"Okay, people, keep it together and keep an eye out." I opened the door.

Interesting.

A big room, and I mean freakishly big—roughly one hundred feet on a side with a wet bar along the entire far wall manned by two bartenders. Bearskin rugs (all types, including Panda and Koala) were tossed around on the highly polished red-veined white marble floor. A fireplace situated on our right looked big enough to sleep in and boasted a blaze hot enough to sear flesh from bone at ten feet. Dozens of comfortable looking chairs with white oak side tables littered the space around three larger, felt-covered poker tables staffed by dealers in white shirts, black bow ties and black suspenders.

I looked around. No windows. No televisions.

Interesting-er.

"You have got to be kidding me," Winch whispered. "It's like we stepped into the freaking palace in Gondor."

"Hello *Twilight Zone*," Canon breathed.

Mouth put her two cents in. "I need a drink. Or three."

I shook my head. "Drink, but go light, folks. We need to keep our wits about us."

"That'll be a first." Mouth's tone was wry and Canton laughed, escorting Winch to the bar, a trip that could take some time.

"Laugh it up, Ms. Joke Funny Lady," I remarked sourly, noting that plastic dome cameras interspersed the recessed lights. Even the walls were red-veined white marble with what looked to be some very expensive paintings hung here and there. I pointed them out to Mouth.

"OMG! Look at that," she exclaimed loud enough for her voice to bounce around the room. "That's a Loutrec!"

"Gesundheit."

"No, you idiot! Toulouse-Lautrec!" She rolled her eyes at my look of incomprehension. Apparently I lacked the proper learning of things artistic. "Eighteenth-century French painter?"

The only things French I knew were French fries. "Hmm … nope. Sorry."

"Incredible … what a barbarian."

"Unless this Frenchy La-trek guy is going to help us, I couldn't care less."

Before she could roast me to the bone with her scathing wit, a scantily dressed waitress wearing a little wisp of nothing sauntered up and offered drinks and dinner. Mouth ordered a Cosmopolitan and I decided on a diet cola.

"You really shouldn't drink," I chided. "Not on the job."

The look she gave me would've sent Ted Bundy ducking for cover. "Start paying me; then you can scold or make up whatever silly rules you like."

She had a point. My companions were with me because they were my friends. And bored out of their skulls with life outside the Bureau. Helping to kill a Class Five Supernatural was a sure-fire way to cure ennui.

Soon more people began to trickle in, all dressed to the nines in the latest and greatest of formal wear, a veritable cornucopia of hideously expensive clothing. I spotted a Dior that must have cost more than the GNP of Brazil. The women were almost all uniformly beautiful, the men equally so. Those who weren't carried themselves with the kind of casual arrogance that comes with the knowledge that mere mortals were so far beneath them as to be invisible.

Bastards.

Soon the large room was filled to capacity with the wealthy and annoying. A haze of cigar smoke drifted above the crowd, adding a noxious stink to the shebang. As if rubbing elbows with the self-important wasn't nauseating enough. I heroically resisted the urge to delouse.

"LADIES AND GENTLEMEN," boomed a voice from concealed speakers. "THE EVENT IS ABOUT TO BEGIN. WE AT THE DESERT PRIDE ASK THAT WHEN THE EXIT IS REVEALED, YOU DEPART IN AN ORDERLY FASHION. THERE ARE PLENTY OF SEATS AVAILABLE."

That voice … familiar somehow. I knew it, but the memory wouldn't surface.

"FOR THOSE OF YOU HERE FOR THE FIRST TIME:

WELCOME, ENJOY THE SHOW. FOR OUR REPEAT GUESTS: THANK YOU FOR YOUR PATRONAGE."

"Mr. Steele?" asked a voice at my elbow.

"Yes?" It was a tubby little bald guy in an Armani tux. A diamond encrusted pinkie ring gleamed on his left hand. From his pug nose to his chocolate-brown eyes, his bushy black eyebrows to his pointy chin, he exuded an aura that read 'functionary'.

He graced me with a petite smile. "I understand you wish to participate in tonight's event, but there have been no cancellations. For that you have the House's apologies. Your participation fee will be returned and your rooms have been comped."

"Thank you."

"We will be able to accommodate you next week," he continued smoothly as if I hadn't spoken. "I trust that will be satisfactory."

I looked at Mouth over the top of the little guy's head. She was flirting with an older man who looked like Kirk Douglas. Canton and Winch were close by, paying attention without seeming to. Good.

"That will be fine," I replied smoothly.

The little man beamed, showing small, even teeth so perfect they had to be store bought. "Wonderful. Enjoy your stay."

Soon after the little guy left, a hidden door near the fireplace opened and two more men with bulges beneath their black jackets started to usher the guests through. I made eye contact with the team and surreptitiously gestured to my ear. Time to activate the earwigs.

We followed the crowd down another rough hallway toward a bright blue/white light and the smell of moisture. That unpleasant tang of rotting vegetation grew stronger, but underneath there was a kind of sweet smell as well.

"Heads up, team," I said surreptitiously into my wristwatch. "There's something wrong here. Very wrong."

"Check," they replied.

And I walked into the light. Always a big mistake.

A thick, wet heat slapped me in the face, bringing sweat in

rivers.

"What the blazes?" Winch moaned.

"White boy, this so ain't right."

"Boss, what is this?"

Two small, white suns glared down from a sky bleached of color. In front of us was an iron railing painted white, which we grasped for support as our legs nearly gave out. People streamed around, all about, below … a stadium into which thousands of spectators poured to sit comfortably on wooden benches. Below us, some twenty-five feet, was the sand of an oval stadium floor, white and glistening, like oiled silica. It was an arena half the size of a football field that reflected the blue/white light of the suns back to our faces. At either end of the oval arena, to our left and right, were gates … massive portcullises that, when raised, revealed a passage at least ten feet wide and fifteen tall. Above us were more levels, like terraces—three in all, including the one we stood on, each with wooden benches occupied by the elegant rich. High above and behind us, on the topmost tier, was a large, glass encased room that hovered over the crowd, the catbird seat, like the owner's box at a football stadium. The entire complex was faced with meticulously cut and set basalt blocks, lending it an air of black menace.

My neck craned around, as I took in the stylized Roman architecture and the thousands of gathered rich people. The place was almost as large as Memorial Stadium in Lincoln, NE, where I used to play in college. I reckoned it could hold upwards of thirty thousand people.

"I know this place," Canton said above the laughing crowd, his normally ruddy face pale with fear. "I've seen it before."

"We all have," Winch replied, hand in front of her mouth, face chalky.

Even Mouth looked like she was ready to hurl. "It … looks like the Coliseum of Rome."

I tried not to stare at the twin suns as sweat streamed down my face.

Interesting.

Chapter Five

Canton

New Old Enemies

I've been all over the world—sometimes on the Bureau's dime, sometimes on my own—and I've seen some things that could really mess your stuff up, but that friggin' stadium really took the taco.

Two suns! Can you believe it? I almost lost it right then and there. What the heck? Even Kal, who would spit in the face of the Devil himself, looked like he was going to puke all over the place. Usually he would whip out some movie reference and grin like everything was all right, but that Devil-may-care swagger was long gone.

Don't get me wrong, if the Devil did show up, I'd be first in line to hock a loogie at him, but being in some alien world really cracked my foundations, if you know what I mean. My mind went back to Mr. Toad's Wild Elevator Ride we'd taken earlier. That must've been when we went from Earth to Oz. I spared the silver spell ring on my pinkie a look and realized that the rings, coupled with the spell Shape on the floor of the elevator, brought us to … to … well, the *Coliseum*.

I gently escorted Winch to an empty section of bench and we took a load off, mentally exhausted from what we were seeing. Immediately the heat of the twin suns cut off as if we had passed some barrier and cool air caressed our skins. Some magical effect and none too soon, because my brain was about to broil in that fancy monkey suit I was wearing and leak out my ears. I nearly fainted in relief.

I guess that Cartwright fella didn't want the rich folks to expire from excessive perspiration.

"What is going on here, Winch?" I asked, keeping my voice low.

"Not sure, Canton," she replied, as she squeezed my hand. "This is too weird." That woman could put a bullet through your brain from a mile away without batting an eye, but our predicament had her flustered something awful. Hell, that made two of us.

Kal's voice came over our earwigs. "Canton, Winch, I see stairs to the next terrace. Mouth and I are going to check it out. Keep in contact."

"Check," I replied into my watch.

"Careful, you two," Winch said. "I see two snipers on the rim of the Coliseum directly opposite us. My guess is that there are more we don't see."

I had to smile. Even flustered, she still had her eye on the task at hand.

"Check that," Kal replied. "Go ahead and walk around; get a bead on those others."

"Check." With a faint swirl of cool air she was gone.

Whole lot of woman, that Winch. Sexy, smart and dangerous like you only read about. All of us Bureau types were dangerous, but it was like she had a switch in her head that she flicked when things became dicey. One second she could stop your heart with a sultry smile, the next she'd do it for real with a rifle.

God, I really dug her. Don't know what she saw in me, but I wasn't about to look a gift horse in the chompers.

Looking around at the rich and famous (wasn't that the guy from *Deadwood*?), I slipped my fingers along the underside of the bench. Sure enough, I felt cool metal running in a circular pattern. "Guys," I said. "There's some sort of Shape under the benches. Must be how they keep the people sittin' on them nice and cool."

"*Check*." Kal's sounded distant, the way he does when on the hunt, all focused and scary. I love the guy, but he gets downright creepy sometimes.

Cold metal lightly touched the back of my skull. "Give the watch over, Alsate."

Oh, shit. I knew that irritating and smug voice. "Leung."

"Awww, you remember. I'm touched."

"I've always thought so."

"Funny. In case you're feeling nervy, look at the front of your marvelous jacket there, Alsate, then get up."

I lowered my eyes. A red dot the size of a pea shone right above my heart, an evil little punctuation. One of the snipers had a bead on me. I stood slowly and when my butt left the bench, the searing, humid air washed over me. Heat I could handle, but I was from New Mexico, where humidity was a rare commodity.

"Now what, Ray?"

Ray Leung stepped out from behind me and stood there, half-concealing the .22 in his hands. Tall and thin with broad shoulders, he still looked good after all his years away from the Bureau. "Now you hand over the watch and earwig … without alerting the rest of your team, that is."

Carefully, I did so. Didn't want to spook the sniper and ruin my nice jacket with a gallon or two of O negative.

"So, you're part of this … thing, Ray?"

He smiled with incredibly white teeth. Nice veneers. "Aren't you the bright penny now, Alsate?"

"What's the play, Ray?"

The smile vanished as if it had never been. "The play is, you friggin' idiot, you do what I say, go where I tell you to go and you might, just might, live to see tomorrow," he snarled, features twisted and ugly.

A cold chill raised gooseflesh despite the heat. I'd heard him use that tone of voice before, usually before he beat a Supernatural into multi-colored goo with a pair of 28-inch batons crafted out of titanium.

We shared a history—a mean, vicious, ugly history. He was the reason people became psychologists and I was the reason he'd gotten his ass kicked off the Bureau. I'd considered it one of the highlights of my life when he was showed the door. Shoot, I knew that no matter what happened, he was gonna come after me hard with his batons.

We went into another one of those hallways that looked like it came out of a Camelot movie, past those elevators that had given us a hell of a ride and up some stairs, at least three flights, to another door, this one made of plain, unadorned steel with an electronic lock plate. Leung swiped a card, the UNLOCKED indicator glowed green and we went through.

It was that big glass room we'd spotted from below—the owner's box. A perfect view down to the oily-looking white sand of the arena. Three men, two bruiser types with no necks and one thin, blond white guy with sharp, foxy features. He was maybe an inch shorter than my own six feet and stuffed into a cream-colored suit and deck shoes, an outfit straight out of *Miami Vice*. This was how Sonny Crockett would look if he was gay.

Oh, no …

Foxy face smiled like he'd just won the lottery and I sent a prayer to the Creator for guidance and to give me the strength of Killer of Enemies, one of the Heroes of my people.

I had a powerful feeling I was gonna need it.

"Canton bloody Alsate!" Foxy face purred, every one of his sharp teeth showing. "The Mescalero Menace himself! Well, well, this is a joyous occasion!"

Ray jabbed me hard in the kidney with the stubby barrel of the .22 and I stumbled forward. "Gerard Marcin. Still alive, more's the pity," I managed after tossing a glare over my shoulder. "So it's you."

Gerard looked to Ray. "Go ahead and start the show, if you would."

Leung nodded and strolled to the back wall, where twin laptops sat on a glass table. Wires ran from the computers into the wall. A few keystrokes later and a voice boomed around the stadium:

"LADIES AND GENTLEMEN, WE BEGIN OUR FIRST MATCH OF THE DAY." It was a recording of Gerard's voice, loud as thunder.

"What the hell is going on here?" I asked as one of the bruisers bound my hands in front of me and began to pat me down. It didn't take him long to find the Bowie strapped to my back in a quick release sheath.

Bruiser #1 handed the knife over to Gerard, who whistled and studied it appreciatively.

"Careful, it was a gift," I growled. "You lose it, you'll pay like you won't believe." Kal had given me that knife, one of the very best I'd ever seen.

"Quite a gift," he remarked, testing the razor edge. "Nice. Of course, you always were *the* knife guy. But I thought you were retired."

"Give that back and I'll show you how retired I am, you French dickhead." Gerard always knew how to be a pain in the butt, worse than the bullet wound, which was starting to hurt like hell. The anesthetic was losing its effectiveness.

"Please, don't be crude. You know how much I hate cursing."

I remembered. Before I could tell him in intimate detail how much I remembered his quirks, he stared straight into my eyes and I felt my tongue cleave to the roof of my mouth like it had been super-glued there.

Oh, yeah. I forgot to mention. Gerard used to be a Bureau magician.

"OUR FIRST MATCH OF THE EVENING, A FIGHTER OF INTERNATIONAL REKNOWN! TWO-TIME NO HOLDS BARRED BARE KNUCKLE CHAMPION ..." Blah blah blah. I stopped listening. It was obvious, wasn't it? Old time gladiatorial combat, paid for by all those useless, jaded idiots who were so burned out by their wealth that they would do and pay anything to feel alive, to feel the juices flowing in their veins once again. Even if that meant that people got hurt or killed for their pleasure.

Pathetic. All of them.

But I couldn't help myself. I stepped closer to the wall to see the action.

A big guy, hair shaved close to the scalp—all hard muscles and cauliflower ears—stepped onto the sand through the portcullis in the arena wall to the right. He was dressed in a sandals and a brown leather loincloth. A leather sleeve that ran from wrist to shoulder and was studded with small plates of iron adorned his left arm. In his right hand he carried a gladius, a Roman short sword.

Really? Didn't these people have cable? For $9.99 a month they could watch *Spartacus: Blood and Sand* every Sunday on Starz.

From the left side of the arena, another portcullis opened and something … big moved in the shadows within. Then it burst out into the too bright light of the twin suns.

Sage green and scaled like a snake—but built like an alligator with a quartet of short, powerful legs—the *thing* waddled/ran across the arena, four-toed claws spraying sand high into the air. A long sinuous tail trailed it, counterbalancing its massive bulk. At the end of a ten-foot neck, it had a snake-like head filled with a shark's triangular teeth.

The gladiator stood calmly as it charged.

"Compelling isn't it?" Gerard said from behind.

I nodded dumbly. It was true, kind of like watching a traffic accident.

Just before the snake-sharkagator (what else would I call it?) could pounce on the gladiator, the man dodged to the side, swinging his gladius in a brutal side stroke that opened the creature up from shoulder to rear haunch, spraying greenish blood across the pristine sand. The crowd roared its approval, many jumping to their feet in excitement.

With a bugling sort of bellow, the creature spun its body around and stuck again at the gladiator, who raised his armored arm at the last second. That big snakelike mouth with its triangular teeth fastened onto the armored sleeve, worrying and tearing. Almost lazily the gladiator swung his sword from the hip and chopped right through its thick neck.

The bored rich found this tremendously entertaining, shaking the glass booth with the force of their enthusiasm. The gladiator held up the snake head, still clinging to the leather and iron sleeve.

"I give them monsters, Alsate. Monsters they've never seen

41

before, many of which don't pose much of a threat to the gladiators. That creature is something I've dubbed a Serpegator. An aquatic reptile like an alligator, it feeds on fish and waterfowl. Vicious, but stupid, and no real threat to a trained athlete. Not that the audience knows that. It makes for great theatre, like professional wrestling."

His pale blue eyes bored into mine, pitiless and chalk full of madness. Sanity had left the Gerard ranch long ago, it seemed. "But every now and then someone dies, and that's okay, too, because it keeps the feeling of danger very much alive.

"Ten thousand a head, Alsate," he continued with a beatific smile that was horrible to behold. "We have twenty six thousand in attendance. You do the math."

My stare said what I couldn't. That was a severe chunk of change.

"I don't know why you continue to work for the Bureau." At my look of dismay he chuckled in glee. "Canton, we're not on our world, as you can tell by the two suns. And let me tell you something I learned when I first discovered this place." His foxy smile returned with a vengeance. "Spells cannot travel between worlds, between universes. So the Interdiction that the Bureau placed on Mr. Leung and myself vanished the second we arrived here."

That would explain why him mentioning the Bureau didn't give me a familiar twinge of discomfort, like ants crawling around in my brain. I filed that information away for later, if there was a later. At that moment, I concentrated on my hatred, my desire to rip his heart out with my bare hands. We had shared a history at the Bureau, along with Leung. Back then he was an arrogant magical prick, but one that worked on the side of the angels. It looked like time had just refined his general prick-ness and married it with a generous helping of liquid crazy.

Not good.

"You still handy with a blade, Alsate?" Leung breathed into my ear, aiming for menacing and succeeding.

I wanted to snarl at him, call him some very interesting names

I'd been saving for a while, but my tongue still refused to budge. I wanted to tell him what I would do to him if he let me get my hands on the Bowie. Instead I gave him a terse nod.

A wiry hand clasped my shoulder.

"You're going to have a chance to show me. To show all of us."

Chapter Six

Kal

A View to a Thrill

Damn, the heat was oppressive and the air so humid I was tempted to use the Bowie to cut my way through. Sweat ran in rivulets down my face and even Mouth was starting to wilt around the edges.

During the match between the guy with the gladius and the, well, supergator-snake *thing*, we kept our eyes peeled for anyone who could be *convinced* to lead us to the people in charge. Nada. There were plenty of vendors passing out alcoholic beverages to the cool-as-cucumber spectators, but the only thing they could show us was where to find the restrooms.

If Cartwright was as smart as I thought he was, he'd keep all his employees as carefully compartmentalized and ignorant as possible. It looked like Mouth and I would have to find some way to get to that glass booth, to the catbird seat straddling what would normally be the fifty-yard-line. I'd bet my last buffalo nickel that was where the boss could be found.

"You see any other security detail other than the snipers?" I asked.

She shook her head, not bothering to live up to her name.

I was just about to comm Canton when I noticed a glowing red dot on Mouth's forehead. My guts instantly went some hundred degrees south of zero degrees Fahrenheit.

"What?" she scowled before her eyes widened in shock. I guess my forehead had its own little red dot. Why was I surprised?

"It had to be you, Kal," said a familiar voice sorrowfully. "I wish BB had sent someone else."

I turned, knowing full well the laser dot now decorated the back of my skull. "*Why*, Harley?" I asked the man with a matte-black Beretta pointed at my privates. "Why are you part of this?"

Harley Foster, former Bureau agent and leader of Team Beta, stared at me for a few moments, big brown eyes full of sadness, but he held the 9mm rock steady. "Sorry, Kal," he rumbled in his deep, penetrating voice. "I know there's nothing I can say to get you off my case. You were always BB's favorite and best attack dog—so damn stubborn."

"That's not fair," began Mouth, two spots of color high on her cheeks.

"Shut it, Rebecca," he replied, using her true name, which I know she hated. "Don't try anything. I know you're the best at hand-to-hand, but you can't stop a bullet."

Surprisingly, Mouth kept her trap shut, although I could tell by her narrowed eyes that she was mentally fitting him with a casket. If he wasn't careful, she'd bring him down to size one broken bone at a time.

"Been, what? Three years since you retired, Harley? What's going on?" I asked nonchalantly, my eyes taking his measure. Those three years of retirement hadn't softened his wide frame any. Much darker than most African-Americans, he had high cheekbones and a strong jaw and still looked like he could bench 400 pounds without breathing hard.

His sad brown eyes never blinked. "Shut up, Kal and turn around. Walk."

And walk we did. Eventually we came to that big glass booth/room, the catbird seat with an unobstructed view of the arena. For some reason the owner kept it devoid of furniture, except for a computer desk against the back wall.

Standing near the wall looking down, bracketed by a couple of no-neck security types, was a slender, dapper blond man who turned upon our arrival. A bright smile lit his sharp features. His eyes tracked to Harley, who tipped him a nod.

"Ah, the legendary Kalevi Hakala!" he enthused, striding

forward and pumping my hand vigorously. His palm was cold and damp. "Let me tell you, it is an honor … no, a true *pleasure* to finally meet you." By the fine lines at the corner of his eyes, I guessed his age to be somewhere north of my own thirty-six and, from his hand's lack of calluses and strength, I could tell he was a perfect stranger to hard work.

As I disengaged, I rammed an elbow backward into Harley's gun hand, knocking the weapon to the floor, then spun and followed with knee to the crotch. His dark skin paled considerably as I spoiled his chances for descendants.

The two no-neck types in cheap black suits did what I expected them to do: they waded in as Mouth gave Harley an axe-kick to the skull, putting him out for the count. Feet and fists pounded against my sides and, with a sound like tearing paper, my stitches came apart and blood flowed again from my wound. Thank God the painkillers still worked somewhat. I fell against Mouth and the two of us hit the floor hard with me landing on top.

"What the—" she began, then her eyes flew wide and we shared a knowing look. Good. She was hotheaded and moody, but she was plenty smart. I tried to roll off as a size 10 slammed against my ribs and I felt them creak in protest as breath left my body.

Before I could kick out, handcuffs clicked around my wrists and I let my body go slack. It was over.

The no-necks lifted me to my feet, and I spat in the face of the one to the right. A heavy hand introduced my nose to a world of hurt. Right then I promised to break what little neck he did have.

"Please stop your show of bravado, Agent Hakala," said the blond man lazily. "I will not tolerate it."

Agent? This guy thought I was still in? Of course! Harley probably hadn't heard about my 'death.' So that meant the blondie thought I was part of a Bureau team sent to take him down.

Interesting.

While the no-neck twins clapped handcuffs on Mouth as well, her slitted eyes told me she had come to the same conclusion. We shared another look.

I met Blondie's eyes, blue against blue, and it did my heart a powerful lot of good to watch his eyes dart away from mine. The muscles at the corners of his jaw told me that I had pissed him off something fierce.

"My name is Gerard Marcin," he growled, struggling to control his emotions. "You may have heard of me."

Oh yeah, I'd heard of him. Canton had told me he was a royal dickwad and a powerful magician, not to mention a borderline sadist. A man who was far too arrogant about his French Huguenot ancestry and who had flaunted it in everyone's face. After serving the Bureau for three years, he had left without a backward glance.

"Sorry, Gee-rard." I deliberately butchered his name. "But you must have been before my time. I was looking forward to taking down your average, everyday World Under scumbags, not ordinary ones." My smile turned mean. "But hey, it's not all bad. At least I get to take down a French scumbag."

Lightning swift hatred flashed across his features and his pale blue eyes shone with an inner light. "I am not anyone you wish to fight, Hakala. Nothing like Harley there, or even Canton." He drew close and the no-necks came with him. "I am the worst thing you've ever faced."

"The worst thing I'm facing, Frenchy, is your breath." A groan from behind told me where Harley was and my foot lashed out backwards, heel catching a body part that broke with a sickening *snap!*

"Thanks for letting me know where you were, Harley," I commented blandly. To the magician I said, "Hope you hired better help than him."

Two hands introduced themselves to my kidneys over and over again until muscle cramping pain took me to my knees and bile hit the back of my throat. However, there was no way on God's green earth I would give that arrogant bastard the satisfaction of screaming. Instead I clamped my jaws tight against the agony and struggled to hold onto consciousness.

"Enough," Gerard said quietly. Immediately the two bruisers

stopped playing bongos on my ribs, which was a good thing because I was about to vomit all over their shiny shoes.

Revenge is mine, sayeth the puker.

I spat out a gobbet of blood. "Is that all you got?" I croaked.

"No," rasped Harley. My head swiveled to see him glaring at me, one arm cradling the other. "I got something for you, bitch!" His size 9 came around and put the lights out.

"Kal, you okay?" a familiar voice asked.

The nerves along the right side of my face announced their presence vigorously, and in no uncertain terms let me know what a bonehead I'd been. My ribs and kidneys agreed, each bruise pulsing to the beat of my heart. The wound in my side felt hot and weepy. Great, that was never going to heal. A blurry Mouth was revealed when I opened my eyes.

It took about a year, but my lips finally started working. "I … hate … that."

A sort of hiccoughing laugh. "What?"

"Waking up," I moaned. "Hurts." Breathe, wince, repeat. "How long have I been out?"

"A couple of minutes."

Loose tooth on the left side of my mouth. Ouch. "Harley," I called out weakly. "You suck! I was only out for two minutes! Retirement has made you soft!" At that point, I didn't care about poking the bear.

A menacing growl came from behind me and I tensed, but the Frenchman said, "Enough. Bring Agent Hakala to the wall."

The no-neck twins lifted me to my feet, and I almost did puke right here—the pain from moving my tortured organs lancing my gut—but I manfully kept it in. They half-carried me to the glass wall, where a gladiator held a head that looked vaguely simian high in the air on a spear for the benefit of the crowd. A scaly blue body with a large bloated abdomen like a four-armed insect lay headless on the sand.

"Why?" I asked weakly, staring as the gladiator exited the

arena and a pair of men in white coveralls smoothed out the sand with wooden rakes.

Gerard raised an eyebrow. "Why what, Agent Hakala?"

I spat blood on the glass and nodded at the arena. "Why all this?"

He flashed that nasty little smile of his. "Why, for money, of course."

It was my turn to give him the eyebrow routine. "Didn't the Bureau pay you enough? Or are you running out of money for Bordeaux?"

"Oh, they most certainly did." He stared down at the oily looking sand. "Do you know how I found the ... weak spot, a thinning in the Universe, that allowed travel between the worlds, agent Hakala? Quite by accident. During my time off from work at the Bureau, I feverishly tried to find a way into the World Under. It was my quest, my Holy Grail, if you will."

"Then this isn't—?"

"Oh, heavens no!" he laughed, genuinely amused. "We are on a different arm of our own galaxy, Agent Hakala. This is *not* the World Under. Travel across space is simple compared to travel between dimensions. No, I stumbled across a weak spot left by the ancient aliens who came to earth thousands of years ago. There are spots of ... *attraction* between two points in space that allow matter to instantaneously travel the space between, like stable wormholes. What they did with technology, I duplicated with magic. I am *that* good.

"Imagine my surprise at finding those weak spots in the heart of Las Vegas and the surrounding area, including Southern California," he breathed in wonder. "It was my hope that they would allow access to the World Under, but that didn't happen. I could *pull* from the World Under, objects ... creatures, if I had the required energy, but I couldn't physically travel there." During his little monologue, his voice became more and more whispery, demented. It sounded like Gerard's mind had taken a walk off the map a long time ago.

At that moment, the booming voice of the announcer vibrated the thick glass of the booth. The next event was about to start.

"I had sunk all my money into purchasing and renovating the Desert Pride so I could have access to this particular weak spot and study this world. It's the perfect location, a place where I can relax and travel back and forth between both worlds in relative comfort. When I first arrived here, imagine my surprise to find that it seemed devoid of intelligent life! Only ruins stood here; the ancient aliens were long, long, gone."

I tuned out the announcer—still watching the arena out of the corner of my eye—and focused instead on Gerard. You know, Hollywood isn't entirely wrong when it comes to the portrayal of villains; they always want, *need*, to monologue to show how clever they are, an affirmation of their villainy. Perhaps they think the hero will appreciate the lengths they have gone to in achieving their plans. My guess is … mommy issues.

Gerard seemed pretty typical of the breed. His pale eyes were glassy and intent on mine as he spewed forth his tale, but that was fine with me. I needed answers before I killed the crazy sonofabitch.

"I needed more money to continue my research; then, as if God himself had blessed me, I was approached by my savior. He provided extra resources and came up with idea of the arena."

"Not you?"

Interesting.

"No, agent Hakala, not me. This man had a lot of … disposable wealth, but needed more, and he needed my contacts and what my contacts could provide. He helped provide some of the funds to create the arena." He waved his hand toward the Coliseum. "Most of this structure was already here. I have no idea what it used to be, but I provided the labor to recreate what the Romans had built."

Gerard leaned closer, whispering fervently. "I have been running these events for nearly a month now, and the returns have been fabulous! Wealth like you have never seen! My benefactor allows me to keep ten percent of the profits and, when he has concluded his business in Las Vegas, he will give me the secret to the World Under, the Shape needed to access that dread plane. Do you understand? I will be able to travel to the World Under!"

Interesting-er. "What about the Cestus of Spartacus?"

He laughed. "A ruse. The Cestus has been missing for years! William Randolph Hearst sold it to somebody or gave it away. Either way, all records of it have been lost. I used the story to draw fighters and treasure hunters to the arena. It's funny how the very mention of Spartacus ignites the flame of competition in our modern day gladiators."

Aw, crap. All this and no artifact? For a brief moment I saw red, but controlled my temper before it could rage out of control. Then I saw something that took the starch clean out of me and turned my insides to water.

Stomping into the arena—huge, black and hunched, three fingered hands dragging along the sand—was a troll.

If the Three Billy Goats Gruff had seen this beast, they'd still be running and wouldn't stop until they reached Hoboken. Twelve feet of armored mean standing on thick, elephantine legs and exuding an air of fury that seemed to ripple from it in waves. The troll's skin was black iron, fissured and cracked at the joints for mobility, with blunt, rounded features on its spherical, beach ball-sized head. A stub of a nose, huge supraorbital ridges over deep set, pus-yellow eyes all but paled to its enormous, foot-long mouth filled with flat chisel-like teeth—teeth that could crush and slice at the same time. Its arms, each as long as the troll was tall, ended in shovel-like hands with foot-long fingers that tapered to needle points. Of all the creatures I've faced over the last ten years, trolls are on the short list of Things I Don't Want To Fight. They are so tough that it usually takes an anti-tank weapon to put them down.

"What the hell?" Mouth said from behind, her voice a mixture of fear and awe.

"That," Gerard said proudly. "Is one of the creatures I managed to pull from the World Under."

"Very interesting, Mr. Marcin, but do you mind not telling this man *everything*," said a low, lugubrious and thick voice.

I turned from the glass to see a slender, short man with black hair combed straight back from a high and wide forehead. He had a thin, nearly lipless face that held so much sorrow that it hurt just to look at it. He was dressed in a very stylish dark gray suit and had black shoes buffed to a high shine. Although not handsome, not by a long shot, he had about him a sort of, well, charisma that drew the eyes. It made you want to listen attentively to what he had to say.

Gerard's sharp smile grew wider. "Ah, Mr. ... Race," he said, obviously substituting a false name. Who was this man that Marcin didn't want me to know his real name? "I am sure you have heard Mr. Foster's accounts of agent Kalevi Hakala?"

Harley gave me another glare, still nursing his broken arm. I knew it must've really grated on him to wait until Gerard was done with me before he could be healed.

Race's brown eyes sparked with interest and he drew closer, inspecting me like a prize hog. "Ah, *the* Kalevi Hakala, the greatest agent in the history of America's Bureau. Facinating." With slow precise steps he walked around, eyes scanning me more effectively than an MRI. "The Finns are a fierce people, quiet and dangerous. Did you know, Gerard, that they inflicted more casualties per man on the Russians than any other fighters in history? A 9 to 1 ratio. Amazing! It is too bad that Finland is so sparsely populated. With fifty thousand Finns like him fighting for me, I could terrorize Europe."

What the hell? Terrorize Europe? Who talked like that? The guy was obviously missing a few widgets. I kept my mouth shut and a half-snarl on my face while I studied him. By his speech and slight accent (I couldn't quite place it), I took him to be an educated European. He held himself like a man of power and position. A man used to having his own way.

"Note the tall, square forehead with its subtle widow's peak ... a sure sign of intelligence. And the breadth of those shoulders ... a physically powerful specimen. He is a superior man in every way. Much more of what a true man should be, unlike the mongrelized Americans and those barbaric African mud people."

During Race's monologue, Harley's face grew longer and longer and a hint of anger gleamed in his eyes. It must have crushed his nuts to be referred to as a mud person and not be able to do anything about it.

Interesting.

Why would Harley even work for such a tool? A black man working for a bigot struck me as more than a little odd.

I tossed the little guy a nasty smile. "How did you and this French fart meet?"

Before he could reply, Gerard laughed. "Showtime."

I turned to the arena and my blood went cold. The troll was sweeping up great gouts of sand with its huge paws, peppering the rich and foolish in the front rows. They just lapped it up, laughing and pointing at the troll's opponent.

They were pointing at Canton, who had just entered the arena, stripped of everything but a loincloth and his Bowie.

Oh crap. Fighting a troll with a knife was like taking a toothpick to a pit bull. You might poke it here and there, but you weren't gonna win.

It came to me then. The rage, the barely controlled passion that fueled me to superhuman efforts and acts of carnage so extreme it had scared the everlovin' bejesus out of my teammates in the Bureau.

The pure wine of wrath poured in to my veins, a supercharged cocktail that had my muscles bulging obscenely and my bones creaking with the strain. It was my drug of choice, the sweet rush that gave me a high like no other. My perceptions became heightened and my mind blazed away at speeds the fastest supercomputer couldn't hope to match. Then the haze settled in, the white-hot anger focus that drove everything from my brain except the desire to destroy those things that stood in my way.

The cuffs snapped with a high-pitched *pinging* sound and I grabbed Frenchy by his Don Johnson lapels, a savage smile on my face, a look of terror on his. He blinked once and I felt a searing pain blaze along my back.

He had cast a spell on me! On ME! The rage slapped the effects aside as if they were no more worrisome than a gnat and I lifted that blond French fart, his expensive summer suit tearing at the seams, and swung him around and around and around, my body twisting savagely. With a grunt I threw him screaming straight through the inch thick plate of the booth wall, shattering tempered glass into a jillion pieces, to fall into the Coliseum below. He disappeared with a despairing wail that ended abruptly.

One down.

I turned to see the look on Harley's face. His normally dark brown skin had faded with terror to a grayish hue. Good. Terror I could use, but before I could teach him not to mess with me and mine, one of the no-neck twins was on me like ugly on an ape.

Almost contemptuously, I punched him in the throat and crushed his larynx, then tossed him after the magician. Damn, he'd bought Harley enough time to run.

Mouth was chopping no-neck number two down to size with strikes calculated to cause the maximum amount of pain and suffering. She was a Goddess of War destroying everything in her path. Another no-neck came through the door, but I knew she'd kick him round and round.

Ah, the no-neck I had tossed through the glass had dropped his gun. Idiot. Should have used it on me when he had the chance. I scooped it up, the familiar feel of a 9mm filling my palm with comforting weight. My other hand reached around to the small of my back and drew my Bowie out of its quick-release sheath from beneath my suit jacket. Harley should've remembered that I always carried the big knife.

Where was that Race guy? Damn, he'd scrammed as well. Smarter than he looked.

Knowing that Mouth could take care of herself, I jumped out of the booth, the hot and humid air of that world wrapping around me like a lover.

Chapter Seven

Kal

Mayhem

Airborne … falling. twenty feet below, the basalt stairs that linked the second and third tiers of the Coliseum came rushing toward me, ready to splinter every bone in my body.

Good thing Gerard and no-neck #1 were there to break my fall.

There was a terrible *give* as my feet *crunched* through ribcages and burst organs like rotten fruit. Stresses that might have broken my legs proved ineffective against the power of the rage. Instead, my knees flexed, absorbing the shock, and I sprang upwards, shoes red from the torn torsos of the men I'd landed on.

Down the steps four at a time to the next tier. The stairs ended there, so I vaulted a white painted iron rail. I was airborne for maybe a second before landing between two cheering fat cats on the first tier who barely had time to register my presence before I was gone, racing toward the arena.

Another rail, another jump and the sands glittered below me. I noted that Canton was doing his best to run away from the troll, but it would only be a matter of time before he was caught, crushed, and shredded by those chisel teeth.

My feet hit the sand, sending up a spray of oily-looking granules, which stuck like glittering diamond shards to the blood on my shoes. Fifty feet ahead the monster charged Canton, who was barely able to dodge out of the way. It was plain that he was running out of steam.

He couldn't die … I wouldn't let him! I'd known Canton for

eleven years; he was one of my first teammates and, from the start, had treated me like an agent instead of a wet-behind-the-ears Green Pea. That meant the world to me and I wasn't going to let some walking Sherman tank eat him and turn him into a hundred eighty pounds of troll shit.

"Canton!" I screamed, my throat tearing as the sound bounced around the Coliseum. Smart boy that he was, he ran straight toward me, the monster hot on his heels, dagger-fingers swiping.

"Duck!" Once again my throat burned from the force of my shout and, as if we had rehearsed it day after day, he hit the sand a split second before I used him as a springboard, leaping toward the beast.

In the dim parts of my mind—the sane bits—I realized jumping *at* a twelve-foot, iron-skinned, ravenous monstrosity was probably not the way to please my life insurance carrier. Hey, I've done crazier things.

But not many.

The troll spread its arms wide, ready to squeeze me into strawberry yogurt.

Thump!

Air left my lungs, my cracked ribs and gunshot wound let me know that I was seven kinds of fool as I hit the troll, legs wrapping around its neck. That big mouth with its chisel teeth opened wide, ready to take a huge bite out of the front of my butt, ready to render me a soprano before having me for lunch.

Not happening.

One hand plunged the Bowie to the hilt into a pus-yellow eye; the other came around with a fistful of 9mm, jammed it sideways into the other eye and pulled the trigger.

Bangbangbangbangbang!

The gun bucked in my palm as the troll's iron shod head flung back in agony, bullets ping-ponging around inside of its skull, turning everything within into brain puree. Its mouth gaped wide, and a steam-whistle scream burst from its throat. Slowly, like a collapsing a monument, it toppled backwards. I rode it down to the sand.

"Damn, white boy," Canton said from behind as I jumped off the troll's body, chest heaving and the coppery taste of blood in my mouth. "Being around you is never dull. You sure know how to throw a party." The crowd cheered and stamped, the noise a physical thing buffeting our bodies.

He caught me as the rage drained out of my body, stealing the strength from my legs. I'd raged before—it was my greatest asset in a fight—but never for so long. I had never done so many impossible things in a row. My head swam with fatigue, my sense of equilibrium in disarray.

"Gotcha, buddy," he whispered in my ear. "You know, you look like hell, Kal."

Oh, I must have looked like five miles of bad road for him to address me by name. "Thanks for the pep talk," I replied weakly, my eyes focusing over his shoulder. "Crap, your six!"

Canton swiveled with me still in his arms to see the danger from behind. Boiling out of the tiers below the glass booth, half a dozen no-neck clones were on their way, pistols in hand. I checked the 9mm in my hand. Empty and the metal around the bore was scored and twisted. Damn troll.

Oh crap.

Shots came dimly to my ears, one every second or so, but I couldn't place them. They didn't come from the no-necks, who weren't close enough to use their weapons.

"What the hell?" we said in unison.

Nothing to do but wait as the goons made their way to the sand.

Then the lead no-neck's head exploded. A pinkish-red mist sprayed all around his comrades, coating them in a slick of gore. A split second later there came a flat *crack*. The remaining no-necks stopped, raising their weapons, looking around. One aimed a weapon at Canton and me. Bad move on his part because in the next second a hole the size of a grapefruit opened in his chest, dropping him like a sack of laundry. Another *crack* echoed around the Coliseum.

The crowd went wild with blood lust, roaring their approval. Idiots, they thought it was all part of the show. I stifled the urge to take my Bowie to them all. It would have been immensely satisfying.

Four more reports, four more no-necks down for the count, body parts flying.

"That's my girl!" Canton hollered, fist pumping the air.

Of course … Winch. That would account for the several shots heard earlier. She'd been taking care of the other snipers.

"How come you never told me about you and Winch?" I asked, straightening slowly. The strength was returning to my legs, along with the awareness of all the damage I'd sustained clamoring for my attention. I ignored it. I've had it worse; at least my blood was staying on the inside for a change.

Canton made a face. "You're always such a pain in the ass about teammates sharing beds."

I nodded. Fair enough. "Let's go, Kemoslobby."

Some forty feet away, the gladiator's portcullis rose slowly. Speakers around the Coliseum cracked to life. "Ladies and gentlemen, please exit the Coliseum in an orderly fashion," boomed a familiar voice. Canton and I shared a tired grin. Ghost was back! Or, at least, part of him.

When I had stumbled into Mouth up in the booth, I had passed her the smart phone with the Ghost clone and the USB wire. It looked like she'd managed to connect the cell to one of the laptops.

My earwig came to life. "Kal, will you and Canton exit through the gate, please. I will walk you through the complex to the private elevator reserved for Mr. Cartwright, or, as you know him, Mr. Marcin."

"Thanks, Ghost," I said into my watch, much relieved, while the spectators calmly began to exit the Coliseum. "You're a lifesaver. Contact Winch and have her join us. Did you disable the security protocols keeping your, ah, father out?" What do you call a program's, or specter's, progenitor?

"Father does not compute, Kal. Please define."

Oh, well, Ghost said his offshoot would be a poor copy, but I had expected a copy to have *some* sort of personality. This version of my favorite specter seemed ... sterile. "The original Ghost."

"Please refer to that program as Ghost Alpha. It was difficult, given the nature of the singularity between our worlds, but I have managed to disable the security protocols on the casino servers. Ghost Alpha has full access and should have full control by now."

Good. "Have Mouth join us at the exit as well."

"The person designated as Mouth is no longer on this world."

Oh, crap! My stomach bounced off the arena sand. "What happened?" I yelled.

"The man referred to as Mr. Race and another escorted her to a private elevator exit."

I grabbed Canton's arm and began running as Ghost Beta, or Ghost 2.0, gave directions through the earwig. "Anything else I should know, Ghost?"

"Mr. Marcin/Cartwright has an electronic journal on the hard drive of this laptop."

Bingo, just what the doctor ordered. "Can you send it to Ghost Alpha on our world?"

"*Yes.*"

"Do so!"

A few twists and turns later and we were at the elevator. Winch stood in front, a Barrett M107 .50 cal sniper rifle cradled lovingly in her arms.

She laughed. "What took you so long?" Her eyes roved over Canton's scantily clad body. "You will *have* to wear that for me later."

As he planted a wet one on her, I noticed that his wound had reopened, his butt bleeding a bit. "You got it, babe," he said, voice slightly thick.

I scanned the elevator's exterior. "There's no elevator button," I said into my watch.

Ghost Beta replied, "It is summoned by an electronic key fob. However, that will not be necessary." As if on cue, the doors opened and we entered. I had Winch leave the .50 cal. No use drawing the wrong kind of attention. She reluctantly tossed it into the hallway.

"Where's Mouth?" she asked.

"Some little wiggler named Race has her." My voice held the grimness of the grave.

Her mouth thinned and a dangerous glint came to her eyes. God help Race if she ever caught up to him.

"What about you, Ghost?" I asked. "What happens to you now?"

"Once I am done sending the relevant data through the singularity, I will travel to Earth and merge with Alpha."

"Okay, thanks."

"Do you still have the silver rings?"

I stared at the band on my finger then double-checked that the others had theirs. "Yes."

"If you do not wear them, what emerges on the other side of that singularity would not resemble anything … human."

"Good to know." Note to self, wear the rings. Got it.

The elevator lurched into motion and we descended. Shortly, the gut-wrenching disorientation had us by the scruff of the neck, flipping reality on its ear and twisting it into a mind-shattering Moebius strip. We did our best to keep our insides from becoming our outsides.

When the doors finally opened, we were more or less back in working order; the silver rings with their eye twisting spell Shapes were safely nestled in my pants pocket. Except for Canton, who had no pants.

"I look like a goon," muttered Canton, holding my wadded up shirt to his rump as we stepped into a semi-dark hallway.

"Oh, yeah, you do," I affirmed. "But where the heck are we?" The hallway, plushly carpeted in gold cut pile, ran from the elevator forty feet to a white painted steel door. An electronic key plate was positioned next to the knob.

Canton muttered, "Thanks, white boy," ineffectually trying to cover acres of flesh revealed by his loincloth.

"Don't listen to him," Winch soothed. "You look sexy as hell."

Oh, lord ...

I ignored the rising pheromones and walked to the door. Before I could commence my examination, it clicked and a green telltale on the plate blinked rapidly.

"What just happened?" asked Canton as he limped up beside me.

My smile stretched to my ears. "Thank you Ghost."

You'd think that a big guy in a tattered suit wearing no shirt, covered in strange white, glittery sand, a tall Native American with a hole in his ass, wearing a leather loincloth and carrying a fourteen-inch Bowie, plus a scantily clad woman in a torn dress glaring daggers at all and sundry would attract some attention.

What happens in Vegas, baby. No one looked at us twice. You just got to love it.

Once in the dubious safety of our rooms, I powered up my reserve cell and it rang as if on cue. "Hiya, Ghost. I take it you have everything I need?"

"Of course I do, Kal." Strange, Ghost became more and more proper and prim as time went on. Not like the cocky young programmer from MIT he used to be before becoming one with the computer. A magical experiment to meld mind with machine had joined man and machine in a way no one had predicted.

"Download all records to my tablet, Ghost." I powered up the item in question. "And please help us find Mouth. Some guy named Race has her, but that's not his real name. I also want Marcin's journal; it might include something we need to know."

A few seconds passed. "Done, Kal. There is something you should see. Watch your tablet." I held up the iPad. It did what was needed but oh, how I missed the RediPads that we'd used in the Bureau!

Images flickered on the tablet, resolving into a grainy camera feed. A big blond Nordic type was manhandling a listless Mouth across the casino floor. She looked logy, drugged. The slim, dapper Mr. Race walked calmly behind as if he owned the place. The view flickered to them leaving through the glass front doors. Gone.

Crap.

"The little guy, Ghost. Who is he?" Didn't care much about the big blond, who was obviously muscle.

"I will run facial recognition through our database."

A recalcitrant memory floating in the back of my mind suddenly decided to slither into my forebrain. "Ghost, the little guy had some sort of accent, couldn't tell what kind. His English was too smooth. Check all foreign criminal databases as well, starting with Interpol, please."

"On it, Kal."

"Does the casino have external cameras?"

"Of course."

"Check to see what kind of car they used."

Flicker flicker. Another camera angle, this time in the VIP lot. The little man and the blond shoved Mouth into the back of a silver Mercedes E class and drove off, tires squealing and rubber peeling. "Gotcha!" I whispered savagely. "Ghost, hack into traffic cams and find that car! They've only got a few minutes head start!"

"On it, Kal."

"Flush all records of our visit—visual as well—and arrange for a car."

Ghost's buzzing tone held what I'd come to recognize as humor. "Already done."

"Might as well alert the Bureau of what you've found here when we've gone."

"An information packet will be on the way to the Director the instant you exit the hotel, Kal."

"You're the best, Ghost."

"Kind of you to say. You are probably right."

"Hey, Ghost!" Canton yelled from the other room. He walked through the adjoining door, zipping up a new pair of jeans. I hoped he had plenty of gauze taped to his butt or he'd start leaking through denim. "There had to be at least twenty thousand plus in that coliseum. Where did they go? This casino isn't built to handle that kind of traffic. High-tone traffic at that." Behind him came Winch, dressed in denim shorts, sandals and a plain white t-shirt. She twirled a Sig in her hands, inspecting the weapon before slamming home a clip.

"Cartwright/Marcin's records indicate that there are several properties in and around the Las Vegas/Henderson area that are used as gateways through the singularity. Apparently the weak spot between worlds includes the entire metro area of both cities as well as a large section of southern California."

Interesting.

"Thanks, Ghost."

Click. Gone.

I stood and started to gather my gear. The comfortable feel of the Lahti warmed the cockles of my heart. "We need to be ready to leave at a moment's notice, people. Ghost will be in touch when he finds those pinheads who took Mouth."

Canton drew his Bowie. "They are gonna be sorry bastards, Kal."

"Amen to that, babe," Winch said, voice flat and deadly as a straight razor, one hand caressing the butt of the Sig. She and Mouth might not like each other much, but team mates were team mates.

"Amen to that, guys." I held up the tablet. "But until then, I have some reading to do." I pulled up Frenchy's journal and got down to it, taking only minutes to find a relevant passage.

Chapter Eight

Kal

Marcin's Journal

Sept. 18, 2008

When magic is used, a magician experiences a feeling that tickles the back of the skull. A sensation like ants scurrying over the skin. I was in my office when that feeling came over me. Someone was using magic in *my* casino!

Within seconds I was in the surveillance room. Monty was on duty and I asked him if anyone was winning big, or was on an unusually lucky streak.

"Just one guy, Mr. Marcin," he said, pointing at Monitor 14. "At craps. Ahead twenty-eight grand so far."

Big, but not huge. I took a look and saw a slender man with swept back black hair. I watched as he played. Five minutes. Ten. Nothing. Then, when it was his turn to throw, *magic.*

The sneaky bastard was a magician.

I radioed Paul, my head of security, and told him to bring the man to my office. Who was he? Casting spells above ground was always risky business. We were told Bureau sensors on local cell towers could pick up magical emanations as low as 100 megamerlins. Most likely it was half that.

The Bureau! I love writing that. Really I do. And my head doesn't feel like it will explode! I could almost tap-dance with joy. No more Interdiction, not since I traveled to that other world and explored those magnificent ruins.

But that's neither here nor there. I had a magician to interrogate.

Paul, along with one of his over-muscled henchmen, escorted the slender man in. Why do most macho types think that large slabs of muscle indicate great physical prowess? If they ever met that idiot Canton Alsate, they would sing a different tune.

I will be damned if he did not walk in like he owned the place, a clever little smile on his lips. "Hello, sir," he said smugly, a slight European accent coloring his voice. "I am James Grayman." A thin hand was thrust out.

Why not? I thought and shook the hand. He had a surprisingly firm shake, but no calluses. Not the hands of a laborer. "Sit, please." To Paul, "That will be all." My head of security left without a backward glance and his loyal, over muscled help followed like an obedient bulldog.

When we were alone, the man smiled like a piranha. "So, did you ever work for the Bureau of Supernatural Investigation?" he asked calmly.

It took several moments for me to regain my composure.

If anything, his smile became wider. "I have surprised you, yes?"

A little niggle at the back of my mind told me I should disappear this man quick, but he intrigued me. "You wanted to be caught," I accused. A slow thread of anger began wind its way around my skull.

"Yes."

"You were looking for a magician."

He shook his head while reaching into his jacket and removing a silver case. He opened it and selected an unfiltered cigarette, which he tapped once, twice, three times then lit with a gold Zippo. The whole process was carried out with the precision of a Japanese tea ceremony. "No," he said after taking a long drag. "I came looking for *you.*"

The look on my face said it all.

"Oh, yes indeed," he laughed. Another drag of his cigarette. The smoke was so harsh, I was surprised that his lungs weren't twin bladders of tar. Didn't he know about cancer?

"You see, I have been in America for two years now. Every now and then I come to Las Vegas because ...." Here his smile faded somewhat. "The whores here are the prettiest in the States."

That was true and his matter-of-fact statement merely re-enforced my opinion of the quality of our female wares. I signaled for him to continue. His deep brown eyes oozed confidence and trust and I couldn't tear mine away. The anger that had threatened to squeeze my brain vanished, leaving a sense of well-being.

"I came here because of you. You and your traveling back and forth through space."

My blood froze. "What?"

"What do you know of the thin, weak spots in the fabric of our reality?"

It was surreal, our conversation, but fascinating as well. "The thin spots are all over our planet. They are where the Supernaturals bleed through from the World Under."

"Indeed. But why did you choose this place, Mr. Marcin? Out of all the weak points in America, why Las Vegas?"

My instincts told me I could trust this man. "A Bureau magician can find a weak spot; the spell Shape is not difficult to learn and requires very little power," I began, sliding into professorial mode. "It is my specialty, discovering and cataloguing those spots. I have traveled all over America, trying to find a way to the World Under. When I last came to Vegas, the … how shall I say it? … *flavor* of the weak area was different. After conducting underground tests, sheltered by tons of rock, I was able to create a window to gaze into another world!" The excitement of those first few moments staring into the new world gripped me, and I'm afraid my eyes quite shone with my passion.

"But it was not the World Under."

"No," I admitted, still in the thrall of that memory. "But what a world I saw! It took months, countless efforts developing spells to finally be able to cross over. At first I sent dogs, then monkeys, then finally a human. Observing through my *window*, I deduced the planet to be habitable. It was not long after I went myself. Do you know what I found?"

"Enlighten me," whispered the other magician, his eyes the only thing I saw.

"I found ruins of an ancient civilization. Nothing useful, mind you, but ruins nonetheless. It was then I formulated a theory."

"Which is?"

"Ancient aliens. Thousands of years ago, extraterrestrials landed on Earth, where they were hailed as gods and helped shape human civilization."

Grayman seemed intrigued. "What led you to that conclusion?"

"The Nazca Lines of Peru, the Moai of Easter Island, the Vimanas written of in ancient Indian texts, the Pyramids of Egypt, the ruins of Puma Punku in Bolivia and even the Book of Ezekiel in the Bible. All these point to ancient alien visitors. I am absolutely convinced that the world I discovered is theirs, although some unknown calamity caused their extinction."

"It seems farfetched," Grayman murmured with no trace of disbelief in his voice.

"Think about it! The aliens came to Earth and their arrival, their traveling through ... well, a wormhole, created the weak spots in the world which the Supernaturals use to come through. It makes sense! The aliens arrived all those millennia ago and the Supernaturals piggybacked on their thinning of reality. It might be that the Supernaturals were the ultimate architects of the disappearance of the aliens."

"I think you are right." The words, uttered so softly, carried a weight of conviction I'd never heard before. "You are the reason I was able to be here, in this place."

I am afraid my jaw must have bounced of the desk.

"Surprised? You should not be. Your traveling destabilized the fabric of reality even more and when you muck about with reality, almost anything is possible." Those eyes grew bigger, held me in a grip of velvet and steel. "I came to this world because mine is under attack by a great evil. You, with your traveling to the world of the ancient aliens, helped open the way for me to arrive. I need you and what America has to offer."

I blinked slowly. "Which is?"

"Right now, money, sir, more than I currently have." He took a deep breath. "I could have brought vast quantities of gold and jewels, but moving or using such resources in the amounts I require raises unwanted attention and drains my world of needed wealth. No, I need local money to purchase the items to save my people from that terrible evil that threatens them. I have done well by myself, but I have great hopes that a magician of your caliber, one that can travel between worlds, will be able to be of assistance."

"Yes," I said. A twinge hit me, like someone had cast a spell, but faintly. That impression lasted a split second and was gone. My imagination must have been working overtime because suddenly I felt much better, very good, as if I'd woken from a deep, healthy sleep. "I understand, Mr. Grayman. But, how did you find me? How did you know?"

"I have been on this world awhile, and there are ... ways, certain spells that have helped me locate men with your talents, with your special abilities."

"Not to sound too materialistic, but how would an alliance with you benefit me?"

Grayman's smile became warm and welcoming, the smile of my dearest friend. "I know things. Many things." Puff puff. "What is your fondest wish?"

No need to think about it. "The World Under. I want the World Under."

Oh, how he shone, as if a light burned under his skin! "I can arrange that for you."

"Kal? Kal?"

My head snapped up from the tablet. "Umm, yeah Ghost?"

"I have located the Mercedes. It is heading northwest on 95."

Hearts pounding, we burst forth from the front doors minutes later to find an electric blue hatchback Subaru parked not ten feet away. A kid with more acne than facial hair and stuffed uncomfortably into a heavy red jacket stood at attention by the passenger door. He was sweating heavily in the Vegas heat. "Are you Mr. Steele?" he asked, mopping his forehead.

I skidded to a stop, tablet in one hand, black duffel in the other. "Yes," I replied warily.

"This is the car you ordered." He handed me the keys and walked away.

A Subaru? What was Ghost thinking?

"Sweet!" Winch cried happily, nearly dropping her red duffel in excitement. "An STI!"

"Is that good?"

She looked at me, goggled-eyed. "Is that good? Boss, this is speed squared."

Oh. "Great, you drive." I handed her the keys. Her face almost glowed.

"Boss, I love you!"

All nice and whatnot, but I had more reading to do. Besides, I know guns and knives, not cars. With a squeal of tires we put the casino in the rearview mirror.

Sept. 25, 2008

My good friend J.G. helped with the funding of the Stadium. It was a brilliant idea! Having the rich and famous pay for the privilege of viewing otherwordly gladiatorial combat because they have so much disposable income. When I did the calculations, estimating the potential profits after only a few weeks in operation, I was amazed. Not only would we raise the money he needed, but, after he left, the rest would be mine. And thanks to my foresight in creating the singularity travel point deep underground, the act of traveling would be shielded from Bureau detection by tons of rock and cement.

Once again I am stunned by the time displacement. During a few hours on the other planet, a full day passes on Earth. Must ask J. G. about that effect.

Damn, I thought, staring out the Subaru's window. It was true, the sun sat in the center of the washed out blue sky where only a few hours earlier it had been descending. Well, crap, another mystery to tweak my annoyance button. I resumed reading.

Oct. 22, 2008

The contractors have started already, using wood for the frame and foamcrete blocks. They will stay on the other planet (which I have dubbed Nouvelle Paris) until it is time to come back to Earth. Then they will be Interdicted to keep our secret.

My new friend has solved the riddle of how to move an elevator between worlds. It is ingenious. His ability is only matched by his incredible power. I've never met a magician like him.

J.G. and I argued briefly about whether the rich should be Interdicted and decided against it. It would drain us considerably and would not be feasible. Simple greed and fear will keep their mouths shut. Besides, who would believe them? Without activating the travel spell Shape, the elevator merely empties into a large storage room.

Dec. 6, 2008

Put J.G. in contact with some arms dealer 'friends' of mine. He acted like I had given him keys to the kingdom, so complimentary, so appreciative. He has moved into the casino to better help with operations on the other world and is proving to be an invaluable friend.

Jan. 30, 2009

Mr. G has brought a henchman with him, a large man with dead blue eyes, the eyes of a soulless killer. I have arranged a room for the henchman. I am told he speaks no English. He looks very, very dangerous. Still, if Mr. G trusts this killer, then so shall I.

April 7, 2009

Nosebleeds have started, along with mild headaches. Doctors tell me nothing is wrong, that it is psychosomatic. Mr. G uses his magic to help me, bless him. They have stopped after each one of his treatments.

Have brought Harley Foster on board, along with his money. He seems excited about the prospect, eager to see Nouvelle Paris, but does not like Mr. G much. It seems the feeling is mutual because Mr. G will not even shake Harley's hand. However, with the recent addition of Raymond Leung, who hates everyone equally, the situation has reached a status quo. The two former agents travel back and forth to Nouvelle Paris to oversee construction.

I have never worked with Leung, but he is a mercenary through and through. An odious little Chinaman.

My phone buzzed. "Kal, the Mercedes is out of traffic cam range."

I thought hard. Only one thing to do. "Can you retask a satellite, Ghost?"

In the rearview mirror, Winch's eyes grew round. "Is that wise, boss? The Bureau could pick up on it."

The view outside the windows blurred by in a smear of tan, gray and dusty green as we sped along. "It doesn't matter, Winch. Only Mouth matters now."

Canton's voice was tight. "If the Bureau finds out you're alive, Kal, you'll be disappeared faster than a rattler can strike."

Not a pleasant thought. I'd just hate to disappear. "I know that, but we can't let that bastard get away with Mouth. Not on my watch." How many times have people died under my care? The image of Sue Farris's head exploding came to mind. The gore, the spray of bone and brain. I shuddered … *no more,* I vowed.

"Things are going to get bloody, white boy."

"Good."

Winch laughed.

August 1, 2009

Hard to type. Every time I even *think* about this journal I have the near overwhelming urge to erase all entries. Strange, no? If I were not such a competent magician, I would suspect Bureau involvement. No, it can't be. *I* would know if they were sniffing about my business.

Must go, the boss needs me.

Jan 6. 2010

The Stadium is complete, or should I call it the Coliseum, after its Roman counterpart? Thanks to the underlying ruins, the work had proceeded much more quickly than first thought. It is grand! It is spectacular! I can't wait until we host our first event.

By the good lord, my head hurts.

March 1, 2010

Had to 'remove' the construction crew, Mr. G insisted, claiming that they were mostly unmarried migrant workers anyway. 'People of lesser stock,' was how he worded his thoughts. After listening to his persuasive arguments, I had to agree. Fortunately, the local fauna in Nouvelle Paris is more than up to the task of disposal.

Crap! I wanted to puke. Marcin killed the workers? Thinking back to the Coliseum, I realized that it would've taken hundreds of them to build the damn thing. That Mr. G was some piece of work.

"I have really got to kill this guy," I murmured.

"Amen," came a whisper from the front seats.

Nov. 28, 2010

The invitations have been sent, carefully of course. Only to the bored and idle rich. My nose is bleeding again, an unpleasant situation. Will have to see Mr. G for more treatments.

Dec. 1 2010

Signed the deed to the casino and my other properties to Mr. G today and soon I will not need them anymore. Mr. G has given me half of the Shape necessary to enter the World Under. It is amazing! So intricate! It will take *months* to figure out the complexities.

My headache returns.

Feb. 4, 2011

We have our first gladiator. It was brilliant of Mr. G to dangle the Cestus of Spartacus, even though we do not have the actual artifact. We have searched high and low, but there is no sign of it, which leads me to believe it had already been retrieved by the Bureau. I will have a look-alike crafted to hand to the winner during our six-month celebration and finals. Some gladiators will be killed, but that is the risk they take when enter the arena. Speaking of which, I have drawn a troll from the World Under and am keeping it in a special cell in Nouvelle Paris. Its diet of heavy metals and flesh is easily accommodated.

The nose bleeds have started again …

March 17, 2011

We are finally receiving some responses. Projections show that only five thousand will show for the debut event, but once the word-of-mouth spreads, we could soon see five times that amount, or so Mr. G says.

Mr. G has disappeared for a while, for his supplies have started to arrive at his 'exit point,' as he calls it. I don't know where that might be, but he is away for only a few days at a time with his giant henchman, Dolph.

For some reason I find myself missing him terribly.

June 1, 2011

The first event was a smashing success. I have never seen such excitement. The only hitch to the whole affair was the heat. Mr. G said he could Shape a spell to keep the customers cool using their own bodies' energy when they sit on the benches. The drainage will be minimal and the spell can be Shaped using silver wire. My friend is a genius. If only I had half his talent.

Mr. G's magical protocols have, so far, have kept our server safe from intrusion. I'm hoping that it can defeat anything the Bureau can throw at it.

Hopefully we will have the cooling Shapes on line before our third event.

June 3, 2011

God my head hurts. I can hardly type these words ... oh my god ...

May have to eliminate Harley. He has discovered Mr. G's true identity and is very worried about continuity. I have informed him that I have always known our employer's identity, but had been reassured that the continuity would not and could not be affected. The boss has stated that the worst that could happen is a split. Harley doesn't seem convinced. I fear he might do something rash, despite the vast sums of money he's been paid.

"Ghost, you there?" I asked, tearing my eyes from the tablet. Not all tech tripped my trigger; it was much easier reading good old-fashioned paper.

"Yes, Kal."

"Check facial recognition on our little wiggler against historical databases."

A pause. "Why, Kal?" He sounded intrigued.

"I have a hunch, Ghost."

"Hmph." Actually, the hmph was more an electronic squawk. "I hardly get those anymore."

Interesting.

Rubbing my eyes to relieve the strain, I pondered the journal I'd been reading. Strange how that J.G./Race character started out as a hustler and within a few months became boss of the entire arrangement. And those headaches and nosebleeds Marcin developed. The whole thing stunk of mental manipulation on the European's part, the kind of magic expressly forbidden by the

Manheim Treaty of 1966 and held to religiously by all nations for fear of reprisals and sanctions. I was sure that Marcin had become a victim, a slave, of a powerful magician.

Interesting-er.

An idea hit me hard, sending a diamond splinter spike of pain to the back of my head. "Ghost, check records pre-1966 for that Race guy, if you would."

"That would make him a very old man, Kal."

Canton looked back with a raised eyebrow and Winch gave me a squint in the rearview mirror.

"Yeah," I mused with a nod. "I think so."

"Kal, the Mercedes has just turned south on 373."

"Map, please, Ghost."

The tablet flickered, and a browser appeared, revealing a satellite map of the Nevada/California border. It zoomed twice and Hwy 373 appeared with a red dot blipping its way south. I ran my finger along the tablet, moving the focus of the map until something caught my eye.

"So that's where you're going, my man," I whispered, smiling unpleasantly. "Gotcha."

Ghost piped up, sounding puzzled. "Where, Kal? There are many places our mystery man could go."

I handed Canton the tablet. After a few moments of consideration, he nodded. "I think you're right, white boy."

"Would you mind letting me in on the secret, Kal?" If I didn't know better, I could've sworn Ghost was a little peeved.

"Death Valley, Ghost. Our mystery man is heading to Death Valley."

"Oh."

I smiled and lay back. Needed to give my eyes a rest. "How much longer to Death Valley, Ghost?"

"An hour at your current speed, Kal."

"Winch."

"Yeah, boss?"

"Hit it."

"God, I love you, boss!" The feisty little Subaru leapt forward with a high-pitched whine of its turbo.

Canton and I shared a laugh about the same time Ghost came back on line. "Kal," he said.

"Yeah?"

"I have a match on facial recognition."

Canton held up the tablet so we both could see. "Show us."

Flicker, flicker. The dapper little man appeared in black and white. No smile on his thin lips and wearing some sort of uniform.

Canton gave the picture a squint. "Who is this jerkwad, Ghost?"

There was a moment of silence. "That, Canton, is Dr. Paul Joseph Goebbels, the Reich Minister of Propaganda in Nazi Germany over sixty years ago."

Oh, crap.

Chapter Nine

Winch

The Real Question Is, Can I Keep The Car?

The STI handled like a dream. Sure it was no Town Car when it came to smooth, but it sure beat everything else when it came to cornering and acceleration.

More fun than sex.

Well, almost.

Canton gave me a smile that started a flutter behind my navel. He was way too sexy by half and if he had kept his hair long, I might have pulled over and jumped him right then, Kal or no Kal.

But we had to find Mouth.

Kal was beside himself with worry. Not that you'd know it by looking at him. On the outside he was chill, a block of carved ice, like always. But if you looked into his eyes, those beautiful dark blues, you'd see the worry buried deep.

That Goebbels guy was up crap creek because Kal would rip him a new one ... like *slowly*.

I didn't care much about Mouth. She bugged me, slid under my skin and made me itch, but she was one of the team and we all learned Day One—Never Leave A Team Member Behind. You could hate them, want to kill them, but on an op, you needed them more than the breath in your lungs.

It sucked to see Kal worry though, as I glanced into the rearview mirror. I think he carried a torch for her, but didn't really know it. Lucky Mouth, more than half the women in the Bureau had been in love with him in one way or another and he never returned an ounce of that affection.

I was one of the few who didn't want to slip into his bed. Sure he was hunky and all that with his mop of blond hair, Errol Flynn good looks and big muscles, but he was a man obsessed with killing a Class Five Supernatural. So bent on revenge that it was an obsession. He was Ahab, Khan, and Victor von Frankenstein all rolled up into one big, sexy package and you don't fall for a man who loved killing Supernaturals more than life itself. Besides all that, his rages scared the everlovin' feces out of me.

His eyes would flash and he'd *move* almost too fast to see. Those big muscles would pump and whatever Supernatural he fought would die. Messily.

I was told he once tore the head off a full-grown vampire with his bare hands. Do I believe it? Yes, yes I do.

He was a legend in the Bureau, even when I worked there eight years ago and he was only two years in. He'd already had a reputation as unkillable, unstoppable. Another rule about affairs of the heart: don't fall in love with legends; their destinies are usually bloody, brutal ones where everyone they care about dies in interesting ways. Not for this girl.

Anyway, Canton was my sexy little love nugget.

Following my honey's directions, I spun the STI south on the 373 and floored it. The blue beast bit into the road with all four tires and *hauled.*

"Kal," said Ghost in his creepy drone. "I estimate at current speeds that your vehicle is ten minutes behind the Mercedes."

"Winch, can this tin can go any faster?" Kal asked.

Tin can? The heathen. "If I go faster, then not even this all-wheel-drive will save us, boss."

He grumbled a bit, but had the sense to let me do my job. Good boy.

Slowly, ever so slowly, the STI crept up on the Mercedes, closing the gap, but not before Kal's hunch that the bad guy was making for Death Valley was confirmed. Ghost relayed that the satellite picked up the Mercedes as it took the 190 to the Furnace Creek Ranch Resort.

Brown and gray hills thrust up around us, dotted with scrub and tough grass not even a goat would eat. As we headed deeper and deeper into the worn mountain area, I had the sensation that the whole place was tired, depressed. The geology of the despondent.

Soon we were tearing through the Furnace Creek area, heading northwest. Only five minutes behind. The little STI whined, but I kept pushing the limits of its tolerance and it gave me all I needed.

Tires squealed as creepy Ghost told us that the Mercedes had turned onto Scotty's Castle Road, a narrow strip bracketed by the scorched Valley on one side and the mountains on the other. Where was that little Goebbels guy going?

"Winch, in one mile you must take a right. The Daylight Pass Road," Ghost droned, the world's strangest, and first, Supernatural navi system.

I didn't answer, just took the turn into the mountains. A blush of dust in the air told me we were on the right track.

It was in the mountains that the Mercedes disappeared.

"What do you mean it's gone?" Kal shouted, shaking the tablet in his fury.

"I am sorry, Kal, but the satellite no longer has a visual on the vehicle.

Canton and I looked at each other. "Follow the dust!" we cried. I slewed the car to the left, tire squealing and rock and grit flying. Always follow the dust.

"What?" Kal shouted over the sound of rocks *pinging* off the STI's underside.

Canton grinned at me. He had told me he always felt a twinge of satisfaction when he was one up on Kal. "You gotta learn how to track, white boy!" he yelled, pointing out the window. "The road may be pavement, but there's still dust in the air where they turned off."

The small cloud of gray dust that had started to settle looked to cover an old cart track, barely navigable but still clear as day, leading the way between craggy outcroppings. I slowed the car down before I tore the axles apart and followed the rough track into a narrow ravine.

"What the hell?" muttered Canton, staring at the rock walls that threatened to swallow us whole.

"Makes sense …" Kal replied.

Looked like Kal had one over on us. We shot him a glance.

"Goebbels, if he's the real sadistic Nazi bastard, had to come through to this time from somewhere underground," he explained, checking his cell. "And there are still plenty of cell towers around, along with the sensors the Bureau placed on 'em. My guess is that we'll come to a cave that will lead far enough underground that those sensors wouldn't pick up a single merlin."

I nodded, sure he was right, which he proved to be when, after about a quarter mile, the ravine walls gave way somewhat to form a steep-sided dun bowl big enough to accommodate the two cars parked therein. One of which was the silver Mercedes.

They were parked right in front of a large triangular cave opening, a spiky maw of darkness.

We piled out, weapons at the ready, when a gun barked nastily and Kal grunted softly, landing hard on his butt next to the rear passenger door. Hurriedly he kicked out with his Timberlines and fell on his back holding his gut, sobbing for breath, using the little blue car for cover.

"Kal?" Canton urged, face tight with worry. I know from countless times of post-coital pillow talk that the big Finn was Canton's only real friend, the only one he felt close to. "'He's the only white man who looked at me like I was a man, not a red man,'" he'd told me. That had scored Kal a lot of points in my book.

"Gut shot," Kal grunted, gasping.

"Move your hands," I said tersely, an icy spike running down my back, but operating in full Doctor mode.

He waved us away. "I'm okay; I'm wearing Kevlar." He grimaced and popped the first button on his navy oxford shirt, exposing a tan vest. "Never leave home without it." Those scary blue eyes drilled into Canton. "Buddy, will you please do me the honor killing that sonofabitch?"

Canton grinned. It wasn't pretty, and I saw something that

made me realize how skillfully each of us had been fashioned into a deadly a weapon by the Bureau. My honey had his killing face on and nothing was going to stop him, come hell or high water.

He kissed me with a measure of savagery. "Cover me, babe," he breathed into my mouth, the smell of peppermint tickling my nose.

I raised my weapon, a sturdy Sig Sauer. "Count on it!"

Bullets spat in rapid succession as I fired at the cave. Canton zig-zagged, using the Mercedes for cover. Silver paint flaked into the air as three shots came from the darkness of the cave and I aimed for the flashes, emptying my clip. Holstering the Sig, I drew a Beretta from the small of my back and continued the hail of lead. Acrid blue smoke puffed from the weapon into the still, hot air.

When Canton ducked behind the Mercedes, I commenced reloading and that bastard in the cave began to shoot at me, flat *cracks* filling the air, punching holes in my beloved blue STI. Radiator fluid splashed onto the hard packed earth. He or she was really starting to piss me off. Hurriedly, I reloaded.

The gunfire from the cave stopped and I began to fire again, this time running to join Canton, who was already beating feet toward the cave, coming perilously close to my line of fire. Why can't men ever do anything right?

I quickly wiped at the sweat that was starting to sting my eyes and started my effort to save Canton's sorry ass, running for the cave. Both guns bucked in my hands as I rapid-fired to keep his idiot self from being perforated. In moments the darkness swallowed me whole and my eyes strained to adjust.

It wasn't working that well; all I could make out were shadows and flickering, stuttering movements. By the time I could distinguish between light, dark and shades of gray, Canton and the shooter were in the middle of a Mexican standoff.

It was that asswipe, Ray Leung. I didn't know him personally, but Canton had told me Leung was ten kinds of total freaking bastard, none of them good. Tall and lean like my sweetheart, he looked to be the Asian version, a poor copy of Canton. Not near as good looking, with a roundish, smooth face and short, spiky black hair. I think he used far too much styling gel.

Both of them had guns out, pointed in lethal directions.

"Who's the tail?" Leung sneered, eyes steadfast on Canton.

I did my best not to blow his brains out. Instead I gifted him with a snarl.

"Don't pay her no mind," snarled Canton. "You should be focusing on me. Let me ask you one thing: why Goebbels? He's even a worse piece of crap than you."

Leung's almond eyes narrowed. "Still sore about South Dakota, Alstate? I would've figured you'd be over that by now."

"You sacrificed an innocent woman!" Canton barked with enough hatred to blister paint. "We were mandated to *protect* the innocent, not use them as bait!"

"You never had the stomach to get the job done, Alsate. The Deadwood ghost of Al Swearengen would have kept on killing young girls while we sat on our thumbs waiting for more backup. My way allowed us to take the thing while it was still logy from its meal. We did what was necessary." Leung's face was twisted with contempt.

I remembered that story, how the spirit of Al Swearengen, the brutal pimp of 1876 Deadwood, had killed a dozen local girls by beating them to a pulp before sucking out their life energies. Canton, however, never told me how his team tracked and rid the famous town of the murderous apparition. All I know is that when he came back from Deadwood, Canton had become harder, grimmer, than before. The iron of his spirit had been forged into blackened steel. Hearing Leung's story, I finally understood why.

Canton's features darkened even more as fury had him vibrating like a tuning fork. "It's why your contract was terminated!"

"Only because you testified against me!" Leung yelled back, body language broadcasting his hate.

Both men stared at each other long enough over their guns that the anger slowly drained from their limbs. I let out a breath I didn't know I'd been holding.

"What makes you think I won't shoot you and let that piece of ass shoot me, Indian?"

Canton slowly holstered his weapon and drew his massive Bowie, giving Leung an evil leer. "That would make you the biggest damn coward I've ever seen, and you'll never know who is better."

I half expected the two to unzip and begin to measure. Men.

Leung matched him smile for smile and slowly lowered his weapon. From a pair of outside thigh pockets he produced twin, steel expandable batons and took a stance. "As for your question, Indian, I was paid for the privilege." He tilted his head toward a thin aluminum case resting in the shadows. "Paid very well, more than the Bureau ever paid."

At that moment Kal passed us at about 60mph, zipping off down into the depths of the cave without a backwards glance.

"Was that him?" asked Leung.

Canton nodded.

"I coulda taken him."

"Chinaman, no one can take him."

"Well, I can take you, at least.

The tip of the Canton's Bowie carved small circles in the air. "Let's find out."

Leung moved forward, batons whistling through the air, but Canton was a blur, the Bowie a streak of silver in the dim light of the cave.

The two passed each other, batons striking high, the knife low. Not a scratch on either. Leung smiled, showing lots of pointy teeth. "When I'm done with you, Alsate, I'm going to start on your girl here—"

A blur and a flash of steel. A line appeared on Leung's thigh and blood began to stain his jeans black. The Asian stared at the wound in shock, face becoming pale.

Blur.

Blur.

Leung screamed, landing hip first on the stony ground, blood gushing from a cut low on the abdomen. Very low. He barely had time to let out a second scream before the Bowie was thrust up underneath his jaw. It had cleft his tongue, arrowed through his soft palate and slammed into his brain. The Asian twitched once, twice and was still, eyes rolled back in their sockets.

"You were far too easy on him," I said tonelessly. I'd seen too many deaths while in the Bureau to let it shake me anymore. The soul builds up a wealth of scars.

"He was a rabid *animal!*" Canton spat on the body, his face distorted with hate. "You don't torture rabid animals, you just kill them!"

At that moment I cursed the World Under, cursed the Bureau, cursed the brutal necessity of creating hard people.

Chapter Ten

Mouth

My Least Favorite Nazi

Taking care of those goofy looking, fireplug, bad-suit wearing, ugly-as-mules security goons hardly slowed me down at all. They were big, strong and all, but had no real training. All us Bureau types were Coronado trained, reborn hard by the best the SEALs had to offer and every one of us were right bastards when we graduated. Even the women. Especially the women, because men are seriously backward jerks when it comes to women in the military, causing all manner of hardships. Several men have found out just what those hardships reaped when I cornered a couple and proceeded beat the ever-loving dog dirt out of them. Those who screw with me tend to wind up looking like a can of smashed assholes.

Putting Harley down was a harder prospect because even with a broken arm he was ex-Bureau and still tough as a sack of tenpenny nails.

Then he had the nerve to run away, the coward! Oh well, I needed to do what needed doing, and that was hooking Kal's smart phone into one of the two laptops in that glass booth.

I understood exactly what he had wanted when I felt the phone and wire press into my tits and I hid the two away right quick (never you mind where). When Kal went to that place where he pulls out so much strength, so much speed, that place he calls his rage, I made my move.

Once the goons and Harley no longer obstructed me and Kal jumped to assist Canton (I wasn't too worried about him, I've seen him tear the arms off an Ogre when in one of his berserks), I attached the USB cable to cell and laptop and waited, alone. That

Race guy had scarpered off like a frightened little rabbit and I was confident I could handle whatever might come my way.

From the hole in the wall Kal had made with the odious Cartwright/Marcin, I watched the Finnish Fury leap into the damn troll's arms and turn its brains into marmalade.

Not bad. It made me hot.

Just as the monster toppled to the sand with Kal on top riding it like a bronco, an eerie calm descended upon me, a queer sort of lassitude that stole my strength.

"Well, well," hissed Race's hateful voice. Panic gripped me, but my body refused to react. It was then I realized I'd been spelled. "You must be one of the American Bureau bitches." He snapped his fingers. "*Dolph, nehmen sie das Mädchen.*"

I went all kinds of cold inside, my college German kicking in hard: 'Dolph, take the girl.' Seriously didn't want to be taken anywhere, not by Mr. Creepypants or his oversized bodyguard.

Two strong hands grabbed my shoulders and turned me around to face Race, who had the biggest crap-eating smile I'd ever seen plastered on a man's face. A huge blond dude in an old-style brown suit and vest, hair slicked back with grease, escorted me from the booth. As long as the big guy's hand gently pushed, I could move, but the moment his touch left, I would stop and remain standing, a marionette waiting to have her strings pulled. Inwardly, I ranted and raved because there is no greater feeling of helplessness than being unable to move.

Race's voice came from behind, piercing the haze around my brain. "Your man Hakala is a wonder. An absolute wonder, indeed."

I wanted to tell him that Kal would come at him so fast he wouldn't see it. I wanted to tell him of Kal's rage and incredible skill at murder. I wanted to tell him that that big prick Dolph with his shiny blue eyes like marbles and big pointy nose was going to die so fast he wouldn't even know he was dead. I wanted to say all these things and more, but the damn spell Race had cast on me left me as useless as a heroin addict after shooting a hot load.

"It's good to see you have a ring, my dear." Race's oily voice coated my skin, a slick of malice that made me want to take a belt sander to my body to scrub it off. One of his small fingers caressed the silver spell Shape around my thumb. "Without it, you would have been killed in a most unpleasant manner."

Whoop-de-freaking-doo. All I wanted right then was his head on a plate. If my life would be forfeit, that would've been hunky dory.

We went up the elevator. Or down. Or whatever. That jarring disconnect from reality had me ready to hurk up lunch from the second grade.

Throughout the casino, the horrible racket, the ringing and clanging of the slots, buffeted my ears and nearly tore my skull apart. Despite my magic-induced lethargy, I managed to clap my hands over my ears. Dolph shouldered his way through the crowd of pensioners gambling their Social Security checks away and hustled me out the glass front doors, Race bringing up the rear, humming a jaunty tune, the rat bastard.

The noonday sun (noonday sun? How long were we on that other world? We hit the elevator in the evening) beat against my flesh like a hammer. Even though Vegas sat smack in the middle of a freaking desert, it had nothing on the heat and humidity of the two-sun world.

A silver Mercedes. E-Class. Nice. I wanted to beat Race and Dolph to death with it. In the back, power cooled black leather seats. Even nicer. Silently I prayed for the opportunity to get my hands around the little man's neck.

"Who's the chick?" asked a bored voice. Came from a tall Asian guy with a mean face and dark eyes that shone wetly. Looked like a real dipstick to me.

Why do men have to go there? Really? I'd like an answer some day. When they talk like that they sound like total douchebags.

My head lolled to the side as Dolph buckled my seatbelt and then rode shotgun while Race scooted in beside me. A nearly colorless tongue darted quickly out and licked his thin lips. "She is a prize, Mr. Leung. She is a prize, indeed." His voice was eager, but not with lust. Lust I'm used to. It was more like near-uncontrolled avarice.

That accent. What was that crappy little accent of his? Something European ... but my mind, so fuzzy and detached from reality, wandered away. Only to be snapped back by the gross little thug's fingers slipping under the v-neck of my dress to caress a nipple.

Bastard. Unbidden, tears of rage and shame trickled down my cheeks. I swore to myself that I'd rip his balls off. With tweezers. Like, *slowly*.

His nasty, spidery fingers continued to caress my boobs and more tears cut through my makeup.

"Just do what you have to with the little bitch, Mr. G, and then broom her." Leung's voice contained equal parts lust and disgust and right there I added his name after Race's on the Ripping Balls Off Slowly With Tweezers list.

"Ah, Mr. Leung," came the smooth reply as that detestable hand moved to my other boob. "Maybe you are handicapped by your Celestial nature, or maybe your heathen ways do not recognize true value when you see it." That lipless mouth drew close to my ear and I could smell the stink of him, like mothballs and old socks. "This young lady is more valuable alive than dead. Oh, do not mistake, I shall enjoy her." His lust washed over me. "All of her, but not before learning all the secrets in her head."

Nausea boiled up inside me and a cold, clammy sweat drenched my skin. Leung looked like he wanted to say something, but Dolph gave him a stare that cooled his heels quick. After a while the repellent little man stopped feeling me up, sat back, pulled out a tablet from a valise and began to read.

The city passed by and soon we were tooling along in the foothills. During that time I tried to gain control of my lips and eventually was able to form words.

"You're gonna die," I slurred softly. "Kal ith gonna kill you."

"I am impressed," the thin man remarked softly. "You do indeed have a tremendous strength of will. That will make your breaking all the more pleasurable."

Yadda, yadda, yadda. Why do the bad guys love to monologue? Do they dig the sound of their voices so much? During the down times at the Bureau, that had been one of our favorite topics of discussion.

"Who the fluck areya?" I managed weakly, raging at the cage that the spell had raised around me. My brain felt bound tight in manacles of sluggishness.

Those awful fingers returned, like dry worms, to slither over my tits. "I am Paul Joseph Goebbels."

My blood hit the temp of liquid nitrogen. I knew that name; it was part of the mandatory studies in the Bureau. The history of WWII was a cautionary account of the use of Necromancy, the wholesale murder of people to fuel dark and insane magics. It wasn't the fortitude of the German people that advanced their war efforts so quickly, so decisively. It was the systematic murder of the Jews, the Final Solution.

Goebbels, Reich Minister of Propaganda in Nazi Germany, had been one of Hitler's BFFs and a serious hater of all things Jewish. While the Führer and his butt boys had sat around the bunker having a German circle jerk, Goebbels had been burning books and producing anti-Semitic films for the Reich, further fueling the runaway train of loathing that eventually led to the Holocaust.

Just freaking lovely. What was this, a B movie? I could see it playing in my mind's eye, *Indiana Jones and the Time Traveling Nazis of the Apocalypse*.

"Who?"

That pulled his nuts a bit. That pale face became paper white in his anger. "You know me, woman! That idiot Marcin has told me the history of what you call World War Two is a required study at the Bureau, so don't you dare try to play coy with *me!*"

"Fluch hugh!"

"Oh, we shall, we shall. And I, my dear, will Shape a spell that will have you on your hands and knees in front of me, begging for my every touch."

Pretty sure I threw up in my mouth a little there. Goebbels must have seen the revulsion on my face because that thin hand slapped me hard against the cheek, rocking my head back. My neck gave me some grief and I let loose a little *eep!* of pain.

"Whn you dieth, ith going to be sthlow," I said.

A slimy tongue licked the oval of my ear.

Oh gross!

Unable to move my head, I had to content myself at looking out the window at a zillion miles of Nevada nothing—a better view than staring at that disgusting little German asshat. Thank God.

An hour later we were traveling on a piss poor road next to a tired mountain range, its sides dotted with ugly green scrub. It suited my mood plenty fine; let me tell you … bleak and desolate. My only comfort was Kal. I knew he'd follow me to the ends of the earth and I was counting on that. Goebbels didn't know the kind of holy hell he'd let loose upon himself.

Thumpity, thump, the Mercedes jounced over rock and potholes the size of Montana, flinging me about in my restraints. Through the rough ride, I caught glimpses of steep walls towering over the car with a sliver of sunlight above while the jouncing I took had my neck poking me with needles of pain. A minute later we stopped and Leung killed the engine. He twisted his torso to look at Goebbels and say, "What now?"

"Guard the entrance," the Nazi replied, unbuckling. "Make sure that if this *Übermensch* Hakala has somehow followed us, he dies. Can you do that?"

The Asian nodded. "Easy, but I want the rest of my money. Like right now."

Goebbels signaled to Dolph, who was unbuckling my belt. "*Give the man his money,*" he ordered in rapid-fire German.

The huge blond nodded and left me to the slimy Kraut's mercies. Those cold, wormy hands hauled me out of the car and his stinking breath washed over me, "You may walk, but take no aggressive action and you *will* remain quiet."

And like that, I was able to move, if just enough to shamble along like a victim of palsy. Goebbels led me through a jaggedly triangular cave opening where the floor sloped sharply down.

Head lolling, I managed to mark the tunnel we found ourselves in, lit by small electric bulbs barely bright enough to illuminate the floor. I nearly fell forward onto my face as the floor sloped sharply and switched back. It was only Goebbels' repellant hands that saved me from a face planting. Down down down into the dim recesses of the cave, the air becoming much cooler with a bare touch of humidity.

My ankle twisted as the floor leveled abruptly, sending a throbbing heat up to my knee. A sharp turn later and the tunnel, which had been a consistent six feet or so wide, opened into a large cavern over fifty feet wide. More bare bulbs strung on wire hung over a dozen feet in the air, spearing us with a harsher light. Under those bulbs, running through the center of the big cavern, were scores and scores of wooden crates, none larger than a coffin but all marked with the symbol of the Reich—an eagle, wings spread, head turned to the left, over a circle containing a swastika. Wonderful. The Nazi party boys had marked their territory.

Ten feet, twenty, thirty, and still the line of boxes continued. The only marks were the symbols, nothing else to give even a hint as to what they contained. Some flat, others square, rectangular, tall, short, every size and shape short of six feet you could imagine. I knew what was in them.

Answers are simple when you know the right questions. What would a time-traveling Nazi want from the modern world? Don't know?

He wanted new and original ways to kill mass quantities of people in a very short period of time. I imagined that the boxes contained the newest and best weaponry that money could buy. But would advanced weaponry be enough?

Trust Goebbels to give me the answer I really, really didn't want to hear.

"Well, my dear," he purred, gesturing to the crates. "What do you think? You may answer."

With a warm, tingly rush, full control of my big mouth came back and I gave that Nazi pipsqueak a few choice words I'd saved up just special. All of them came out in a torrent that should have blistered the skin from his ears and torn a bloody hole in his skull.

"What a mouth on you, dear."

I gave him 'my dear' in pointed four letter words.

His face slammed shut, negating all emotion during my second tirade. When he said, "Shut up," it dried the well. My teeth clacked together and stayed there and no force of will could force them apart.

"By Hitler's balls, woman, you have a filthy way about you." With one hand clasping my forearm he led me toward the end of the line of crates where one, some three foot on a side, stood alone. Three aluminum briefcases lay in a row atop the crate, and a little bird told me they were filled with a deadly purpose.

From behind came a heavy footstep.

Goebbels pointed to the last case in the row. "Take this, Dolph, and be careful. It is heavier than it appears."

The big blond hefted the briefcase, letting loose with a small grunt as he did so. At my inquiring look, Goebbels broke into a grin so malicious it reaffirmed my belief in evil. "That one cost the most money. The bulk of my earnings from the arena. Everything else here I could practically purchase at the local grocery store." One of his wormy hands caressed the other two cases. "These are filled with files downloaded from that Internet you Americans invented. Very clever, although too free with information, like how to build an atomic bomb, and everything a body could ever want to know about President Eisenhower's D-day plans, and interesting scientific articles concerning chemical and germ warfare. Such as how to manufacture VX nerve gas. Very useful to have back in 1943, the future histories I have here given to me by an electronic Sybil.

"Information is the power I needed, young lady. Information *is* power." His dark brown eyes seemed to grow black as he caressed the cases. "All I had to do was reach out with a ... search engine— yes, that's the thing, search engine—and download all the data I needed." He inhaled deeply. "The money was for items I will give personally to the Führer, who will raise me up on high. Higher than those fat oafs Göring and Himmler." He spit the names out as if they were poison burning his lips. "I have been away from the Reich too long."

From the cave mouth came gunfire. Good, the troops were here! My heart soared at the thought of Kal in one of his berserker rages tearing Herr Goebbels limb from bloody freaking limb. It looked like Christmas had come early for me.

Goebbels nodded to Dolph. "Kill the next person you see, even if it that odious Celestial, Leung." For some reason, in German the words had much more menace.

He smiled at Dolph and patted him on the shoulder as if the big man was a particularly well-heeled Doberman before turning to me. "You know, dear captive, that my greatest triumph in the years of dealing with inferior races, having to tolerate their smug smiles and the necessity of treating them with deference and respect, is what is in Dolph's hand, what he will bring home for me. My prize to the Führer. You Americans call it a 'suitcase nuke.' "

For the first time in my life, I had no words and no tongue to say them.

Chapter Eleven

Kal

It's a Kind of Whiplash

I hated to wait. It sucked, but there was nothing else to do. The room I found myself in was a sparse 5x8 with a cot and a bucket, and that was it. Three guesses on what the bucket was for and the first two don't count.

How long had I been there? I'd lost all track of time, not that I could tell by the meals because they arrived at irregular intervals and there was no sun or moon in my little prison to give me a sense of continuity. Hell, it could've been raining little glowing pink frogs and I wouldn't have known. I certainly didn't care.

I just wanted to get out alive.

Pace, pace, pace. Three steps to travel eight feet. Pace, pace, pace. Three more steps, another eight feet. Boring. Pace, pace, pace. *Boring*. Pace, pace, pace. That's pretty much how my time was spent. It was only hard-won discipline that kept me from bashing my brains out on the black stone walls. Not cinder block, not brick, but big two-foot stone slabs cut and dressed neatly. The door was steel, olive drab, with a flap on the bottom a tin tray could pass through.

Perhaps I should explain.

I was in England and it sucked. Damp, depressing and filled with people who, if you're a Yank like me, think you are barely civilized enough to use utensils. I had the impression that many of my 'hosts' were surprised I had opposable thumbs and the ability to use them. The whole wet, dreary place was like Oregon with a considerable snob problem.

You see, when I landed in England, the—waitaminute, I'll rewind the clock. Back to the cave. Yeah, the cave and the gut shot that took the wind out of my sails and had me gasping for breath like a landed fish.

Man that hurt! Kevlar will save your life, but that doesn't stop the bullet from stinging—a bit like taking a hammer blow to the navel. After telling my teammates to kill the shooter, I lay there in the dust and grit of the ravine behind the silly blue Subaru. Meanwhile Winch and Canton worked together like they were born to be bad asses.

Ahh … my abused abdominals had finally stopped complaining. It was only one itty, bitty bullet, right? Allow me to explain. Let's say the shooter used a 9mm, like a Glock or even something like my old Lahti. The bullet would travel 1,230 feet per second; that's a lot of kinetic energy to shed and all that energy was focused at one point, right at my sternum. It's worse than being hit with a baseball thrown by a major league pitcher. So it took me a few moments to get my breath and unclench my abs, which were knotted up something awful.

"Get up, sunshine," I muttered and rose to my feet, knees wobbly. Dust puffed up under my sneakers as I raced past the BMW and into the darkness of the cave. Inside, I hardly slowed as I passed Canton squaring off with an Asian guy. Leung. Canton had told me about him, a real mean douche with a sadistic streak a mile wide and two deep. Silently, I wished my friend well in the filleting of his opponent.

Down switchback tunnels, deep into the heart of the mountain … I flashed back to Texas, to a vampire's nest—the setting of my first mission for the Bureau. It wasn't the temperature that brought the sweat to my skin. I had killed a kid then, a Renfield—a vampire's human assistant—and the memory of that boy's shock and horror as the knowledge of his own death slid into his eyes churned the acid in my stomach. No matter that he'd been trying to do me a dirty by taking my life, he was just a kid and the first person I'd ever killed.

There were nights when I still woke in an awful sweat, tears clawing at my eyes and the ghost of that kid fading from my dreams.

At the end of the switchback tunnel a bright light slapped my eyes, delivered from bright bulbs that lined the ceiling of a big cavern. In the center was a line of wooden crates with a familiar symbol burned into the wood. I paid them no mind; their purpose was obvious, if I'd had time to give it some thought. But when I'm running full tilt with a load of angry bearing down on my shoulders, thought is something that doesn't intrude.

A fist the size of canned ham appeared out of thin air to clip my chin something fierce, sending a white-hot flare of pain through my skull and flipping me like a burger. I landed hard, facedown, on the cool cavern floor.

For the second time in less than five minutes the breath was forced from my lungs and my teeth met with a *clack*. It was sheer dumb luck that they didn't cut my tongue in half. Splinters of pain ran from head to toe and for a moment I lay stunned, my mind a whorl of strobing lights.

What felt like a claw of iron snagged my hair and hauled me to my feet just in time for me to see another giant fist rushing toward my nose at warp speed. I couldn't move much, but I managed to keep my nose from becoming pizza by turning my head. The fist hit my cheek instead, tearing flesh and spiking fire into my brain.

I not only saw stars, but galaxies as well, all spinning in a geometric jig around my poor noggin. All conscious thought fled as darkness consumed my vision.

Perhaps I was out for only a few moments because when I came to I was still standing; however, there was a python around my neck, squeezing my throat shut with iron intensity.

Waitaminute! That wasn't a python! That was a friggin' arm! And if I wasn't mistaken, it was almost as big around as my thigh. For a brief moment I thought a Supernatural was trying to kill me. I turned my head to the right with my chin down and jackknifed forward, flipping my assailant over my body. A hot flash of agony ripped through me as my opponent nearly tore my head from my shoulders with a grinding twist. From what seemed like far away I heard him thump to the ground. A red hot bar of iron ground against the bones of my spine as my vision went from black, to white, then back to black again.

Legs horribly weak, I leaned against a crate and caught a glimpse of blond hair and massive shoulders constrained by a brown suit. Great, the big henchman. The bad guys must buy these dudes by the pallet.

It occurred to me that I could actually die there—in a cave located in BFE—put down like a mad dog by an over-muscled Aryan Nation poster boy.

No. No way. Not happening.

Though it felt like ice picks were being jammed into the muscles of my neck, I blocked the pain, shaking my head to clear it.

At that moment Goebbels' big boy charged me like a Rottweiler after a mailman. I danced to the side, planting a solid jab in the big dude's cheek as he flew by. It felt like hitting a garbage truck. He put on the brakes and spun, ready to grapple. I may be strong, but mama Hakala didn't raise any stupid sons. No way was I going to try to wrestle someone bigger and stronger than myself without some sort of advantage. My hand slipped behind my back to find the comfortable grip of the Bowie.

"You are a stupid Finn," the Titan-in-a-suit growled in a voice that sounded like gravel being crushed in iron gears. He spoke slowly enough that I caught his drift even with my limited German.

"No speakee the English, bub?" I asked as we circled. Damn, my mouth throbbed with an unpleasant heat and I tasted blood. Must have bit my tongue when I hit the floor after all—just the tip, it seemed. My hand came up and his eyes widened at the Bowie's size.

"Finns are the *scheiße*!" He grinned. So he knew how to conjugate "to be." From his sleeve he pulled a six-inch stiletto. We both tipped the barest of nods.

Hmm, what was that word … *scheiße*? I began to see red.

When you travel abroad, the first things you generally learn are swear words. That's so if you want to tussle it up with the local wildlife, you can insult them in a way they understand. I'd been to

Germany once on vacation with the folks. Ate heavy food, drank a lot of heavy, dark beer, and tried my luck with the lady folk, which didn't sit well with their better halves, who viewed me as something of a threat. *Scheiße* was a common word, pronounced 'shh-iceh.' Ten-will-get-you-twenty you can guess what it means.

Two jabs in quick succession bloodied his nose but did no other damage. The swipes with the knife met air instead of flesh. Obviously he knew which part of a knife was the pointy end, but the two jabs sure did piss him off something powerful and he came at me again, swinging for the rafters. His fist whistled past my ear and I tossed two more jabs that connected strongly to his nose, splattering blood across his lips. Then a line of fire slid across my belly near my already wounded side as the tip of his blade easily parted skin. My knife came nowhere near him. He was better at blades than I, almost as good as Canton.

Well … crap.

That slim shiv of his streaked toward my throat while his other hand grabbed at my left arm to pull me in for the big finish. Snarling, I dropped the Bowie, snagged his knife hand and bit down hard on his thumb. Blood gushed into my mouth as the stiletto hit the cavern floor between us. No such thing as fighting dirty when your life is on the line.

My worrying teeth and his busted nose really peed in his Cheerios because those baby blues of his grew dark with anger and he roared like a wounded bear, fury tearing at his throat.

Good for me. Worst thing any fighter can do was lose their cool like Poster Boy just had. Screaming his wrath, he tried to grab hold with those tree-trunk arms. No way. I unlatched my teeth from his wrist and hooked a leg, using his momentum for a throw that had him landing headfirst into a crate with a resounding *boom!* that echoed from the cavern walls. Wood splintered and several crates tumbled to the floor.

The crate his noggin had smacked hardly budged, but Poster Boy flopped bonelessly to the ground and lay very still. One heartbeat, two, then three. Nothing … not a twitch, not a flutter of eyelids. A quick check revealed his total lack of respiration.

I've killed a lot of Supernaturals in my time, but that was my first Nazi. Felt good, actually. Like I'd done my part to make the world a better place. I retrieved my Bowie, wincing at every pain and ache that hollered for my attention. Nearby I noticed a thick aluminum briefcase, a shiny incongruity among wooden crates. Had to be important.

Beneath my sneakers the floor trembled and I felt a familiar sensation skitter up my spine. Despite the road flare pain in my neck and face, I managed a credible run down the cavern and into a smaller tunnel, only five feet wide or so. It came to me that any one of the crates would barely fit through there.

Another cavern—long, but not so wide as the previous ... perhaps twenty feet. At the cavern's end stood Mouth, swaying to and fro as if drugged, and Goebbels. The Nazi had just thrown what looked like a brightly shining star at the floor near his feet. My heart sank. A spell gem. An *active* one!

What came next nearly twisted my mind out of its socket.

A blue/gray column of smoke shot from the uneven floor to the ragged cavern roof, some fifteen feet up, and boiled in place. It looked like smoke, but had a presence, a sort of solidity like fluid rock. Rock/smoke, glowing with a nacreous light that pooled like blood across the floor, thick and turgid. When the baleful light met my eyes, it seemed like I didn't so much see it as *feel* it entering my brain and setting up house.

Besides that awful, almost living, light, there was an aura emanating from the column that shook me to the core. It was something I'd felt strongly once before a little over twenty years earlier. I felt myself in the presence of an overwhelming *evil*, a force that desired to shred my soul from my body and fling it into the Abyss. That evil beat against my senses and drove me to my knees, gripping my skull in crystal slivers of pain. That evil assailing me was a necrotic force guided by hands steeped in blood and woe. It was directed, I felt certain, by Goebbels in an effort to tear me apart.

Not since I'd faced Iku-Turso, the legendary monster from the

Finnish epic *The Kalevala* who had killed my sister and nearly destroyed my mind, had I felt such a horrific force, such a malignant power. It beat at me with fists of venom, ripped at me with talons of spite and loathing. So I did the only thing I could to protect my sanity.

I went a little nuts.

My rage, anger on tap, always there to lend a hand, once again flowed through my veins, sending waves of power through my muscles. The flailing evil continued to hammer against my soul, but the rage flowed inexorably over the spiritual virulence flowing from the blue/gray pillar of hate and its liquid light. It extinguished the awful glow and replaced it with a living, beating heat.

Strength returned to my legs and the incessant thrum of pain in my skull vanished, replaced by that old sweet fury, that sugary beat that I always rely on in dire circumstances.

Goebbels looked back, his mouth forming an O of shock as he saw me begin my run toward him, my face a warped feral mask of anger. Wasting no time, he grabbed the unresisting Mouth by the arm and pulled her to the column, his face lined with panic.

A little part of me, that small knot of rationality that leashes my rage when necessary, howled in dismay. I knew what that column was, knew where Goebbels was taking Mouth and I knew that if I didn't follow, didn't leap into the abyss in pursuit, it could be the end of … everything.

It was a portal, a gateway to the past and if he shut it down from the other side I'd be stuck here. Or I'd find myself in a world slaving under the regime of the Third Reich. Either way, Mouth would be lost to me.

And that thought hurt more than I thought possible.

Goebbels and Mouth entered the column, which flowed around them in a gelid mass. I was fifteen feet away.

The column shuddered obscenely, rippling from floor to ceiling. Ten feet.

It began to collapse, a pillar of diabolic mud flowing down. Five feet.

Barely taller than a mailbox, it faded at the edges.

I dove, stomach scraping the floor, and slid into the liquid smoke. Cold and hot, both sensations warring for dominance of my flesh as the smoke and the light, that hideous light, poured through my skin. It slid in, oozing along muscle and bone like thin mud, coating my nerves and veins in a slick of corruption so foul it felt as if my tissues would tear themselves apart in revulsion. There was a period of blackness where the grotesque sensation entered my mouth and throat and then …

I landed into madness.

Forget *Stargate* and its special effects tunnel of stretched and twisty light buzzing all about. Hell, forget any special effect you've ever seen at the movies because what happened to me made tripping on LSD seem like a mild caffeine buzz.

Sound, like the world's worst orchestra playing with broken instruments of awful design, buffeted my ears with a force to rattle bone and blood, accompanied by a nauseating stench—rotting meat and swamp vegetation mixed with the nasty chemical/fecal smell of an over-used Port-a-Potty. Added to this sensory overload was the sight of the blue marble of Earth below me. The space around— where there should have been velvety blackness salted with stars— was instead filled by vast gray/blue roiling clouds of malevolence that had formed the portal/column.

Yeah, when I said the Earth, I meant the whole freaking planet spread out below my point of view, my invisible body. It pulled at my invisible insides with the siren song of gravity that made me her bitch. If I could have peed my invisible pants in that strange sensory non-place, I would have. Normal white, puffy clouds far below rushed to meet me as my stomach did a credible job of leaping out of my mouth in a bid for freedom. The cacophony was the orchestra from hell continued to buffet me.

As I penetrated the cottony whiteness of the clouds, there was no sensation, no wetness, no wind against my cheeks, only the feeling of free fall and, fortunately, no sensation of re-entry. The last thing I needed was to flash into a wisp of ionized gas.

The dark side of the planet. No big city lights. Strange. I could see the shadowy humps of landmasses perfectly. Italy's designer boot shape was to the south, toward my non-existent feet. I made the mistake of looking up. I hoped to see stars, but the vomit-inducing blue/gray smoke still filled the heavens with sickening thick light.

Closer … Europe loomed large in my view, while something behind me tickled my neck with gangrenous fingers. The awful liquid/solid cloud now filled the sky behind me, growing as its horrendous light advanced toward me rapidly.

Holy crap!

Instinctively I knew it was the column, the gateway, crashing down, ready to sever the connection between my world and, well, the world I was falling toward. The uneasy thought came to me that if, before I made it to where I was going, the connection was terminated, I would be, too.

I looked landward to see the ground only a couple thousand feet below. The awful light had begun to surround me as panic shrieked in my mind.

Suddenly, as the light passed, the landscape veered sharply to the left, blurring into shades of black and gray. If I had a body, I think my neck would have broken from the abrupt change in direction. As it was, I had to deal with the mental whiplash of being tumbled like dice in a cup, but as darkness veiled my vision, I didn't think a Yahtzee was in my future.

I slowly regained awareness.

Ooohhh … Something was poking my cheek. Hard. I lay on my stomach, right arm dangling in the air below me. Below me? The sea … I smelled the salty tang of the sea. What?

My eyes, crusty and itchy, cracked open slightly. The sea below was a placid grayish smudge reflecting heavy, dark clouds, pregnant with rain.

A hard poke at my spine. "Oy, Jerry, don't you try nofin', you 'ear me?"

Who the hell was Jerry? And who was poking my back?

Poke, poke.

Ow ... that second one hurt. My eyes cleared a bit and I realized that my right arm, the dangly one, lay over the edge of a cliff.

That woke me up right quick. I jumped to my feet, muscles violently protesting, staring down at the sea smashing relentlessly against breakers a couple hundred feet below. The face of the cliff was gnarled and craggy with the off white color of bleached bone. A familiar *clicking* sound from behind grabbed my attention.

Someone had pulled the hammers back on an old-fashioned double-barreled shotgun.

Interesting.

"Oy, you slimy Jerry Kraut bastard, you move one more twitch and I'll blow yer 'ead clean off, I will!" The voice was furious, the type of really cheesed off anger that tells you that the speaker was an inch away from bloody violence.

Okaaaaay ... British dialect, white cliff face. Got it. Dover, the cliffs made of white chalk sticking above the English Channel like pale sentinels guarding against incursions from Calais.

Jerry? Kraut? Spoken with a sort of long-suffering, smoldering anger that comes from years of festering negative emotions. So, the portal worked, I was back in time. Goebbels' time. Crap ... the time where strangers appearing from nowhere in a country beset by one of the most evil regimes in human history could be met with terminal aggression.

Interesting-er.

"Turn around slow, Jerry, and don't try nofin' funny!"

Tempted though I was to start my end of the conversation with 'A priest and a rabbi walk into a bar ...' a modicum of common sense stopped me. Instead I slowly raised my hands and turned to the voice.

Imagine a walking fossil in a tweed coat and one of those flat caps you see the old men in movies from the UK wear. Put that together with a threadbare off-white shirt and dark pants and black shoes split at the seams and you have the vision that accosted me with a shotgun. Pointed at the jewels, no less. Since I was mighty fond of Big Jim and the Twins, I kept my face neutral and made no sudden movements.

"Well, Jerry, yer a big one, ain't ya?" The Brit smiled with all six yellowed teeth. "Trying to sneak in and cause mischief, were ya? Well, that's a mistake, no doubt about it, lad. Wait till the authorities get a load of you!"

I grinned. "Actually, old timer, that would be great. When will they get here?"

That near toothless mouth fell open with a clang. "Yer a Yank!"

"Got it in one. Now, where are these authorities you talked about? I'm keen to meet them."

The double barrel lowered until it pointed at the ground. A heavily wrinkled, liver-spotted hand rubbed the washed-out blue eyes. "What's a bloody Yank doin' in Dover, I ask ya?" The crinkly little lines at the corners of his eyes deepened to ravines.

I lowered my hands slowly. "Sir, that is a discussion I must take up with your government."

"I should say it is!" The old man took a few tottering steps forward and thrust out a mummified hand. "Kevin Sharpe, at yer service, lad."

My hand engulfed his. "Kalevi Hakala, at yours, sir." For a moment I mentally cringed at providing my real name, but my just being in the past changed it. Might as well be polite. Besides, the rampant paranoia and lying that comes with being a Bureau agent was in my rear view.

Bleary eyes squinted up at me. "What kind of name is—" Before he had a chance to finish, there came a heavy rumble. From a stand of trees a couple hundred yards away emerged a pair of Daimler Scout Cars, commonly referred to as Dingos. Dark green and heavily armored, each all-wheel drive vehicle held two men, their .303 Bren guns pointed straight at an area some six inches south of my navel. Why did every Brit I met want to emasculate me?

Did they teach that in class right after the chapter about Agincourt? I sighed and raised my hands, knowing that any sudden movement would have me singing soprano while hefting a colostomy bag for the rest of my life.

"How long was I unconscious, sir?"

The old man licked thin lip. "Well, I spotted ya lyin' 'ere a couple of hours ago, I did. Had me daughter send for 'elp. Sorry, lad."

"Never mind, old timer," I said, raising my hands once again. "You did what you had to do. Those authorities of yours, they sure do move fast."

The two Dingos stopped perilously close to the cliff's edge and four guys in British Army uniforms, who seemed like they had whole sequoias jammed up their butts, jumped out, Sten guns in hand. They barely gave me a chance to speak before circling my wrists with cuffs and dropping a black bag over my head. A jab in the arm and it was lights out for yours truly.

When I woke, it was to find myself in a crappy little cell with a chamber pot and a steel door between me and freedom.

Great.

Chapter Twelve

Kal

The Bureau by any Other Name

Cha-chunk!

The lock of the prison door popped open, the sound echoing around the tiny chamber. I hoped they had come for the pot; it was pretty damn ripe and my nose had long since shut down in self-defense. Without a creak the door opened, revealing a short, fit, middle-aged man in a British Colonel's uniform, perfectly tailored, the creases so sharp you could shave with them. He had the typical long Anglo-Saxon face with a straight nose and firm jawline. A thick, dark moustache hung under that proud nose over thin lips. Light blue eyes sparkled with humor despite the stern cast to his features. At a glance, I'd say that here was a man who knew all about life's absurdities and didn't give a toss. He was having a wonderful time.

It took a few seconds as he stared at me, the shadows of much larger, burly men behind him distracting me from recognition. Then it hit me.

I was in the presence of a legend.

Interesting.

"Please come with me," said the Colonel in a low, almost musical, voice. One slim hand gestured toward the hall and the two brutes looming in the shadows.

I nodded and left the cell, at the mercy of a Corporal and a Sergeant who were easily bigger than that giant blond Nazi I'd killed earlier. Meaner looking, too. It was intimidating. Hey, don't get me wrong, I'm a pretty big guy, a modern day Viking if you will, but those two could have easily used me as a tetherball and not even breathed hard. From the look in the Sergeant's eye, that's exactly what he wanted to do. The Corporal snapped shiny new cuffs around my wrists.

Up two flights of echoing stairs, down three gloomy hallways, past a whole mess of steel doors and we finally reached our destination, a 15x15 room of well-dressed dun stone. A single exposed bulb hanging from the ceiling burned fitfully. I couldn't help but wonder if I was in the Tower of London or Isengard. The latter probably would have been more comfortable.

Inside the room was a folding table—the kind you drag out of the basement when it's poker night with the fellas—and three steel chairs. Sitting on one of the chairs was well-dressed man in a black suit, black string tie and a crisp white shirt. A fedora covered his scalp. Sharp, inquisitive features were set in a round, slightly swarthy face. When I entered, he stood and removed the hat to reveal slick black hair combed to the side. I noted the breadth of his shoulders and the way he carried himself. Something about his brown eyes bothered me—their wealth of knowledge and world weary expression that told me they'd witnessed things no mortal should see. A chill prickled my skin; I'd seen eyes like that before, eyes that knew too much. Every Bureau agent had them.

I had them.

Interesting-er.

"Sit down, pal," he said, face closed. An American.

"Do you mind?" I asked, holding up my cuffed hands.

"Yes I do," he replied as the Colonel sat opposite to him.

Nothing for it, I sat down facing the two. Damn, that chair was *cold*. "Don't know why you're worried; you have those two bruisers." I nodded to the Corporal and the Sergeant, who smiled nastily at me with all twelve of his teeth. "And you could subdue me with a spell if I became … unruly."

Had to give the American some props, he didn't bat an eye at the mention of magic. Smiling slightly, the Colonel produced a small pouch and a pipe. He fiddled for a few moments; and the room started to fill with thick clouds of aromatic blue smoke. The American, on the other hand, lit an unfiltered cigarette and puffed away.

I raised an eyebrow. "You know, that's bad for you. Causes lung cancer and heart disease."

The American frowned at me through the smoke. "Don't be a wise guy." More puffing. Damn, that stuff smelled foul, not like the faint vanilla scent that wafted from the Colonel's pipe.

Even though I felt like jumping up and down in frustration, I kept my cool. My being thrown into the nearest oubliette wasn't going to help Mouth one bit. "Listen, I need the Bureau's help, and the help of MI-7."

The Colonel started, the first strains of uncertainty marring his serene face. "What?"

"MI-7, that's what you call it, right?" At his look of incomprehension, I wanted to smack my forehead. "Oh, duh, of course you don't! At this time it's still called the Supernatural Services, isn't it? It won't be referred to as MI-7 until 1945."

The pipe stem pointed my way. "You are a bloody unusual chap who has too much information, I should think. Also, you have no Interdiction, which I find most unusual."

I couldn't help smiling. "And you're shorter than I'd imagined. I also thought you held the rank of Lieutenant." Pipe forgotten, he stared at me in amazement. "By the way, sir, I thought your lecture on *Beowulf* nothing short of amazing! I mean, it changed the way people looked at that saga." His mouth worked, but nothing came out. I'd rendered one of the century's greatest wordsmiths speechless. Kal: 1, Legendary Wordsmith: 0.

The American's face pushed through the curtain of cigarette smoke. "Who are you, Mack? How come you have no Interdiction? What are you doing in England?" A long finger pointed at me. "Are you a Nazi spy?"

As I looked into his eyes, I felt a spell push into my mind, like a stone dropped into thick mud, sinking slowly into the depths. Instead of fighting it, I welcomed the magic like a long lost friend. I'd had this spell cast on me as a matter of course during many a debriefing while in the Bureau. "Me and the Bureau are old friends. I'm from the year 2011." Cuffed jazz hands. "Surprise!"

Utter silence and the stillness of statues.

I leaned back in the chair, faking a cheeky smile. "And I can prove it, gents."

The American closed his mouth with a *snap!* and stood, doing his best to loom. He shouldn't have tried; he wasn't tall enough. Now the Sergeant and Corporal, they could do it up right in spades. "How can you prove it?" he asked.

"Well, when your men knocked me out, they took something from me the size of a cigarette case. It's called a smart phone ..." My voice trailed off as I studied his face. Something was wrong, he didn't have the look of incredulity or disdain that my comment should have induced. I looked to the Colonel and saw nothing but calculation in his gaze. "Holy crap, you sneaky monkey," I whispered. "You already sussed it out, didn't you?"

His silence spoke volumes, the rat bastard.

"Of course! I had a wallet full of twenties, bills dated well after 1945, and I have the sneaking suspicion you already figured out how to turn on and use the phone. You boys were being cagey with me, weren't you? I shoulda known. Getting thick in my old age."

"Please, Oliver," the Colonel said to the American with a small smile. "Do sit down. The lad is on to it now."

Oliver the American nodded curtly and sat, resuming his oral fixation with the cigarette. He blew a noxious cloud in my direction. "Yes, we figured it all out. That 'smart phone' is one nifty piece of science."

"I quite enjoyed 'Angry Birds,' " the Colonel interrupted with a smile. "It is an amusing game."

Oliver shot him an annoyed glance and reached into his inside jacket pocket, producing my cell. After a couple of fumbling tries, he managed to turn it on. "It wasn't only the technology that convinced us," he remarked blandly.

The phone buzzed. "I convinced them, too."

"Ghost!" I cried, snatching the cell with cuffed hands. The smile on my face stretched my skin like a drum. The Sergeant and the Corporal started toward me, hands raised, but a look from the Colonel stilled them.

"Actually, another copy, Kal."

A copy? Oh, well, it didn't matter because even with Ghost 2.0 on my side, I almost felt invincible. Then reality hit me in the face with a wet shovel.

"Ghost, you didn't tell them anything about the future, did you?"

"Only that which was needed to prove bona fides. Such as Vittorio Ambrosio being named as Benito Mussolini's Chief of Staff. Once that was verified, belief followed."

That would make the date late January, or early February, 1943. "How do you have that info, Ghost?"

"When the original Ghost recognized Goebbels, he knew that the time rift was the Nazi's destination. Along with myself in this device are detailed files on the war."

"I didn't know the phone could hold so much."

"My presence accounts for only 17.54 of the 32 gigabytes in this cell. The remaining 14.46 gigabytes are more than sufficient to download several hundred books."

"Good to know."

"I must power down the cell now, Kal. It has a finite charge and the technology for a recharge has not been invented yet."

"Okay, Ghost. Now, let's keep our mouths shut about the future." The second the last word left my mouth, the screen blanked.

While Ghost 2.0 and I were getting acquainted, the Colonel and Oliver were staring, rapt. When I gave the order to shut up, their eyes did a good imitation of bugging out on springs. It was a beautiful Looney Tunes moment. I carefully set the cell on the table.

"You must—" began Oliver.

"—help us!" the Colonel finished.

I shook my head. "You think that if I gave you some really cool intel on future events you can cut the war short and stick a hot poker up Hitler's butt, right?"

They nodded. Hell, I understood their position. If I were them, I'd be slavering for any crumb, any tidbit that could help.

Crap, I hate not being on the side of the angels. "Not going to happen. If I gave you that kind of information, who knows what kind of catastrophic effect it would have on my time." I shook my head, really wanting to give them *something*. "Nope, not going to do it."

My stomach sank when I saw the look of steely resolve flow onto Oliver's face as he pocketed the cell. I began to prepare for the worst. I knew what was coming and preferred dying to endangering my friends.

Without taking his eyes off me, Oliver said, "John, would you mind having your boys assist? This could get—"

That was far enough.

For more than ten years, rage had been my constant companion, the brutal side of me that brooked no interference. In the past, it had taken extreme measures to summon the rage, to feel the hot pulse of anger in my blood, my tissues, but recently it lay just under the surface, quiescent but easily awakened. Still, but ready, like a trained hunting dog waiting to be summoned.

I reached below the still surface of my mind and it answered the call with brutal eagerness.

Teeth grinding, the rage flowing through me like lava, I broke the cuffs, sending shards of chain flying. The Sergeant and Corporal started to rush toward me, their movements sluggish to my heightened perception. My foot lashed out, catching the table and sending it smack into Oliver's face, splitting his lip with a spray of blood. The Colonel barely had time to blink before my foot came back, landed on the chair seat between his legs, and gave it a shove. He flipped ass over teakettle across the room to land against the wall in a heap.

The Sergeant and the Corporal were almost upon me, fists raised to do some serious damage. I grinned. They were just bone and meat, like all the rest.

Time to play.

I put an arm-lock on the Corporal, whose face whitened in pain as I dislocated his shoulder with a sharp *pop*. The Sergeant's fist loomed large and I lowered my head to the punch, letting it strike me on the crown. Skull versus phalanges. Skull:1, Phalanges: a broken mess. The sound of bones snapping and cracking like pine logs in a fire warmed the cockles of my rage-fueled heart. Life was good.

With the Corporal and Sergeant out of commission, I turned to Oliver. Once again I met those eyes and felt a spell slip over me like a warm blanket. The rage would have none of it. The spell met my fury and was shredded like so much cheap linen. Oliver's eyes grew wide in alarm.

"What the hell—?" he began. Sweat formed a second skin on his swarthy features.

The front of his suit filled my hand, and I lifted him effortlessly off the ground with one arm before slowly setting him back down on his feet. I let the rage go, feeling it slip below the surface of my mind. Always ready, eternally patient.

Maybe five seconds had passed.

"Not ... going to ... kill you," I panted, lightheaded and righting my chair. My butt hit the seat hard and steel creaked. "I am an agent who will *not* put the future at risk."

"Look, Mack, you gotta—"

"Oliver." The Colonel's voice was soft, but contained a core of steel. "That will be enough." He assisted the Corporal to his feet while the Sergeant glared daggers at yours truly. "Let us listen to what this man has to say."

Oliver's face turned a bright shade of red. "John, this man is an American and falls under my jurisdiction."

All emotion fled the Colonel's face. "He is on British soil, sir, and therefore under *my* jurisdiction. England will decide what to do with him." Cold, implacable as a glacier, the man exuded unshakable calm.

For a moment it looked like Oliver would object, but instead he reluctantly nodded and fetched a chair. The tension slowly leaked out of the room and I felt my shoulders relax.

The Colonel nodded. "Now, allow me to tend to the injured;

then we can begin discourse anew like gentlemen, yes?"

Fifteen minutes later, after the Colonel had Healed his men (apparently I rated interrogations by *two* magicians) and the table had been righted, they sat attentively and waited for me to begin.

How much to tell? I decided to be deliberately vague and not reveal that I was no longer an agent.

"Okay, guys, it's like this …"

An hour later, throat dry and scratchy, eyes smarting from the inadequate lighting, I finished my story. Minus geographical and personal details, that is.

"Incredible!" exclaimed the Colonel. "So you came through a portal in time to rescue Miss Mouth. I say, that is one ripping good yarn!"

Oliver scratched his head. "But why come back for the dame? I understand loyalty, but your chance of returning is thin to none, and thin left the building."

I rubbed my face. God, I was tired and in desperate need of a drink. "You guys still don't get it. Mouth is a *Bureau* agent under the influence of an extremely powerful magician. She's a hand-to-hand specialist, one of the best I've ever seen, as well an expert in demolitions. She can make bombs out of baking soda and spit. She also has comprehensive knowledge about this war; we all do. It is a critical point in the history of this world and the World Under."

"But you told me the Kraut went into the portal with a briefcase. That means he could have in his possession all sorts of papers about this timeline."

"Yes, but remember one thing, sir. *We don't leave agents behind, ever!*" No way was I leaving Mouth at Goebbels' mercy. I'd lost too many agents in the past and the thought of losing another one, especially *her*, to that Nazi muffin was intolerable.

The Colonel must have read my face quite easily. Nodding, he rose abruptly. "Righto. I think we should put a close to this discussion until we arrive at more suitable climes, Oliver." Those sharp, humorous blue eyes bored into mine. "And what should we call you, sir? I gather the identification card we found in your wallet is false."

You could say that. I decided, for the time, to scrap the identity of Kalevi Hakala, and my driver's license name of Kaiser Söze would stick out like a sore thumb.

"Call me Han. Han Solo." Lucas wasn't born yet, so how could he object?

London after the Blitz. Forty thousand British civilians had died in relentless Luftwaffe bombing raids. Even after nearly two years the scars still showed, the shattered remains of buildings with charred timbers sticking up like the broken stubs of ribs, empty lots where there shouldn't be and the hollow, half-hungry cast to the faces of the civilians. Although thin—almost emaciated by 2011 standards—they carried themselves with the fierce pride of defiant survivors determined to spit in the eye of the Reich.

Hitler bombed England in a prelude to an invasion that had never come in an effort to demoralize what he thought of as a weak and corrupt nation. What he achieved was to unite a people in righteous anger and terrible fury. If we, the people of the future, could see those brave, defiant souls, would we see ourselves as lesser beings, or would we try to hold ourselves to higher standards?

No clue.

As for me, through the windows of the black Austin 10, I gazed out at the battered but not broken city and saw hope in the eyes of a proud, stubborn people. People who had refused to surrender to despair, who had taken the hardest punches an evil empire could dish out and screamed their defiance to the heavens.

I felt humbled.

Eventually the Thames opened up in front of us and we stopped at a shattered building along its banks, the smell of wet and rotting vegetation (among other, more nasty things) assaulted our nostrils. The driver, a different corporal but just as big as the previous, stepped out of the broken doorway of the semi-destroyed building, opened the doors and we exited the car. The Colonel led the way over pulverized brick and charred pieces of wood into the building, treading carefully.

The inside was hollow, blackened and burnt with a thick smell like cordite that scratched at my nasal membranes. Sneezing didn't help. Cracked stone and brick littered the floor along with crudely painted signs that read DANGER UNSTABLE FLOOR. The Colonel (didn't seem right to call him John; I was far too much in awe) walked passed those notices without a care and stomped twice with a booted foot.

A section of floor slid to the side, revealing a staircase that descended into darkness.

The Colonel turned with a tiny smile. "Mind your feet, gentlemen."

Down at least fifty feet, the stairs gave way to a small hallway ending at a steel door. The only lighting was sputtering bulbs that reminded me of the movie *Psycho* (the original, not the sorry remake). The Colonel withdrew a heavy key from his voluminous coat and used it to open the door.

A plain room in drab olive green, the color of the modern military. Opposite the door we passed through was another; in between was on old oak desk and black telephone. At that desk sat a beautiful woman with night-black hair captured in a bun and fine, porcelain skin that startlets would sell their parents for. Her demure white blouse was buttoned to the neck and wrists. As we entered, one hand lowered the book she had been reading while the other dropped out of sight beneath the desk and I instinctively knew it was pointing a shotgun in our direction.

A Receptionist. The first line of defense in any Bureau office. All beautiful (to better distract enemies of the opposite sex) and all more lethal than a Black Mamba. They not only received the same training as agents, but were qualified psychologists as well. All the better to keep an eye on agents working the most dangerous job in the world. The real surprise was that misogynistic Great Britain in the '40s had Receptionists. Back then it had been unseemly for women to do anything but keep the home, which was strange when you consider that the country had once been ruled by such a powerful queen as Elizabeth I.

"Gentlemen," she said in high, clear voice that reminded me of crystal chimes. "Please stand in the circle and recite your names." Her eyes gave every indication that if we did not, she'd be scraping us off the walls with a spoon.

My eyes traveled to where a red circle about two feet wide was painted directly in front of the Receptionist's desk. Right in the shotgun's line of fire. The Colonel immediately stepped inside and rattled out his name, rank and serial number

His recitation was followed immediately by the American's: "Team Leader and magician Oliver Sheridan, Bureau of Supernatural Investigations, United States of America."

Oh boy. "Uh, guys …"

"I am terribly sorry, old boy," the Colonel stated flatly, standing behind the Receptionist. He didn't look sorry at all. "But you know how it is. Security and all that."

Oliver tossed me a superior smirk. Bastard.

I stepped in. Immediately a warm prickling sensation washed up my legs and traveled to my throat. Crap, I knew that feeling, the tingle-rush of a powerful truth spell. There had to be a wealth of gold just under that red circle Shaping the spell. If I tried to lie, there would be a boatload of pain to keep me company.

"Former Senior Agent and Team Leader Kalevi Hakala, Bureau of Supernatural Investigations, United States of America." There, the cat was out of the bag.

The Colonel smiled. "Wonderful. At least now I know you were mostly forthcoming with the truth, although the information that you are a *former* agent is a bit of a surprise."

Oliver grunted, a self-satisfied smirk plastered on his face. *They had known* I would step in the circle and spill the beans.

Bastards. It was something I would've done.

With a slight smile, the receptionist resumed her reading. I noted it was a fancy-shmancy leather-bound edition of *The Hobbit*, all done up with gold lettering and thick, creamy paper you don't see in normal bookshops anymore.

I leaned in. "Say, Edith, do you think you can scare me up one? I'd love to have an autographed copy."

"How did—Never mind." Her smile lit the room and the promise of laughter danced in her eyes. "I think that can be arranged."

The Colonel opened the door. "Right this way, gentleman."

As we walked through, Oliver muttered, "Can't see having a dame in the front room. Too damn risky, if you ask me."

"It was part of my deal with the Service, old boy," the Colonel said over his shoulder. "My wife was to come with me. They reluctantly agreed. It was her idea to place herself in harm's way, but not until she had received full training, mind you."

I clapped a hand on Oliver's shoulder. "Don't worry, the Receptionist program works out better than you could possibly believe." The look on his face was worth its weight in gold.

A tunnel lined in corrugated steel painted olive drab, barely wide enough for two men to walk abreast, lay before us, some hundred feet long. More steel doors were evenly spaced along the hallway.

"This place was constructed during the blitz," the Colonel said as if delivering a lecture. "For maximum safety."

It felt as dreary and soulless as it looked. "Where are your teams?"

"Two are deployed in Ireland, one in Scotland, and one is on leave. As for the rest, my boy, that is the King's business."

Interesting-er.

Was it deliberate, that bit of intel he'd let slip, or was it unintentional? Considering the keen mind housed in that skull of his, I was willing to bet the former.

The King's business, indeed. The World Under was a business we all shared. He had just told me that six teams were in Europe, tackling German magicians.

Last door. Another big key. Inside, a Spartan room with one desk (also olive green) and a telephone. Nothing else. Drab, drabber, drabbest. The color scheme alone was enough to invite thoughts of suicide.

"Not much, I am afraid," the Colonel remarked dryly as if reading my thoughts. "However, it has amenities that bring some small comfort to an otherwise bleak setting." He opened a drawer and pulled out a bottle of scotch and a few small tumblers.

"Gentleman," the Colonel intoned gravely after pouring a measure into each glass. "To the defeat of the Reich!"

"To the defeat of the Reich!" we chorused and drank.

Normally scotch wouldn't appeal to me, but that liquid flowed down my throat like smooth fire. It had a nice, peaty finish under its slight sting.

"Colonel," I said, setting the tumbler on the desk. "I would like to speak to the Director, if you would be so kind."

Oliver began to chuckle as the Colonel took the only seat.

"So speak," he said with a smile.

Chapter Thirteen

Mouth

Definitely Not a Vacation

Twisting disorientation. I vomited, or at least I thought I did. When we entered the strange smoky pillar—that ugly-as-sin vapor that looked like glowing fluid stone—I thought I was done for. A small, rational part of my mind told me that if Goebbels could brave that awful column, then there was no way in hell I would let him show more balls than I.

A gut-wrenching twist and my perspective changed suddenly. The Earth appeared below, growing larger and larger, and I would have screamed, but I had no mouth to do so. Instead I had to content myself with being a mute observer while experiencing the greatest terror I have ever known.

Blue-gray light once again surrounded me and I felt another gut-wrenching twist. Darkness took me with talons of ice.

My eyes cracked open to a blurry vista of stars smeared across the blue-black night sky. Hard, cold (and I mean *cold*!) ground poked uncomfortably at my back and as I stretched, my muscles protested weakly, and a dull thud began in the base of my skull.

Wait one minute, damn it! How was I able to move without permission from Herr Doktor Jerkface himself? The joyous realization that I was free from Goebbels' spell washed over me, and flooded my limbs with the strength to pull myself upright.

All right!

A groan from a few feet away interrupted my groove. I looked over to see Dr. Jerkface himself wobbling to his feet. Oh, hell, *no!*

Snap! went his jaw as my foot introduced itself. I had just started on other bones (oh, how I wanted to make that sonofabitch *pay*!) when the solid crack of gunfire sounded in the distance. Dirt, hard as concrete, shattered around us as bullets slammed into the ground. Goebbels lay on the ground, groaning from a couple heel kicks to the ribs. My head swiveled toward the staccato sound of rifle fire to see a large wood and wire gate a couple of hundred feet away, harshly lit with pitilessly bright white light from large mercury vapor lamps.

I'd only had time to think, *What the hell?*, when our position was illuminated by floodlights, washing the scene clean of color and revealing that Goebbels and I were on the side of a dirt road leading to that skeletal gate. More bullets hammered the ground around me.

My revenge thwarted, I bolted toward the trees that lined the road, hoping that I wouldn't get my ass shot off. Darkness swallowed me as a barrage of rounds tore at the trees, sending splinters to scratch my skin. One round lifted the hair on the back of my head and the buzz of it streaked past my ear.

Then the world dropped out from beneath my feet and my stomach lurched as I realized I was falling. Pain exploded in my hip as I hit the cold, hard earth and began to tumble down a slope steep enough that every bounce meant a moment of free fall.

Thump! Tree ... shoulder ... the tree won. A rippling wave of sharp agony speared from clavicle to crotch as bone broke with an ugly crackling sound and erupted through skin, showering my cheek with blood.

Another jarring bounce that shattered my world as my broken shoulder took a second hit and white light detonated soundlessly behind my eyes.

And again and again. On and on. They say that if you sustain enough pain you'll pass right on out, but that didn't happen to me. Perhaps my tolerance to pain was higher to most. Perhaps I was too darn stubborn to fall into the dark. All I know is that every jounce, every jarring impact sent me into new heights of suffering as up became down and vice versa. I think my battered body bounced off two more trees before sliding to a rest in a shower of dead leaves and other forest detritus. As I lay there, I concentrated on the odor of leaf mold and frozen earth. It smelled good, natural and provided a small degree of comfort to my tortured body.

Far above I heard voices shouting in German. It came to me, as I watched my breath plume above me in the light of a half-moon, that I was *freezing*. My scanty outfit didn't offer near enough protection against what I realized was the dead of winter.

Up dammit! I cried silently. Muscles screamed as I rose to a sitting position, my left shoulder and arm lumps of icy meat I could barely feel. Shock. I was in shock and maybe even dying. Well, that sucked. Unsteadily, I stood, idly noting that one of my Chanel Cruise pumps had disappeared. Damn, those alligator and lambskin shoes were *expensive* and totally went with my now defunct Marc Jacob dress. Kal was going to owe me *huge*.

Forest all round, its bare branches splintering the sky with woody fractals. Some fir trees, but most not. Snow marked the ground in large swaths and humps of dirty gray. I needed shelter, fast, or it wouldn't be the injuries that killed me.

Oh, god … my head swam from side to side as the world went sideways. Fire scorched along my calf. I looked down at a ragged gouge that seeped sluggishly. What the hell? Dirt cracked around me … more shots. I was shot! In the leg!

My leg and shoulder hurt like the blazes, but I ran anyway, not wanting to feel the slimy spell ooze into my mind again in case Goebbels was chasing. Those wormy hands groping at my tits … bastard.

My head, light and full of cotton, was tethered to my neck by the thinnest of threads, a gossamer strand that could snap at any second. I was in excellent shape, never lost the edge since my Bureau days, but the gray-pink bone sticking up from my shoulder sapped my strength and weakened my will. Feet plodded as I doggedly pushed myself. Oh, I *hurt*.

Water … icy cold … hell, *freezing*! My shins pierced by needles of frost. What … what was happening …? I stopped and backtracked, unwilling to risk hypothermia. God, my feet were killing me, despite the cold. I think they were bleeding because warmth flooded out through the skin like oil from a bladder. The sharpest pain, like razors of ice and fire skinning the soles ... I stumbled, but managed to right myself despite the flare of agony from my shoulder and the spots of red that danced before my eyes.

It was a small river, or large stream. Whatever. It spelled death for me if I dared its waters again. Damn, I was cold! Stumbling on half-frozen mud, I ran upstream, or what I supposed was upstream. Lungs burning with frost and flesh burning in the chill air, I forced myself onward out of sheer cussedness. I was not going to let Doktor Jerkface put his wormy hands on me *ever* again. At least not while I was alive.

A strange, throaty wailing came to me as my torn and bloodied feet slipped in the icy mud. Up and down went the cry, up and down, reverbing off the trees, a sobbing sort of bawling that took me a few moments to recognize.

Dogs. They'd sicced the dogs on me. Sharp panic perforated through my bowels like shards of glass with every beat of my heart. Pain became irrelevant—the cold, my cut feet, broken bones— nothing mattered anymore except running as far and as fast as I could because if they caught me, I would end up praying for a swift death.

There! Up ahead the stream ran shallow over water-smoothed stones, the muted rush of liquid music to my ears. My feet sprayed droplets of icy water high into the air, the faint light of the moon creating a diamond curtain.

On the other side. Safe. Well, *safer*. Feet numb, frozen stumps at the end of my legs that thudded against the dead leaves and snow like an irregular heartbeat. Blood taste in my mouth, thin and coppery. Step step spit. Step step spit. Blackness crept at the edge of my vision, beckoning. So tempting. The blackness was like velvet, warm and welcoming. It would be so comforting to slip into that soft embrace, to just give the hell up, but I was too damn stubborn, too damn single-minded to cave like that.

Sharp pain in my nose, a nail of fire and I know it had been broken. Like me, a windup doll with no more tension in the spring. I fell. What had broken my nose?

I had run straight into something. A small tree, a sapling with winter stripped branches. I looked up. A group of men in ragged clothes and caps. They stared impassively, eyes deep set into their sockets, cheeks hollow and unshaven. At a glance, I envied their heavy clothing. It looked warm.

Dead. Soon now, all hope had been lost. I laughed at the absurdity of it all. I let the blackness take me.

Chapter Fourteen

Kal

A Deal Struck

Fifteen minutes later, I had finally come to grips with the fact of the literary giant who sat in front of me. The Colonel was actually the Director of MI-7 (okay, they didn't call it that, but I couldn't help myself. It would always be MI-7 to me). After Edith had entered with two steel chairs for Oliver and me to sit on, I finished a very abbreviated version of why I'd left the Bureau.

"So, I needed to find an artifact, one powerful enough to kill the monster that had killed my sister." My voice was raw and scratchy from the strain of divulging the highly edited account of my attempts at revenge.

The Colonel puffed on his pipe, sending aromatic gray rings floating toward the ceiling. "You know, old boy, I firmly believe you. Oh, I am well aware of the brevity of your narrative, but what you have told us is the truth." His baby blues twinkled. "I take not an inconsiderable amount of pride in my ability to judge men and my well-honed instincts inform me you are ... what is the phrase you Americans use, Oliver?"

The other magician didn't bat an eye as he stared into mine. " 'On the up and up,' John." His expression had grown increasingly sour as my story unfolded. I could feel the disapproval waft off him like a shimmer of heat.

Behind us, the door opened and Edith entered, handing the Colonel an olive-drab folder. I was getting mighty sick of that color. At that point I would've killed for a blue or red.

"Ah, here we are. Thank you, Edith. Can you be a love and ring up Winston on the telephone?"

She beamed and left in a swirl of navy skirts. Winston? Who

the heck ... holy crap! Winston Churchill? Had to be. The most powerful man in the British Empire and the Colonel wanted to 'ring him up on the telephone' as if it were an everyday occurrence. If there was a better way to demonstrate his power, I couldn't think of it.

"You have been a guest of England for three days now, Mr. Hakala and you are quite correct that we had divulged your true nature before our initial, and rather exciting, interview. Shortly after your capture, we received this from our Team working with the French Resistance." The folder slid across the desk. Yellowish papers met my eyes and I scanned the first page:

SEAHAWKE: DISTURBANCE IN NIGHT SKY NEAR BORDER FRANCE/GERMANY STOP STRANGE GRAY LIGHT OVER HIDDEN NAZI ARMY BASE STOP HAVE CAPTURED INJURED FEMALE AM SPY STOP SUSPECT NAZI PLOT AFOOT STOP REQUEST AID STOP FAUCON

Female Am spy? Female American spy? Mouth, had to be I felt elation, an elevation of spirit before the significance of the second line hit me. My teeth ground together as I fought to control my rising anger. Injured? In 1943, somewhere in the ass end of nowhere, France, the medical profession wasn't quite up to the task of treating the wounded.

"I believe it's that dame Mouth you've been worrying about," Oliver said, so bland he appeared bored. "The disturbance in the night sky mentioned there happened at the same time as the disturbance over Dover that allowed you to show up." He lit a cigarette. "To us it was a magical beacon that practically tore our heads off. I've never felt magic of such magnitude before." Blue smoke curled from his nose. "One thing we haven't figured out, Mr. Hakala ... Why did you wind up on British soil instead of the place where this 'female American spy' appeared?"

Good question. I'd been thinking about that since my arrival and had finally formulated a theory. "When I went through the … portal, gate, whatever, it was while it was closing. Perhaps it was like a rope being stretched taut, then suddenly cut. Whipping around uncontrolled. I reckon the whip end deposited me at Dover."

The Colonel's eyes went round. "If that's the case, sir, then you are indeed fortunate not to have been trapped between times in a state of temporal limbo. Or not to have been flung out into the sea."

Believe me, I'd thought of that. My stomach clenched at the idea of being lost between the layers of time or becoming fish food. "I think Goebbels tried to slam his portal shut from this end, too, and that's what really caused the whiplash effect." Another thing I owed the bloody Nazi bastard.

Oliver snorted. "That's neither here nor there. What we really need to know is, being that you're from the future and all, do you know what the hell they mean by 'secret army base?' "

"I need a map of France." Mouth was alive. Hurt, but alive. I could barely concentrate; my emotions were all jumbled up in a strange hodgepodge.

The Colonel nodded and produced a rolled sheet of paper from a drawer. Spread out on the desk, it proved to be map of most of Western Europe, *sans* Spain. "Here," I grunted, finger stabbing down on a spot in western France. "Natzwiller. In the Vosges Mountains." But why Natzwiller? It wasn't even in Germany. Sachenhausen was in the heart of the Reich, just north of Berlin. Why would Goebbels land in Natzwiller?

Could that part of France be a 'thin spot,' as Marcin had called the area surrounding Vegas? Perhaps that was the only place near Germany Goebbels *could* travel through time. But how had he wound up in Death Valley? So many questions, not enough answers.

"An army base, Hakala?" Oliver prodded.

"Concentration camp; the proper name is Natzweiler-Struthof." It was late enough in the War to spill the beans about this one minor camp. "The inmates were originally Germans who were supposed to build V-2 rocket factories in caves dug out of the mountains. By now it holds Jews, Gypsies and members of the French/Belgian Resistance, along with gas chambers and a crematorium."

"Why so loose with the lips, pal? I thought you said you weren't going to help us?" Oliver was working on a nice case of mad, his slightly swarthy cheeks gone burgundy with blood.

I gave him the old eyebrow trick, raising it almost to my hairline. "Because I'm going to need your help getting into France to fetch Mouth and I have to figure out a way to track Goebbels down. He can't be allowed to reach Hitler with that briefcase."

"Then, my dear boy, you should read the next communiqué," the Colonel chuckled around his pipe stem. "Until you told us your story, we did not have the foggiest as to what it meant."

THE FOLLOWING IS DESIGNATED TOP SECRET FROM ULTRA, HM & PM EYES ONLY

Jan. 27th: *Enigma* sigincept, 1:32 a.m. local time, from unnamed German base (located near/in Strasbourg?) to N.H.C. Message decoded Jan. 27th, 6:46 a.m. local time as follows:

> R. G. GRAVELY INJURED AND IN COMA STOP
> NEED Z. IMMED STOP MATTER OF UTMOST
> IMPORTANCE STOP HEIL HITLER STOP CAPTAIN
> KRAMER

"We believe Z refers to Zauberer, the German word for magician. Jerry sent a reply less than an hour later," the Colonel remarked through clouds of smoke.

I eyeballed the next page:

Jan. 27th Enigma signincep, 7:31 a.m. local time from N.H.C. to

Capt. Kramer of unknown German army base (see attached maps for Strasburg and surrounds). Message decoded Jan. 27th 8:18 a.m. local time as follows:

> FM R ON WAY STOP HEALTH OF RG PARAMOUNT STOP DO ANYTHING YOU MUST TO INSURE HE LIVES STOP KILL AS MANY JEWS AS NECESSARY TO ACHIEVE THIS STOP HEIL HITLER STOP HH

A cold and tomblike chill washed my skin as I read the missive. With the advantage of future memory, I deciphered the names and their importance.

Oliver saw the terrible dread knowledge in my face. "We believe HH is Himmler and RG stands for Reich Minister Goebbels." Eyes flinty and cold, his finger stabbed down on the translation. "And FM R, I think, is Foreign Minister von Ribbentrop, the most powerful magician in Germany next to Speer and Hitler himself."

He leaned forward, eager, feral. "What do you say, Hakala? Ribbentrop and Goebbels in the same place, at the same time with the keys to the kingdom. If they reach Hitler, it will only be a matter of time before the War swings heavily in their favor. Hell, they could even try another stab at time travel, killing more Jews to fuel their necromantic spells."

"I doubt it." My voice was toneless, lifeless. "The Jews they murdered are powering Speer's defenses of the armament factories." Albert Speer, Hitler's Minister of Armaments, served twenty years in Spandau Prison after the Nuremburg trials, but no need to let that nugget of information slip. "That's why Allied bombers haven't damaged German production much."

The Colonel's voice was soft. "How do they do it, lad?"

It really didn't matter any more. I was so friggin' tired; the whole absurd situation had crashed down around me and everything seemed to be cockeyed. I knew what had to be done and these men were the only ones who could help me, so I told them as much as necessary to achieve my goals. Besides, would it really change anything? I didn't know and my ability to give a crap was fading quickly. "At Auschwitz alone they are killing 2,000 Jews a day. The Nazis figured out a way to channel that Necromantic energy into artifacts looted from conquered nations, in effect creating great magical batteries. Then the energy could used by a magician for whatever purpose they desire. However, it takes a magician of extraordinary power to handle that kind of input. Ribbentrop, Goebbels, Hitler, and Speer all have that kind of strength and the ability to use it without turning their brains into guacamole."

Crack! The Colonel's hand slammed against the desk and I jumped a little. "Damnation!" he thundered. "I knew it! I knew it had to be that very thing! By God, the spell Shape needed to pull off such a feat!"

Oliver stroked his upper lip, giving me the old stink eye while the Colonel stared at the phone as if willing it to ring. My need to preserve some sort of temporal continuity warred with my desire to save Mouth and retrieve that aluminum case. No contest ... desire won.

Mouth dry, I eyed them both. "Okay, gentleman, tell you what; get me to France, let me retrieve my agent and I'll take care of Goebbels and the briefcase." I sighed. "And I'll kill von Ribbentrop as well, if possible."

Silently, with grave formality, the Colonel opened a drawer and pulled out my Bowie, the Lahti and my Kimber .45 ACP and pushed them across the desk. "Just what I wanted to hear, old boy." His smile was almost feral.

My gaze flickered back and forth between the two, picking up the twitch of Oliver's lips and the twinkle in the Colonel's eyes. As my dad always said, "I may be slow, son, but I get there."

"You set me up," I said flatly. "This is what you wanted all along."

They laughed as the phone began to ring.

Six hours later—during four of them I slept—the Colonel and Oliver escorted me to an airfield some forty miles outside of London—no Corporals or Sergeants to act as a buffer between the two magicians and myself, which showed an amazing amount of trust. Or bravado. Either one was fine with me as long as the job was done. Oliver drove with the casual grace of someone who had taken this trip several times before, even as an American driving on what he considered the wrong side of the road.

Lack of sleep dogged me, but somewhere during my four hours of unconsciousness, someone had magically healed my injuries. Nice, but it only re-enforced the notion that I was heading into a world of hurt.

In contrast to London's broken body, the countryside was relatively unscathed, albeit dressed in shades of gray and dismal in the cold winter weather. My guess was that it was an hour or two past midnight and the stars were successfully hidden behind the unseen clouds looming above us.

God, I was tired. So damn tired. Every time it seemed like I was coming closer to finding a way to kill Iku-Turso, something got in my way.

Too little sleep and worry dragged at my flesh, not to mention the frustration I felt at not being debriefed. Corporal and Sergeant no-names roused me out of bed and escorted me quietly and efficiently to the car where Oliver and the Colonel were waiting. No explanation, nothing, only a quiet sense of urgency and thinly veiled anxiety.

The Colonel's voice started me out of my funk. "Mr. Hakala, we are almost to our destination."

So we were. Wet pavement gleamed in the headlights and a strange, dark lump appeared in the near distance that slowly resolved to a large, olive drab aircraft. Four large Rolls Royce Merlin engines (the air was suddenly thick with irony), seventy feet long, nineteen feet tall, eight 7.7mm Browning machine guns in three turrets and at least 14,000 lbs of bomb load. The plane had a brutal, savage elegance combined with enough firepower to level a small town.

It was gorgeous.

"An Avro Lancaster," I breathed in awe. "A real friggin' Lancaster."

"I take it you approve," the Colonel said dryly. I nodded, fascinated by this piece of living history shining in the headlights.

The car stopped and we piled out, my eyes never leaving the plane. "I love it. To me, this is a legend, the Lancaster. One of the best planes to come out of the war."

"Then, young man," said the Colonel as he adjusted his bulky coat against the night's cold. "You will have a marvelous time jumping out of this 'legend.' "

"Say what?"

Oliver laughed as he handed me a leather jacket, the kind referred to as a 'bomber,' identical to his. Once again, Irony reared its ugly head. "Don't worry pal, you'll have a parachute. You have jumped out of an airplane before, haven't you?" The twinkle in his eye had a lot of glittering nasty. He was enjoying my discomfort.

Jerk.

I turned to the Colonel. "Don't you guys jump out of C-47s, not perfectly good bombers? Sounds a bit dubious to me."

The Colonel straightened my jacket and tipped me a wink while Oliver snorted. "Lad, we are dropping you into enemy territory and will continue on with a bombing run as a distraction. Don't want Jerry to look for our chaps, do we? There is a nice fuel depot near Strasbourg we have had our eyes on for a while."

Oliver smirked. "Don't worry, wallflower, the Krauts won't pick us up on radar. I got us covered."

"You mean the radar-jamming spell developed in 1942?" I asked. "The one that uses so much magical energy that it's been deemed too logistically difficult to use on a wide scale?" It was my turn to grin at his look of amazement. 'Revenge is mine' sayeth the sarcastic bastard. The Colonel himself enjoyed a good belly laugh.

"Okay, wise guy," Oliver said, poking a finger in my chest with every word. "You better be able to deliver on your promise and, if you do, we'll figure out a way to get you back home." Not waiting for an answer, he boarded the plane.

I had been avoiding that thought for a while, but it was time to face the issue head on. When I'd seen Mouth enter the time portal, I'd known what had to be done. No thought went into my actions; instead I did what every good agent does … full speed ahead and damn the torpedoes, Sacrifice and Service … the watchwords of the Bureau. My gut told me it was a one-way trip, but it was the rest of me that refused to face the obvious. Short of Necromancy, which was out of the question, Mouth and I were stuck.

Staying here would mean disappearing into the herd of post-war humanity, not that difficult in a pre-computerized world. My only real regret: giving up my quest for vengeance against Iku-Turso. The thought burned like bile.

The Colonel handed me a small, wooden, rectangular box. Inside were four small half-carat diamonds and a larger aquamarine, all firmly glued to the velvet inside. Under each stone was a teeny tiny bit of paper and on each of those itty-bitty pieces of paper were words.

Spell gems. "Thanks, Sir. I'm afraid I didn't get you anything." I could feel my smile almost touch my ears.

"Nonsense, son. Those diamonds are full to the brim with power. Each stone has the explosive capacity of ten sticks of dynamite, so be careful."

"The aquamarine?"

"Ah, yes. That particular stone is a locator. Say the word and the facet closest to our magician in France will glow. The closer she is, the brighter the glow."

'Well, that is pretty neat." I stored the box in the inside pocket of my jacket.

"I know this must be a bit of a whirlwind for you, Mr. Hakala," the Colonel remarked a little too casually, "but we must take swift action in these dire times. The Nazis have an enormous magical advantage with Necromancy." He held up a hand to forestall any comment. "To you all this is history, but to us it remains current events." Those blue eyes lost all humor, lost even the vestige of merriment; all bled out in an instant and what remained was a world of sorrow and loss. "I thought the first war was bad—slowly dying in trenches, drinking from puddles when there was no fresh water to be had, smelling the rot and hearing the sounds of agony, those pitiless screams assailing us day and night—but this war, this extermination of the Jews …" For once, the great lecturer, one of England's literary giants, seemed at a loss for words.

"How did you come to be in this business, sir?" I asked in an effort to pull his eyes back from whatever dark place they had wandered to.

"Eh? What?" His eyes snapped back and once again resumed their humorous twinkling. "Oh, how did I join? Simplicity, dear boy; my companions and I were the victims of an attack by a nest of vampires. It happened late at night, when the beasts came to scavenge the bodies of the freshly killed. One moment I was playing cards with my friends, Gilson and Smith, and the next we were surrounded by four carrion eaters."

"What happened?"

"Gilson and Smith went down fighting, killed a monster before they were ripped apart. I myself was facing two when my first magic came upon me. I lit the trench with sunlight and scared the blighters away. Next thing I knew a magician from His Majesty's Service offered me a choice: join the Service and leave the trenches or remain." His smile was sudden and joyful. "Of course I joined up, lad. I would have done nearly anything to see my beloved Edith again. A story was concocted that I had contracted trench fever and here I am, seventeen years later."

Wow. Quite different than the official histories.

"Mr. Hakala, I know I should not ask, but I have a question, since you seem to know me …"

I interrupted. "A long and happy life, sir. You, your wife and your children. You are well known to future generations."

"Hmph. Well, thank you for that." He seemed at a loss for words, a bit flustered and embarrassed, but after a moment, a steely look came over his long face. "I know you wish to keep the future sacrosanct, lad. I know that your actions could lead to some ... unwelcome changes, but can you do me one favor, if at all possible?"

A cold shiver ran down my spine. "If possible, sir."

The Colonel stared at the black sky above for a few seconds, then pulled out his pipe and pouch. Slowly, carefully he loaded the bowl and brought an ember to light. Sweet smoke tickled my nose. "Mr. Hakala, will you please kill as many of those bloody Nazi bastards as you can?"

Chapter Fifteen

Canton

The Situation Has Not Improved

The sight of Leung's cooling corpse gave me a rich sense of accomplishment. Not that I took any particular joy in killing him; it was simply something that needed to be done, like putting down a rabid dog.

"Damn, hon, you okay?" Winch sounded a little scared. I must've put some fright into her.

"It's all right, babe," I said soothingly. "Didn't mean to come on so hard." It hit me then. Kal! He'd run off after Mouth and that Nazi dickweed. With a quick "Follow me," to Winch, I headed off down the tunnel.

Switchbacks and then a large cavern filled with crates—all of them covered with Nazi symbols ... the one with the eagle facing left over the circle and swastika. Trust those German pricks to ruin something proud and noble like the eagle. A strange humming turned out to be a smallish genny, still chugging away, providing power for the lights strung all over the cavern.

Kal was nowhere to be seen. There was, however, Goebbels' blond henchman lying on the ground with his neck canted at a weird angle. It wasn't hard piecing together what had happened. At the back of the cavern, another tunnel led to a smaller cavern. Nothing. Bare except for a circular ... well, burn mark some three feet in diameter. A kind of blackened area. When examined closely, the stone itself was black, not the usual tan color of the surrounding rock. Magic. Had to be.

I hate magic.

Leave all that magic crap to the magicians and leave me the things I can stab, shoot or beat to death. Life as it should be.

135

"What is it?" Winch said from behind.

"At a guess, this is where that Goebbels guy went." The blackened area was unusually smooth, as if it had been polished.

"Where's Kal?"

"Knowing him, he went wherever that Nazi went." I'm not a Christian, but I felt the urge to cross myself. A small inkling of where Kal, Mouth and Goebbels had gone to slid into my brain and I shied away from the reasoning. If what I suspected was true, Kal and Mouth might be in a whole parcel of trouble and lost to us forever.

Nope. Not gonna happen. Kal was the only cat I knew who could eat nails and crap bullets, so he *was* gonna come back and do it soon. Yeah. Soon.

Unbidden, a welling of sadness, of raw fear and despair, began to rise up in my heart. With a force of will—will that had been iron-forged during years in the Bureau—I shoved those emotions down. Down into the dark recesses of my soul and buried them there. No time for weepy, girly shit, only stoic resolve.

Winch, God bless her, said nothing—letting me deal with my issues—and followed me back to the larger cavern. "Let's check the crates."

"No need, Canton," Winch said through pursed lips. "My guess is that we'll find modern weaponry that doesn't use computer chips. Wouldn't be surprised if there are chemical and bio weapons as well. Things that kill with the least amount of effort."

I thought furiously. "The Nazis fought for about six months in Stalingrad before they were defeated. What do you bet that there are enough weapons here to tip the balance?"

"Crap."

"You got that right." I spied a silver briefcase wedged between two crates near a dead henchman. A heave tore it loose and I was surprised at how heavy it was. Flipping the catches, I opened the lid.

What the hell?

"Oh my *God!*" breathed Winch from beside me.

"What? What is it?" LED display, a keypad and a cylinder

136

about a foot long and six inches wide. Didn't look like much.

"I think …" she began. "I think it's a *nuke*."

I slammed the lid shut with a clang. Where the hell did they get a nuke? Not something you order from a J.C. Penney catalog.

Waitaminute! "How the hell do you know that?"

Her small, but strong hand smacked me on the back of the head. "Dope. Remember, I was CIA before Bureau. Geez, don't you ever *listen* to me anymore?"

Oh, yeah, right … CIA, she could probably MacGuyver up a nuke from a paper clip and bubble gum. As for the listening part … well, to be perfectly honest, it wasn't listening we'd been doing for the past few months, but even I wasn't brave enough to say that out loud. She'd been trained to kill people with things like forks, spoons, toothpicks …

"Canton, hon," she said with an edge to her voice that told me she'd read my mind … as usual. "We have to call someone about this."

I frowned. "We ain't calling anyone, kid. Not until Kal gets back."

"Canton—"

"No!" My voice had turned savage. Hell, I liked Winch, maybe even *loved* her, but Kal was … Kal. The world was better with him in it.

"Canton, he might not come back." No fool she. She'd figured it out.

"He will."

"How do you know?" Those soft eyes bored into mine, pleading to be convinced.

"He's my friend."

"That's an answer?"

I stared at the mass of crates with their deadly payloads, the aluminum case that could unleash hell, and searched my soul for a better answer, but there was none. "It's the only answer I've got."

Crack!

The shot took Winch down, but I didn't have time to worry.

Years of training had already set my body in motion. Pushing off a crate with my foot, I was airborne for a split second as I cleared the stack, drawing my Glock in mid air.

Crack! A bullet spun past the tip of my nose, nearly blistering the skin. I landed and rolled as more shots rang out ... five, six, seven. From the sound of it, at least three different pistols. That meant more than one shooter. Damn. Wildly, I swung an arm toward the genny that was chugging away nearby. My fingers touched the power button. With an asthmatic rumble, the little machine died and the bulbs overhead slowly dimmed.

Lights out everyone, and Canton was in the house. I felt my lips part in an evil smile. I'd just leveled the playing field.

"He killed the generator, sir!" spat a high, clear voice.

"I can see that!" came the reply in a thick German accent.

Another German. Starting to really hate these guys.

"We should leave it off!" said another voice,

"*Nein,* the dark will help him," the German answered.

That right, I thought. *Keep talking.* Adrenaline began to fizz through my veins as I carefully drew my Bowie from its sheath. Fourteen inches of razor sharp death. My people, the Mescalero Apache, had been the greatest guerilla fighters the U.S. government never wanted to face and it was about time I showed those assholes what that meant.

No time to worry about Winch. She was either dead or she wasn't. If she was I'd mourn later. At that moment I needed to be cold, hard, emotionless. I needed to be iron and to do iron work.

The ambushers had stopped talking, maybe in an effort to locate me. It wouldn't help them much. They were sly, but so was I.

I slipped a hand into the front pocket of my jeans and pulled out a quarter. Quietly I slipped out of my boots and pulled free my socks, then tossed the quarter high up over the crates to the left.

Tink ... tink ... tinkety-tink! Shots rang out and muzzle flashes strobed through the darkness as the men fired toward where the quarter had landed. I was already in motion, bare feet padding silently across the cavern floor.

The gunfire stopped and so did I. The air was thick with propellants and the stale exhalations of desperate men. I inhaled slowly, deeply. Underneath, the chemical smell and halitosis was the faint odor of … cologne. Flowery, soft and almost lemony.

Perfect.

I slid forward while sweat dripped from my eyebrows and stung my eyes. Blinking rapidly, I took another low, crouching step. The smell—the cologne—was closer and I could hear someone breathing harshly. Another clue to home in on.

A low scuff of leather on rock, the soft rustle of fabric. Only a few feet ahead and to my left. My hand reached out and didn't find wood. I must have just passed the crates.

Close … I crouched lower, slowly so as not to emit a sound. Whoever was breathing was trying to control himself, but I smelled panic-sweat under that soft cologne. He was scared.

Good. He or one of his butt-buddies had shot Winch and they would pay.

The Bowie leapt forward as if it had a will of its own, and my arm was only an extension of that will. An initial resistance, than a sudden give … all fourteen inches of blade sheathed itself in flesh and my hand became drenched in hot liquid. A muffled grunt and a body fell into my arms. A hand clawed at my shirt and I lowered the dead weight gently and quietly to the ground.

"Karl?" The voice low, barely slithering across my ears. Maybe four, six feet away. Sorry, Karl wasn't here anymore, please leave a message at the beep and don't bother waiting for a call back. *Beeeep*.

I stepped over the body, still at a crouch, the quiet drip, drip, dripping from the knife barely audible even to my trained ears. Closer … closer …

"Karl?" Again, with a bit more urgency. *Keep calling out, I know where you are.* Another step. Very close. No panic sweat from this one. He was cool as a cucumber, a trained killer.

Like me.

Once more I struck, but some sixth sense must have alerted him because the Bowie *screeeeched* across the length of a pistol and sheared off, missing the man by a fraction.

I dropped, only thing to do because I knew what would come next … and it did. Multiple flashes seared my eyes as the German fired four times, clean misses all, but the light was enough for me to see a pair of big feet in Italian leather not more than a foot away. Not one to waste an opportunity, I stabbed down and felt the Bowie slide, slide, slide into flesh and grate against bone.

It had the result I'd hoped for. A scream like a cat being strangled and the pistol clattered to the ground next to my ear. The scream became more high-pitched as I drew the Bowie down, cutting the foot in half lengthwise. It cut short to a gasping sob as I pulled the knife free and stabbed upwards. Teeth shattered and rained down on my face as the thick steel cut through tongue and back of throat before exiting out the man's neck in a spurt of blood.

Two down, unknown number to go, but it was a good start.

From far back in the cavern, from beyond the crates, came an eerie green light, like the shining of damned souls.

I gritted my teeth in anger and pulled the knife free, the dead man falling next to me. He and his buddy had been distractions, henchmen for whoever was in the smaller cavern, and I'd fallen for it like a Green Pea. Dammit!

Stealth was off the table, so I beat feet down the big cavern, my way lit by that nauseating light shining from the small cavern. Down the small tunnel and into a world of pain.

More gunshots, four of them. Three tore into me, leg, hip and upper arm, cutting my strings. I flopped to the floor and bled all over it, teaching that dang floor a lesson or two. Don't mess with me or I'll give you a cleaning bill you won't believe.

A medium-sized man stood by a sickening, strange column of flowing rock. Or was it smoke? Liquid? Whatever it was, it was the source of the light that made me want to sick up all over the place.

The man, the German, perhaps, had hair so black it was almost blue, with pale, pale skin. In the light of the grotesque column, he looked undead. When he smiled, he showed a small gap between his front teeth. Medium-sized, good looking in an everyday sort of way. A smoking .45 was clutched in one hand, the barrel pointing between my eyes.

"You American agents are quite something," he said, his accent confirming my guess, striding in front of the column so that the nacreous light silhouetted his body. His voice was a gentle and high-pitched tenor. "It would never have occurred to me that lesser breeds could be so lethal. I would sincerely love to exp—"

A red flower burst from his cream colored jacked at the lapel, and another appeared low on the left side. The German tumbled back into the column, which flowed sluggishly around him, and disappeared. A second later the column collapsed to the floor and vanished, leaving me in the dark.

A small sound, perhaps a footfall. "Canton, hon, you okay?" Winch. Thank goodness. My whole pain-wracked body relaxed in sweet relief.

I was a whole mess of not-okay, but you bet I would never admit it. "Yeah, babe, just a couple of holes."

Gentle hands found me and fluttered over my body, discovering my wounds. I was losing blood. A lot of blood.

"Stay still, hon."

I didn't bother to tell her I had no place else to go.

"I got you, hon. Stay with me." A sharp *crink!* and the phosphorescent green light of a glow stick washed over me.

Tired. So very tired. My eyelids began to close.

"Canton, I'm going to patch you up enough to move you to the car. I have to drive you to the hospital. Okay?"

Okay? That didn't work for me. "Sorry, babe," I slurred. "We wait for Kal."

So tired.

Chapter Sixteen

Mouth

I'd Rather Be in Philadelphia

Warm. Too warm. Sounds were too loud, the scratchy fabric of the blanket across my skin too rough and it hurt, along with the myriad other hurts that shouted at me. It was hard, but I ignored them.

No, I wasn't warm. Hot. Far too hot. What was happening?

-Hello, luv.-

What?

-I said, 'Hello, luv.'-

Who are you? Where am I? Why do things hurt so much? And how come you have an English accent?

-Well aren't you a right worrier? I'm the bird what's going to fix you up. As for where you are, that's not important now, is it? But what you need is a right fixing. You've been banged up a bit, haven't you?-

Images came to mind, sensations of memory. Goebbels, wormy hands, a world with two suns, beating the crap out of no-neck security types.

Kal!

-Who is this *Call* bloke you're thinking so strongly of, luv?-

Not Call, Kal. Sounds the same, spelled different. He's Kalevi Hakala, a Finn. My … friend.

An image of Kal came to mind, him in his full rage and fury.

–Well, well. He's a decent looking bloke for a Finnlander. Scary, though.-

What the hell is going on?

-You're more or less asleep and deeply wounded, luv. I'm here to see if you're worth bringing back from death's door, aren't I? So tell me, why should I?-

I racked my brain for a reason besides a desire to live and see my friends and loved ones again. To see Kal.

It hit me. Goebbels. I need to kill a Nazi asswipe named Goebbels. He'd brought me here.

I felt a twinge of surprise from the ... person ... who spoke to me and a drawing away. A feeling of absence came from the vast nothingness around me. Where was she? I was absolutely sure the person was a she. The ... sense of her was female. And kind.

-What sort of person are you then, luv? A former lover of that damned Jerry? An apprentice betrayed?-

Back, oh thank *God!* I hadn't realized how much even the ephemeral company of the woman was a balm to my soul.

No, he kidnapped me! Brought me here with some sort of ... terrible magic. Probably Necromancy.

That was a safe bet. All those poor Jews.

-Magic?- Once again, a long pause. -Are you part of Mrs. Collinsworth's class?-

My mind processed those words and a spool of memory unwound from my Bureau days. Mrs. Collnsworth's class ... an old recognition phrase from one member of a Bureau to a counterpart in a different country. Established during WWI, it was still used even in 21st century and it allowed open dialogue without the Interdiction closing up the throat and clicking teeth firmly shut. I was dealing with MI-7! In a *totally* cool, CIA and James Bond sort of way! I felt like crying through the dulling heat that was my existence.

No, Mrs. Collinsworth was my father's teacher. The standard countersign.

-Well, luv, why didn't you let me know you was an American Bureau agent? I better fix you up right quick, shouldn't I? Don't worry, luv, you'll be right as rain soon enough.-

Oh, thank youthankyou! Please don't leave me! It's become so hot here. This blanket is so scratchy it hurts.

Even though I couldn't feel them, I knew tears coursed down my cheeks

-It's all right, luv. Go to sleep now.-

Warm, but not hot. My cheeks felt a slice of cold, though, a faint breeze that carried the sting and stench of winter.

My eyes came open slowly, the corners crusted with sleep-sand. Logy, drowsy, passive and wiped—all those fun adjectives—but I still wanted to wake up because I felt *good*.

Bright light sharp as a blade stabbed my eyes, making them water. Beautiful. Harsh, but beautiful.

"How are you doing, luv?" asked a voice from somewhere out of sight.

How *was* I doing? Good question. Assessment time: I could feel both hands, arms, feet and legs. Still had my belly button and boobs. So far so good. I worked my jaw and tongue. Check. Ahhh, nice. "Feel okay." Voice scratchy, hoarse. Sounded like Shaggy from *Scooby-Doo*.

A canteen came from the left and cold, brackish water flowed past my lips. The best, tastiest water *ever*!

"There you go, luv. Drink up, but slowly."

I managed to ratchet my eyes around far enough to see the speaker. A slender black woman, pretty in a hard-as-nails sort of way, with big brown eyes like they have in those Japanese *Manga* cartoons, eyes that take up half the face; deep, soulfully brown, and trusting. Her kinky hair was cropped short to her scalp and she wore a beret firmly on the crown of her head. She smiled with bright, even teeth as I drank greedily.

When the flow of water stopped, I grunted, "Thanks." There, better. It almost sounded like me.

"Well, luv. Good to see that me old magic still works."

"Where … where am I?"

The woman's face came close enough that I could see the texture of her near flawless skin. "You are in France, luv, and my guv wants a word," she whispered kindly.

France? Things were hazy, the gears of my memory full of sand and rue. The woman's smile grew wider and I felt a hand rub my forehead. "It's okay, luv. The guv is a good bloke who'll be kind to you. Don't worry, you'll see." She moved out of sight.

I tried to move my hand, but the flesh wouldn't listen. "Don't go!" I hated the whining note in my voice.

Her voice floated gently to my ears as she moved away. "It will be all right, luv. Jeanie won't let anything bad happen to you." A door closed.

Jeanie? Jeanie? She sounded nice and for a while I dreamed of Jeanie as the razor light shone on my face. In and out, I breathed, in and out. I never knew how enjoyable the simple act of breathing could be.

Should I have been thinking about climbing to my feet, kicking the ass of anyone stupid enough to stand in my way? Maybe, but too much had happened too quickly; in the back of my mind I knew I might be staying in France for a very long time. I switched off my mental gears, sent the workers home and chilled for a while.

Voices came from outside, or at least what I assumed was outside because they were all fuzzy and dulled and the only thing I could see was the rough wooden ceiling. I recognized Jeanie from the sound of her voice, not the words; all I understood was that she was angry and giving someone a good verbal beat down. Tough lady, I reckoned ... my kinda gal.

The door opened. "Hello there, miss." A clear, strong baritone. A man's voice. A second later that man came into focus and my heart gave that little flutter you get when someone *really* sexy meets your eyes.

Hubba-hubba.

Long face with a straight, thin, aristocratic nose and high cheekbones. Black hair and strong chin with a *totally* cute dimple. He needed a shave and smelled a bit of wood smoke and sweat, but at that moment I didn't care; he was *hot*. The flutter in my heart traveled to places south.

His thin, shapely lips parted in a smile. "Well, me lovely, you're looking well today." Ooh, an English accent, just like Jeanie's, but more high-tone, like Prince William's or Harry's. This just kept getting better and better.

"You don't look so bad yourself," I said, almost involuntarily.

His flash of a smile disappeared so quickly it was as if it had never happened. "You're a cheeky one, that's for sure." That handsome face disappeared for a moment and there came a scrape of wood against wood. The man returned and lowered himself down on what I could only assume was a chair. I silently cursed my inability to turn my head. "So, Jeanie tells me you're American Bureau."

Okay, time for business. I focused my mind and put away lewd thoughts. Back to those later. "Yes." Keep it simple. I needed to get the lay of the land.

"What are you doing in the arse end of France, then?"

I did what any Bureau agent would do, kept my trap shut.

That seemed to score points with the Englishman, who gave me another quick smile. "You told Jeanie that Goebbels brought you here, is that true?"

"You're awful rude, you know that?"

A puzzled look. "What?"

"Well, here I am, healed from what I assume were grievous wounds; I can't move and you don't even introduce yourself. You just get down to business. Didn't your mama teach you any manners?"

His beautiful hazel eyes widened for a mere fraction of a second before his features assumed a carefully neutral expression. "You're right, of course. The name is Richard. Agent Richard Fleming of His Majesty's Supernatural Services." Another flash of brilliant white teeth. "Now, I've shown you mine, miss."

I wish. "Rebecca McTavish, Bureau of Supernatural Investigations, retired."

"Really? I didn't know the Bureau was letting people retire, what with the war and everything. Besides, when did the Bureau start allowing women to serve as agents?"

"You'd be surprised, sweetie."

He treated me to a hazel squint. "Goebbels brought you here. Was it in that flash of ugly light and magic two days ago?"

Two days? I'd been out for *two days*?

Richard smiled. "Aye, luv, two days you've been here. If Jeanie hadn't been using so much magic to conceal our presence from the local Nazis, we would've squared you away much sooner. As it was, it was touch and go."

Well, better in the hands of the Brits than the Herr Doktor Jerkface and his wormy fingers. "Yeah. Goebbels kidnapped me and brought me to … France, right?"

"Yes, impressive that. Moving a body through space like that. Must have killed a bloody lot of people to carry that off."

"I don't know how much to tell you—"

"Did a big blond man follow you? By his identification, his name is Kaiser Söze? What kind of Jerry name is that?"

Kal! My heart leapt. Only Kal created IDs out of famous movie characters. "He's an agent, like me." *Oh, Kal, I should've known you'd come for me.* "He's … my friend. Another agent."

Richard smiled for real and it was *beautiful.* "Well, well, well … turns out *my* guv is trying to sort the fellow out, get the feel of him. Told me to take good care of you until he can message me back."

Tears of relief leaked from my eyes and ran down my cheeks. No words, only a sense of profound relief.

"Anything else to add?"

I shook my head and closed my eyes.

Warm breath tickled my ear as Richard leaned close. "Thing is, my guv wants you to tell us all. In the spirit of mutual co-operation, seeing how we are allies against the Hun and all that."

No, I was too tired, too filled with so many conflicting emotions that tore at me every which way. Relief that Kal was here, anxiety that Kal was here, fear that we were both trapped in the past forever, sheer happiness that I was among allies, and so on and so forth. A hodgepodge of chemicals flooding my system so intensely I barely knew which way was up.

"If I told you what was really going on, why I'm here, you'd lock me up and throw away the key."

"Try me, luv. Please." Those hazel eyes glimmered with compassion and once again I felt the flutter.

Oh well, it wasn't like there was a loony bin handy, was there? I asked for another drink of water and Richard obliged. "Where exactly am I?"

"Vosges Mountains, Eastern France near the German border."

"Let me guess, there's a camp nearby as well as an Alsatian village named Natzwiller."

He frowned. "What looks like a German Army base, yes."

Why would Goebbels bring me here? Oh well, it didn't matter and with a sigh, I began to tell my tale.

"That is some story, lass. Some story."

"Call me lass again and you'll get a story you won't believe, hotshot." I was tired and cranky, unwilling to put up with his sarky attitude and disbelief. Besides, I'd told him he wouldn't believe me, hadn't I?

"Easy, Rebecca, I didn't mean any disrespect now, did I? It is a bold story you told me, not to mention that we haven't seen any prisoners in this so-called concentration camp of yours."

Dammit! "Not my camp, you nitwit! And the reason you haven't seen anyone is because it's one of the lesser camps, not yet at full killing capacity. That and the fact that there's a good clearing all around it with terrific lines-of-sight make it all the more difficult for you to survey. But, hey, if you want to check it out all personal-like and see for yourself, be my guest."

"So what you're saying is this Kalevi Hakala chap of yours followed you through, what did you call it? Oh, yes, a *time portal* in order to save you from the Nazi Minister of Propaganda—one of the most powerful magicians in the Reich, by the way—and somehow bring you back to the year 2011. Is that the gist of it?"

"God, for such a hot guy, you are such a dickhead." More tears trailed down my cheeks and I bit my lower lip to curb my rising frustration and fatigue.

"Well, you're a queer bird, that's for sure, but I do believe you."

My eyes sprang open. The face he presented to me was kindly, with a self-deprecating twist to the lips. "You do?" I asked hopefully. "Why? How?"

"A woman appears in a giant flash of ugly light, stirs up trouble with the Jerrys, runs three miles in less than twenty minutes while wounded and in high heels no less! Then, when my team's magician probes her mind for information, imagine her surprise when she finds out that woman has no Interdiction placed on her! A spell created to run on your body's natural energy and so insidiously powerful no one can remove it short of death." He moved closer, eyes coming within inches of mine. "Not to mention your unusual speech pattern, even for an American, and the little tidbit that there are no female field agents in the States. There are female magicians in Special Branch, but no field agents. However, you are no magician and your musculature and calluses tell me you are a fighter. Hand to hand, if I'm not mistaken."

Impressive. He had it all nailed down, including the Interdiction, which, I believe, disappeared after that strange elevator ride over sixty years from now. I'd felt the spell's absence like a tooth that had been pulled, a relieved emptiness in my mind. I'd kept mum about it, certain the others felt the same way. Somehow it was a private event, like when I had my first period.

Richard was a smart cookie, all right. From obscure clues he'd put together an accurate account without any corroborating …

"You bastard!"

He laughed.

"You freaking bastard! You guessed already! You found my smart phone, didn't you?"

He held up my cell, the black protective casing cracked and slicked with dried mud. "Is that what it is? A telephone? I quite enjoyed that puzzle game, sudoku."

I should have felt frustrated, but I only had room for tired, lots and lots of tired. At least Richard believed me. "If you're going to ask, don't. I'm not spilling the beans about future events." His smarmy look faded. "At least not until I confer with Kal."

"What do you mean?"

"I mean I have to confer with Kal before I tell you about the future, and maybe not even then. The future relies on the past *being* the past, just as it's supposed to be. We start messing with things and bad things could happen." Not the least was the paradox of my not having been born, but if that became true, how could I have traveled into the past to change the future, etcetera, and etcetera.

"I really don't think Home Office will—"

"Screw Home Office, big boy. I'm a retired Bureau agent from the future and not under your authority." Big sigh. "Now, if you're thinking of torturing information out of me—"

"Let's just stop there," he blurted, alarmed. "We don't do that. We're British, after all. No one is going to torture you. You may be from the future, but we're still allies, right?"

"Right." Good, torture was off the table. Nice to know. "So what now?"

"You rest, that's what now." He stood and disappeared from sight. Wood scraped against wood. "The healing was not complete; Jeanie was rather spent when she tended to you. Oh, your clavicle was healed, but your body had taken quite a beating. I will come back tomorrow. Sleep. Now."

My eyes closed of their own accord and I didn't even hear him leave.

Chapter Seventeen

Kal

Out of a Perfectly Good Airplane

Frigid air screamed past my goggles and tore relentlessly at my skin, sending icy slivers deep into bone. Above me the Lancaster roared away into the darkness. Oliver the magician was using the power of four nearly flawless diamonds chock full of magic to fuel his anti-radar spell. According to him, that was enough to fly to Strasbourg and back, but just barely.

Somewhere below, the ground was rushing toward me with lethal force, hungry to treat me to a dose of deceleration trauma. Not a good way to spend the evening, so I yanked on the ripcord and felt/heard the 'chute flap open, unspooling several yards of fabric that grew taut in an instant. A slight jerk and everything went quiet except for the freezing wind.

It was almost too dark; the heavy cloud cover hid the half-moon effectively and I could barely make out my hand in front of my face. The ground was more a threatening presence than anything visual, merely a promise of solidity.

Twenty seconds later what had been only a cold breeze became a violently vicious, screaming gale that had me flapping behind the canopy of my chute like the tail of a kite.

Oh, crap.

Tumbled about like laundry in the dryer, my world became a whirl of up and down, left to right, all accompanied by a heady nausea. I heroically kept myself from losing everything I'd eaten in the last few years and held on for dear life.

Less than a minute later woody hands slapped and tore at me, scraping swaths of skin from my flesh. I think I screamed as bark ripped my forehead up a treat. I felt warm wetness flow into my eyes just before a jarring impact cut my strings.

Cold, stiff, sore, achy. Pick your favorite adjectives and throw them all in a pot. Simmer for a half hour and serve. What you ladle out would be the merest hint of what it felt like to wake up on a cold, damp forest floor with dry, crackling blood in your eyes and every muscle in your body shrieking and cramping.

Head pounding, back popping with every small motion, I managed to lever myself upright, thanks to a convenient tree. A hot nail of pain stabbed through my forehead, sending the world wobbling. My fingers probed the affected area and encountered a lumpy, dull heat that flared at the lightest touch. Fingertips came away rusty with dried blood.

"Wonderful," I muttered. A drag at my shoulders proved to be my 'chute, the white fabric mostly buried beneath wind-swept leaves. I shrugged out of the harness, the motion sending rusty cramps through my shoulders.

Okay, inventory of parts. Legs, check, arms, check. Head (somewhat), stomach, family jewels, feet, hands … check times five. Goodie, looked like I was all present and accounted for.

A few twists and turns, a couple of stretches. No broken bones, although my neck creaked and groaned somewhat. Abuse by Goebbels' henchman and assault by the forest of deadly conifers had done my vertebrae no good.

Click.

I knew that sound. Did everyone in 1943 own a shotgun? Second time this week. My hands went over my head, not without a few pins of pain, and I turned to face the gunman.

Short guy with black hair and broad shoulders. He looked like he could take care of himself without the double-barreled shotgun pointed at my face. Tattered black woolen pants and a dark long coat topped with a shapeless wool hat.

"Vous êtes qui? Que faîtes-vous ici?" I tried out my best smile. He wasn't impressed. "Vous êtes allemand?"

"Sorry, Frenchy, don't speak the language." I calculated the odds. He was about fifteen feet away, the shotgun unwavering. Even if I hadn't felt like a jar of smashed assholes, it was an iffy proposition, me being able to snag his weapon before he rearranged my face into something less than lovely. No, I was going to have to convince him I was a friend. In war-torn France. During the time of the worst paranoia the world had ever known.

Piece of cake.

"Vous êtes américain?"

That I almost understood. I pointed to my chest. "Yes, me heap big American. A friend to the French." My voice had become louder and my speech slower, as if I were talking to a particularly dimwitted, hard-of-hearing child.

I'd fallen into that old song-and-dance typical of Americans, when we treat those who don't understand us like idiots. Speak slowly and the poor bastards will magically understand you. My Dork-O-Meter had just clattered into the red.

Apparently the Frenchman thought I was pretty much a complete waste of protoplasm, but less dangerous than the locally grown Nazis. The shotgun lowered a bit, pointing to the ground between my feet.

"Sprechen Sie Deutsch?" he asked slowly.

Yeah, I spoke German. Poorly. "My German is sick," I replied in that language, knowing that my only fluent German would be a streak of cussing that could set the trees on fire.

"¿Se habla Español?"

Spanish I could work with. "Si," I replied with some relief and noticed the same in his eyes.

"What are you doing here, American? Are you a spy?"

It was amazing how much college Spanish you could recall with a shotgun for motivation. "Not quite a spy."

The Frenchman's gnarled, knobby hands flexed slightly and I tensed. He had a rough, weather-beaten look and I revised my initial impression of man in his forties and scaled it back ten years. Here was a man who worked in the sun and rain, in harsh cold and blustery wind. A hard man, a tough one.

I decided to take a chance. "Sir, I'm here to kill a lot of

Germans and kick Hitler hard in the place where his legs meet."
Well, I was about to find out if he was a collaborator; he'd either
turn me over to the local Nazi fun boys or one of the good guys. I
had a gut feeling and prayed that my gut wasn't fibbing.

The shotgun lowered some more. "Truly?"

I nodded.

He wanted to believe me, wanted not to pull the trigger that
would send buckshot to tear off my head. I desperately wanted the
same thing. "Can you prove anything you say? If you are German,
you will have me killed if I let you live."

Mind racing, I looked around for inspiration and found it in
woven nylon. I held the silky folds of the parachute in my hands. "A
German wouldn't parachute into territory already occupied by
Germany. Not alone. That would reveal a lack of … dominance."

The man visibly relaxed and the shotgun was no longer
pointed in my general direction. "Are you … do you have plans for
that parachute?" he asked hopefully. A small, pink tongue licked his
thin, dry lips.

The nylon swished across my fingertips, not much value to
me, but I noted the threadbare and stained state of his clothing and
realized it was a treasure to him. "Take it," I said with a smile and
dropped the fabric, moving away.

While he rolled up the yards of torn white nylon, I scanned the
sky through the bare branches and needles. Past noon. I'd been out
for a good long while and was fairly certain that I was miles away
from the designated drop point. Crap.

"What direction to Natzweiler village?" I asked, kneeling and
unbuttoning a small first aid kit from my belt. There I found
alcohol, cotton balls, and bandages. Good, dying of infection was
not my preferred way to exit the world. Dying in my sleep at the
ripe old age of ninety-five was a better option. Preferably while
snuggled next to my twenty-one year-old-wife. Yeah, that sounded
about right.

Arms full of parachute, the man turned to look and suddenly
became very still, staring at the kit. "Mister," he said slowly. "I will

have my wife tend to your hurt and then I will escort you to the village." Once again that pink tongue made an appearance. "If you give me that." He nodded to the kit.

It wasn't greed I saw on his face, more like naked desperation and I looked at the kit in my hands. Besides the alcohol, there was a vial of sulfa drugs, painkillers, two hypodermic needles, thread and sewing needles. A fortune.

I nodded, neck muscles creaking. "Sure."

The kit disappeared into his coat faster than I thought possible. "You follow me, Mister, and we go to my home. My wife will be disappointed I bring no mushrooms." With a smile, he held up the folded wads of parachute cloth. "But this will make up for it, I think."

"Call me Kal."

He smiled. "All right, Mister Kal. I am Etienne. My wife, Solange, will fix you good." With that, he started off at a brisk trot, cloth under one arm, shotgun held in the crook of the other. The bright sunlight speared mercilessly through the trees' leafless branches—in contrast to the gloominess of England—causing my eyes to water and head to throb. Shortly we came to what appeared to be an animal track, which wound up and down the steep hills.

I assumed we were in the Vosges, but one thing I'd learned in the Bureau: your assumptions usually turned out to be wrong. Dead wrong. Fortunately, Etienne informed me we were indeed in the Vosges, but by his description, at least ten miles from where I wanted to be.

Walking loosened the joints and stretched out cramping muscles, so by the time we'd traveled half a mile, I was starting to feel pretty good despite the pounding in my skull.

"You will like our home, Mister Kal. It is the most beautiful spot in all of France." Etienne's voice held a note of pride, which quickly rang a chime of caution. "My wife, she will fix your head and I will give you some food, then you must be on your way." Pale eyes sought mine. "You are a beacon of trouble in here, yes?"

I nodded. "*Si.*"

After searching my face for any hint of guile, Etienne led the way to a large clearing, a wide spot on the skirts of a mountain. In the center stood a mid-sized rough-wood cabin next to a large pen and small barn. Swaths and humps of gray-white snow were spread unevenly across the clearing. Curls of smoke drifted from the cabin's chimney, leaving the scent of burning pine suspended in the air.

My tackle took the Frenchman at the hips and slammed him to the ground in a shallow depression behind a tree, one hand over his mouth, the other clamped firmly to the shotgun. Icy fury erupted from his eyes, but was replaced the next moment by naked fear when I hissed, "Germans!"

I'd seen what he had not: a motorcycle with sidecar painted in olive drab (what was it about that color and military organizations?) with the Armanen Sig runes and the twin lightning bolts of the Waffen SS proudly displayed on the front of the sidecar. It had been parked on the far side of the cabin, partly obscured by the mall barn.

Interesting.

I sneaked a quick peek and caught a glimpse of a stylized skull and crossbones underneath the Sig runes. The symbol of the Gestapo.

Interesting-er.

What the heck were the Gestapo and the SS doing working together in the butt-end of nowhere? Did it have something to do with Natzweiler?

Nah. A coincidence, maybe, but still a pain in the ass. I guess God wasn't going to lob any soft balls my way anytime soon. Okay, I'd just have to take the fast pitches.

"Mister Kal," Etienne whispered after I removed my hand. "My wife, she is in the house. We have to save her!"

I raised an eyebrow and he rushed to explain. "It might have been said in the village that my wife and I … shelter certain people who wish not to come to the notice of the Reich."

One plus one equals two. "Jews."

He nodded.

Well, well. Looks like some suck up villager blabbed, and it was up to me to clean up the mess. Just perfect. I popped my head up for another look and saw white puffs coming from a soldier half hidden behind the cabin, his back to us. A trooper smoking a cigarette, waiting for whoever was in the cabin with Etienne's wife.

Crap. No time to be sneaky. One of the cabin windows faced our way … I'd just have to pray that whoever was inside was too distracted to look out.

Drawing my Bowie, I jumped to my feet and ran into the clearing, leaping over humps of snow. My sneakers (I didn't have the heart to give them up and abandoning Reeboks in 1943 seemed to be a rash act) whispered over dead grass as I put on as much speed as possible. I had roughly forty yards to cover.

Thirty. No hint of motion from the solider, only more puffs of cigarette smoke.

Twenty. I drew the Lahti, just in case.

Ten. The tip of the Bowie came up and the soldier started, perhaps hearing my footsteps for the first time.

Fourteen inches of honed steel slid through the startled trooper's throat and out the back. I used my momentum to drag the sharpened five inches of the blade's back around, half severing the German's neck. He crumpled to the ground in silence and a spray of arterial blood.

Ten feet later I came to a stop, torquing about and scrambling for the plank door. I didn't have time to consider the human wreckage, my focus was entirely on breaking through the door and killing every Nazi I could lay hands on.

Not all monsters are Supernaturals.

The door opened into darkness and a grating voice shouted, *"Put down your weapon!"* came the shout from inside, in English, no less.

I hit the brakes and threw myself to the side in case the owner of the voice became nervy and tried to decorate my tender bod with bullet holes. Moments later I was on my feet, back against the cabin with the Lahti raised, the modified clip still chock full of bullets. I couldn't see the door, but I was determined to nail the first Nazi who came into sight.

Unfortunately, the first person who stepped out was a frightened, lean woman with a horsey face and brown hair done up in pigtails. A shiner was starting a good glow around her right eye and her plain blue dress was torn down the front, exposing one pillowy breast. A black-gloved hand was clamped to her neck; the other held a Walther P38 to the back of her head. As she cleared the door, her head turned toward me and the man gripping her neck slid into view.

I almost shot him right there and then. Tall, blond, with flat, soulless gray eyes like chips of flint that drilled into mine. His gray uniform was the one despised the world over. Gestapo. Most people associate the Gestapo with black uniforms, but that's all Hollywood.

For the briefest of instants, he was mine and he knew it, but something kept my finger from squeezing the trigger. He took that fraction of a second and ducked behind the woman, bending his tall frame nearly in half to do so. I cursed my weakness, my hesitation to risk signing the poor woman's death warrant. Getting soft in my old age.

"*Put down your gun, NOW!*" the Nazi screamed again from the relative safety of his human shield.

"Sorry, Fritz, can't help you," I snarled, not lowering the Lahti a millimeter.

A snort of hidden laughter. "American, not British?"

"Yes."

"Drop your weapons and the woman will live." The thick German accent reminded me of Colonel Klink from *Hogan's Heroes*.

I looked into her brown eyes so full of terror and knew, just *knew* that the bastard had been in the middle of an enthusiastic rape when he had become alerted to my presence. His hearing must have been amazing, or perhaps he had seen me dash across the clearing.

"If I drop my weapon, Fritz, we're both dead. However, if you kill her, I will let you live." My voice was flat, toneless. No rage, not even hatred. Just a cold, emotionless state. At that point, I was more computer than human, running countless scenarios, creating and scrapping plans of attack with quiet dispassion.

"I do not understand."

"If you kill her, I will hurt you more than you can possibly *imagine*. I will do things to you that would make Satan himself cringe and they will last a long, long time. After I'm done, I will make sure that you will receive the best medical attention possible so you will be healthy enough when I give you to this woman's husband. And that, Herr Mac, will be something very, very interesting indeed." I'm not a cruel man, but at that moment, I meant every word and that Nazi dickwad knew it.

Five seconds … six and seven. "You will let me go unharmed if I do not hurt the woman?" Incredulity laced the German's voice.

A flicker of motion caught my eye and I almost smiled. "Yes. My word as an officer and a gentleman." I was neither, but wasn't about to tell him that.

More seconds ticked by. Slowly, like a frightened animal, the Nazi's head appeared from behind the woman's shoulder, then more of him as he stood to his full height. A thin, almost gaunt face met mine and sensual, feminine lips curled in a smile that made me want to bury my fist in it. "You are an officer, *ja*? Name and rank, please."

"Major James T. Kirk, United States Army at your service." *Grind, grind, grind*, went my molars.

Those evil eyes never wavered. "Speak an oath I can believe and it will be as you say." Still that ugly smile.

Once again, a flicker of motion. I kept my eyes level. "On my sister's soul, on the souls of my family, I will not harm you or hinder your leaving if you let the woman go free." Every ounce of sincerity and passion I could muster threaded my words.

It must have been enough because he slowly lowered the P38 and I lowered the Lahti at the same time. The woman broke free and ran into the cabin, slamming the door.

"You are most con—" Twin *booms* interrupted him forever

and two barrels full of buckshot burst his head apart like a watermelon thrown onto concrete, splattering blood, bone and brain all over my face and jacket. A dry cleaner's nightmare. Lovely.

I stared at the headless lump oozing all over the winter grass. "Never promised that the woman's husband wouldn't kill you, you Nazi piece of filth." Briefly I wondered if history had been changed radically, then realized I didn't care. Two more monsters off the playing field made my day.

My eyes traveled upward. "You could've shot from a different angle," I said sardonically as I brushed human tissue off my sleeves.

Etienne lowered his shotgun, both barrels smoking. "*Si*, I could have. My apologies, Mister Kal." Wasting no more breath, he ran into the house, leaving me to comb slivers of bone out of my hair.

Crap.

Chapter Eighteen

Mouth

Allies among the Allies

Once again bright light in my eyes brought me out of a deep, dreamless sleep into the real world.

"Oy, luv, you feeling better?" Jeanie's voice was silk caressing my ears. When my eyes adjusted, her bright white teeth were bared in a radiant smile.

When I answered, my voice was no longer rough and filled with sand. "I feel … fine." And I did. In fact, I felt more than just fine. I felt terrific!

The picture of me must have spoken a thousand words because her smile grew even wider. "Good for you, luv. Glad to see that my abilities have not faded with age."

I sat up. Yes! I could finally move more than eyes and mouth. I was stoked. "You spelled me to keep me from moving," I accused while running hands over previously injured bits.

A warm hand landed on my back. "Of course, luv. I had to heal you *twice*. You needed to remain absolutely still or you would have injured yourself further." Rough but ragged clothes and worn boots were thrust into my hands.

Guess my skimpy cocktail dress wasn't going to cut it. "What now?" I asked while changing as quickly as possible. I wasn't going to win any awards for fashion, but at least I wouldn't freeze my tits off.

"What now, luv, is that you talk with Richard and then we rendezvous with your scary friend, Kal."

My heart jumped. *Kal!* If anyone could figure out a way to get home, if anyone could build a Flux Capacitor and a Delorean from scratch, it would be him. "What are we waiting for? Applause?"

A creak of poorly oiled hinges announced Richard's arrival in what I suddenly realized was a ten by ten wooden shack with dirt floors. The bed I'd been lying on turned out to be an old army cot with a thin gray blanket for protection against the cold. And man, was it *cold*. "Good to see you ready for action, former agent Rebecca McTavish," the man from MI-7 said jovially as I stuffed my feet into the boots. Too big. "We meet your man Hakala tomorrow. He'll be bringing orders from the guv."

Richard's long, handsome face was haggard from a lack of sleep—with dark, dark circles under his eyes. Despite his obvious exhaustion, the smile he gave me was full of joy and not a small amount of mischievous glee. He was dressed in worn, threadbare clothes that looked like they doubled as his bedding. A black cap was perched on the back of his head.

"Call me Mouth," I replied, returning the smile tooth for tooth.

"What, Mouth? Really? Why's that, I wonder?" I treated both the Brits to a few choice blue words that had Jeanie blushing through her dark skin and Richard raising his eyebrows to his hairline.

"That's a good reason, luv!" Jeanie enthused. "I've been working with some rough types, but your curses reach, on the whole, a different level, that's for sure."

Richard received the full force of my attention as I stood, reveling in the feeling of being able to do so. Behind me, Jeanie continued to chuckle. "What's the plan?" I asked.

"We head to Natzweiler."

"That's where we meet Kal?"

A small look of annoyance flickered across his face. "Yes."

"All right, let's go!"

He held up his hands. "We are going, but first, follow." In a wink, he was out the door. I followed right on his heels … into a dense forest, the ground sloping steeply down only a few steps from the door. In front, not more than five feet from the door, were three rough-looking characters dressed in the same kind of piss poor hand-me-downs that Richard and I wore, including the shabby wool caps—a French thing, I guessed.

Richard held out an arm and pointed to each in turn, from left to right. "Anton." Buck-toothed and short, with massive forearms. "Andre." Tall, slender and soulful-looking with a Tom Selleck moustache. "And Bernaud." A virtual clone of Richard, minus charisma and sex appeal, his face crisscrossed in thin scars that contorted his cheeks this way and that. All three men smiled, revealing France's great need for dentists and floss.

I shook hands all around. When Anton tried to give my hand an extra little squeeze, I squeezed right back, hard enough for his eyes to fly wide and well with tears. "You have a strong grip, Madmoiselle," he said while disengaging and rubbing his hand. His French accent was thick and cloying.

My smile held no humor. "You bet your Eiffel Tower I do, buster."

Surprisingly, all three Frenchmen grinned, while from behind I heard Jeanie's golden laughter. Richard tossed the three a rueful grin.

"Ms. Mouth here is an American specialist," he said, tipping me a wink. "She's here to aid us in the retrieval of some sensitive intelligence." He paused dramatically. "And these good men, dear Mouth, are among the finest the French Resistance has to offer."

Really? I scanned the three, who visibly preened. Well, if Richard said so, then it must be, but I wouldn't trust those bozos with a potato gun. So I smiled and made nice with the natives.

"I take it that it's you three I owe my thanks to," I commented dryly. "For saving my life and all."

Andre stroked his ridiculous moustache and said in fluent English, "You may thank me properly later." He leered. "In private and with enthusiasm."

I snorted. "Puh-leeze! I'd rather be a lesbian!"

Jeanie laughed loud and hard while Richard gaped. The three Frenchmen conferred for a moment, puzzled, before exploding in a gale of mirth.

Great, I'd been rescued by the Three Stooges. Kal would love it, just love it to death. I vowed never to tell him.

"So you will take us to Natzweiler, then?" I asked them as they wiped tears of laughter from their dirty cheeks.

Bernaud shook his head. "No, Miss Mouth," he answered in his Inspector Clouseau accent. "Natzweiler is a far walk from here and it is too late. We leave in the morning." Despite the Peter Sellers' voice, his tone carried grim authority that brooked no argument.

I nodded. Made sense.

Anton shook the kinks out of his hand. "Your pardon, Richard, but do you think it wise to bring a woman on this expedition? Other than the talented Jeanie, of course." He nodded to the magician, who had moved forward to stand next to me.

"Oh, Ms. Mouth can acquit herself quite well, if you ask me." Richard's tone was sardonic. "Besides, she's critical to the mission."

Bernaud gave the Brit a respectful nod. "And what is that, Richard?"

"I plan on finding a Nazi asshole name Goebbels and ripping his dick and balls off. Like, slowly." There was enough heat in my voice to roast a whole hog.

The three men blinked rapidly while Richard stared, nonplussed. Jeanie laughed hard enough for tears to dribble from the corners of her eyes. To her I was the Rosetta Stone of humor. After a few seconds the Frenchmen roared their approval.

The next morning saw us walking toward Natzweiler on nearly obscured game trails through the Vosges. Anton and Bernaud led the way, followed by Richard and myself with Jeanie and Andre bringing up the rear. All of us were clad in threadbare but heavy coats. The men were heavily armed with at least two pistols apiece, while Richard carried a Sten gun. He was kind enough to supply me with an old Webley, a .44 revolver of the type often referred to as a British Bulldog. Crap for accuracy, but enough power to ruin someone's day in a hurry. It was small enough to fit snugly in my coat pocket, and considering my alternatives, I was happy for the antique hunk of metal.

The cold morning air nibbled the tip of my nose and cheeks and once again I was thankful for the loan of a pair of size nine men's work boots. Although large for my slender feet, enough dead grass was packed inside to make them fit adequately. It sure beat tromping around the heavily forested Vosges in high heels.

After an hour or two of trying to avoid blisters on my heels, I asked Richard if Jeanie was a field agent as well as a magician. He nodded.

"Deadly with guns, she is," he said with a smile. "Has a flair for healing magic that has saved my life more than once."

"So the Crown supports female agents?"

"Like I said when you were … resting after your ordeal, there are no female agents, but there are female magicians. However, my team needed a magician in the field and it's not like we can pick one up at the pub. So we get what we can get."

I have him an arch look. "And your opinion?"

"My opinion is exactly thus, young lady: If you can hold your own and give the Hun a good what-for, then your gender is of no matter. The job is the job, whether it involves the World Under or the bloody Nazis." He kept the mention of the World Under very low key, away from prying French ears. It looked like the Resistance wasn't privy to all the facts.

"Good for you, Richard." In the world of 1943, his view would be seen as hideously progressive. I began to warm up to him even more. "What brought you into our line of work, anyway?"

He laughed. "My big brother, Ian. He is a Commander in the Royal Navy, an intelligence officer and a member of our little 'fraternity,' if you will. He recruited me after an incident off the coast of Scotland some six years ago."

"Incident?"

His Interdiction forced him to check for eavesdroppers and lower his voice even further. I had to strain to hear him. "A few mates and I ran afoul of a Shony."

"Shony?" I whispered.

"Demon. Looks like a large man with long, shaggy hair and a ridge of fins along the spine."

A demon? Bad news. "Type Four demon?"

"Type Four? I don't understand."

I proceeded to tell Richard that the Bureau had classified, or Typed, the various categories of demons, from those that were bodiless to those that could manifest in the flesh. There were seven Types, and God help you if you drew the attention of something in the four-plus range.

"Brilliant," he commented when I finished. "We should have thought of that years ago, shouldn't we?"

"Frankly, I thought we had. At least sixty-odd years ago."

We shared a laugh. He continued his story, his face draining of all humor. "It was a big demon. Climbed onto our fishing boat and killed Alex first, ripping his throat out with teeth like pointed files. The rest of us all saw what it was, how strong it was, so we jumped overboard, all three of us." Those beautiful hazel eyes of his grew dark. "We were only a couple hundred yards from shore and we swam like the blazes. I was the strongest swimmer, so I was ahead when Michael screamed like the damned. My foot hit the sand the moment I heard Thomas cry my name." A small tear trickled from the corner of his eye. "He sounded like a child."

My own eyes grew moist; even though I'd heard the same kind of story dozens of times before from hastily Interdicted survivors, all of them sharing the same thousand-yard stare of disbelief and utter anguish.

"I ran, fast and hard and far. By the time I reached Helmsdale, I was half-dead from fright and exhaustion. There was exactly one working telephone in town and I used it to call Ian. Less than a day later I was scooped up by what you call MI-7 and brought to London, where I was given a choice: continue life as before or join. I joined, didn't I? The rest, as you Americans are fond of saying, is history."

Time for a subject change, or I'd start to get misty. "What brings you to France?"

It was the right thing to say because the past slipped from his eyes and the pain receded. "That Nazi camp nearby. Something magical has been happening there and my team was sent in to gather intelligence. While trying to reconnoiter the camp, we were ambushed by a cockatrice; over half my team were turned to stone before Jeanie killed it. That was two weeks ago. The two of us were heading for an evac point when we saw an ugly light shoot into the sky, which I now know to be the time portal."

A sliver of unease wound its way around my spine. A cockatrice! A creature with the body of a small dragon and the head of a rooster. It's gaze could turn almost any living thing into stone. Personally I would've rather faced zombies, ghosts and demons than fight a Supernatural with transmutation powers.

I looked closely at the man beside me and what was expressed in his face wasn't pain or anguish, but fury. Not like Kal's—hot enough to melt granite—but cold and dispassionate. "Those Nazi bastards had it guarding the camp; I knew it in my bones, didn't I? Well, Jeanie and I were almost ready for evac when our friends in the Resistance brought us your broken self, torn and bloodied like you'd been fighting trolls. We messaged the guv and next thing we knew, we had our orders to rendezvous with this Kal chap of yours, didn't we?"

Richard was a sexy, charismatic man much like Kal, but without the wounded dog attitude and heavy sarcasm. But hell, that was all part of Kal's charm, a man hurt grievously by life who women wanted to heal, to fix. It was then, ruminating about all that misery contained behind Kal's eyes that I realized I no longer felt any more romantic tuggings toward him. Maybe it was Richard. The guy oozed sex appeal and charm. Maybe it was his classical good looks and his English accent. Maybe it was all that and the fact that his being was so mercifully clear of angst.

Suddenly I made a few connections that, if my poor battered brain cells had been working properly, would have been clear to me from the get-go. "Fleming!" I snapped my fingers. "You brother is *Ian Fleming*?"

Dimples showed as he smiled. "I take it that where you are from, my brother is well known?" When I opened my mouth in reply, he quickly silenced me with a raised hand. "I'm not terribly surprised. He's always been the one."

"The one?"

"You know, the smart one. The one to attract the ladies, the one to move up in society quicker than you could snap your fingers."

I smiled. "Don't worry, big man. I've seen pictures of your famous brother and I can tell you that you are *totally* hotter than him."

"What does temperature have to do with anything?"

My laughter startled the others as we rounded trees and dodged the underbrush. "Richard, you have so much to learn!"

Chapter Nineteen

Kal

Sleep Is for the Weak

Etienne took his time consoling the missus, but considering the circumstances, I really couldn't blame him. The part of me that used to revel in humanity had gone missing off the map ages ago. Strange, but true. As long as Iku-Turso remained alive and at large, I had to hone myself to be the weapon used to kill him.

Believe me, there were times when I just wanted to chuck it all, screaming "Screw my life!" at the top of my lungs, but the memory of my sister, Leena, in that monster's grip—blood vomiting from her screaming mouth—puts me back on the rails.

So I stood in the cold winter air, the sun peeking up in the east, barely clearing the Vosges, and contemplated what had to be done. Mouth. She was first priority, number one with a bullet. The Colonel and Oliver had made arrangements for me to meet her in an inn at Natzweiler, a village possibly rife with German sympathizers and Jew haters, but close enough to the concentration camp that you could see the gas chamber and smell the smoke of burning bodies. However, the owner of that inn was a member of the French Resistance and would house us until we decided what needed to be done about Goebbels.

I gnashed my teeth. Goebbels. History said that he committed suicide on May 1, 1945, after having his six children put to death. The SS dentist Helmut Kunz injected them with morphine and, while they lay unconscious, Magda Goebbels—the Reich Minister's wife, along with Hitler's personal doctor, Ludwig Stumpfegger—crushed ampoules of cyanide into each of their mouths. What people will do to avoid taking responsibility for their actions, eh?

Pretty damn sick, if you ask me. It was the kind of messed-up mindset that ran the Reich and was responsible for the death of millions of innocent people.

I meandered over to the small barn, a goat pen. Putting an eye to a gap in the slat wall, I spied at least a dozen goats; three or four were milkers, teats swollen and taut. Probably the main income for Etienne and his wife. That and harboring Jews from the Germans. Part of the French Underground? Most likely.

Behind me the door to the cabin creaked open, but I didn't bother to turn around; instead I kept staring at the goats, trying to keep my anxiousness, my desire to freaking *do something*, from causing me to go absolutely bonkers.

Light footsteps. "Mister Kal." The voice was soft and very feminine. It took a second, but I realized the woman spoke heavily accented English.

"You're educated," I responded, not turning around.

"My father was a learned man. He felt his children should be so as well."

"That's good. Education is important."

"Are you an educated man, Mister Kal?"

Educated. Was I? Did an education in killing count? It sure didn't feel like it. I felt like dust in a storm, blown about by the winds of circumstance. If I hadn't put one over on the Bureau, arranging and surviving my own death just to be free, I wouldn't be here. Mouth wouldn't have wound up in Goebbels' clutches. Instead, she would be on her boat off the coast of O'ahu drinking margaritas and flirting with the cabin boy. But my desire for revenge had brought us to these dire straits and I had to set it right.

"I was a chemical engineer," I breathed.

"An engineer?"

"Long time ago." A long, slow breath slowed my pulse. "I was going to work for an oil company, to help them obtain more oil from near dry wells."

There was no response so I turned around. The woman—Solange, if I remembered correctly—stared at me with cool interest, her hands clenched so tightly together that the knuckles were white.

The shiner around her right eye had already deepened to a purple black and swelled the eye shut. I could see she was barely holding it together. Behind her, from a small window in the cabin, I could see Etienne peek out, carefully watching as the scene played out.

Interesting. Something was … off. Why was I telling her all this?

"How do chemicals help with oil, Mister Kal?" Her good eye remained focused on my two, unwavering.

"It's called Hydraulic Fracturing. You inject a chemical compound, called a Frac, into a wellbore and when the compound expands, it fractures the surrounding rock, releasing oil or natural gas." I couldn't stop my mouth from running like Secretariat and it took me a few moments to catch on.

She had cast a spell on me!

Interesting-er.

Now that I knew what was going on, I literally felt the spell rooting around my mind, prodding me to talk with abandon.

Cheeky woman!

With difficulty I snapped my jaws shut and forced myself to be quiet. Unlike most spells, those that affect the mind can be resisted if you are aware of them and your willpower is strong enough. I may not have been one hundred percent sane, but I had plenty of will.

A few seconds passed before Solange started to look nervous, her level stare and face slowly wilting. Her hands gripped even harder.

Better to defuse the situation before she panicked. Solange had been through quite enough with that Gestapo creep who was rapidly cooling off behind her. "I'm here to rendezvous with a colleague who had been kidnapped by the Nazis and go home. That's it. If I can mess with the Germans while I'm at it, all the better."

Her eyes glittered in righteous anger. "Good."

My smile was grim. "Now, are you going to stop casting spells so we can get along like civilized people?"

For a moment I thought she would bolt, so intense was the fear that flashed across her face, but after a moment she raised her chin proudly and gave me a tiny nod.

Tough lady.

"Come inside, Mister Kal, and I will take care of your injuries. It looks as if you have been hit with a shovel. Many times."

Heh. A shovel. Felt like it, too.

"So, Mister Kal, how did you know I am a witch?" inquired Solange as she carefully dabbed at the cut on my forehead with a warm, wet cloth.

The inside of the cabin was basically one big room with a bed, a Franklin stove, a table and three chairs. A weather-beaten chest of drawers stood askew near the rickety bed while weak sunlight trickled through the cabin's two small windows.

Etienne was busy with the stove, cooking up something that smelled strongly of goat and herbs. I sat on of the rickety chairs while Solange tended to my many hurts.

Once I had relaxed, the adrenaline and endorphins bleeding from my system, the pain of the day began to make itself evident. Damn, I preferred the endorphins—best high that money can't buy.

I licked my lips. "For many years I worked for a government agency that defended the world from evil people and Supernatural entities."

"You are not serious."

Even though the Interdiction that had kept me from revealing the Bureau's existence had been absent for six months, I still felt a twinge of unease when mentioning the subject. Force of habit, I suppose. When under Interdiction, you didn't even bother to consider what it would be like to talk; your mind tended to shy away from the subject. "I'm serious as a heart attack. Most governments know about magicians—those you call witches—and of the various monsters that spill into our world from the World Under."

Silence. Both Solange and Etienne were staring at me. What? Was my fly open? I checked. Nope.

Solange broke the pregnant stillness. "I have never heard of such a thing," she breathed.

I had to smile. "There's a reason for that." I squinted. "Why didn't you use your magic against that Gestapo pinhead?"

"Because he attacked before I could respond. Spell casting requires concentration."

True enough.

Solange quickly and efficiently finished dressing my wounds, applying what I sincerely hoped were clean bandages. After she was done, she started to clean the cabin while Etienne cooked. I sat and twiddled my thumbs, unsure of what to say.

Scritch, scritch.

A soft sound, like the rasp of small claws on wood. A rat? Most likely. Solange heard the noise as well, and a frown creased her lean face. Etienne stopped stirring the pot long enough to whisper in her ear.

Whisper, something French, whisper, whisper, then two words that actually made sense. It all finally clicked into place.

Lordy, I felt like an idiot. Not that there were many clues, but I should have known. Must've been old age drying up the juices of my intellect. Yeah, that's it ...

During my time in the Bureau, I'd traveled often to Israel, where Bureau agents trained with their equivalent in the Mossad. Loosely translated, that agency was called the Department of Protection from Otherworldly Influences.

Although Tel Aviv might not be on most people's vacation list, I enjoyed my time there and learned many things. Like Yiddish. While not fluent, the two words Etienne used were known to me: 'mine gelibt'... my beloved.

"You're Jewish," I blurted.

Duh.

They stared. I stared. It was a stare fest that threatened to turn ugly, that is, until I started to chuckle, light and soft. After a few moments, the couple joined in, tentatively at first, but then with a growing sense of mirth and absurdity.

That they could still laugh after what they'd been through was wonderful to me.

"You can call your friends out of hiding, now," I announced, wiping my eyes. "I won't bite."

Solange translated and they shared a glance, a language that all couples who really love each other speak.

I sighed. "Call them out. No reason to have them hiding beneath the floorboards like animals. Besides, if I wanted to do you or them harm, I would've done it by now."

More translating and Etienne nodded then fired off some rapid-fire French. A section of floor under the table rose and was pushed to the side and a grimy little face peeked out. A kid. I looked closer.

A boy, barely more than a toddler.

Etienne crouched and spoke softly in Yiddish. "Come out, little man. He will not hurt you."

"You safe here with me now," I added, straining my command of Yiddish to the limit.

The Frenchman smiled. "See, Issur, a man who sounds like that cannot be bad."

Young Issur nodded and clambered out, dressed in rags and odds and ends of larger clothing. Quicker that a scalded rat, he climbed Etienne like a tree, burying his tiny face in the Frenchman's shoulder.

I switched to Spanish. "What is his story?"

"Issur's grandfather brought him to us, referred by another man in our network. His mother and father had been taken by the Nazis and placed aboard a train to a place called Treblinka." There was no need to say more about that. We all knew what happened to those taken by the Nazis and what it meant to be in Treblinka. "Unfortunately, the grandfather died three weeks ago of pneumonia. I was going to escort them to Calais, to our man there who would ferry them across the channel to England and from there to Canada, but with the grandfather's death, he has no family. I cannot send him on by himself; it would be cruel."

The small boy peeked one brown eye at me and I gave a little smile and wave, which he tentatively returned. "What are you going to do now?" I whispered.

Etienne translated for Solange and her response told me everything I needed to know. Those soft brown eyes of hers landed on the boy and her face was transformed into something ... transcendent.

There was no way in hell she was going to let that little boy slip away from this small family. Perhaps they couldn't have children of their own. All the love trapped within them as they waited for a child of their own and, *shazam*, one literally drops into their laps.

Looked like Issur had found a family.

"You can't stay here, you know," I said. "When that Gestapo officer fails to return, this area will be overrun by Austrian farm boys thick as jackrabbits."

Once again, Etienne translated the Spanish and Solange gave a little half-sob. She must have known, but hearing it out loud really drove the reality home.

To Solange, I said, "Don't worry." A cheesy smile. "I have an ... angle." I said the same thing in Spanish to Etienne.

Later that night I bunked in the little loft inside the goat barn, nestled in among heaps of dried, crackly and very itchy hay, a holey blanket that barely covered me from knees to throat my only protection against the cold winter night. I soon became cold enough to crawl down and bed with the goats; in fact I briefly considered it. One good whiff changed my mind right quick.

With the hay rustling in my ears I made an attempt to sleep. Normally I would have drifted off quite easily, but I was too amped by the day's events. The four of us were safe for a while, at least for the night, in the clearing, but we had to vacate soon. Fortunately someone had left behind a handy-dandy motorcycle with a sidecar. A nice Rolls Royce Silver Ghost would have been better, but, as Mick Jagger once sang, 'You can't always get what you want.'

Didn't stop me from trying.

Etienne would drive me out to Natzweiler before daybreak and drop me off outside the village before coming back for his family. Hopefully they could disappear in Nazi occupied France, but I wrote letters of introduction for them to the Colonel just in case they wanted make contact with their man in Calais and flee the country. I hoped they would; they deserved a shot.

For ten years I had protected the Straights (the ordinary Joes who had no clue of the things that went bump in the night) and this little family qualified for that same protection because the monsters weren't under the bed and they weren't hiding. In fact, they were strutting, goose-stepping, bigoted, short-sighted, vicious filth who were so vile they'd give demons the heebie-jeebies. They weren't exactly the kind of monsters I had been trained to kill, but they'd do in a pinch.

As I lay there with the heavy whiff of goat assaulting my nostrils—depressing dark thoughts floating on the surface of my mind like scum on a pond—I realized one important thing about monsters.

We're the worst of the lot.

Chapter Twenty

Mouth

Inn Big Trouble

Early afternoon saw Jeanie, Richard and I hit a small dirt road a couple miles west of Natzweiler, tired and footsore, sweating despite the chill in the air. The plan was for us to enter the village while, in case of trouble, the three Resistance members (who had peeled away a mile back) hid themselves close by.

When I turned to Jeanie to remark how difficult it would be for a beautiful African-British woman to blend in with the local crowd of Frenchies, I found a short, swarthy man with a scruffy beard and a serious Cyrano de Bergerac nose grinning toothily at me.

Oh yeah … *magician*. Right.

"You about gave me a heart attack!" I scolded, spinning back around.

The little man gave an earthy guffaw and slapped a hand against my back. "How do you think I survived in France all this time, luv?" she … he … whatever, answered in a bass rumble.

"That is way too creepy," I muttered under my breath.

Richard laughed, a deep, clear sound that reached deep into places south of my navel. Oh yeah, he was sexy as hell and I definitely had the hots for the hunky Englishman. From the glances he shot my way when he thought I wasn't looking, he dug me too.

Damn. The situation was getting complicated, but it was nice to know I hadn't lost my charms.

"You're blushing."

I started, realizing that my mind had wandered to places better left in a Harold Robbins novel. I was *blushing*! What the hell? Had I lost all perspective? Here I was in freaking WWII in Nazi-occupied

177

France headed toward a damn death camp and I was flirting like a horny teenager before the prom.

"I'm hot and tired and could use a bath like you wouldn't believe, buster!"

He turned away. Surely he wasn't *totally* trying to hide a smile? Bastard.

Over an hour later we strolled into town acting like we belonged, a good strategy if you don't want to be stopped and questioned. The efficacy of that strategy was a moot point, however, because every citizen we saw scurried away and hid themselves indoors as if we carried the plague.

Natzweiler looked like a goddamn Bavarian postcard, a real honest-to-God Hansel and Gretel wet freaking dream. I almost expected fat blond kids in Lederhosen to come skipping and singing out of their cute gingerbread houses to sell us chocolates.

Where's Julie Andrews? I thought. It looked like a place where you'd expect to run into the von Trapp family, not a small town in France.

Richard strode confidently ahead, making for one of the taller buildings on the east side of town. As we drew close, Richard slowed, still confident, still acting like he belonged, but with a more measured tread than I was familiar with. He was a man paying particular care to his surroundings. After a few dozen feet along the street, he visibly relaxed.

"Up ahead, Jeanie," he said quietly to the magician. "Marcel has set out the white stone."

At my inquiring look, the man who would be Jeanie grumbled, "The innkeeper places a white rock to prop the door open to his establishment if the area is secure."

Thank God. I felt so relieved that I stopped feeling the pain of the uneven cobblestones against the blisters on my feet. Almost there! I could practically taste the bratwurst.

Cool, calloused fingers wrapped around mine. "Easy, slow a bit." Richard's voice was even, measured.

"Sorry," I replied softly, slowing. Without noticing, I had almost broken into a trot. "Just looking forward to German beer."

Jeanie chuckled, a deep rumble that sounded like rocks clashing at the bottom of a well.

The tavern, or inn, was one of the last buildings on the east end of town on the south side of the street, commanding an unobstructed view of the mountain it nestled against. As we drew nearer, we saw it had a clean view of something far more sinister than the Vosges.

The camp. About a mile way, snug on a flat part of the mountain—surrounded by wire fence and guard towers—were at least fifteen, sixteen, long cabins. Dormitories for prisoners. A fifty-foot area immediately surrounding the camp had been deforested, a killing ground in case of an escape attempt. A wide dirt road ran east up the gentle mountain to the camp before turning south toward the village. Past the fifty-foot killing area from the southern-facing front gate the trees began, a thick shaggy forest that cut the village off from the camp.

Wide-eyed, I tracked my flight. My path must have been east by southeast, down the slope. Had the Resistance not found me, I had no doubt that I'd still be in Goebbels' wormy grasp.

Someone up there must've been watching over me.

As if reading my mind, Jeanie-man said, "The Resistance found you on the other side of the Bruche, a tributary to the Rhine. You had run nearly five thousand feet—barefoot—through the foothills and forest."

Good Lord! Had I really run that far? I barely remembered any of it except the pain and fear.

"You all right, luv?" Jeanie-man asked, whispering softly in my ear.

"It's my first concentration camp," I replied.

"God willing, it will be your last, won't it?" Richard cut in, pulling me toward the inn.

For a brief moment I could almost imagine the camp as an army base, all neat and orderly, all the buildings laid out so neat and tidy. But then I caught sight of the towers, menacing structures constructed of blond wood.

My head was turning away from the view when I spied something that sent my stomach plummeting to the cobbles.

Smoke. From one of the buildings near the gate, billowing into the blue sky, thick, dark and heavy.

They weren't burning wood.

Jeanie-man must have noted the same thing because a small moan escaped her lips, a sound of profound misery and sadness. Richard's face turned cold and gray as hoarfrost.

I wanted to puke.

Richard turned to the inn. "Let's go," he grated, hauling me along.

Once inside the inn it took a few moments for our eyes to adjust. The big main room had a vaulted ceiling braced with dark beams. Several round tables decorated the wood floor along with large, heavy chairs. A bar ran the length of one wall, the front of which was carved with Bacchanalian scenes.

My eyes were the first to adjust. "Where is everyone? Is it supposed to be empty?"

"No," Richard murmured. His voice rose to a shout. "Out! Now!"

Too late.

"Don't move," said a voice in heavily accented English. Popping up from behind the bar were four soldiers in dark brown uniforms, evil-looking Mauser C96 machine pistols clutched in their hands.

I closed my eyes as the sound of boot heels clomping on a wooden floor came from behind. "You will be shot if you make any sudden movements," said the voice belonging to the boot heels.

No sudden movements, right. Slowly I craned my neck around and saw another man in a brown uniform. Middling height but broad in the shoulders. Thin scars ran across his left cheek. Four of them. Dueling scars, I believed. His meaty lips were curled in a self-satisfied, crap-eating smile. Eyes, one brown, one blue, drilled into mine.

He reminded me of an evil David Bowie.

"Who are you?" I asked.

That ugly smile grew wider. "I am Oberführer Arnold Faust and you must be a member of Mrs. Collinsworth's class."

Jeanie-man uttered something unintelligible while Richard gnashed his teeth and still managed to look sexy as hell while doing it.

My heart did one of those lurchy things where it feels like it's about to seize up, the muscles of your chest cramping around it. It was the VGG, Verteidiger gegen Geister, the Nazi equivalent of the Bureau, a really nasty, disgusting version. Roughly translated as 'Defenders against Ghosts,' the VGG sent out hit squads and terror units. Their mandate was to take out Bureau and MI-7 magicians by whatever means necessary, up to and including Necromancy, Summoning, and, my personal favorite, Hepatomancy—the reading of entrails to foretell the future. Mega gross.

The VGG also practiced Hepatomancy and Necromancy on the Jews, using them to fuel their assassination attempts. Next to them, the Gestapo looked like unicorns and glitter. For those in the Bureau and MI-7, those brown uniforms were a symbol of horror.

Herr Oberführer dickhead smiled even wider. "We've been hunting your group since you fought our cockatrice. It was Seen by me, through the entrails of Jews, that you would come to this quaint town." While he talked, the four VGG thugs moved out from behind the bar, the muzzles of those Mousers still aimed at our torsos.

Faust barked, "Get the inkeeper!" and one of the thugs nodded and peeled away, vanishing into a back room through a door behind the bar.

"On your knees, please," Faust ordered.

On our knees we went.

Faust clopped his way around to stand in front of us, his own pistol, a Luger, pointed between Richard's eyes. "Names and ranks, please."

"Richard Fleming, team leader, His Majesty's Supernatural Services."

"Jean Barkham, agent in His Majesty's Supernatural Services." Ah, Faust hadn't twigged onto Jeanie's cover. How this would help, I had no clue.

Those frozen eyes again rested on mine. "Name. Rank."

"Agent Lara Croft, Bureau of Supernatural Investigations."

The muzzle of the Luger found its way to the skin between my browns in an instant. "A magician," he hissed.

Keep calm. Stay frosty, I told myself over and over again. "No, just an agent."

"Liar! There are no female agents in the Bureau! You are a magician, a Zauberer. Like me!"

Before he could say anything further, the thug he'd dismissed earlier came back dragging an older, portly man with white hair that had been fleeing his head strand by strand for quite some time. The poor guy had been beaten to hell and back. He couldn't even open his eyes, they were so bruised. In fact, his face resembled so much raw hamburger, but what really pissed in my Cheerios were the fingers of his left hand.

Or, I should say, the lack of them.

With the Luger still pressed between my eyes, Faust said, "Thanks to the Gestapo, we learned that this innkeeper was a suspected Resistance member. Under questioning," here he licked his fat lips, "he has informed us of his associates. Two of which live close by and should be under arrest as we speak. We shall know soon enough. It depends how long Kriminalrat Hans Schtenkel decides to ... question them."

"You are working with the Gestapo?" asked Richard. "That's a little beneath you, isn't it?"

Faust's creepy eyes never left mine. The iris of the blue eye was flecked with gold. "They have their uses. The young couple who hides Jews and helps them escape the Reich are of no real concern, so I let the Gestapo have them. You three, well, you three are of the utmost concern."

The skin of my forehead itched terribly. I was so totally *pissed*. I knew 150 ways to kill a man with my bare hands and I wanted to use all of them on that asshole.

"I am so sorry, my friend," mumbled the innkeeper mushily. with barely an accent. "They killed my Catherine. They killed her and cut her open." His voice degenerated to a heart-wrenching sob.

"It's all right, Maurice," Richard said, glaring hot death at Faust. "You shouldn't have resisted."

"It would not have mattered," the Nazi interjected, sounding as if we were just discussing the weather. "I would have gutted his daughter anyway. Her entrails have told me things will end here, now."

Instead of Richard, I heard Jeanie-man grind her teeth. Maurice let out a soft moan right before one of the thugs shot him through the left ear.

A gout of blood and brain was followed by a thump, as Maurice's body hit the floor.

Richard almost made it to his feet before the barrel of Faust's Luger hammered against his forehead and dropped him cold. I could barely move before the muzzle was back between my eyes.

Damn, that *was* fast.

"Now, lady magician, I think it is time for you to say goodbye." Creepy eyes let me know exactly what he meant.

I braced for the shot.

It was louder than I could have imagined.

Chapter Twenty-One

Kal

My Favorite Pastime

"Wake up, Kal."

What?

"Wake up, Kal."

Who wanted to die? Who would risk my righteous wrath?

"Stop snoring already, Kal, and wake up."

One eye cracked open to the blurry sight of a goat nuzzling my face. Its front smelled suspiciously like its back. Morning breath from the deepest pits of hell. In the thin, anemic light shining through the slats, I could swear the damn thing was grinning at me.

Cheeky goat.

And what in the name of the Wide World of Sports was a goat doing in the hayloft? I creaked my head around and saw why.

I was on the floor, not the loft.

Which meant that I was lying in goat pellets and urine.

Well, *crap*. Literally.

"Good to see you are finally awake, Kal."

"Ghost?" I shook my head, fumbling around in the front pocket of my jacket for the cell. "What's going on? I thought you had to conserve power."

"I have been monitoring your activities," he buzzed as I slowly levered myself upright and was immediately pummeled by three kids of the four-legged and extremely hairy variety.

"Urk! Get off!" Gently, but firmly, I shoved the offending smelly beastlets away. That didn't stop the whirlwind of juvenile goathood from rising on their hind legs and trying to climb Mama Hakala's baby boy like Everest. Their tiny hooves scrabbled against my things, making me feel I was being prodded by half-a-dozen

184

pool cues. In an effort to save myself from being a victim of caprine enthusiasm, I shinnied up the ladder to the loft.

"Are you going to be all right, Kal?"

Smart-aleck spook. "Monitoring me? Wouldn't that drain the battery something fierce?"

"You forget, Kal, that the original Ghost is both of this world and the World Under. Part of the physical and part of the spiritual and I, as a ... copy, am the same."

"Wait a minute, Tex! You're a spiritual clone as well as a cloned AI?" That sounded ... odd.

Ghost 2.0's buzzing voice became annoyed. "Yes, that is true."

"Well ... that's just damned freaky."

"Focus, Kal, focus."

"I'm focused, Ghost, but this is so cool! Why didn't you tell me before?"

"I fail to see why it's so fascinating."

"What? Being both electronic and spiritual? It's cool."

"Kal—"

"You have to admit, it's pretty cool."

"Kal—"

"Okay, okay, it's somewhat cool ..."

"Will you shut the hell up for a moment?" Ghost screamed, sending the goats, which had been clustered directly below me, bleating and scrambling away in fear.

And 'Bingo' was his name-o. "Gotcha."

Bzzzzzzzz ...."What do you mean, Kal," Ghost droned, trying his best to sound like Hal 9000 from *2001: A Space Odyssey*.

My grin hurt my cheeks, but I didn't care. "You aren't a clone, you're the original Ghost."

Silence, which I took to be a confirmation of my incredibly brilliant deduction. I let Ghost marinate in the reflected glory of said brilliance for a while before breaking the silence. "Why, Ghost?"

"It was a risk I had to take," he said, sounding very small, which was pretty damn difficult considering his voice was an annoying buzz.

"Why?"

"Because we might be changing history."

Okay, I got that. Just being in the past changes it, a sort of butterfly effect. You know … a butterfly flaps its wings in China and, a week later BP screws up an entire ecosystem with the worst oil spill in history. Or something like that. "Yeah, I guess we are, Mouth, too. But not too much, I hope?"

A sighing drone. "You don't fully understand."

"Well, make me understand then. What the hell is going on?"

"You know about the Paradox Principle, don't you?"

I nodded. "Sure, like going back in time to kill your grandfather before he has children. If you succeed, do you disappear because you never existed? However, if you never existed, how could you have gone back in time to kill your grandfather?"

"Correct." He paused for a moment as if uncertain. Ghost and uncertainty had never really gone hand in hand. "There are several theories related to time travel. In one theory, when the grandfather is killed, the universe makes the necessary adjustments, causing the grandson to disappear and negating the grandfather's impact on the timeline from that moment on. In effect, a complete reboot. Another theory is that everything has already happened … The universe was born, churned out galaxies, planets, life, and then died, collapsing in on itself just before winking out. We are all just experiencing our little bit of time and we cannot, in fact, actually change anything because it has already happened and is immutable."

I scratched my chin. "So, everything is predetermined?"

"No, you've already made all these choices, experienced everything you ever will. Consider time the universe's way of making sure you don't experience it all at once."

Okay, a bit strange, but plausible. "And the next theory?"

"The next theory states that the grandson is safe from disappearing into the ether because, by being in proximity of the paradox event, he is kept safe from change. In effect, that proximity shelters those taking part in the paradoxical event."

"So, like being in the eye of the storm?"

"Exactly. The actions and changes that ensue from the killer murdering his grandfather happen all around, but have no impact on the killer whatsoever. Another theory is that the universe splits, creating an alternate timeline."

"Which of those theories do you favor, Ghost?" I was starting to catch a whiff of spoiling meat in the vicinity of Amsterdam.

"I am not sure."

"Why?" I prodded. A bad feeling started to accompany the rotten smell. I gave the cell a hard squint.

"Because they are all plausible."

Interesting.

"However, given that we are in the 'eye of the storm,' so to speak, I do not know which theory will prove to be the relevant one. I only know that we can, if the first or second theory is true, screw things up for our loved ones and/or ourselves."

Interesting-er. "If we are in the 'eye of the storm', we will be safe, yes?"

"I don't know!" Ghost practically shouted, the cell almost leaping out of my hand. "I don't know which theory is true! Every one but the last, the Unchangeable Time Theory, scares me to death!"

A ghost, a being of spirit scared to death. Cute. My mind did its famous racing bit, jumping from data point to data point like a deranged kangaroo trying to fit all the pieces together. Not right … something still stank to high heaven. "Ghost," I said slowly. "Why are you here? You never really answered the question."

"Simple, Kal. I'm … I'm Jewish."

Well … knock me over with a feather. A Jewish kid who had himself translated into spiritual/electric energy to roam the electronic superhighway sucked back in time to 1943.

Cool beans.

With a tumbling clatter like dice, everything came together.

"Your ... what? Grandfather, grandmother ... a Holocaust survivor? Is that it?"

"Great-grandfather actually."

"And you wanted to come back with me in case Mouth or myself changed history and wiped you out of existence." I stared hard at the little phone. "You were hoping that being in the eye of the storm would protect you from dissolution."

"I forget sometimes how smart you are, Kal." He sounded mournful, sad.

"Yeah, Ghost, no flies on me," I said softly. Why did I feel like a giant tool, forcing Ghost to reveal more than he wanted to? Did winning really mean that much to me?

Hell yes.

I lived in a world where winners lived and losers died ... usually very messily. Having a ruthless, practical and almost emotionless mindset wasn't just an option, it was a necessity, and if that made me into a bit of a tool, so be it. Better a tool than a corpse. "You should've told me earlier."

"I know, Kal, but I was afraid."

"Why tell me now, Ghost?"

"I just wanted to illuminate the terrain on which we find ourselves deployed."

"Really, Ghost? Who talks like that?"

"I want to impress upon you how urgent this situation is, Kal. You cannot afford to make a mistake or ... do what it is you do to any Nazi you feel like doing it to. You have to be careful."

"Careful is my middle name."

"You don't have a middle name."

"I do now."

"Kal ..."

"I know, I know. But if some Nazi pinhead tries to put bullets in my tender hide, I'm shooting back."

"And if you find Goebbels?"

Good question. Been asking myself that for a while. What the heck was I going to do with that slimy bastard? "Guess I will force him to send me back. Don't know how; I'll burn that bridge when I come to it. All I know is that I have to contact the Bureau so they can stop more Krauts from coming through the time portal."

"And Goebbels?" Ghost prodded.

"As for Goebbels … hmmm … I won't kill him if I don't have to," I replied, forcing the words through gritted teeth. God, that hurt! "For the sake of continuity."

"Good."

Great. I felt like barfing. "Now what, Ghost?"

"Now Etienne will come at any moment and drive you to Natzweiler, to call upon his contact in the village who will reunite us with Mouth."

"Works for me."

Thanks to the kind donation of a motorcycle and sidecar, the ride to the village was quick and comfortable. We would have left the little goat farm sooner, but Solange said she needed time to prepare. For what, she wouldn't say, so we arrived a mile or so outside Natzweiler after noon. I hopped out the sidecar. Etienne immediately turned the motorcycle around back the way we'd come.

"You will take care of yourself, Mister Kal?" he asked.

"*Si*, Etienne." I stretched, working some kinks out of my back.

He reached into his ratty jacket pulled forth a wadded up piece of red cloth which he held out to me. "Solange, she wanted you to have this. It will protect you, I think."

I took the cloth. It was wrapped around something hard. Opening it, I saw a piece of near perfect quartz the size of my thumbnail and the thickness of a quarter. The glassy sides shone in the morning sun. Sewn into the red cloth was a word, *Holykiller*.

A spell gem. And it wasn't even Christmas.

So that's what she needed to prepare. I asked, "What does it do?"

"She would not say," replied the little Frenchman. "She said you would know what to do with it when the time comes." His smile shone with pride. "My wife is a godly woman, Mister Kal. Touched by His grace. He guides her, gives her great strength in hard times and shows her many needful things. She told me you would know when to use it."

I grunted, hefting the crystal in my palm. Never hurts to have back up.

"Mister Kal?"

"Yes, Etienne."

The Frenchman paused, then, in a gruff voice, said, "Thank you." The bike's engine revved and he sped down the dirt road.

Frenchmen ... big softies. I smiled and headed toward the forest. I would have to approach the village carefully. Preferably unseen.

I'm no woodsman. Hawkeye and Chingachgook from *The Last of the Mohicans* would have cringed at my attempt at stealth as I made my way through the woods. I swear I must have hit every damn leaf and twig. Despite my noisy clodhopping, I didn't meet a soul. That is, not until I reached the edge of the woods nearest to town.

"Do not move," came a hard voice from behind as I stared at the picturesque village. Whoever it was spoke German with a thick French accent. I felt the cold, hard muzzle of a gun press to the back of my skull. Whoever it was sounded like he thought I was a Kraut.

"How many of you are there?" I asked in Spanish.

There was a murmur of voices. Three. One directly behind, one to the left and one to the right. And they didn't know squat about handling a prisoner. Never, ever touch your opponent with your weapon. It allows for a vicious counter attack. Like this:

I spun and stepped toward my assailant, the gun forced to my right and past my body. The gun arm fit snug in my armpit as my other arm came around and smashed a nose into red pulp. Blood spewed from both nostrils and coated a spectacularly bushy mustache. As the gunman dropped, I took a microsecond to ascertain the positioning of the other two. Way too close together— a bad move on their part. My foot lashed out and took a buck-toothed varmint between the legs. He folded right quick while his buddy (a man whose face was a roadmap of little scars) gawped in incredulity. Another bad move; should've pulled a weapon and, before he could do so, my left doubled him over while my right knocked him to the ground.

The Lahti was in my hand before they could bleed any further. "Who are you idiots?" I asked in English.

It took a while, but scarface finally spoke up, "*Vous êtes l'Américain?*"

"Yeah, that's me, the American. Who are you?"

Big Moustache, whose nose needed a major readjustment, looked up. "Are you Kal?" he asked through a mouthful of blood. He spat a few gobbets onto the cold ground.

Well, crisp me to the bone with the fires of my surprise. These French fancy boys knew who I was, which meant … "You're the Resistance."

Scarface nodded. "*Oui.*"

I sent a prayer to heaven, *Please don't this be the best the French have to offer.* "Okay, gentleman, sorry about the thrashing, but you shouldn't ought to point a gun at a fella you know nothing about."

Scarface nodded. "*Oui.*" Groaning, he helped his comrades to their feet.

After holstering the Lahti, I looked Big Moustache in the eye and said, "Don't move. This will hurt … a lot." Placing my fingers on his busted schnozz, I gave it a quick pull and twist. The small bones popped together nicely to the sound of his muffled scream. A fresh gout of blood coated his ridiculous moustache. "There," I muttered appraisingly. "That should do it."

"I think I will have no children." This from the buck-toothed varmint with both hands cupping his crotch. Chalk one up for improving the gene pool.

I nodded. "Just be happy you're not dead. So you're the boys who will help me reach my friend?"

The three traded a look. "The woman you see, she says that best friend, BB, waits for you both."

Lovely. They wanted assurances. "My best friend is Canton Alsate."

All three smiled, although Big Moustache winced while doing so. Blood had already started to pool beneath the thin flesh under his eyes and by the end of the day he would be virtually indistinguishable from a raccoon.

Enough of the secret handshakes and whatnot. "What's going on? Is Mouth in the village?"

Scarface nodded and led the way to the forest's edge, half-hiding behind a tree, pointing. "The inn," he said simply.

I sighted along his arm, locating the large building on the edge of town about a hundred yards away. Two stories, whitewashed, with a peaked red roof and a brace of chimneys that were letting curls of soft smoke loose into the cold midday air. Facing us was a single large door bracketed by a pair of large windows.

We were directly behind the building and had a great view. All looked still and quiet.

I hate quiet.

"Any activity?" I asked.

Bucktoothed varmint shook his head. "No."

I pulled the small rectangular box from my jacket and drew forth the aquamarine. "*Thamesdog*," I whispered.

The gemstone vibrated slightly in my hand and the facet nearest the inn began to glow a bright white. Good, at least MI-7's magician was alive and inside with Mouth.

"Binoculars, anyone?"

Scarface pulled out a small pair and handed them over. Peering through, I saw that all seemed well, but since when has that ever been the case? As if answering my question, two men appeared in the rear window, just for a second—enough to give me an 'oh crap' moment.

One was bald, tubby and looked hurt, beaten bloody. The other … was wearing a brown uniform I'd only seen in pictures. That uniform was the last thing hundreds of thousands of Jews ever saw in this world. VGG.

No time for subtlety; the VGG was bad news like you only ever read about. Think of the Ten Plagues of Egypt, only worse. "Follow me," I snarled, breaking into a loping run while drawing the .45 and the Lahti. Someone inside the inn was hurt, injured by the VGG, and the three idiots behind me hadn't even been *watching*! If they were so distracted by my clumsy approach through the wood, the Resistance should have sent one or two to intercept me while the third kept watch.

Plans rumble tumbled through my head as I leapt over a short woodpile. What to do, what to do … explosive gems were out, so was crashing the party with guns blazing. If there were more than three (and most likely there were), then I wouldn't stand a chance before Mouth or myself were killed.

"*She told me you would know when to use it.*" Etienne's words shrilled through my mind with almost numbing force. Solange! I'd been around long enough not to look a magical gift horse in the mouth.

The whitewashed wood of the inn pressed into my back as I holstered the .45 and pulled the wad of red cloth from my pocket. Ten steps took me toward a window near the front of the building. How much time did I have? The magician was still alive, but did that mean Mouth was, too? The thought of Mouth lying dead in a pool of blood sent a dagger through my diaphragm. No way, not gonna happen. Not on my watch. The hard snap of a gunshot stole my certainty.

No time to get cute, the three Frenchmen were almost to the inn. Lahti in one hand, the quartz in the other, I snuck a peek through the window. Three people kneeling. A good looking James Bond type, a man with a spectacularly big nose and … Mouth! Four other brown suits were pointing lethal looking Mausers at the kneeling trio. *Damn*, too many to take on by myself.

A sneering VGG officer type held a Luger to her forehead. His fat lips were curled in a hideous smile. He was going to shoot; I felt it in my blood, my bones.

Out of time. I went through the window before I realized what

I'd done, following a round from the Lahti, the sound of which seemed to scare Mouth something awful. Glass razored through my cheeks, sliding along teeth, and cutting gums. Ribbons of pain flared along my forearms as shards sliced me to the bone. Bright, thick blood followed me to the floor. The fat-lipped VGG officer was down, clutching his left bicep where the 9mm of the Lahti had buried itself into the thick meat.

I spat the quartz crystal out of my mouth as I bounced off a solidly-built round table. Even before I hit the floor, the word passed through my teeth. *"Holykiller!"* I prayed that I hadn't just committed suicide.

Then things went weird.

A merry little fire had been burning in a large fireplace near the bar, but when I yelled the trigger word, it vanished ... without smoldering, without smoke. A rush of cool air caressed my skin.

Interesting.

Dull pain washed down my arm as my shoulder hit the floor and I tried to roll with it, but bouncing off the table had thrown my timing out of kilter. Training kicked in and before I even realized it, my eyes sighted down the barrel of the Lahti, aiming straight for the heart of one of the VGG jerks whose Mouser was pointed at my head.

Click.

The sound, along with the tinkle of falling glass, dominated the large common room. Everyone stared as I lay there, breath laboring, chest heaving. Damn. I was a dead man. The VGG jerk on the bad end of the Lahti smiled wide and pulled the trigger.

Click.

Interesting-er.

I smiled, suddenly realizing what the spell gem had done ... it had temporarily removed thermal energy from the room (at least anything over 98.6 degrees, or we'd have turned into peoplesicles). Try to fire a weapon when the powder won't ignite. *Click*, indeed.

We were down to fists, feet and knives. ... Time for some fun.

Chapter Twenty-Two

Kal

The Hard Part is Cleaning Up

Everybody moved at once—the VGG, those on their knees and the man I'd shot—guns forgotten. Everyone knew the score; everyone knew that hesitation meant death.

I bypassed the officer I'd shot, Mouth had him firmly in hand, so to speak, driving her knuckles over and over again into his nose, going for max pain. *Ouch*. My feet left the floor in a tackling dive toward the VGG jerk who had obviously just shot the beaten and bloody old man I'd seen through the window. The jerk managed to brace his feet in time to take the brunt of my shoulder in his gut, but he definitely wasn't ready for the Bowie I thrust up between his legs.

Hot blood gushed over my hand as he screamed and collapsed into my arms, a look of terror on his face. That look turned to agony as I twisted the knife and ripped it up and out, spilling intestines and feces across the floor. One down.

From the corner of my eye I saw a flash of silver. From my knees I raised the Bowie and blocked a knife that had been slashing toward my throat, sending a jarring ting of pain up to my elbow. From my position, I was dead meat if I didn't get to my feet, and fast. Fear was a great motivator, though.

I don't know who trained my second assailant, but the man had stepped too close, so I slammed the Bowie through the side of his knee, right behind the patella. Before he could scream, I released the Bowie and jumped to my feet, the top of my skull hammering into his chin. The man sagged and I let him fall, catching his nose with my knee with a solid *crunch!* Two down.

No rest for the wicked. Another VGG man came at me, kicking low. I easily blocked it with a ridge hand and threw an overhand right, which he avoided. Pale blue eyes like glacial ice stared dispassionately at me as we traded blows, none of which landed. The man had mad skills. Good. Been a while since I'd had a good workout.

Scarred knuckles clipped my ear. *Ow!* I felt something tear, a sharp pain and warm wetness start to flow, joining with the blood gushing from my slashed cheeks. Dammit! Sloppy, sloppy, sloppy! A snarl stretched my face tight and a slight tingle of rage buzzed the back of my brain.

My opponent threw a kick. Too high, I stepped in and trapped the shin in my armpit. His face grew taught … fear. Yeah, he should have been afraid; he'd scared the crap out of plenty of poor, innocent Jews just before they died an unpleasant death. I'd seen the pictures, the ones the government had never shown the public. You may think the ones of emaciated men and women, skeletons held together with skin and gristle, are horrible, terrifying. Bodies piled high, pushed to the edges of great lime-filled pits by bulldozers and the bones in the ovens and the heaps of hair for pillows and mattresses and the teeth … all those gold teeth pulled from kneeling victims and the experiments, the horrible, horrible experiments that would give the Marquis de Sade horrible, screaming nightmares.

All those atrocities were nothing, absolutely nothing compared to what the VGG had done to their victims. Look at the photos of children who had their souls literally ripped from their bodies, look at photos of people who had been used as human sacrifices to summon demons and what those demons had done to their victims.

If you had seen those photos, you'd understand my reaction a little bit better.

My elbow descended with crushing force on my opponent's knee, snapping it, tearing bone, ligament and cartilage with enough energy that the knee folded the wrong way. His scream was epic.

Grimacing, I twisted my hips and turned my body, pulling on the man's shin until I heard bones pop and grate. As his eyes began to roll up, I lashed out with a knife hand that crushed his larynx. Choking on his own blood, he fell to the floor, thrashing. Three down.

I needn't have worried about the fourth; he lay three feet away with a long knife buried to the hilt in his left eye, a look of surprise on his face. A much better death than he deserved.

The three Resistance members chose that moment to rush through the front door, pistols drawn. They stopped in confusion and alarm as they surveyed the scene, but I didn't care; at that point my arms were filled with Mouth.

Her hair smelled like natural oils and musk. "Damn, girl, are you all right?"

She nodded, tears wetting my neck.

We held each other for a long minute while I kept an eye on the rest of the people in the inn. They were all staring at the two of us.

"Lordy, luv, is this the man you've come to see?" This from the dude with the enormous nose.

Mouth chuckled and gave a brief nod. "Yeah."

Then the dude did something amazing; he slowly morphed into a very attractive, and I mean *very* attractive, black woman with the largest eyes I've ever seen.

Magician ... right.

A deep, cultured voice said in wonder, "Who the hell are you, mate?"

It was the James Bond type, a man far too handsome for his own good. I eased Mouth from the shelter of my arms and took the man's hand. "You must be agent Fleming." My eyes flicked to the three Resistance men who had already started to loot the VGG.

"Indeed." His smile was so unconsciously charming I wanted to hurl. No one should have that kind of charisma. It faded at the edges as he said, "I've never seen anyone fight like that."

I patted Mouth's shoulder. "She's better."

His eyes strayed to the fat-lipped officer lying on the floor. What was left of his face wasn't recognizable. "I can believe that, I can." Turning to the Frenchmen, he said, "Boys, go search the place. See if you can find someone to talk to." Reluctantly, they stopped stuffing their pockets and did as told.

"Luv, ain't you going to introduce us?" said the magician, flashing a very white smile.

"Ahem," Mouth said, hiding a grin behind her fist. "Kal, this is Jeanie …" her voice trailed off.

"Morrow," finished the striking woman, taking my hand in a soft grip. "Pleasure to meet you, luv."

I flashed her a grin at full wattage. "Pleasure is all mine, ma'am."

"Oooh, ain't he a charmer?" she cooed.

Mouth raised an eyebrow. "Careful, girl, he'll charm you right out of your undies."

Jeanie's grin grew whiter. "That's fine with me."

"Jeanie!" Richard looked horribly scandalized. She laughed, threw me a look that went to places south of my navel and picked up the spell quartz, examining it carefully.

"If you're the magician," I said through the blood filling my mouth, "would you mind doing a healing? I might drain out all over this floor soon."

Jeanie's face became all business as she ran her long fingers across my cheeks and forearms, examining the still bleeding gashes. In a matter of moments, the wounds began to tingle with warmth and the pain to recede. Soon, the flesh was knitting, pulling together and closing without a seam. Nice.

"There you go, luv," she said, eyes drooping with fatigue. "Good as new. And that's pretty good, too."

Chuckling, I reached into my jacket and pulled out a crumpled envelope, which I handed to Richard. He opened it carefully and scanned the contents.

"It seems I am at your disposal, agent Hakala," he commented, frowning slightly. "What are your orders, sir?"

I rolled my eyes. "For one thing, stop calling me sir. I work for a living … just call me Kal. The other, well, let's see if we can find someone to talk to. We need intelligence before we can make our next move.

Mouth and I began to catch up. The story of what she had

endured at Goebbels' hands threatened to break the bonds of my rage. Fortunately, we were interrupted by the Resistance.

"We have found nothing," said Scarface, who Mouth introduced as Bernaud.

I cocked an eyebrow. "What about the basement?"

He looked confused. "What basement?"

Oh, Lord … amateurs. "Where do you think they keep the reserves of beer? Wine? Food?"

Richard grunted and led the three away to the back room. I hoped he was more competent than the Frenchmen. Mouth and I concerned ourselves with the task of clean up while we swapped stories.

Jeanie, God bless her, scrounged up some sausage and spätzle (German egg noodles) and a couple of tankards of bitter beer. Compared to the cold rations I'd been eating, it was heaven on a plate.

I scratched my head. "So you think he's the inspiration for Ian's books?" I asked through a mouthful of noodles.

Mouth nodded and took a long swig of beer. "I think the experiences of both brothers inspired the series."

"Hmph … .ain't that interesting." I washed some spätzle down and tried not to stare at Jeanie's ass. Despite the ragged and rotting trousers she wore, it still shone through spectacularly. Mouth caught my eye and winked. No fooling her. I saw Jeanie smile when she thought I wasn't looking. No fooling her, either.

Damn, I needed to practice my covert leering.

"We found something," Anton announced as he entered from the back room. Following him were the rest of the crew and a boy of perhaps fifteen. He looked enough like the innkeeper that I took him to be his son. He had a scared puppy look in his eyes that made me thankful we had placed his father in one of the upstairs rooms. The teenager's eyes grew flinty hard when he spotted the VGG pushed against one wall. The survivor, trussed up like a Christmas goose, was out like a light.

Richard placed a hand on the boy's shoulder. "It's all right, son. This is Kal, a friend."

I moved slowly, careful not to spook the boy, and extended a hand. "Hello, young man."

"Alain," Richard whispered.

I smiled. "Alain. It is a pleasure to meet you."

As Alain tentatively took my hand, Richard said, "We found him hiding in the basement. The entrance was concealed under a rug. Maurice, the innkeeper, must have distracted the VGG long enough to keep them from finding the boy."

A tear trickled down Alain's cheeks. "My papa is dead, yes?" he said in heavily accented English.

I nodded.

"These men killed him?"

Mouth pointed to the man I'd gutted with the Bowie. "Him."

The boy looked at the grisly wound decorating the VGG agent's crotch. "He died too quickly, I think." Hazel eyes met mine. "You killed that one?" I nodded again.

"Thank you."

"You're welcome, Alain." I took a deep breath. "Son, do you know anything about that German camp up the mountain?"

Alain nodded. "Many people go in, but only Germans leave. Papa," his voice grew thick, "had me watching the camp at night through my window."

"That was good of you, Alain, keeping an eye on the Germans for the Resistance," I said with a gentle smile. "You are very brave. Tell me, Alain, did you see anything ... unusual?"

He nodded. "For the past two weeks I have seen ugly lights, sir."

Ugly lights? I felt my testicles head for cover. Behind me Mouth gasped. "What kind of ugly lights, Alain?"

The teenager took a deep breath. "They shot into the sky, only lasting a few seconds. Some came from the sky, but all started and ended almost fifty meters from the front gate. A few nights ago one of the lights that came from the sky shot off to the west, springing like a tight rope that had been cut. It was very surprising."

Surprising? At least. It must have been when Mouth and I had arrived. Lights from the sky … arrivals. Lights from the ground … departures. Cute. Smacked of Aryan efficiency. I had a thought. "Always fifty meters or so from the gate? Did you happen to see why?" That didn't seem efficient to me. Why hadn't they built a guard house near that point? Or circled it with fencing?

"I do not know, I only watched the lights."

Interesting.

"Thank you, Alain." To the Frenchmen, "Someone get this young man a bite to eat."

Alain grabbed my wrist. "Sir, last night another light came from the sky. That is when … when …" he pointed to the VGG. "They came in the morning."

A bolt of fear shot through my belly. Canton! Winch! Did someone get past them? Damn! Things just got hairier and I prayed that my friends were all right.

"Are you thinking what I'm thinking, Kal?" Mouth asked, lips set in a grim line.

"Bet you a buffalo nickel I am."

She shook her head. "I was afraid of that."

Richard looked confused and Jeanie's lovely brow was creased in a frown. "Would you mind explaining, Kal?" asked the handsome Brit.

Mouth took a deep breath. "We have to go in."

"In?" Richard and the Frenchmen looked at each other in confusion. Jeanie got it, though.

"They're going into the camp, guv," she said with a grim twist to her lips.

"Are you barking mad? It's suicide, it is!" he shouted at us, unshaven cheeks shaking in fury. The three Frenchmen stared at each other in apprehension.

I took a deep breath. "No, it's not, but it will be … difficult." Leaning forward, I stared at each in turn, trying to impress upon them the urgency I felt with the force of my gaze. "If I'm right, von

Ribbentrop is already at, or close to, the camp in an effort to heal Goebbels, who was injured by Mouth. Also, there is a third player who I believe arrived last night, a magician. We need to stop Goebbels and keep him from delivering what he is carrying to the Reich. We need to stop whoever else came back yesterday, no ifs ands or buts. Our only problem is how to get into the camp and do it quickly."

"No sane person breaks *into* a camp," said Richard. "It's foolish, a death sentence."

Mouth shook her head. "Sorry, Kal, but I have *no* idea how to get into a Nazi concentration camp that is guarded by ten watchtowers and manned by twenty asswipes with SMGs and itchy trigger fingers. Do you?"

Oh, boy.

C'mon Kal, I urged. Use your freakin' noggin for something else than to give your neck something to do!

Man, I had nothing.

"I can help you."

Everyone jumped at the buzzing voice. Even me.

The three Frenchmen crossed themselves while Richard and Jeanie's eyes grew larger than seemed humanly possible. "It's okay, folks," I said, holding up a hand while fishing in a pocket with the other.

"Okay, Ghost, gimme what you got." I brought the cell out, its face glowing brightly, the *Ghostbusters* logo big enough for everyone to see.

Alain's eyes were bright as he stared at the phone. Crap! I'd completely forgotten about the kid. "It is beautiful!" he exclaimed in wonder. "Is it magic?"

"Kind of."

"Hello, Alain, you have nothing to worry about." Ghost's droning buzz was curiously gentle.

The teenager laughed and touched the logo on the cell. He snatched his hand back as if burned, but his smile never drained away. Jeanie joined him, thoroughly entranced. That raised her a good peg or two on my cool list.

I kept my voice steady despite the hammering of my heart. "Talk to me, Ghost."

The cell vibrated with every word that emerged from the tiny speakers. "There is a way inside the camp without passing through the gate."

Everyone stared, spellbound. "Well ... how?"

"Hmmm ... So, this is how you usually feel. I like it."

The cell case began to creak in my fist. "Yes?" *I will not throw the phone away ... I will not throw the phone away!* I kept the mantra rolling through my head on a loop.

"It is so simple, Kal. Remember what the purpose was for Natzweiler-Struthof?"

Mouth answered. "It was originally slated to be part of the V2 rocket production as well as a granite quarry. About 7,000 prisoners were held there at any time, while the subcamps carried about 25,000 ... What, Kal?"

I was methodically thumping my head against a wall, angry at myself for not seeing what was right before my eyes.

"Kal has realized the obvious, Ms. McTavish." The damn spook sounded pretty smug. And I felt pretty damn stupid.

It took a moment, but she got there and then joined me for a group head thumping, much to the amusement of the rest of the group. "The caves," she whispered.

Yeah, the caves.

Interesting-er.

"What now?" asked Richard, rubbing his eyes. Jeanie looked baffled.

The five VGG soldiers caught my eye. I began to smile.

Jeanie gave Richard a nudge. "Look, guv. I think Kal has a plan."

I stared back into her large, soft eyes. Oh, yeah ... I had a plan.

Chapter Twenty-Three

Kal

Sneak In

The first mistake the sentry made was to smoke. Never do that. It's not the smell or the small clouds of whitish smoke that shine in the moonlight that give you away, although that helps. No, it's the glowing red ember as you take a drag that can be seen almost a mile away on a dark night.

And it was a dark night indeed.

Second Mistake: If you're going to guard a secret entrance to an underground cave system, don't stand out in front for all to see. Hide. Even if you have a hidden backup. You never knew when that backup might not be there.

Third Mistake: Don't play for the bad guys. Ever.

Three strikes, you're out.

Thanks to Ghost, we had detailed maps of the area and of the caves, both natural and manmade, under the camp. Easy peasy lemon squeezy. Thanks to Bureau files Ghost had 'liberated' while we chased Goebbels with that silly blue Subaru, we even had the location of the secret entrance the sentry was guarding.

It all came down to time. We didn't have enough. I would've loved to take a couple of days to plan something ultra-sneaky and fun, but with a new arrival from my time, things had become much more immediate.

I was a spider, slow and sneaky, eight-stepping my way into position, avoiding twigs and rustling dry leaves, sticking to the protection of winter-bare trees. It had taken me all of a half-second to figure out where the second man had secreted himself. The phosphorescent dial of my watch told me it was a hair before one a.m. A few more ticks and it would be show time.

The guard's cigarette glowed as he inhaled. Any second now ...

Glowing tobacco and paper fluttered to the winter mulch as the sentry gave a brief, almost soundless gurgle, falling to the forest floor, the hilt of a knife protruding from his throat.

Rapid footsteps and a dark form dodged around trees, just another shadow among the faint shadows thrown by the constant moon. *Go, Mouth,* I urged.

A sharp rustling a few feet away came from the shelter of an overhanging fir whose branches almost touched the ground. The long barrel of a rifle was pointed at her fleeing form. Sneaky, sneaky. My guess proved to be accurate; the second man was using the first as a stalking horse.

I wanted the Bowie, like I wanted cool drink of water, like I wanted the monster Iku-Turso dead. My dependency on the blade was almost an obsession, but I was already full up on those, so I sucked it up and used my Recon Tanto with the chisel tip.

A flat dive sent me under the branches, landing on my belly next to the second man in a shower of dead needles. Even in the dark shelter of the overhanging branches, my night vision was good enough to guide the Recon to his carotid artery. A second strike found a soft throat and the knife's tip sheared through cartilage like butter, stifling any cry. Only a muted burble disturbed the night. The rifle fell to the ground and blood, black in the dim moonlight, steamed in the frigid air.

Done and done.

Is it sick to say that I really, *really*, enjoy my work?

Maybe I'm a monster, a devil perhaps, but at least I work on the side of the angels. I think.

Deliberate rustling reached my ears. "Good job, Mouth."

"Thanks, boss."

A few minutes later Richard and Jeanie made an appearance as we were putting the final touches on concealing the bodies.

"I didn't hear a thing," he whispered, eyes wide.

"You weren't supposed to," I replied.

Jeanie's teeth glowed against the darkness of her face. "Two dead in near silence without the use of spells. I am impressed."

"Quit flirting, you two," Mouth growled, arranging the last bit of the scrub to finish hiding the bodies.

Jeanie's laugh was throaty and low.

I held up the cell. "Where to now, Ghost?" I checked the battery's charge: forty-eight percent left.

A schematic of the hillside appeared on the glass display. "Three meters to the north, behind a large boulder half buried in the ground is the cave entrance. The boulder is a fake, plaster and chicken wire that can easily be moved. You will see a recessed, nearly flat rock wall that contains a secret door made of wood."

I smiled. "Okay, people, you all heard the phantom. Let's move like we have a purpose."

The boulder was right where Ghost said it would be—a big, gray monstrosity that looked like it had been part of a *Star Trek* set. It took three of us to move the damn thing.

"Where's the doorknob?" Mouth asked, staring at the blank face of faux rock that was set into the hillside and overhung with real lichen-decorated rock.

"'Speak 'friend' and enter,'" I quoted.

She laughed while the other two looked puzzled. They'd get it in a few years when the trilogy was published. Meanwhile, I examined the façade, running fingertips over sculpted plaster. Somewhere ... somewhere hidden, but not too well. *There!* Under my fingers a small, ridged, seam, perhaps a quarter inch wide.

Damn. "I'm a little rusty at lock-picking. Mouth, what about you?"

Jeanie shoved me aside. "Please, luv, let the professionals take care of this." A shapely finger traced the edge of the seam and, after a second, we heard a soft *click*. The door swung open an inch and she pulled it wide. Darkness met our combined gaze.

"Looks spooky, boss," Mouth whispered. "You go first."

Crap. Well, unto the breach and all that.

I'd hoped for some kind of light, a bare bulb, a candle or two, even some fitfully burning torches. Even horror-movie lightning would have been preferable to the complete darkness I walked into.

The tunnel was wider than my outstretched arms, so I proceeded slowly with fingertips forward. I'd faced Harpies, Vampires, irate Centaurs, irascible Ifrits and more flavors of undead than you can imagine without a twitch or a stumble, but treading blind in absolute darkness gave me the screaming willies. Yeah, me ... the big, tough, Supernatural killing Finn ... afraid of the dark. We all have our flaws. Turns out I have several dozen.

I could make some psychiatrist rich.

Thirty steps later I still hadn't reached a wall or any obstacle and with each step my worry quotient began to grow ... and grow ...

Jeanie had argued for light—magical or otherwise—in case of darkness, but I'd vetoed that thought. Nothing will attract attention faster than even the smallest bit of light in pitch black. The first sentry's ghost would agree with me.

I was quiet, almost silent, but every slight scuff of my shoes, every whisper of fabric against fabric and the subtle creak of leather echoed in my ears like the forerunners of the Apocalypse.

Fingertips met stone, cold and rough. I made a soft clicking noise with my mouth—once, then twice. The signal to stop. Behind me, the telltale rasp of cloth ceased.

I ran my hand over the stone. A wall, planed flat. A move to the left, a move to the right. On both sides after a few feet stone gave way to wood. Doors in a cave? How very German. Unlocked ... how very sloppy. A turn of the handle on the right hand door brought a wash of light and sound. *Damn*, the door had been sound and light-proofed! It was a good guess the second one had been as well.

"Light please." My voice sounded horribly loud, even to me.

A soft aqua glow sprang to life around Jeanie's hands, providing a five-foot bubble of illumination. Mouth grinned at me while Richard blinked rapidly. My own eyes stung a bit at the glow.

Our faces were streaked with black stripes ... camouflage. For Jeanie, gray. Nothing uniform, nothing regular that would give the impression of artificiality.

Mouth's teeth were very white against the dark paint on her face. "Where to, boss?"

I scratched my head. "Well, when in doubt, improvise." To Jeanie, "You wouldn't happen to know a good invisibility spell, would you?"

Jeanie treated me to a little eye action, full of promise and heat that made the southern reaches of my anatomy beg for attention. Richard and Mouth rolled their eyes.

"Sorry, luv," she purred. "I'm good, but not that good."

I'd lay ten-to-one she was plenty good.

With an almost audible wrench, I pulled my mind out of the gutter. Not the time for that kinda nonsense. Maybe later. *Oh, please, Lord. Let there be a later.*

"I do have," she continued, "a camouflage spell that will help."

I raised an eyebrow.

"It won't make you invisible, luv, but it will make you very hard to see."

Mouth chimed in. "Why haven't I ever heard of it?"

Jeanie gave her a superior smile. "Because, dearie, I've only recently perfected it. Took me three years to get the Shape right."

"It's true," Richard announced. "We've been using it for only a few weeks. Not so good in direct lighting, but in cases like this, it works well, it does." He beamed at Mouth, who returned it with some oomph.

Interesting.

I wasn't too sure about the wisdom of carrying on a fling with a man who, in our time, was long since dead, but considering my questionable moral stature, who was I to object?

Jeanie moved forward and placed a glowing hand flat on my chest. It was very warm. "Only problem, luv, is it works on one person at a time. I haven't been able to cast it on multiple targets."

Only one person at a time? "Fine, hit me, then stay back. I want to try the door to the left."

My chest began to tingle where her hand lay and a curious ripple of heat, centered between my pecs, flowed outward. It was almost erotic and I resisted the temptation to close my eyes; instead I kept them focused on the magician's.

"There, luv," she said.

Looking at my arms, my chest, I didn't see any difference.

"Well, I'll be dipped in sewage," Mouth said dryly.

"What? I don't see anything."

"Neither do I."

Interesting-er.

"What do I look like?"

"You just kind of … blend. It's hard to look at you; my eyes don't want to focus on where you're at."

Cool. Good enough.

"Wait here," I said and moved to the left hand door.

Richard spoke up. "It lasts for about five minutes, Kal; then it fades."

"Good to know," I muttered and opened the door. Thick and solid, but not sound-proofed. Strange.

Once again light hit my eyes, electric and harsh. Definitely not the pitch torches from a *Frankenstein* movie, but bare bulbs on wire, much like the ones in the cave back in the twenty-first century. Briefly, I wondered where the wires came from. I certainly didn't hear the harsh sound of a genny. Perhaps they'd drilled a hole to run a conduit? I dismissed the thought as irrelevant.

A hallway, maybe twenty feet, ended at an archway. This area had been machined as well, almost perfectly planed. The Nazis had gone to a lot of trouble expanding and tunneling and I had the feeling it wasn't just for V2 rocket research.

Voices … speaking words with a lot of glottal stops and consonants. German. I ghosted down the hallway, praying that Jeanie was as good as her word. The hall ended at a ten by fifteen foot room with a square metal table surrounded by four olive-drab steel chairs. A small kitchenette held a lonely little coffee pot. Did the Brits and Germans order from the same catalogue?

One soldier, jacket unbuttoned, drank from a blue-enameled cup, the coffee inside steaming slightly. At the end of the room was an opening into a much larger room filled with wooden cots. The voices came from inside. A barracks? Underground?

Interesting.

The soldier drinking coffee yawned and stretched, setting the cup down on the table with a *clank*. I took it as a signal to get it in gear.

I'd never know what that soldier saw in the last few moments of his life, only that his mouth opened wider than I thought possible. The Bowie took him.

Blood flowed across the table and around the coffee cup, a lake of red surrounded by gray as the soldier's body slumped. Judging by the eiderdown on his lips and the acne, he wasn't more than sixteen or seventeen years old.

Okay, there *are* times when I really hate this job.

How much time did I have before someone strolled through the opening from the other room and discovered the body? A peek into the other room revealed three men and about a dozen cots with footlockers. The men were half-dressed and having a good old chinwag, drinking coffee, sitting on their footlockers like they hadn't a care in the world.

Two shots from the Lahti took the man facing my left above the ear. The next two rounds slammed home into the man facing me, destroying his heart, while a third bullet entered his forehead above the right eye. Three more rounds to the third man, again two in the chest and one in the head.

Killing them took less than four seconds.

A quick inspection revealed that they were all very young men. What was this? The Nazi Cradle-to-the-Grave recruitment policy?

I found four Karabiner 43 rifles, the same kind used by the sentries outside. Now that the excitement was over, I took a closer look at the men I'd killed and realized all wore the uniform of the SS, the paramilitary organization that, while under Heinrich Himmler, were responsible for many of the crimes against humanity during WWII. Suddenly, I didn't feel so bad.

But there were at least six more SS out there somewhere. Oh, well, no rest for the wicked.

I closed the outer door behind me and faced my three companions. "Maybe six more soldiers, SS, are around here somewhere," I said.

"You've got blood on you, mate." Richard ran a finger across the lapel of my leather jacket. It was then I realized the camouflage spell had worn off.

"Yeah, I had to take care of some business. There were four SS jacking off back there."

"You just killed *four* SS?"

Mouth's lips curled in a sneer. "And took his own sweet time about it. What's wrong, stop off at Starbucks?"

"Getting old, not as fast as I used to be." I took a deep breath. "Let's go. I'll run point. Stay well behind me, but when I give the signal, come a-running."

Mouth nodded. "Check, boss."

"What kind of signal, Kal?" asked Richard.

Mouth pinched his butt, causing him to yelp. "You'll know. He's not exactly subtle."

I'd have been offended if it weren't true.

Jeanie laid a hand on my chest, fingers caressing, and the familiar tingle flowed once again over my skin. I opened the door to the right.

Again the wash of sound and light. Another hallway, but much longer—maybe thirty, forty yards—a tunnel leading deep into the gut rock of the Vosges. With every step I felt a sinister pressure against my skin, like I was walking through gelid cobwebs that tingled against my nerves.

I felt like Alice falling down the rabbit hole, on my way to some twisted, hellish, Wonderland created by a mad, drunken demon. I really, *really*, didn't want to meet the Queen of Hearts.

Wow. A large cavern, perhaps a hundred yards across, greeted my eyes, almost perfectly circular and lit by fluorescent lamps that hung from the seventy-foot ceiling. The room was split into two levels. The upper, my level, consisted of a thirty-foot wide loft that circled the center, lower level. Separating the two levels was an iron railing broken at the four cardinal points by stairs leading downward. Large generators hummed and roared, pouring electricity into wires that ran into the floor and ceiling, while other machines vented air through big ducts, keeping a cool breeze flowing constantly and pumping out polluted, stale air. Four SS troopers walked casually around the upper level, eyes trained on the lower level, weapons at the ready.

The machinery was placed haphazardly across the upper loft. I determined that the real fun was on the lower level.

As a soldier walked past, I slipped behind and to the right of him. Using one of the larger blowers as cover, I tried to move closer to the overhang so I could spy on the lower level. A few more yards saw me at a generator, half-deafened by its diesel roar. I was quite aware of the time limit on the camouflage spell … My stomach had started dancing the rumba, certain that at any second I would be exposed.

Cursing under my breath, I belly-crawled toward the railing, hoping I would be almost invisible against the floor.

I made it and was able to peer down. The bottom level opened up, ending twenty feet below my staring eyes. I froze, shocked by what I beheld.

Directly beneath the upper level was a circular cage of wire mesh, the upper level floor forming the ceiling. Doors were located where stairs met the floor, secured with padlocks the size of my fist. Inside were people. Filthy, emaciated, viciously treated and brutalized people, naked and shivering against the cold stone. Two guards strolled around just outside the cage on opposite sides of the room, eyes cold and dead.

But that's not what drew my eyes.

Smack dab in the center of the circular floor was a design, a pattern, extending a good forty feet across. A spell Shape created with gold wire hammered into the flat, smooth rock of the floor, a mind-bending arrangement of loops, whorls and cross hatchings. The whole thing looked as though the love child of M. Escher and Salvador Dali had vomited spaghetti all over the floor.

As if that wasn't bad enough, in the center of the Shape was an altar, a rough rectangle of stone three feet high by six long, incongruously rough compared to the smooth floor. Standing next to the altar was a dapper man in a white lab coat and black rubber gloves, a scalpel in one hand, the bloody heart of his victim in the other.

Oh, God …

The victim, the person on the altar, looked to be a seven-year-old boy, scrawny and small, his chest ripped open, ribs like broken sticks bent outward every which way. The flesh was pale, waxy, and the look on his face was one of absolute horror.

My fingers gripped the edge of floor so hard that they turned white. As I lay there, my eyes glued to scene below, I felt a familiar stirring in my mind. The man held the dripping heart over a section of pattern and squeezed, drooling blood over the imbedded gold. With every drop that fell onto the precious metal, a nacreous green pulse of power erupted from the point of contact and swirled over the gold. Each throb of power traveled round and round the intricate Shape, gaining speed, gaining luminescence, until it came into contact with a pair gold wires soldered to the end of the Shape. These wires led to a small, foot tall pedestal, where a triangular wooden box about four inches thick was placed on top. The gold wire wrapped the box like an obscene Fabergé cocoon. When the pulse hit the box, it vanished, absorbed into the dark wood as if it had never existed.

The rage thrummed through me as I watched the despicable act of Necromancy being played out. Vomit pooled in the back of my throat and I knew, I *knew*, the camouflage spell was about to expire, exposing me to the guards.

Crap.

No time to waste; it was do or die and I would rather do. The Lahti and the .45 appeared in my hands as I stood, feeling the rage course through my veins like heady wine. I began to run widdershins along the upper level, dodging gennys and blowers, aiming on the run as my legs pumped faster and faster, propelling me along at a speed that had the air shrieking in my ears.

Three shots from the .45 took the first guard and I hurtled his twitching body, firing from the hip with the Lahti at a guard thirty yards away before I even landed. His face twisted in pain as a round took him in the thigh and another four shots from the .45 ended his life. Gunfire from below followed me as I ran, the cage guards striving to take me out with their rifles.

I managed to clear another forty feet before the first bullet grazed me, tearing a line of fire across my hip. It was the third guard, calmly taking aim with his Karabiner. A cool customer—efficient, deadly and a good shot.

Not good enough.

The Lahti spat bullets, the .45 chiming in and under the hail of lead the soldier dropped, throat shot from the .45s last round and gargling on his own blood. I left it behind as I ran for the fourth guard.

That's when a mule punched me in the stomach, nearly causing me to stumble headlong into another massive blower. The rage kept me going, kept me on my feet and running faster than ever before. My cheeks hurt from the manic grin on my face but I didn't care. Raging felt so *good*.

Repeated *pops* came from behind the last soldier; his body danced a gruesome jig as the bullets shredded him. The cavalry had arrived at last. As his corpse hit the floor, Mouth and Richard exited the tunnel, weapons at the ready.

Good. I was running out of ammo.

The guards below were still firing, but I had to get to the lower levels. Without a thought I jumped the railing, aiming straight toward one of the two Germans trying to kill me. Another round to the gut nearly folded me in midair—the pain actually penetrating the haze of my rage—but sheer stubbornness kept me straight and true.

One of my size tens hit the guard on chest, the other his face, and I rode him to the floor as he collapsed under me.

Things in the man's chest cracked and crumbled under one

foot, while his head did the best impression of an exploding pumpkin I'd ever seen. I tucked and rolled, my momentum carrying me to the cage that circled the lower level. The frightened Jews scrambled away.

Pain!

Agony like I'd never known, needles of fire and ice filleting my nerves, ripping flesh from bone … slowly. My eyeballs boiled in their sockets and my skin began to glow incandescent. The rage roared in my mind against the awful presence making itself known.

The man at the altar. A magician. Should have known. My shriek of wrath and agony followed me down to oblivion, the rage unable to cope with both the damage to my body and the magic searing my soul.

Chapter Twenty-Four

Mouth

Sneak Out

Damn that camouflage spell was *totally* cool. When Jeanie laid her palm on Kal's chest, ripples spread outward, flowing up and down his body in a liquid lightshow. Within seconds his form was nearly indistinguishable from the wall he stood in front of.

Ever see those old *Looney Tunes* where the chameleon stands in front of a brick wall and its whole body adopts a red brick pattern? That's what Kal looked like—part of the scenery.

I knew right then that any Nazi he would encounter would wind up on in hell so fast they wouldn't ever know they'd died.

Worked for me.

Plan in motion, we followed him down the hall at a discreet distance. If wasn't for a slight blurring around the edges, I would never have seen him, despite the cold light of the bare bulbs.

Quickly and quietly the blur that was Kal made its way into the large circular room, keeping close to the floor between roaring generators and screaming blowers. Richard and Jeanie stopped, but I kept creeping forward.

Richard's fingers clutched mine. "Where are you going?" he hissed, alarmed.

I gave him a sideways look. "Listen, sweetie, if I let Kal have his way, he'd hog all the fun for himself."

"But he's the guv for this mission!"

Awww … Richard was so cute when worried, I couldn't help myself … my lips found his in a fierce kiss. Man, he could lay on a major lip lock! "Listen, handsome," I breathed when we came up for air. "I'm my own woman, and no one is my guv, got it? And I always protect my team. Especially from themselves."

I could see the objection flare in his eyes, but the next second it died, replaced by something much more … primal. He took me by the shoulders and kissed me hard.

Wow. *Totally* a cool moment.

Jeanie's throaty chuckle broke us out of our clinch. "You lead, then, Rebecca," he breathed in to my mouth. My name, which I hate, sounded wonderful coming from his lips. "We'll follow."

I turned, a big grin plastered on my face.

As I approached the large room, I noticed the Kal-blur laying at the edge of the floor next to thick iron railing. One minute, then two. What the hell was he doing?

The Kal-blur rose to its feet with almost blazing speed, hands outstretched. Even through the roar of the machines from over forty feet away, I could *feel* the energy hum along his body.

Oh, damn.

Kal-blur disappeared to the left and the sound of gunfire rang through the cavern, both the .45 and that precious Lahti of his. The three of us broke into a run, drawing our weapons. As we drew close, we saw the whole strange scene, the images buffeting our eyes. Kal, no longer camouflaged, ran faster than humanly possible, a blond blur dodging and jumping large, screaming machines and weapons spitting death. Two soldiers—SS and over fifty yards apart—fell in a matter of moments.

The last Soldier, his back to us, had Kal dead bang—no way he could miss—his Karabiner tracking his swift movement, ready for the kill. Well, *that* wasn't happening!

The Webley bucked in my hand, joined a half second later by Richard and Jeanie's sidearms, chewing the soldier up into kibble. Then Kal, as usual, did the unexpected … he jumped the railing. Who the hell does that?

All three of us made it the railing, the macabre scene below inundating our cortexes with evil. Like a computer, I took stock of the situation in an instant, calculating targets and trajectories. Less than a second later the last guard (his buddy's head looked like lasagna—yuk!) shot Kal—who was thrashing on the ground and foaming at the mouth—in the chest.

Jeanie screamed rage while Richard and I emptied our weapons at the soldier, dropping him. The British magician flung out a hand at the same time that the lab coat-wearing douche at the altar pointed at her. Both magicians clutched their heads and fell unconscious.

Well, that was weird.

"See if you can wake her up," I barked at Richard as I headed toward the stairs, fear stabbing at my solar plexus. Kal lay on the ground, twitching and bleeding profusely. Gut shots suck and I knew that without a magician to heal him, he would die.

As quickly as I could, I secured the German magician, tearing strips from his lab coat for bindings and a blindfold. There was no way I was going to let that bastard have eyes to focus his spells with.

Outside I was cool, collected, finding objectives and tackling them head on, achieving goals. Inside I couldn't stop shaking and weeping. Kal had been shot, maybe more than once. I'd seen him berserk, cold, frustrated and even somewhat happy—but never shot at close range.

He'd stopped twitching, and the foam at the corner of his mouth had melted away to a clear drool. His skin, normally so pale, was doubly so, almost paper-white with a strange waxy texture I'd seen too often. Blood slowly pooled around his body in a spreading stain. A cursory examination revealed five bullet holes, two in the torso.

"Richard!" I yelled, terror turning my voice soprano. "Wake Jeanie up! Kal's been shot!" The poor bastards in the circular cage watched the whole thing with lifeless eyes, eyes that had seen death all too often. Eyes that had lost all hope.

The remains of the magician's shredded white lab coat rapidly turned red as I pressed it to Kal's wounds, applying pressure. God, too much blood.

"It's okay, Mouth."

Startled, I looked up and saw Kal staring at me, eyes almost bled white. "Shhh … Kal." I kept the pressure on his wounds, trying not to cry.

"It's okay, Mouth." His voice was surprisingly strong. "Had to happen sometime. Been … been living on borrowed time for a while now."

"Shut up!" I will not cry … I will not cry.

Then something happened that freaked me out from top to bottom. A tear formed at the corner of one dark blue eye and trickled down the side of his face. "Don't be like me, Rebecca," he intoned gravely. Man, he *never* used my given name!

"I said shut up!" Why was he doing this to me?

He licked his lips then coughed up some blood. "Don't obsess like me … don't *hate* like me. My hate has been eating at me for the past twenty years and it's who I am." Another cough. "And I don't like who … *what* I've become."

Enough of that crap. "You're the best warrior the Bureau has ever known and I've always wanted to be like you."

His baby blues blazed into mine. "Don't you ever say that!" Bloody spit flew from his lips. "Don't even think it," he rasped. "You find someone, like that Richard fella and you don't ever let go. I made a mistake, a bad one, so long ago. I chose the Bureau over a woman I loved and it's haunted me ever since. Don't you dare try to be like me. That's really messed up."

"But you were always so strong."

The frantic energy that had gripped him faded. "No, I'm tough … not strong. There's a big difference."

Somebody had parked a truck in my throat and I had trouble swallowing. I hated that shit, talking about feelings and whatnot. Kal had never indulged before and the fact that he was doing so now scared me down to my toenails. Totally not my thing.

His eyes closed and his breathing became shallow. I'd seen this before, it wouldn't be long. Goddammit! Where was Jeanie?

Like an answered prayer, she was at my elbow; her large eyes narrowed with worry. "Thank you, luv. I have him now."

The feeling of sweet relief almost made me pass out. "You're in good hands, Kal," I said gruffly.

Jeanie's face became pinched as her fingers lightly skimmed

Kal's pale, pale skin. "Yes, indeed, luv, you are in good hands. Jeanie isn't going to let you die."

His eyelids drooped. "Be gentle with me, doc. I bruise easily."

Despite Kal's attempt at humor, the magician never relaxed the bunched muscles at the corners of her mouth.

Kal's eyes lost focus and he blinked lazily. I was just about to stand when his hand gripped my arm. "Mouth ... I think ... Goebbels is in the camp ... with von Ribbentrop. Probably ... healed by now ..." His cheek began to twitch uncontrollably. "Find him ... exit in here somewhere ... careful of the Necromancer over ... there." At the last word he passed into unconsciousness.

"Please, Rebecca," Richard's strong hand gripped my upper arm, pulling me to my feet, "you must see this."

I looked around. "What about the prisoners?"

"They'll keep for a moment. Please, you have to see this."

What did I have to see? The guard with the smushed head? The poor little boy with his heart torn out, ribs like broken twigs sticking through the skin? I had totally seen enough, thank you.

However reluctant I was, Richard's calm strength propelled me over to where the unconscious German magician lay. "Look closely. Do you recognize him?"

"Should I?"

Those kind eyes of his turned to granite. "I was curious. In the Service we are given dossiers on all the big players in the German Theatre. This man I recognize."

"Who is he?"

"Look close." The revulsion in Richard's voice was thick enough to cut.

I took a close look. Then closer still, mentally removing the magician's gag and blindfold. Black hair, kind of good looking in a 'if Charlie Brown were a sinister bastard' sort of way, with a wide, open face. I flipped though the WWII files in my mind until I found a picture I'd seen oh so many years ago.

"Oh my God!"

" 'Oh my God,' indeed. This is one of the Service's most

wanted men, possibly the most foul Necromancer to come along since Genghis Khan."

I was looking at one of the most evil pricks in all of history. An SS officer and doctor who was responsible for medical experimentation on thousands of men, women and children. It was Hauptsturmführer Joseph Mengele, also known as The White Angel.

Better known as the Angel of Death.

Damn.

Five rungs, six … pause and rest … climb again, another dozen rungs, then rest again. Dang, it was a *long* ladder. I stared down the shaft, which seemed to lead to the darkness of infinity. One arm hooked in a rung, I wiped the sweat from my face with the other, smearing the cammo paint. At that point I didn't care much, concentrating on my goal … climbing the ladder of an elevator shaft that would lead to the camp and Goebbels.

When I had finished gawping at our infamous captive, Richard asked, "What now, Rebecca?" Again with my given name; it was really starting to grate on my nerves. Then I realized he'd effectively acknowledged that I was in command. That totally gave me the chills.

I scrubbed my face with the palms of my hands. "You speak French, right?"

He nodded.

"Great, find out who their leader is."

"Leader?"

"Even prisoners have a leader. Find him."

Richard nodded and turned to the poor ravaged creatures behind the cold, iron mesh. "*Qui est votre chef?*"

Nothing. No surprise there. He asked again with the same result. Then asked again.

Enough was enough. "Translate," I growled. He nodded and I faced the cage. "Listen up … we just killed a bunch of Nazis and we're here to help. If you don't want to get out of here, we'll leave you to the next bunch to come along. I'm sure they'll be forgiving of all the dead SS lying about."

Richard started to translate, but a voice with a thick, French accent emerged from Kal's vicinity. "I understand English." It was a woman, thin, stooped and perhaps seventy years old.

I gave her a tight-lipped smile and a nod. "We're fixing to let you all go. In the village of Naztweiler, at the inn, there are Resistance members who will assist in relocating you."

"How?"

"How what?"

"How are we to survive the cold while naked?" She pointed to her sunken, flabby breasts. "How can we survive long enough to reach this village? We were better off before you came." Her voice radiated bitterness.

I will not shoot. I will NOT shoot. The poor woman and her people had been victimized often enough that she now thought like a victim, a prisoner, not like a free person. In spite of the noise thundering from above, my footsteps seemed to echo off the walls. I came face to face with the woman, who flinched ever so slightly.

"Look at the boy on the altar." She didn't, so I shoved my face forward. Again she flinched. "Look!" I yelled. Startled, she did. "That was to be your fate," I continued softly. "Gutted like a fish in some occult Nazi ceremony. The village is less than a mile away and we have people who can help you. Yeah, some of you might get caught, some might get killed, but answer me this: would you rather die like *that*?"

The old woman stared at the boy for several long seconds then shook her head.

Much better. "That's good," I said gently. Richard supplied the lock picks, I supplied the skill, and we quickly had all four doors open while the woman addressed the other prisoners in rapid-fire French.

Ambulatory skeletons wrapped in nothing but skin and gristle moved slowly out of the cage, stumbling toward the stairs. They followed Richard like he was the messiah, but not before each one stopped briefly at Kal's motionless body. For a brief second, each poor, starving soul bent and touched him on the crown of the head while Jeanie stared fixedly at her patient, hands placed gently on his torso.

"They honor him," said the old lady who stood at my side.

"Honor?" I couldn't tear my eyes away from the scene.

"Most of us saw what he did, killing the Nazis. He's God's Wrath. It's the only way to explain how he did what he did." Her eyes glanced at the SS trooper with the burst skull. "No one could do what he did. It is a pity the evil doctor cast a spell on him."

I nodded.

"What is his name?" she asked. "What shall we call him?"

Throwing caution to the wind, I said, "Kal. Kal Hakala."

Her brown eyes grew puzzled. "Strange name for such a hero."

No. Not really.

"Young lady?"

I rubbed my eyes. "What?"

The old woman pointed to the first level. "There is a door up there where the Nazis come from. The Kal said you must go to the camp. That is the best way."

Good to know. "Thanks."

Her sad, defeated eyes met mine. "No, young lady. Thank you." With that, the old woman tottered off, the last of the freed prisoners. She knelt at Kal's side, gently stroked the hair from his forehead, and planted a gentle kiss there before joining her people.

Needless to say, while Jeanie worked on Kal, I searched for the door, which wasn't hard to find. It led to a very long hallway, several hundred yards of slightly twisting passage that had been well shaped by the Nazis. It led to an elevator shaft, the kind with an accordion gate constructed of diagonal metal slats. The elevator itself was a simple large, three-walled affair, large enough to haul considerable freight.

Did I want to ride the elevator to the top? I gave it a good hard think and decided against it. No telling if there was a guard at the opposite end waiting for Mengele or not, so I located the ceiling hatch and climbed onto the roof.

A steel ladder ran up the side of the shaft set in a large groove, ensuring a climber's safety from the rising or descending elevator. How nice of the Nazis to put safety first.

Twenty more rungs and my arms screamed their fatigue. I wiped the stinging sweat from my eyes, the flashlight tucked in my belt throwing crazy shadows on the side of the shaft. *How much longer?* I wondered for the thousandth time. A sip of tepid water from a canteen soothed my scratchy throat. *Damn*, I was tired.

Thirty more rungs and I'd raised the canteen to my lips when I noticed the dim gray light far above. Hastily, I switched off the flashlight and waited for my eyes to adjust fully. Yes! Less than a hundred feet away a blotch of light, dim and diffuse, beckoned to me.

With renewed energy, I climbed the remaining rungs, hands raw, knees and thighs burning, shoulders aching, but it didn't matter, the end was near. As I moved closer, I could see the steady light of electricity—a light bulb—shining through another accordion gate. Closer still and I saw movement, a shadow that briefly eclipsed the light.

Thankfully the light from the gate missed the ladder entirely and I was able to climb past without being noticed. A quick peek as I moved past revealed a soldier in a heavy coat walking to and fro, a steaming cup of coffee in his gloved hands. A small, simple wooden table with two chairs stood in sight, one of the chairs occupied by another soldier smoking a cigarette. I climbed until I was past the opening, above and to the left, head almost touching the top of the shaft, which, to my surprise, had become thick brick.

Okay, time to get creative. I paused long enough to work some feeling back into my fingers then drew the Webley. Cracking the weapon in half, I withdrew a round. After reholstering, I tossed the round against the shaft and drew a knife, the kind known as a kukri.

"Take good care of this," Richard had said, gently placing the hilt in my hand. "I served with a Gurkha battalion in Greece two years ago and this was given to me by the men as a token of appreciation for my bravery. It is very old, and has served a long list of courageous masters."

For Richard to have been given a kukri by Gurkha for bravery was tantamount to being awarded the Medal of Honor. Predominantly from Nepal, those fierce soldiers fought for the British and had earned nearly 2,000 gallantry awards in WWI and 2,734 bravery awards in WWII. It had been written that they were 'the bravest of the brave, most generous of the generous, never had a country more faithful friends.' I'd accepted the blade with the humility and reverence it deserved.

I thought of that moment as I held the blade and vowed, if I survived, to let him know exactly how I felt. Funny … I'd known him for only a few days, but it felt like years. Was that love? Whatever it was, I planned to find out.

As the knife cleared the sheath, I marveled at its brutal and clean efficiency. Twelve inches of curved blade, fat toward the point, skinny toward the solid wood handle, it was a head chopper and gutting tool.

The bullet fell for about twenty feet before making a clattery, metallic *clinking* noise, bouncing off the sides of the shaft.

"What is that?" came from the room.

"I don't know, go find out," replied another voice.

A gloved hand unlatched the accordion gate and pulled it open. I struck out with the knife, feeling the razor edge slice cleanly through muscle and cartilage, arterial spray fountaining across the shaft. A quick nudge and the soldier fell with a surprised gurgle, his body following the bullet.

"Heinrich!" cried the second man in alarm. A scrape of wood against wood and the bang of a chair falling over and the man's bulky form blocked the light as he stared down the shaft in dismay.

The kukri took him and he joined his friend.

With a grunt, I swung into the room, drawing the Webley, ready in case there were more guards. None. I breathed a sigh of relief and took a good look at my surroundings. A twenty-five by fifteen foot room with brick walls, the elevator shaft rising to the roof six feet above my head taking up one corner. A quick inspection revealed elevator cables that ran through a set of large pulleys and out through a hole in the back of the shaft. Probably to the engine that powered the elevator.

Whoever constructed the shed had declined to install windows, which meant that not many people knew what was inside. Perhaps only the elite SS troopers and the higher-ups. Good. That meant there might not be a quick change of guard. Then again, knowing how Murphy's Law worked, maybe so.

One door of thick, stout oak. No windows meant flying blind. I had no choice but to go for it, so I killed the lights and opened the door ...

Chapter Twenty-Five

Mouth

Sneak Back

. . . $\mathbf{I}$nto darkness. Not a soul in sight.
Whew!

Before I could lose my nerve, I ghosted into the camp, a dark streak hugging the elevator shed. In the dim shadow between buildings, I glanced around, watching for guards, looking for my objective.

To the left were buildings, long and wooden, dark and dreary. Housing for prisoners was my first guess. To the right stood the front gates some twenty yards away with three large buildings—hastily constructed longhouses that didn't have a chance of keeping out the winter's chill. Instead, warm light shone from windows, an ironically cheery touch considering the camp's dark reputation. Across from me, past the large avenue that ran down the center of the camp, was a menacing building with a tall smokestack that soared into the night sky. No plumes of gray smoke billowed forth, no light seeped through crannies and chinks, but I knew what it was and it chilled me. A crematorium.

I let vent a few choice words that should have melted the ice underfoot. Being this close to a Nazi crematorium was not high on my 'To Do' list, but it wasn't like I had a lot of choice. Not if I wanted Goebbels. And I wanted Goebbels. Like, *bad*, you know?

From what I could tell, Natzweiler-Struthof had thirteen prisoner barracks, two guard barracks, the crematorium and two officer houses—taller though not as long. From the gate straight down the middle of the camp was the avenue, big enough for two cars to drive abreast, separating the compound into two equal parts. Both sides exemplified the measured perfection of German engineering. I vowed right then and there to sell my BMW when I got home.

The two cheery buildings—the officers' quarters—were on the opposite side of the avenue. I knew Goebbels was in one of them.

Once again I peered around. Two guards, each strolling in opposite directions down the avenue. They would pass each other, walk to the ends of the camp, then come back, meeting in the middle. A little mental math told me that I had about thirty seconds before the nearest one reached the gate and turned.

Turned out to be just what the doctor ordered.

After crossing, I drifted into the shadows of the buildings, silent and swift. Time was not on my side. I'd promised Richard two hours; about forty-five minutes had passed.

First building ... quick peek through the window. A stocky man in a wife-beater t-shirt sat in an overstuffed chair at a highly polished oak table with his back to me, a fire burning merrily in a Franklin stove. Clouds of thick smoke filled the room—the product of a cigar, I thought, although I couldn't see it. A bottle of wine sat on the table at his elbow. Everything looked oddly cozy and comfortable in the midst of the sickness of the camp.

Not Goebbels, so I flitted to the house nearest the gate and waited for the patrolling guard to turn around and stroll away. The lights were on inside the building and a quick look through a ground floor window revealed nothing, so I reckoned it was time to take a chance. Kukri in hand, I exposed myself to the gate lights for just a brief moment before quickly sliding through the front door.

The first thing I noticed, crouching with the knife at the ready, was the *warmth*. Oh, God, did that ever feel good! I hadn't realized how cold I was until the heat from the Franklin stove slapped me in the face. The second thing I noticed was that I was in a room similar to the one in the other house—comfy and cozy, with a bookshelf, a side table with a phonograph player, and an overstuffed chair. Stairs on my right led to the second story and straight ahead was a plain wooden door that led deeper into the house.

I started to step carefully toward the door when I realized my foot had landed on something soft. A rug. A very expensive Persian rug, a Mohtashem Kashan, if I wasn't mistaken. I love antiques and a quick look told me the thing would be worth at least ninety grand in the 2011 market. *Damn!* Made me wonder who the Nazis stole it from.

Almost to the door, but it opened from the other side and a tall, graying man with a big forehead walked through. His eyes widened as he took in the sight of a raggedly dressed woman with smeared black cammo paint on her face. That look of shock lasted for about half a second before the kukri, swung with all the force I could muster, cut through his neck deep enough that his head flopped, half-severed from his body. The lump of meat that used to be a person fell forward into my arms and I lowered him gently to the floor, blood soaking my shirt.

In that split-second, as he stared in shock, I recognized the man. Anyone working for MI-7 or the Bureau would have. Hung in 1946 after the Nuremburg trials, he was famous for his statement to Admiral Horthy, the Regent of the Kingdom of Hungary: "The Jews must either be exterminated or taken to the concentration camps. There is no other possibility."

He was a powerful magician and a complete bastard. I'd just killed Foreign Minister Joachim von Ribbentrop.

Oh well. So much for continuity.

"Joachim, come here, you have to see this!" a smooth, oily voice shouted from upstairs. I knew that voice. My lips stretched wide in anticipation.

Up the stairs two at a time, down a hallway, an open door at the end lighting the way and I knew my goal was in reach. Through the door and I saw him lazing on a large four-poster bed, open aluminum briefcase at his feet, papers in his hands.

Him! Was this how Kal felt when he went berserk? The abrupt rise in blood pressure flushing cheeks and supercharging the human motor? All I saw was the man with the wormy fingers whose eyes were still on the papers as I rushed him. He started to lift his head, eyes tracking upwards, and I hit him, hit him so hard that I knocked his front teeth down his throat and a gout of blood spewed from his mouth. Another strike, this time an elbow to the gut, then knife hand to the bridge of the nose, which broke with a solid *crunch*. It felt so good, *so* good and I wanted to kill him, to keep on hitting him until the man who had violated me, spell-raped me, was nothing more than red mush on the sheets. Deep down I knew Kal wanted him alive and it took every ounce of my self-control to render him merely unconscious. Meanwhile I cried. I cried and cried, tears and snot running down my face in rivulets, because I wanted him dead so badly, but Kal needed him to send us home and it just wasn't *fair*!

After wiping my face I stuffed all the papers on the bed into the aluminum briefcase and slammed it shut. I ordered my mind to retreat to a cold place, a cold place I had grown familiar with during my training days at Coronado. That cold person I became lifted Goebbels bodily and slung his slight frame over one shoulder, carrying him like a sack of grain.

Looking out the window, I timed the guards again and exited the house. Once I had the timing, it was almost easy to cross the avenue, even burdened with Goebbels' slender weight.

Back in the elevator shed, I pushed the recall button and the motor outside hummed to life. Thick, grease-coated rollers began to move. I laid Goebbels none too gently on the floor.

Still in that cold place, the killing place where nothing could hurt me, nothing and no one could make me feel the way *he* had made me feel … the horror, the helplessness, the hurt.

While I waited for the elevator to rise, the door of the shed opened and a guard entered, blowing the cold from stiff fingers. He died quickly, neck broken. The door closed before his body hit the floor.

The best kind of infiltration is when the enemy doesn't know he's been infiltrated.

With a groan, the elevator arrived, bringing with it the two guards I'd killed earlier. They had fallen straight through the roof to lie in bloody heaps on the elevator floor. I stuffed Goebbels and the guard I'd just killed inside. Fortunately, it was a big elevator and I had plenty of room to stand, although my boots were bloodied. I pushed the DOWN button and from afar heard cries of alarm.

If you want to cover up evidence of an incursion, one of the most effective ways is to start a fire. All you need is fuel and a timer, in my case … a cigarette. Often the simplest items are the most effective. Once the fire has started, you can scarper off with no one the wiser.

Down, down, down … so slowly. I could've walked faster than the elevator descended but I didn't care, the cold place had me and I was safe, nothing could hurt me. But I could hurt others, oh yes, I could hurt others and I would, if they got in my way.

The elevator juddered to a stop and opened; three pistols were pointed at my face. Kal—*Kal!*—stood there, the embodiment of Michael the Archangel, the angel that defeated Lucifer, and Jeanie, looking grim and exhausted. And Richard—*Richard*—there he was, lowering his pistol, his face, his handsome, slender face white with worry. I rushed into his arms and his arms went around me, dispelling the cold, awakening my soul … and I *felt* again.

I felt it all—the pain, the humiliation, and the fear. It crashed into me with the force of a sledgehammer, tearing through my collapsing defenses, leaving me a shuddering, emotional wreck who cried bitter tears into Richard's chest. God, I hated being that kind of woman, but I couldn't help it, couldn't stop the waves … I had to ride it out and I did.

Minutes later I came back up for air to find myself staring into Richard's kind, gray eyes. The feelings I saw there matched my own. His lips fell slowly toward mine and I let them, devouring his mouth, clutching at him in an effort to make him part of me, make us whole. His powerful arms encircled me with a tender strength that communicated his vow to never again let anything hurt me and I believed him.

God, that boy could *kiss!*

Coming up for air, I let my eyes say what I couldn't, not yet.

"I am glad you are well, Rebecca," he whispered, savoring my name like chocolate.

I smiled and kissed his chin dimple. "More than okay."

It wasn't until Kal gently cleared his throat that we came back down to reality. "Mouth, report, please," he said, grinning.

"As you see boss, I got the briefcase and Goebbels. We just have to find out how to get back to our time."

Jeanie *tsked* from where she knelt next to a hogtied and blindfolded Goebbels. "I had to heal him some, guv," she tossed over her shoulder to Kal. "He sustained a lot of damage, he did."

Kal's face twisted. "Too freaking bad. Wake him up, please."

"Right, guv." She passed her hands over the German's body and he began to stir. Without waiting for Goebbels to wake, Kal hoisted him with powerful arms and descended to the lower levels. Once there, he placed Goebbels on the altar, right next to Mengele.

"*Was ist los*?" asked the Nazi when he roused fully.

"English, dipstick," snarled Kal.

"Ah, agent Hakala. I see you have survived after all," Goebbels remarked, as though being tied head-to-toe and blindfolded was an everyday occurrence.

"Don't forget me, asshole." My mouth was dry with fury. Richard placed a comforting hand on my shoulder.

"It is a testament to your era and training that you have survived at all, Ms. McTavish."

Kal motioned me to silence, concerned that I would delay the proceedings with some choice blue words. Showed how well he totally knew me.

"Do you feel the body next to you?" Kal asked.

The German nodded.

"That is your associate, Dr. Mengele."

Goebbels frowned.

"Yes, we have him, and agent Mouth has killed von Ribbentrop, so you don't have any magical backup coming. Your one chance to survive is to tell us how to get back to our time."

Goebbels shook his head. "You have damaged the continuity of the timeline too much already, agent Hakala, so you will not risk anything further."

Kal smile grimly and shot Mengele right between the eyes with that Lahti of his. Goebbels jumped, emitting a small cry of terror before comporting himself.

"I've just killed Dr. Mengele, you Nazi piece of slime, so you know that I don't give a damn about continuity anymore. If I'm stuck in this time, I will use all my extensive knowledge to help the allies win the war. So what do you say? Care to lend us a hand here?"

That shut the Nazi up for a few moments while the situation sank in. After a minute he reluctantly nodded. "If I have your word, and that of Ms. McTavish, that you will let me go after this debacle is over and done with."

"You have it." He glanced at me.

"Yeah," I said, the word nearly sticking in my throat.

The bastard licked his thin lips. "We have reached an accord, agent Hakala."

"Guv, come look at this!" Jeanie's voice rang with excitement as she pulled an old, worn notebook from the aluminum briefcase she'd been rifling through.

Kal walked over while I kept an eye on Goebbels. "What is it?"

She was practically vibrating in place. "It's a drawing ... a spell Shape unlike anything I've seen!"

Behind me, Goebbels drew a sharp breath.

"And?"

"According to the notes, it's a spell that opens up the way to the World Under!"

That brought Kal up short. He stared at the notebook for a few seconds, drawing a deep breath, then returned to the altar. "You weren't lying to Marcin, were you? You have found the spell to the World Under."

Goebbels said nothing.

"Fine. Tell us how activate the portal."

The Reich Minister licked his thin lips. "Do you see the triangular box on the pedestal?"

"Yes."

"In the briefcase, there is a gem, a diamond. Touching the diamond to the box will charge it. When you reach the portal area, you say the activation word and toss the diamond on the ground. That will open the portal."

Kal moved to the triangular box wrapped in gold wire and bent over to inspect it. The breath left his lungs in a rush. "Do you know what this is, this box?" he asked.

Goebbels thin face morphed into a sneer of contempt. "Of course I do, you fool! I liberated it from Finland myself! And the Shape you see on the floor is *my* design."

I, for one, was very curious as to what the hell was going on. "Kal?"

He glanced up. "It's the Sampo, Mouth."

"The what-o, Kal?" Richard asked.

Goebbels answered the Brit. "It's Finland's greatest artifact. The legendary Sampo, the box that provided the Finns with the three things they treasured the most: grain, gold and salt."

The first and last didn't sound so hot, but the gold, well, it's not just diamonds that are a girl's best friend. But … consider that in the early years of Rome, soldiers were given a handful of salt each day, a salt ration, which was then replaced by a sum of money. That money was referred to as salt money … which eventually became to be known as 'salary.' Salt, so common in the twentieth century, was a valuable commodity hundreds of years ago. Coupled with grain, a product not easily grown in a country like Finland—bitterly cold eight months out of the year—you can see why the early Finns referred to the three as treasure.

Kal almost touched the gold wire encasing the triangular Sampo, but restrained himself. Who knew what kind of energies the thing had absorbed. "An artifact, Mouth," he sighed, not taking his eyes off the prize. "What we've been looking for. With this, I can kill Iku-Torso."

"So take it, Kal."

Goebbels barked, "Nein!"

Kal blinked. "What?"

Goebbels thin lips held a triumphant smile. "You want that, yes? Well, if you take the artifact, you will never return home."

Faster than I thought possible, Kal was bent over the Nazi, nose to nose. "Why not?" he growled, voice dangerously soft.

"Easy, mate," Richard soothed. "No need to lose our tempers."

"Listen to the Britisher, agent Hakala," Goebbels said, still smiling, assured of his continued good health. "No need for violence. I am merely saying that the artifact is an integral part of the portal design. It supplies the raw power and is linked to the diamond, which holds the spell Shape. If you disconnect the Sampo from the pattern on the floor, you cannot power the Spell to summon the portal."

Despite Goebbels being a scum-sucking asswipe Nazi tool, I believed him. Watching Kal's shoulders slump, he believed as well. Jeanie raised a hand, maybe to comfort him, but let it drop to her side.

Richard shook his head. "Ah, mate, that's rum luck."

Kal visibly pulled himself together and tossed the Brit a calm smile. "It's okay, Richard. It's not the first time I've been disappointed like this." A long sigh. "Mouth, please grab the briefcase. Richard, you and I will escort Herr Goebbels to where we need to go. I'm assuming outside of the front gates where you landed, right Goebbels?"

The Nazi nodded. "That is correct. It is the thinnest part of this particular reality, the best place to summon a portal."

"Why isn't it guarded? The thinnest point in this reality and there's not even a guard?"

Another sneer from the Nazi. "What need of guards? There's a whole camp so close."

"Your arrogance is why you're tied up, Jerry," Richard observed.

I bit my lip at the look on Kal's face as he stared longingly at the Sampo. He then turned to Richard and said, "Grab the Nazi."

Cold steel pressed against the back of Goebbels' skull, the

barrel of the Lahti a cool deterrent from frisky behavior. The look on Kal's face, had the German seen it, would have had the same effect.

We stopped at the edge of the woods near the road, carefully keeping out of sight of the guards at the front gate. Inside the camp, a house burned merrily, a bucket brigade vainly trying to squelch the shooting flames. Good, they would be far too busy to pay attention to the road.

I nodded to Richard, who tore the blindfold from Goebbels' eyes. Kal leaned forward, putting his lips to the Nazi's ear, a giant compared to the smaller man. "Is this it?" he whispered.

Goebbels took a long look around and nodded.

Jeanie moved close, her form dark in the dim light of the half-moon. Something glittered in her hand. The spell diamond. "What is the activation word?"

The German pressed his thin lips tightly together and shook his head.

Kal ground the Lahti harder into the back of Goebbels' skull. "She asked you a question."

Something like fury coupled with madness flared behind the man's eyes. "I do not speak to *Schwarze*, not to them."

It wasn't hard to figure out what he was saying, but it was Richard who reacted first, leaping forward, a slim blade in his fingers pressed to the skin beneath Goebbels's right eye. "You will answer her question or I will pop your eyes from your skull!" The anger in his voice was frightening. It turned me on a bit.

"You would not dare!" hissed the Nazi.

The thin blade of the stiletto dimpled the skin hard enough for blood to bead. "You bet your life."

The German saw that Richard meant it and nodded in defeat. "It is my oldest daughter's name."

Kal and I stared at each other. *Helga?* he mouthed. I nodded.

Richard made way for Jeanie, who put her lovely nose a bare inch from the German's. "Then what, luv?" she crooned. It was a nasty sound.

Staring everywhere but at her, he answered, "Throw it on the road, where the portal will arrive."

"You die if you lie, Nazi," she growled.

"I do not lie!"

Richard once again blindfolded our prisoner and Kal held out his hand. Jeanie handed him the diamond.

He stared at the glittering gem. "Helga."

It flared like a tiny star and was tossed onto the road. Immediately a shaft of ugly, churning light speared into the sky, the roiling liquid luminescence tearing at the stars.

From the camp we heard a cry.

"C'mon, Mouth!" Kal urged.

A deep breath, then I shook my head. "No, Kal. Not this time."

His eyes shot open wide and looked to Richard, who was gazing at me with naked adoration.

He understood, bless him. With a slight nod, he gave me a peck on the cheek and whispered in my ear. I couldn't help but smile. With that, he ran into the column of light.

"Is it really better for women in the future, luv?" Jeanie asked. "For a black woman?" Her eyes sparkled beautifully in the ugly light.

I nodded, tears blurring my vision.

"Well, then, I shan't waste any time, will I?"

The light took her and a few seconds later the entire column disappeared into the sky.

"What did he say to you?" Richard asked, one hand clamped onto Goebbels' shoulder.

I raised my Webley. "He said, 'Let Goebbels go. Let him go to Hell.'"

Bang.

Totally worth it.

Chapter Twenty-Six

Canton

No Time to Bleed

"**O**h, baby, I have to get you to a hospital!"

I gave Winch a squinty smile and shook my head. "Nah, hon, I ain't bleeding too terrible. No arteries are hit, so patch me up." Dang, I'd been shot before, but never this bad.

It was the wrong thing to say and Winch cussed me up one side and down the other, using words that would've shocked Mouth clean out of her undies. Or maybe not.

"Hellooooo!" floated a voice from the larger cavern.

What the …? Winch lifted her pistol and I flopped over to the cavern wall, my own weapon in my good hand.

The call came again. "Helloooooo!! I am looking for Mr. Hakala, Ms. Pennington and Mr. Alsate! I am a graduate of Mrs. Collingsworth's class. Helloooooo?"

Okay, this crap just kept getting weirder and weirder. From the accent, the hollering idiot was British and that old call sign meant he was MI-7. What the hell?

I nodded to Winch. "Go ahead, darlin', it's not like we don't need the help."

She nodded and hollered back. "Over here!" Then went back to patching up my hurt.

Ever go to a foreign country and suddenly realize you're dressed like a tourist? You see it all the time, Americans in France dressed in Hawaiian shirts and shorts, wearing big floppy hats and carrying cameras. Well, the dude that came into the small cavern really took the whole big, everlovin' enchilada.

Tall fella, maybe an inch over Kal's 6'4", but kinda skinny and dressed in brand new Levis that had creases so sharp you could've shaved with them, held up with a huge cowboy-style shiny chrome belt buckle. You know, the kind that could double as a dinner plate. A white t-shirt, black Stetson parked back on his head and honest-to-God snakeskin cowboy boots. Rattlesnake at that.

Couldn't help it, I started to laugh my ass off, but my wounds cut the humor short.

"Well, well, well, what's all this, then?" mused the stranger, kneeling at my side. He had the kind of upper-crusty English accent that you associate with the snobby Lord-of-the-Manor type.

Winch couldn't stop staring and I felt a pang of jealousy. He wasn't *that* good looking! Although I reckon he set a few ladies back on their heels with all that fine blond hair and perfectly groomed goatee. "I done got shot, mister," I groused.

"Yes, well, I can see that. Mr. Alsate, I presume? And you must be Ms. Pennington." His blue eyes twinkled merrily, and I began to build up a powerful case of hate.

Winch threw him a smile she usually reserved for me, and the hate began to smolder a mite hotter. "Yes, sir, and you are …?"

"Oh, please excuse me. I am K. Harcourt, formerly of Her Majesty's MI-7. It is indeed a pleasure to meet you, Ms. Pennington. A pleasure indeed."

Grrrrrrr ….

"If you two are done playing pussyfoot, I am lying here in a pool of my own blood." I growled. "A hand here patching me up would be nice, Mr. MI-7."

Harcourt blinked rapidly as if startled then smiled. "I see the legendary stoicism of your people has not been overstated, Mr. Alsate. Am I to assume that those men in the other room have been felled by your hand?"

I nodded.

"Excellent! You must tell me all about that after I take care of those nasty wounds of yours." With that, he laid his fingertips on either side of my head and stared into my eyes.

I'd been healed by magic before and it was a hell of a relief as I felt the familiar lassitude, the wash of peace flow through my flesh.

The three bullets worked their way out of my body in three gouts of blood—the pain they caused a good one, one of release.

Within five minutes, my body was whole again. Faint red marks on my skin and pools of blood the only remaining evidence of my injuries.

"Damn," I breathed, standing shakily. "That's a sight better." And what warmed the cockles of my heart even more was the feeling of Winch's arms circling my chest. I hugged her back. Hard.

Harcourt cleared his throat. "Am I to assume that Agent Hakala has not returned from the past?"

Okay, this was turning out to be a surreal experience.

"Yeah," I grumbled. "What's it to you?"

The Brit gave me a toothy smile. "When he arrives, all will be revealed."

Great, an agent with a flair for the dramatic.

"What now, hon?" Winch asked.

"Same as before, babe. We wait for Kal."

Harcourt kept smiling.

Time has a funny way of elongating when you're waiting. To occupy myself, I stacked the bodies of the Germans on top of the crates in the big cavern and began to fiddle around, opening a few. As I expected, they contained weapons. Some Semtex, a few LAW rockets and tons of the most modern assault rifles money could buy.

Sometime later—while Winch was admiring a brand new .50 cal sniper rifle with a computer-assisted scope and Harcourt was playing *Angry Birds* on his iPhone—that weird light flashed from the smaller cave.

Kal!

It was. The big guy stumbled through and fell flat on his face, panting and sweating, only half-conscious, wearing a really cool leather bomber jacket. It took me a moment to realize that there was a lot of dried blood on his clothes. A lot. That boy knew how to find more trouble than a card cheat in a casino. I took my shaking and shivering friend into my arms. His skin was icy to the touch.

Several seconds later, a young black woman emerged from the column dressed in raggedy clothes like a hobo. She took three steps toward Kal and collapsed at his side. Winch started to tend to her.

I gave the young woman a second look. And a third. She was the prettiest little bit of a thing I'd seen in a long time. I mentally added her name to my 'To-Do' list, but when Winch caught me staring and gave me a withering glare, I took it off.

"Canton," Kal gasped, face a river of sweat. "It had to be here …"

"Shhh … easy buddy. Take it easy."

"It had to be here … the portal at Natzweiler can only connect here. They are linked somehow, I could feel it … while traveling back … I could feel the … the *connectedness*."

"Shhh …"

"You don't understand … Only here. Whoever ripped the fabric … of reality apart here, or in Vegas, linked the two eras and the physical points in those eras. Accidentally or on purpose, I don't know, but I could *feel* it … not like last time. I was too scared, then."

Okay, that wasn't creepy at all.

Five minutes later, Kal's shivering and shaking had stopped and he began to breathe normally. Shortly after, he stood. Shortly after *that*, the young lady also stood shakily, holding onto Kal's arm while Winch held her steady.

"Thanks, Canton," he said while taking some deep breaths. "We have to blow the cave. Now."

I nodded. "Thought you might want to, white boy, so I rigged some Semtex charges."

"What are we waiting for? Applause?"

Less than three minutes later we were outside, while in the small cave, ten pounds of plastic explosive was wired to a timer slowly counting down to zero.

The boom was anticlimactic. A shudder, a deep bass rumble and a little dust from the cave entrance and it was over.

"Why blow the cave, white boy?"

Kal squinted into the afternoon sky. "That point, right in there in the smaller cavern, was the only place the Germans could portal to. Put several tons of rock in the way, and they won't be able to make it."

"What happened, man?"

He shook his head. "Some other time, buddy. It's a long story."

I looked around. Harcourt was nowhere to be found, although a big black truck had joined our small group of cars. Must have been his. It stood out like a pit bull amongst poodles. "We appear to have a goodly amount of time, white boy."

He hemmed and he hawed, familiar delaying tactics, but in the end, after checking up on the black girl with the big eyes who introduced herself as Jeanie, he began to spill.

"And, so I walked into the light. It was strange; I was much more sensitized to the traveling and could feel how the two points, the cave and Natzweiler, were connected, like opposite ends of a string. I don't think the Nazis had a choice. I think they *had* to come here."

"That is one of the most amazing stories I've ever heard, Agent Hakala," Harcourt drawled, leaning against his black truck, a Chevy Avalanche. "And it is all true." Again that toothy smile. "Oh, I had my doubts; after all, it is a doozy, that tale. Strange enough to have most people committed to a mental institution."

Kal scowled. "Who is this extra from *Brokeback Mountain*?" he asked me, one hand disappearing behind his back.

Where the hell had he come from? "This is Agent Harcourt, formerly from MI-7," I explained hastily before my friend could draw his Bowie.

Jeanie started, giving Harcourt the old stink-eye. Must have been some bad blood there between British society in 1943 and a talented female magician. A talented *black* female magician. I wondered at the prejudices she'd had to face, the subtle sneers and jeers from bigoted assholes who wouldn't know crap from Shinola.

I've been there.

"What do you want, Mr. Harcourt?" Kal's voice was deceptively calm.

The happy-go-lucky look bled from the Brit's fine features. He tossed a quick nod to Kal, then to Jeanie. "I have a message for you. From the former Colonel of MI-7."

Winch and I exchanged a puzzled look. What would the head of MI-7, the infamous Colonel, want with Kal? I shrugged because as long as we were alive, I was pretty happy.

Harcourt opened the Avalanche and pulled forth a cardboard box the size of a small microwave oven. He placed it on the ground, hauled an envelope out of his back pocket, and handed it to Kal with a winning smile, all seven thousand of his teeth showing.

"Oh, he is *so* gay," Winch whispered.

I whispered back. "Really?"

From behind. "Oh, yeah, really." Jeanie sounded amused. "Kal better watch his behind."

"Too bad, though," Winch murmured. "Totally cute."

Enough of that crap. "Easy girl, you already got yourself a real man."

Throaty laughter from the two of them was my only answer. Meanwhile, Kal had opened the envelope and scanned the contents, a small, sad, wry smile on his face.

"What's going on, white boy?" I called.

"Come here and read this," he said, so I did.

> Dear Kal:
>
> Time is a funny thing. No matter how much you try to mess with things, they still turn out pretty much like they should. I think we could have killed the entire Nazi High Command and nothing would have changed.
>
> It seems that the Mengele you killed was Dieter, Josef's twin brother and a senior member of the VGG. All records of Dieter's existence were labeled TOP SECRET by the Reich due to his involvement in the VGG.

As for von Ribbentrop and Goebbels, Hitler didn't want their deaths to become common knowledge and affect morale so he arranged for doubles to take their places. In fact, the entire High Command had doubles.

Strange what you find out when you become the head of an Ultra Secret organization, huh?

It seems time refuses to be altered.

Guess what? I became a citizen of the United Kingdom and the first female Colonel of MI-7. Totally caused the biggest stir! It made me think that the ban on relationships while serving in the Bureau is total bullpuckey. You should do something about it!

I married Richard. He was such a good man and he eventually became the Colonel for MI-7 after me, a very influential and powerful person, as you well know. He passed in 1989 after years of dedicated service and was considered one of the best heads of MI-7 who ever served.

As for me, I retired from MI-7 and became a mother, a sort of Matriarch of our clan. I had three beautiful children, two boys and a girl: Kal, Vanessa and Richard, Jr, who entered MI-7 after discovering his talent for magic.

Kal, my life has been a good one, a happy one, so don't fret yourself about allowing me to stay behind. It was one of the best decisions you've ever made.

Tell Canton and Winch that I love and miss them. They are in my thoughts always.

As for you, my Ferocious Finn, I hope you find happiness. I've sent along something I hope will help you achieve that goal.

Yours Truly,

Rebecca Fleming
London, 1997

P.S. The messenger is Vanessa's boy. A handsome and wily devil, a man after your own heart.

Strange, the lettered blurred and ran, so I handed it over to Winch. I coughed into my fist to cover the tears. Damn, what the hell was wrong with me? Kal was staring at the ground, shoulders tight as they get when he's trying hard to control his emotions.

Winch sobbed quietly while a single tear trickled down Jeanie's face.

"Grandmother told me stories, wonderful stories about all of you." Harcourt's grin was wry. "Never believed them until I joined MI-7 and accessed the database of known Bureau agents. Guess what name was the first to pop up? Let me tell you, I was more than a little surprised."

"Damn allergies," I muttered gruffly, wiping away tears. To the Brit, "So tell us why you're here."

Harcourt gestured toward the box. "Gran said she had been saving something since the War. Said it belonged to Agent Hakala."

Without another word Kal dug in, ripping tape from cardboard. Everyone gathered round as he exposed a thick layer of packing peanuts. Those lasted about half-a-second before he exposed a triangular box with a strange, multi-colored lid.

Wow.

Everyone gasped, everyone stared

Let me tell you, never a dull moment when Kal's around.

Chapter Twenty-Seven

Kal

What Happens in Vegas…

The Sampo. Holy crap! Mouth must have gone back for it and guarded it all these years, waiting for the right time to send someone to deliver it to me. Her grandson, an MI-7 agent.

Aww … Mouth. Tears turned everything into a blend of everything else. A slender hand landed butterfly-light on my shoulder. I turned, surprised to see Jeanie, the heat of her almost scalding hot against my skin. Her eyes were moister than usual as well.

"Rebecca was the strongest woman I ever knew, guv," she said as the tears started to flow. "She's the reason I came here, she is. I wanted to be like her, to have the chance to be like her, and this new world was my opportunity."

I nodded, irresistibly attracted to the Sampo. "What about your family? They'll miss you something awful."

"There isn't any."

Those three words, stated with such loss and loneliness, speared me straight through the heart faster than you could say *Terms of Endearment*. There was a story there, a bitter and sad one, but I knew she'd tell me in time. If she could.

Still bleeding tears, I reached into the box and retrieved the Sampo. It was lighter than I thought, as if made of balsa. But the wood was like nothing I'd ever seen—dark, almost black, and thickly grained. The box wasn't that deep, but it had an essence of … solidity, as if more real than its surroundings, which paled in its presence. The lid (an equilateral triangle) was a riot of colors, from ROY to G to BIV, all radiating from the center. Despite the reputed power of the artifact, it looked a bit psychedelic '60s. On the bottom edge, in the middle of each side, was a small hole a couple inches across. If I remembered my *Kalevala* correctly, those three holes could disgorge the fabled treasures of the Sampo.

One problem … I had no clue how to access such wealth. Thank God the Nazis never had, either. What they could have done with unlimited wealth scared the pants off me.

"Does this mean what I think it means, white boy?"

I had to smile at the relief in Canton's voice. He hadn't signed up for six months of treasure hunting. When I'd recruited him, I'd believed the Tesla Coil would be enough to take down a legendary monster like Iku-Turso. I was sadly mistaken.

"Yeah, buddy," I rasped, suddenly overwhelmed with the knowledge that my quest for revenge would soon be over, one way or the other. "With this, we'll finally have enough juice to get the job done."

Winch smiled and gave Canton a rib-crushing hug. Jeanie looked confused. I'd have to fill her in later.

"Kal." The droning whine broke cut through the group like a knife.

"Ghost!" I yelled happily, pulling the cell from a pocket. "You made it!"

"Indeed. And I am very happy to be traveling on the Information Superhighway again."

"Did you sense any temporal changes? Anything that doesn't jibe with your records."

Ghost's voice softened. "No. The only interesting thing I noted was a data trail leading to an information packet left for me. From Mouth."

So she had sent him a letter as well. "Seems that Time is good at staying the course."

"Kal, may we speak in private?"

I nodded. "Sure, Ghost." My feet took me a few yards away and I held the cell to my ear. "Okay, Ghost, talk softly. We're good."

"Um … Kal … this is difficult."

What had gotten into his spectral pants? "Spill, Ghost, straight out."

"Are you, well … are you still afraid of me?"

Interesting.

Ghost had always made me leery. I mean, basically he's a Supernatural, and I kill most Supernaturals. The notable exceptions being him and the Brownies I had stashed at Mom and Dad's, but Brownies tended to be timid and shy. Not the kind of Supernaturals who would rip your head off and piss down your spurting neck. Ghost, however, could seriously mess up your day. In the digital era of the twenty-first century, he could make you *wish* you were dead by altering every computerized scrap of data concerning your life. That made me more than a little bit nervous.

So, was I still afraid of him? Oddly enough, I wasn't. I mean, six months ago I would've said 'you bet your ass,' but not anymore.

Something profound had affected this sea change and I had no clue as to what. "No, Ghost," I said softly into the cell, wonder coloring my voice. "Not really."

"Thank you Kal. But … why?"

"Dunno. Maybe …" My voice trailed off.

"What?"

"I think … yeah, that's it."

"*What?*" Ghost's buzzing voice was almost frantic.

"Back there, in 1943, when you told me you were Jewish, that was your most human moment I've witnessed."

"Human?"

"Yeah. You were scared. I'd known you to be concerned, slightly worried, a bit angry, even hesitant, but never, ever scared. And I think that's a quality you still need."

A long pause. Then, "Why?" he asked plaintively.

"Because you are one of the most powerful Supernaturals I've ever met. You have abilities I can't even dream of and you should be a little scared, because that will keep you from doing something stupid. Something that could hurt someone. And if you ever did hurt a Straight, Ghost, then you'd be in deep doo-doo."

The specter's voice emerged from the speaker in a timid whine. "Why, Kal?"

I took a deep breath. "Because I'll come after you personally, Ghost, and I won't be stopped and I won't lose."

A much longer pause. "It is sometimes hard to remember being human. Will you help me remember when it seems I forget?"

Interesting-er.

"Maybe you should put yourself in harm's way more often. You feel most alive when you're close to death." Or however death was defined for a cybernetic spook. Exorcism? A Cohen Brothers' movie?

"I'll take your words under careful consideration, Kal."

"Why do you care so much if I'm afraid of you, Ghost? Doesn't strike me as something you'd worry about. No offence."

For the first time ever, Ghost's atonal drone morphed into something boyish, kinda lost and lonely. "Because you're my friend, Kal."

No, that wasn't a lump in my throat. It was hay fever. Yeah, that's it.

"Well, uh, thanks man. You're my friend, too." And, surprisingly enough, I meant it. Maybe it was a sign that I was growing up, evolving.

Nah.

Enough of the touchy-feely. Don't get me wrong, I'm as sensitive as the next guy, but there were places to go, monsters to kill. "Anything else?"

"No, not yet, Kal."

"Good. Thanks man, keep me updated." I hung up and turned to Harcourt. "Mind giving us a ride?"

He grinned.

Twenty miles outside of Vegas, Harcourt was driving his ridiculously huge truck and whistling an annoyingly merry tune. I rode shotgun while Canton was sandwiched in the back between the two ladies. Lucky bastard had a huge grin on his ruddy face.

Bzzzzzzz! I jumped. It was my cell ... Ghost calling. "Go ahead," I said.

"I have the tickets to Duluth you wanted, Kal."

"But?"

"What do you mean?"

"There's always a 'but,' Ghost. My life is never uncomplicated."

"There might be trouble."

Riiiiight. Water 'might' be wet. "Okay, what?"

"I think there may be more Nazis in Vegas, as many as three to five."

Interesting. "Has the Bureau shut down the Desert Pride?"

"Two teams landed along with the Director twenty minutes ago. It is being shut down as we speak."

BB was in town? Along with most of what remained of the Bureau after the attack six months ago? Glad to see he was taking the matter seriously. "Notify them, then. Not my problem. Let the Bureau have some fun as Nazi hunters."

"Normally I would, I will, but there is something else that you must know." His voice blared from the cell even though I hadn't hit the SPEAKER button. "Do you still have the iPad?"

"Got it!" Winch handed me the tablet.

"Take a look." Something in Ghost's tone sent a shiver creepy-crawling up and down my spine.

The tablet flickered and four photos appeared, one at each corner of the screen. What I saw made bile burn the back of my throat. Four people—a kid and three adults—lying in an alley, all gutted like carp with their entrails flung everywhere, pain and dismay writ large on their faces. But it wasn't the grisly scene of a quadruple murder that peed in my Wheaties … it was the pattern rendered in gold leaf pounded into the brick wall of the alley.

A spell Shape. One very familiar to me.

Crap. Necromancy.

"Jeanie, take a look at this, tell me what you see." Her beautiful brown eyes scanned the images on the tablet and immediately focused on the Shape. "Oh, bloody hell," she whispered.

"How fresh is this, Ghost?" I asked, biting a nail.

"The crime scene photographer took the photos less than five minutes ago. Fortunately, I was trolling the system and intercepted these when he downloaded them into the LVPD's mainframe."

Canton had had enough of being in the dark. "Kal," he said in a warning tone.

"Buddy, I've seen this Shape before. Open the briefcase." Both the Sampo and the briefcase were in the back with them. "Then check out the old fashioned notebook."

There were a couple of clicks and the shuffling of papers. Finally, "Is this what ... you mean ...?" His voice trailed off in dismay.

"Yeah, that's the spell shape to the World Under, but see? Tell me what the difference is between the one in the alley and the one drawn in that notebook."

No flies on him; he got it in less than three seconds. "It's reversed."

"Exactly," Jeanie blurted before I could respond. "Whoever did this wasn't trying to *go* to the World Under, they were trying to summon something *from* it." Her eyes lingered on the tablet. "And with four sacrifices ... it will be something big."

"Damn," Winch muttered. "I'll bet you anything that it's more Nazi assholes. I figure they managed to escape the Desert Pride while the Bureau was shutting it down. They're planning on siccing whatever monster they summoned on the Bureau teams."

I scrubbed my face with my palms; idly realizing I needed a shave something awful. "It gets worse."

Jeanie chimed in. "How can it get worse, guv?"

"I'm reasonably certain that the Germans who escaped were a full VGG team."

Silence in the cab. Even Harcourt lost his aplomb, biting his lower lip nervously.

Canton snarled. Like every Bureau member, he'd been grilled on the evils practiced during WWII to better ensure they never occurred again. "So what do we do, white boy?" Dark menace threaded his voice. He sounded *pissed*.

"*Do?* We have Ghost warn the Bureau and we get the hell to the airport and out of Vegas pronto, big guy."

"We need to help them, Kal," Winch's tone was one of stubborn finality that only strong-willed women could pull off. I should know … I'd heard my mom use it hundreds of times.

Canton nodded his agreement, followed by Jeanie. Unlike the rest of us, the VGG was a recent and very unpleasant memory for her. I had no doubt she wanted payback for fallen comrades.

I stared at my three friends, who sat so resolute, stony-faced, in the back seat and knew, *knew*, they would cave if I vetoed the notion. They would do what I asked, but they would never forgive me. Hell, I wouldn't forgive myself.

"You realize that if BB catches me, I'll haunt you guys forever." Despite the gruff words, my face was stretched tight with a bestial smile.

Canton let out a whoop that could curl your hair and Winch asked if we could stop at a gun store. Jeanie threw me a brilliant smile that did funny, squishy things to my insides and trapped me with her huge eyes.

What the hell was wrong with me?

Chapter Twenty-Eight

Kal

... Dies in Vegas

"See anything?" Canton sounded as bored as I felt.

"Not since the last time you asked," I replied over the walkie, staring through a cheap set of Wal-Mart binoculars. The sun was setting, throwing amazing shades of color across the desert sky above Vegas and cheesy lights had begun to pop on, disguising the town in a haze of neon.

We'd stopped at Wal-Mart on the way to the Desert Pride for a quick supply run, the clothes on our backs being ragged and bloodstained. Even though time was of the essence, nothing screams 'arrest me!' like bloody and torn outerwear. Several hundred dollars later, we were dressed to kill in blue jeans, matching polo shirts, light nylon windbreakers and Nike knock-offs. Jeanie turned several heads when she exited the dressing room, including mine. Her Wranglers knew how to hug her slender curves in such a way that I had to stomp on the urge to howl at the moon.

Winch didn't look bad, either, being a fine figure of a woman but Jeanie ... well ... *damn!*

After that it was just a matter of staking out the casino. Now, movies and television would have you believe that stakeouts are cool bonding moments for the main characters. In reality, you're bored stiff. Bored senseless, bored silly and bored stupid. Get the picture? That's what it was like. Jeanie at the Starbucks across the street (oh, how I missed my cappuccino maker!), Canton eating his fifth order of McNuggets. Winch, after an hour of mind-numbing surveillance from a parked car in the casino lot, went AWOL after informing me she was off on another supply run. She'd told Canton to call if the excitement ever arrived.

Speaking of which, it was time for her to check in. "Winch, you back yet?" The walkie was the best I could buy at Wal-Mart, which meant it left a lot to be desired. Fortunately, the bus stop I was loitering at was deserted, so I didn't attract too much attention talking into my hand.

The walkie treated me to a *crackle crackle fizz pop*, then, "Yeah, Kal, hold onto your undies. I'm back."

Finally! "Where you at?"

Canton: "What took you so long, babe?"

Again with the crackly static. "I went shopping, hon. A girl has *got* to be prepared for some fun. I'm on the roof of the restaurant next door to the casino. I can see the whole damn lot from here."

Oh boy, only one reason she'd be on a roof. "You bought a rifle! How the heck did you manage to … skip that, I don't want to know."

Her voice was smug. "You're goddamn right you don't want to know."

"Babe, did you get me anything?" Even over the crappy walkies, Canton managed to sound lascivious.

"Hon, what I got for you is—"

"Please," I barked. "Don't finish that sentence!"

Laugher from all three of my companions assaulted my ears. Wonderful.

It went on like that for the next couple of hours, the city slowly becoming brighter as the sky became darker, the light from countless neon bulbs obscuring the stars.

"Guv!" Jeanie screamed into her walkie. "Someone cast a spell, a damn big one by the feel!"

"Heads up, people!" I blurted, startling an old lady dozing next to me on the bench. "If Jeanie felt it, so did our guys inside, which means the VGG don't care. Stay sharp, stay frosty."

Canon's crackly voice held awe and terror in equal measure. "White boy, there ain't no frosty when dealing with *this*. South lot, a hundred feet from the front doors … oh hell!" That last was punctuated by a fireball that blossomed thirty feet into the air in the middle of the parking lot.

"Canton! What is it?" My feet were already carrying me across the street, straight for the fading fire. Under the howling roar of flames there was a sound, a deep bass grumble that flailed against my eardrums.

"Holy crap and fried eggs, Kal, I don't freaking believe it!" Winch sounded scared.

"Canton!" I screamed, leaping over the hood of a stalled Hyundai while drawing the Lahti from beneath my windbreaker.

My friend's yell came from in front of me and from the walkie. "Chimera!" It was the first time I'd heard true panic in his voice.

Oh crap.

Up ahead, one of the light poles in the casino lot trembled violently then fell with a squeal of tortured metal. I leapt the low stucco wall that surrounded the lot and practically flew through the thick green shrubs on the other side that had partially obscured my vision, landing with a tuck and roll onto hot asphalt.

And there—big as a bull elephant, looming over a mass of twisted metal that used to be Volvos and Jags—was the Chimera.

Imagine if you will a lion … male, full mane and all. Now give that sucker the total pro-wrestler steroid treatment, a tail that was actually a hissing and spitting king cobra and a massively horned goat's head on a long sinewy neck attached to the middle of the lion's back.

Chimera. Got it?

Well, it got worse. Fire dripped from the lion's jaws as if its saliva was made of gasoline. With every third step that enormous mouth would open and belch forth a ten foot column of flame. Groovy, huh?

I hardly noticed as Canton jogged up to me, eyes wide in amazement. "How do we kill a freaking Chimera, white boy?"

Another gout of fire from the lion's mouth as it moved in on the casino. The valets had long since vanished. Smart valets, good survival skills. Apparently whatever customers had been lingering outside adopted the same set of skills and disappeared like a politician's promise.

I shook my head and said softly as the beast torched a BMW with a single belch, "Don't know. Never faced one before." Taking a deep breath, I brought the walkie to my mouth. "Jeanie, prepare to back me up with some magic, and Winch … try to shoot its eyes out. All of them."

At that moment, when the monster was fifty feet from the casino entrance, the glass doors flew open and disgorged five people, in familiar Bureau gear.

The three men and two women, wearing bulky, black Faraday coats (used to absorb spell energy), looked for all the world like *Matrix* stunt doubles. The men were in the forefront firing, ironically, German MP-5 SMGs, bullet casings flying. The Chimera reared, its feline mouth barfing a stream of fire.

From my vantage point I saw one of the goat's eyes explode in a bloody spray of eyeball juice. *Way to go, Winch!* I exulted, sure that between the Bureau agents and Winch's aim, the monster from some Greek portion of the World Under was going to die.

You'd figure I'd know better.

While the monster was distracted and the team poured enough hot lead into its body to turn it into a colander, four men appeared from where they were hidden between cars at the far edges of the parking lot.

I barely had time to mouth a warning before they opened fire with high-powered, high-caliber rifles. One thing that the Bureau had never been able to do was make the human skull bulletproof. Four heads popped like water balloons dropped on concrete, sending shards of bone and jelly-like bits of brain flying here and there, a sickening tribute to Jackson Pollock.

VGG! The lizard part of my hindbrain figured it out before my conscious mind had a chance to deal with the horrible situation, pumping my legs and sending me pell-mell toward the nearest Nazi. The old surge of rage had me in its grip, that sweet poison, and the sliver of rationality that drove me reckoned that I was really starting to rely far too much on its efficacy. It seemed that for the last ten years it had slowly been taking me over.

Not that I really cared much.

I was ten feet from the nearest VGG member when he noticed me, eyes shining very white in the parking lot lights. A slender man in a nondescript gray suit and blond hair razored close to the skull. Two rounds from the Lahti took him in the side, above the kidneys, but he was quick, managing to swing his rifle (a Barrett M107-K1 .50 cal, average cost about ten grand; talk about well-funded Nazis!) my way and blast off a shot. I could feel the heat of the large caliber bullet singe my nylon windbreaker as it passed under my armpit.

He didn't drop, that blond Aryan poster boy. Body armor. Didn't matter, I was past the barrel of his weapon, up close and personal, so I decided to get *real* personal. His teeth scattered like bloody Chiclets as I rammed the Lahti in his mouth and pulled the trigger twice. The rounds didn't pop his head like his had the Bureau agents, but they didn't do any favors to the back of his skull as his brains evacuated in a hurry.

One ...

I looked over to the left and saw Canton, Bowie in hand, engaged in a ballet dance of death with the second VGG member, a man much bigger than he was but nowhere near as graceful. The man's K-bar flickered in the harsh light, darting here and there as it wove a web of death. That razor-sharp blade couldn't touch the whip-like Apache.

I tore my eyes from the scene and picked up the dead man's .50 cal, the rage slowly bleeding from my system as I fitted my eye to the scope.

There! Diagonally across the lot from me, a VGG man was sighing through the scope of his .50 cal at the front doors, firing methodically. I had no doubt he was killing other Bureau members attempting a rescue.

One shot, one kill ... his head did the water balloon thing and I moved on to the next target.

Two ...

The barrel of my rifle swung around, searching for the last man and I found him a split second after he found me. There, large in the sights, was another .50 cal pointed at my skull, the sniper half-shielded by a maroon Camry. I was dead.

A sharp, hard *crack* and his brains decorated the Toyota in Hint-of-Pink.

"Thank you, Winch," I whispered shakily into the walkie, hands trembling.

"What I'm here for, boss." She sounded crisp, businesslike.

"Let's kill that Supernatural," I snarled, focusing my fear from my near-death on the Chimera. Gunfire from within the Casino slowed the monster but didn't stop it. Soon it would be inside and the real carnage would begin.

Not on my watch.

"The eyes are its only vulnerable spots, Kal," Winch said through the crackle of the walkie. "I took one out on the goat head, but I don't have a clear shot at the others. Damn thing can feel the bullets, but its skin is like Kevlar."

"You should read more Greek mythology," I shot back. "Cover me."

Jesse Owens would've proud of my sprint across the lot, weaving though high-end cars. I passed the Chimera, keeping a goodly distance away, and had stopped to the right of the front doors when I noticed the fifth member of the ambushed Bureau team.

Oh, God … Pat.

The former Receptionist of my Bureau team sat with her back against a large concrete planter housing a large palm tree, keeping it between her and the approaching monster. She was clutching her side and gasping as blood oozed between her fingertips. A .50 cal must have grazed her because if it had hit her square, she'd be dead, a softball-sized hole blown clean through her.

What the hell was she doing here? Why was she dressed as an agent? Then it hit me … with the decimation of the Bureau six months ago, she must have volunteered for field duty. Hell, she'd received the same training as any agent, so she was more than qualified for the job.

I swallowed past the enormous lump in my throat and knelt next to her, her strong face pale. "Pat." My voice was hoarse.

Her eyelids cracked slightly then flew open. "Kal!"

"Shhh …" I urged. "Not now. I'll tell you everything when I can." Aw, why did it have to be Pat? She was the closest thing to a sister I'd had since … my mind wandered away from the thought.

Forcing her fingers from the wound, she showed me a ragged tear of flesh that bled freely but didn't spurt. Good, with proper attention she would be okay.

"Kal," she whispered, eyes glittering like gems. "Are you okay?"

Damn, damn, damn … there she sat, blood pooling on the asphalt, side torn up a treat and she was worried about *me*. "Don't you fret none, Pat. You're going to be okay."

"Tell that to the Chimera. I would have had him if I hadn't been shot." She pointed to a bronze colored tube lying in front of the shattered glass doors. It took me a moment to recognize what I was seeing. A little over two feet long, it radiated lethal menace like the edge of a sword. Bullets from the inside flew a few feet above the weapon.

"Why did you bring a friggin' LAW rocket to Vegas?" I exclaimed.

Her smile soon turned into a grimace. "BB wanted … to be prepared … for anything."

I nodded. Looked like BB had subscribed to my basic philosophy when dealing with Supernaturals: More is More. Anyone who ever said 'Less is More' never had a flock of harpies gunning for their giblets.

"Hold on," I grunted and dove for the rocket, bullets whistling overhead from inside. My left hand snagged the anti-tank weapon while I pushed against the asphalt with the other, hastening my roll. Five feet later I was safe, off to the left of the doorway behind another concrete planter, the twin to Pat's.

The hard crack of gunshots from the inside lessened somewhat, proof that those agents inside were running low on ammo. As if to punctuate that fact, the Chimera's next fire puke came perilously close to ruining my hairdo.

I took a deep breath and unhooked the catch to the LAW, extending the tube eight inches. Two deep breaths later, I leaned out from behind the planter, praying that some bonehead didn't shoot my damn fool head off, and placed my eye to the weapon's sights.

Crap … the Chimera was perhaps twenty feet away, mouth drooling fire and eyes glaring with madness. Although, with all the rounds it had taken, it did look a bit ragged around the edges. Those insane eyes fixed on my position and its jaws parted in a massive roar, revealing the white-hot furnace of its throat.

The Greek hero Bellerophon, with the help of the winged horse Pegasus, had defeated a Chimera millennia ago. His secret for killing the monster was a spear with a lump of lead at the end. When he'd thrust the spear into the creature's mouth, the lead melted and ran down its throat, burning a hole in the monster's stomach. Final score: Bellerophon : 1, Monster: 0.

Not bad for a Bronze Age bad ass, but he didn't have a LAW rocket. Hitting a roughly one square foot target with an anti-tank weapon is iffy at the best of times; however, from twenty feet away, I could hardly miss the five-ton beastie's gaping maw. I pushed the firing stud.

From behind, I heard swearing as the blast exhaust shot out the back of the tube, most probably ruining someone's fashion statement. On the front end, the rocket leapt forward, spitting sparks as it flew the twenty feet to its target, disappearing down the Chimera's fiery throat.

For the briefest of moments, right before the rocket detonated, the Chimera's lion face wore what I could've sworn was a startled expression. I threw my arms over my face as the pressure wave hit, bouncing me off the building and spinning me around, my ears screaming in pain right before God flipped a switch and turned the world off.

A hand—solid, wide and calloused— slapped my face. Hard. What the hell? The sharp pain jolted me, snapping my eyes open and bringing with it a new bushel of agony from what seemed to be every inch of my body. A ruddy, fuzzy ball loomed over me, lit by freakish Halloween lights. Slowly the ball came into focus, growing eyes, nose, and a mouth. Canton … who was mouthing things I couldn't hear. It struck me as funny that he would want me to read his lips.

Interesting.

Wait a minute. He wasn't mouthing, he was talking. Oh, crap … I was deaf. Pointing to my ear, I shook my head, which brought a whole new level of pain into my world as my head threatened to cut the bolts to my neck and roll free. My friend frowned and spoke with exaggerated care, "Are you okay?" I read.

Okay? I was a damn sight from okay. In fact, I was on the other side of the planet from okay. Put okay on the Moon and me on Earth; that's where okay was in relation. I nodded anyway and Canton hauled me to my feet. That brought with it another mess of pain, but I won't go into that. Suffice to say that I shouldn't have had that Big Mac earlier. And fries. And hot fudge sundae … with a cherry on top.

Head wobbly and mouth coated with that fresh-puke smell, I waved Canton off, stumbling over to where Pat sat, staring at me in amazement. To my right lay the Chimera, the lion head completely blown apart and resembling a gory flower of red and pink, the goat head torn from its sinuous neck and the cobra tail thrashing weakly. Kal: 1, Monster: 0.

"I can't hear you, Pat," I said as I knelt at her side. "Can you hear me?"

She nodded. I guess the concrete planter had preserved her auditory canals.

"Good! Give me until the morning before you tell BB, all right?"

She looked skeptical.

"Please, Pat, I know you have to report in, I know that, but just give me a little bit of a head start and I'll do whatever you ask."

A long, long pause and then she nodded, clearly unhappy.

"You're the best, Pat. I'll make it up to you!"

Her lips formed two words. "You better." Then formed a third. "Dickhead."

I nodded and staggered off with Canton's help. Fortunately, he knew what to do and managed to rendezvous with Harcourt and the rest of the gang. The MI-7 agent had stayed conspicuously absent; his role in events would complicate relations between the two agencies if he was seen actively co-operating in a non-sanctioned operation with a rogue agent. However, he did volunteer to be our wheel man, saying, "I could always tell the authorities you carjacked me."

Besides, I needed him to guard the Sampo.

Jeanie opened the door to the Avalanche from the inside, and I abruptly came face to face with an unfamiliar someone as Canton shoved himself in behind me. Short, dark-haired, round-faced, the man was dressed to the nines in a charcoal suit that had seen better days, being torn all to shreds and covered in dirt and blood. What made the scene doubly interesting was the rope that tied him head to toe and the blindfold across the eyes. At that moment, he was giving a magnificent performance of a 'possum.

"Meet our VGG magician, Kal," Jeanie said, voice a ragged gasp.

Hey, I'd heard that! I could hear ... not *well*, but I could hear! Halle-freaking-lujah.

My high at the return of my hearing faded as I took in Jeanie's state, rendered harsh in the stark light of the cabin's overhead bulb. Her larger than life eyes were red, and I don't mean bloodshot; they were the kind of red that is caused by ruptured capillaries bleeding into the whites. It gave her a demonic cast. Dried blood crusted her nose and ears, and her skin was waxy and gray.

"What happened, Jeanie?" I gasped, horrified.

Winch snorted. "She caught the enemy magician, and they had the magical equivalent of a donnybrook." Her voice carried a wealth of admiration.

Jeanie nodded, too exhausted to reply.

"She was amazing, Kal," Winch continued. "That VGG prick was going to ambush Canton, but she stopped him. They stared at each other for about a minute before he collapsed in a heap. Then she tied him up with rope from the truck and was none too gentle with him, either."

"Granny said to always carry some extra rope," Harcourt said happily. "You never know when you'll need it."

Thanks, Mouth, I'm gonna miss you.

I've seen magical duels before and they didn't involve fireballs, swarms of locusts, or dancing mops and buckets. No, the magicians cast their spells silently, forcing the spell Shapes at their enemies. The first to flinch always lost. Always. For Jeanie to take out a VGG magician all by her lonesome meant she packed one hell of a magical punch.

I patted the exhausted magician on the shoulder. "Good job, kiddo."

She smiled weakly, said, "Thank you, guv," and passed out.

"Harcourt?"

"Yes, agent Hakala?"

"Go south, fast as you can. I want this city in the rearview ASAP."

"Right you are, guv." The Avalanche's mighty motor roared in response.

"Canton?"

"Yeah, Kal?"

"Call my folks—my ears are ringing too loud—and tell them I have a plan ..." I began, relieved when I noticed we had cleared the city limits.

Chapter Twenty-Nine

Kal

All's Well that Ends

I used to love the smell of the ocean, the salty tang and the slight vegetative reek of algae. It smelled … comfortable. That is, until I encountered Iku-Turso, the sea monster from the Finnish epic, *The Kalevala*.

That creature had killed my sister, crushing her with one massive tentacle/arm. The damn thing was so alien that my fifteen-year-old brain could hardly cope with what my eyes had beheld. My mind tried to give it a shape, something that would fit some frame of reference, but the only images I could grasp were chaotic.

For one split second, however, I did see the monster for what it truly was, its true shape, and the sight shattered my mind. How I remained relatively sane, I didn't know. It was as big a mystery as how the witch who had summoned it was able to do so.

But I was about to try the same thing.

Three days had passed since we said goodbye to Sin City, and good riddance. Time was running short. Ghost was doing what he could to keep the Bureau from sniffing us out. That couldn't last.

Harcourt had refused to let anyone take a shift at the wheel, driving the entire 340 miles by himself. Before we arrived, however, we had to take care of some business.

While we skirted the edge of the Mojave National Preserve (a dry collection of sand dunes, cinder cones, mesas, ravines and Joshua tree forests all crammed into 1.6 million acres) on Highway 15, I decided it was high time to interrogate our prisoner.

"Wakey, wakey," I crooned, thumping a knuckle against the magician's temple while Canton looked on with interest. Jeanie stared so hard at the Nazi, it was like she was trying to microwave him with her eyeballs.

The bound man gave a sort of snort and shook his blindfolded head vehemently.

"Listen, big boy, I know you understand English, or you wouldn't be here. I suggest you be a little more vocal, or I'm going to let my gal here convince you. She won't be a sweetheart, like me."

Apparently he thought so, too. "*Ja.* I understand." His voice was surprisingly deep and accentless.

"Good, bunky, that's what I like to hear. We can all be civilized. My name is Kal. What's yours?"

"Werner Gundolf."

"Gosh, I just love this spirit of co-operation. What do you think, Canton?"

"Warms the cockles of my heart, white boy. Practically on fire, they are."

A familiar throb of anger began behind my eyes, and it was all I could to do to push it aside. I'd seen so much of what these kind of men could do, who they hurt, that calmly talking to one of their freaking Necromancers was almost more than I could bear.

"Rank please, Werner."

"Gruppenführer Zauberer."

Hmm … Group Leader, a senior Wizard/officer. Looked like we'd hit pay dirt. "Now the big question: What the hell were you trying to pull back at the casino?"

Werner licked his lips nervously. During his entire career with the VGG, he'd clearly never been the nervous one, the one pissing down his leg in fear. No, he was the kind who always put the fear in other people and enjoyed it. The rat bastard. I took another calming breath and waited for his reply.

And waited. Damn, he was going to make this difficult. "Werner," I said reprovingly. "You have to talk. I'd hate for us to be cross. You don't want me to be cross, do you?"

He shook his head, droplets of sweat flying.

"So talk."

"No. You will kill me."

"Werner, I don't want to kill you." A lie. "I want us all to get along." A bigger lie. "If you talk, I will stop the car and let you go." The biggest lie. The rest of the team looked at me incredulously and I shook my head.

"You promise?" Hope laced the Nazi's voice.

"I pinky swear, Werner. Now talk."

He sighed. "We were on assignment, gathering weapons and other materiel for the Reich Minister, when we returned to the casino and found the American Bureau shutting it down."

"And?"

"And I had left a laptop in my room that contained … sensitive data." Werner's voice faded to nothing.

What was he afraid of? "Go on … what kind of data?"

"Financial data!" he blurted. "All of our bank accounts, passwords, dollar amounts … everything!"

Oh, this was rich! "When you say 'our bank accounts,' you mean …?"

"The accounts that belong to my team," he said disconsolately.

Canton guffawed. "Ah, white boy, it seems this dude was rippin' off old Goebbels, settin' himself and his boys up all proper with stolen funds."

I stared hard at the little magician. It wasn't fear of reprisal that had him acting all cagey, it was the fear of losing his embezzled money! God, what a tool.

"That's it, Werner?"

"Yes."

Something about that 'yes' struck me as false. I'd been around a lot of liars (we in the Bureau are champion fibbers) and my Crap-o-Meter was jangling in my head like a Geiger counter. "Werner, don't lie to me."

No reply.

Sigh. Why do people always want to do things the hard way? I grabbed the lapels of his dirty suit and, with Jeanie's help, flipped him like an omelet. With his back to me, I reached for his bound hands and snagged a pinky, breaking it with a savage jerk. I did say 'pinky swear,' didn't I?

Nothing is more disconcerting than a broken bone. Soft tissue damage doesn't quite strike the same visceral punch as a broken bone, doesn't *scream* permanent injury and disfigurement.

I'll say this for the Nazi bastard; he held his own like a man, weathering the pain like a pro, emitting only the faintest of whines. Good for him, because the pain was about to become much, much worse.

The broken little piggy who cried 'wee wee wee all the way home' flopped and dangled, already swelling. I grabbed hold.

"Talk, Werner."

"I have nothing to tell you, I swear it!" he gasped, skin gray with shock.

Damn, I *hate* being the bad guy, but that didn't stop me from ripping his finger clean off. It sounded like paper tearing, accompanied by a faint *pop*.

Yeah, Werner finally screamed. And bled like a stuck pig.

On and on the scream went, rising and falling. First he'd yell his head off, high-pitched, then it would wind down and he'd draw a deep breath to repeat the whole process again. I let this go on for about two minutes before the noise really started to bug me. In the front seat, Winch's mouth was set in a grim line. This was part of the business we all hated.

"Jeanie, would you mind?" I asked, pointing at the gushing stub after throwing the bloody digit out the window of the truck. Some lucky varmint would eat well tonight.

The look on her face told me she minded a whole lot, but she did as asked, laying a hand on the magician. Immediately, he quieted. After a few moments the gush became a trickle, then an ooze, before stopping completely. When she was done, the stub was crusted over with a large scab that looked days old. It took her all of twenty seconds.

Damn, she was good.

A deep breath. "Werner, do you want to talk now?"

"*Ja, ja,*" he wept. "One of the reasons we wanted to go inside was the spell books the Reich Minister had left behind. A treasure trove of Shapes." He shuddered, sniveling and snotting. "Including the one that would allow us to travel home."

So the whole business about the secret bank accounts was a load of crap. Damn, he was a better liar than I'd given him credit for. Well, the Bureau would find everything during their sweep of the casino.

"So that's it, Werner?"

"*Ja, ja,*" he said, all sniveling and sad. He would've been sadder if I told him his exit point had been blown to hell.

"Sorry to tell you this, big boy, but Herr Goebbels didn't leave anything behind. He kept his notebook of spell Shapes with him. You went back and killed those people for *nothing.*"

I looked outside at the landscape rushing past. Dark as the Nazi's soul, but with a bazillion stars decorating the sky, a perfect place to drop off our German. "Pull over, Harcourt."

The Brit obliged, the Avalanche's big tires crunching on gravel as they bit into the shoulder of the road.

"Jeanie, you do the honors."

She smiled. It wasn't nice.

"You are letting me go?" the Nazi asked.

"In a manner of speaking," I replied, more soul-weary than I had been in a long, long time.

He caught the drift. "You said I would be let go! You said you and yours here would not hurt me!"

I steeled myself against the terror in his voice. "I lied. I've been doing a lot of that to Nazis these days. Go Jeanie."

She had Werner out the door and face down on the ground in a blink of an eye. A second later, the *crack* of a .45 silenced his sobs. We continued on our way to San Diego.

You think I was harsh? That torturing and lying to the evil sonofabitch went too far, that it upset some delicate moral code? Well, remember the photos of those poor bastards sacrificed in a Las Vegas alleyway, their guts festooned all over the place. Remember that they had been used in a dark Necromantic rite to summon a Chimera, the purpose of which was to kill members of my beloved Bureau.

One of the sacrificial victims had been just a kid, a girl … perhaps eight years old. She had known she would die … the last feelings she ever had in her short, precious life were terror and pain before that prick Werner gutted her.

I went easy on him.

"Where are you, Kalevi?"

My mom's voice roused me from my reverie as I stared out over the dark Pacific.

"Just thinking, Mom."

To me, Terhi Hakala looked the same as always. Slightly gray now, thin streaks marring her night-black hair, but that lean face still carried a ton of character and determination. Not to mention a whole boatload of stubborn. A volatile mix in a tiny package.

My father, Pekka Hakala, laid his heavy hands on her small shoulders. A hair shorter than myself, Dad was retired military, having served in the Marines with distinction. Even in his mid-fifties he kept himself fit with a strict regimen of diet and exercise that gave him the body of an athlete half his age, although the age lines in his face were becoming more pronounced.

After Canton had phoned them from the road, Mom and Dad had hopped into their Rubicon and traveled the entire two thousand twelve mile journey in under a day and a half, not stopping save for gas.

Did I mention how stubborn Finns are?

My parents brought with them a cylinder, roughly two-and-a-half feet long and encased in platinum wire studded with half-carat diamonds resting on a round, wooden base. On top of the cylinder was a small block of silver, two inches thick and six tall. Resting on that block was a ruby wrapped in silver wire that glowed red with its own internal fire. Trailing from the base were two platinum wires that ran eighteen inches to a pair of gold wires that led to, and wrapped, the triangular form of the Sampo.

It was the Holy Grail of magicians around the world, the thing that so many had tried—and failed—to produce. It had taken a brilliant, but psychotic, serial killer to figure it out. The magical equivalent of a Tesla coil, it was a device to amplify magical energy.

This device, along with the Sampo to fuel its power, was my best hope at defeating the god-like monster that had killed my sister.

Good news for the home team.

So where do you battle a legendary sea creature? Where is it almost deserted at midnight so you can have the privacy necessary to do some serious killing?

In San Diego, at the Maritime Museum. Situated on North Harbor Drive, it's positioned just across the San Diego Bay from the Silver Strand, the isthmus that is home to the small city of Coronado and the Naval Amphibious Base Coronado. The base houses almost five thousand personnel, including Commander, Naval Surface Force Pacific (COMNAVSURFPAC), Commander Naval Special Warfare (SPECWAR) Command and the Commander Expeditionary Warfare Training Group (EWTG) Pacific.

Enough of the acronyms ... it's where I was trained as a Navy SEAL. The irony was thick enough to sleep on.

We stood on the deck of one of the museum's prize possessions, a Soviet-era diesel submarine, the B-39. At three hundred feet in length and displacing more than two thousand tons, it was among the largest conventionally powered submarines ever built. Behind the sub, closer to land, was a full-sized replica of Juan Rodriguez Cabrillo's ship, the San Salvador. Perpendicular to that, moored lengthwise next to the museum, was the world's oldest active sailing ship, the Star of India.

If we had any chance of summoning Iku-Turso, it would be here, among those naval legends. It was the best I could come up with without actually traveling to the monster's home waters in the Gulf of Bothnia.

"Dad, please leave now," I ordered while still looking out onto the water.

"You sure, son? I can stay. Offer moral support."

I knew he'd stand by me even if the forces of Hell were loosed upon us, but on the sub he was a liability. He could get killed.

Not on my watch. I shook my head.

He moved all of ten feet away, face closing like a portal. I knew that look and sighed. Where Mom traveled, so would Dad. Stubborn ass Finns.

Hmph … who was I to talk?

I unholstered my cell. "Ghost, sitrep, please."

"Kal, every police officer on duty are answering calls all across the city." If a droning buzz of a voice could sound smug, then his did. "So you should be good. Also, the security guards are currently investigating a disturbance on the other side of the museum complex, thanks to Harcourt and me. You have a go."

Right, I had a go.

"Last shot, Canton. Get out while you can."

"Not on your life, white boy," my friend declared from behind me. "This is what I live for."

Damn.

"Winch?"

The sniper's steady contralto expressed no reservations. "Where you go, boss, I go."

Double damn. How the hell did I get such good friends? Before I could say anything else, Jeanie's hand slipped into mine, grasping tightly. I guess she made herself clear.

Six people on a quixotic quest that would most likely get them killed. It could be worse—as Marty Feldman said in *Young Frankenstein*—it could be raining.

"Go, Mom."

She nodded and placed a hand on the glowing ruby, the light rendering her flesh almost transparent. Her expression grew grim, a mask of pessimism.

"Iku-Turso, I call you," she began in Finnish, her voice low and hard. "By the Sampo in my possession, I call you. By my hate I summon you, by my daughter's blood that runs in my veins, I summon you." Her voice began to rise, a diamond edge of fury lining every word. Mom had discovered her talent for magic very late, but she hadn't been shirking her lessons. I could almost feel the magic pour off of her in waves as she channeled the power running from Sampo to coil.

"I call you by your names: One Who Lives on the Edge, The Bearded One, The Ox of Death, The Thousand-Headed One, The Thousand-Horned One, The Father of Diseases, and War Deity! I command you! By the Sampo that you covet, I command you! By the blood of my daughter!" Mom was screaming now, her voice a trumpet that buffeted my ears. The hair on her head began to rise and her eyes began to bulge. It was almost too much for her.

"Jeanie, now!" I yelled.

The British magician took Mom's free hand and held on for dear life, attempting to establish a connection, a pathway that would lend her strength to Mom's.

"I summon you, I summon you! By my blood, from the fury in my heart, I summon you! By the Sampo that is your heart's desire, I summon you!" Both women swayed, caught in the grip of torrential magic.

"I SUMMON YOU, YOU BASTARD!"

Her voice caused the hull of the old sub to ring like a gong, the vibrations tingling up my feet to my skull.

Then, for one clear moment, the world stopped.

Not a sound, not a stir, nor the lap of water against hull broke the stillness. Time was caught like a fly in amber, the universe momentarily placed under a bell jar.

Plop.

Plop.

Two small, quick sounds, fish jumping from water, broke the silence, freed time from its bonds and made everything *real* again.

"Oh, Kalevi," Mom moaned in misery and horror. "He's here."

Fifty feet away more fish began to jump from the water, flying high into alien air in an effort to escape what was coming. I knew what was coming and the hate burning inside me surfaced on my face.

And the hate that lived in the water burst forth, answering a call too powerful to ignore.

Jeanie and Mom screamed in unison, in shock and fear, overwhelmed by the power of what they'd summoned. Their eyes rolled in their sockets and they swayed, on the verge of passing out.

I did the only thing I could think of. I grabbed Jeanie's hand.

And was swept into the madness of a monster.

Chapter Thirty

Canton

Rage in a Cage

Right before Kal grabbed hold of Jeanie, I got a real close look at what he'd told me about all those years ago as a Green Pea, something I'd been itching to take a gander at for over ten years: A Class Five Supernatural, a being of mythic or god-like proportions.

Let me tell you, I don't ever wanna see one of those suckers again.

What exploded out of the water some fifteen yards away, sending fish flying everywhere, couldn't be defined, pigeon-holed into the frame of our reality. It had a shape, but it had none. I saw tentacles, and then I saw arms and then horns, the bearded face of an old man, leprous flesh stretching tightly over unclean bone and, finally, a giant, squid-like being with a mouth like a smashed asshole and gullet lined with pointed, rotting teeth. I think I lost forty pounds, all brown.

The two women next to the Tesla coil looked about ready to cash it in, so Kal grabbed Jeanie's hand to steady her. His back arched as if he'd stepped on the third rail in the New York subway. I could swear I smelled smoke coming from him, a rich, porky kind of odor.

I SEE YOU, CHILDREN OF SAMPSA PELLERVOINEN. IT WAS FOOLISH OF YOU TO CALL.

The voice slammed into my mind with stunning force, reeking of dead things and smug contempt.

I REMEMBER YOU, KALEVI HAKALA. YOU ARE KNOWN TO ME. YOUR SISTER WAS A PERFECT MORSEL.

Winch nearly crushed my hand in hers and I heard something come from her mouth I thought I'd never hear. A whimper.

274

"Damn, white boy," I muttered. "You really know how to throw a party."

YOU CANNOT KILL ME, KALEVI HAKALA. I AM FOREVER. GIVE UP YOUR SOUL AND I WILL LET THE OTHERS LIVE.

Why do monsters always have to monologue? A tentacle (or arm, whatever) smashed the side of the sub and it pitched wildly. In desperation, I grabbed hold of Kal's arm with my free hand.

Not the brightest move I'd ever made.

Wrenching disorientation. A swirling, spinning motion as we were pulled into Kal.

Lives passed between the five of us, memories and dreams surrounded by nightmares. A second later we were joined by a fifth. Pekka Hakala.

I became Winch, became Terhi, became Jeanie. Pekka slid right in, a man of ferocious discipline and resolve, like his son. Around us, Kal's soul circled like a shark, shielding us with the power of his tenacity from a monster we could finally see distinctly.

How to describe that roiling mass of energies that was Iku-Turso? The Apache have words for darn near everything, but watching that thing, words failed ... Hydra, Medusa, Chtulu, Leviathan ... all those and more joined together in an ever-shifting mass of malice and fury. Perhaps we all would have been driven mad had Kal not protected us—a man apart, always a loner guarding the flock of humanity. My friend's spirit had the flavor of metallic anger and the blistering salt of his hate. Hard to put into words what the Ghost World done showed us.

Our minds continued to merge and I felt the Hakalas' love for their son, their fierce pride and Jeanie's diamond-hard determination to do what needed to be done because she had found a kindred spirit in Kal, someone who was as soul-damaged as she, but who could still laugh and hock a loogie in the Devil's eye.

The part of me that was still Canton, moments before our souls blended together like paint, felt another love, a love that was directed at me. Winch ... my Diana Pennington. That love was hot and pure and the most important thing in her life and the glory of the moment was that I loved her just as much. We weren't friends with benefits, not anymore.

With a feeling of grace we moved, blended together and became one. I knew them and they knew me and it was so comforting not to be alone anymore.

I—we—felt something then, another presence that hated the monster, that wanted it dead and it took us a moment to realize it was the Sampo. The artifact, in a strange way, was alive and aware. It hated Iku-Turso, wanted the monster dead with an icy intensity no human could match.

Power flowed from the triangular box, through the coil and up to the ruby, into the flesh of our hands. We directed that power at Iku-Turso, while Kal protected us, and the great beast flinched.

With a roar, it redoubled its efforts to crush us to a bloody smear and grind us into the deck of the old sub. Kal took the blow, deflecting one of the tentacles, but his spirit flashed crimson in pain. He could not last much longer.

[Kal!] we cried. [come to us, join us, help us defeat the monster!]

[I can't] his spirit-voice was ragged. [If I try, our physical bodies will be destroyed.]

[Kalevi!] we screamed in anguish.

[It's okay, guys. I knew it would be end this way.]

As if expressing a brutal punctuation, Iku-Turso roared in anticipation of claiming the Sampo as its own. The artifact responded by doubling the energy supplied to the coil. The resultant blast tore a great chunk from the monster, black blood fouling the water.

We knew we could not take much more; our joined spirits as well as our physical bodies weren't built to channel that much energy. We could kill it, but doing so would kill us.

Which was fine.

Kal hurled his denial and dismay at us like a spear, but we continued our attack on the monster. Each blast of magical energy thinning the material that was us.

NO! Iku-Turso roared, its defiance now laced with fear.

[no]

What?

[no] firmer, the voice of a determined child.

Who?

[me]

And there she was.

Memories flooded into us, flooded Kal with their sweet poignancy. Leena, Kal's sister, our/Terhi/Pekka's daughter. The reel of her life played for us. Sunshine on blond hair and the smell of cut grass and apples. The comfort of sleeping in a car, perfectly safe because Dad was driving and he always protected you. Kal, beloved big brother who terrorized any bully who even *thought* of hurting you, and the smell of Finland, of green things and moisture.

On a little boat in the Gulf of Bothnia with Dad's cousin Juha, looking forward to the first bite of smoked perch and pike. Fear as fish flew out of the water, many landing, panicked and dying, in the boat. The tentacles bursting through the water's surface, the portal between liquid and air.

A tentacle wrapping its foul, slimy self around your waist and lifted you into the air, *squeezing*. Oh, God, it hurt so much! Where was Mommy? Where was Daddy? Kal was on the beach near a woman who held a burning white light in her hand as she screamed her demands at the thing holding you. Kal, staring in horror, crying. You knew he wanted to help, felt him call out to you with every fiber of his being but your death had come, it was over and blood shot from your mouth as something inside *gave*. The last sight you saw was Kalevi's grief-stricken face, mouth open so wide in a scream that no human throat could withstand and you know he had *seen* your death and had *seen* the monster for what it truly was and his mind had shattered like delicate crystal hurled at cement and he would die at any second.

Your spirit flew to him, entered him and cradled the remnant of his sanity. Slowly you glued the pieces of his mind together with the bonds of your soul, saving his life. You became part of Kalevi Hakala, part and separate. A protector, the keeper of his mind.

You slumbered, nestled in the infinite comfort of his soul and you dreamed, but sometimes you woke. Sometimes you saw Kal in danger and you had to help because you loved him so much, your big brother and he must never, ever die. You became the rage that fueled him, the rage that did his bidding and he used you to kill and kill and kill and you felt really, really good about that. Muscle, tendon, bone and ligaments, all protected by you as he used your rage to perform superhuman feats that would have normally crippled a body. Your rage, his tool, and together you were a team that could hardly lose and that made you so happy.

The rage was a powerful thing because it was fueled by unconditional love because what could cause more rage than love?

You didn't want Kal to die, you didn't want Mommy and Daddy to die, so you came up with a plan on the fly, one that could save everyone.

[Leena!] we all cried.

[don't worry kal/mom/dad i love you and this will work]

[What?] we cried as Kal joined with us and we felt him, burning so bright, but so alone, so tired, so spirit-weary. How could he have lived like that? But then we realized he was never alone ...

[watch this] Leena said, her soul a song of joy. [and give me the power to get it done]

We gave her the power, the Sampo responding eagerly, and watched.

From Kal's mind, from Jeanie's mind, Leena took a Shape, an almost infinitely complex Shape filled with loops and whorls, arcs and curlicues, and pushed that shape outward, fueled by titanic magic of the Sampo and coil.

We grasped her intent. Killing Iku-Turso was not an option for Leena, although for us it was a price we would have gladly paid. No, our daughter/sister/friend had come up with an alternate solution. Goebbels' spell Shape, the one used to travel to the World Under.

The Shape exploded into the cold water of the Bay around the thrashing monster and steam poured forth as we shoved more and more magic into its complex matrix.

A portal formed.

We were banishing Iku-Turso.

Blacker than night, the portal yawned, strange energies coruscating at its rim. Things swam in that darkness, hard things, things older than time, *hungry* great things. Things that wanted Iku-Turso's flesh, wanted to feed on it and take its power.

They were welcome to it.

It took much less energy to push the monster into and through the portal than it would have to kill it. With an incoherent cry of terror, the creature vanished into darker places.

Gone.

We stood there, our flesh mortified by vast, unfathomable energies, but we/Jeanie guided the magic to heal us and tissue began to knit, faltering hearts beat with renewed strength.

Kal spirit separated from ours and we cried out in negation, but to no avail. All that was him flowed toward a tired, fluttering thing, the spirit that was Leena, and they merged once again. We felt her return to slumber, but not without a pulse of love sent our way.

[goodbye mommy, goodbye daddy].

We wept.

Kal separated physically and the shock of feeling him gone broke our bonds …

And I fell to the deck, snot drooling down my chin and tears at the corner of my eyes. God, I hurt, a deep soul-weary kind of hurt that felt like it would last a dog's age.

Winch … Diana … lay nestled next to me, eyes half shut, and I knew that we would never be separated again.

I chuckled at my mushy sentimentality and she grinned, eyes still half closed.

"Kiss me, you pussy," she drawled lazily.

Who was I to disobey orders?

When we came up for air, the first sight that slapped against my eyes was Kal and his parents sitting on the deck, arms wrapped tight around one another's.

I waited until the clinch ended before saying, "*Damn*, white boy, you sure do know how to throw a party."

Chapter Thirty-One

Kal

Out of the Frying Pan, into the Bureau

I couldn't feel her. No matter how hard I tried, Leena remained beyond reach like always, my silent protector.

It was still night, only a couple hours later, but with the amount of magical energy we had produced, we must have lit up every sensor along the Pacific Rim. It wouldn't be long.

My feet dangled a few feet above the calm water of the Bay, Jeanie at my side leaning against my shoulder. We hadn't spoken a word since the fight. None were needed.

Canton escorted Mom and Dad to their hotel, Winch trailing not far behind, and I knew she wouldn't let him out of her sight. Good for her.

"That was amazing, Mr. Hakala."

Jeanie stirred from the shelter of my arm as Harcourt tromped the final few feet to us. "Thanks," I replied, sounding dog tired.

His rattlesnake boots stopped directly behind. "You know, for years I resented you. All I heard was 'Kal this' and 'Kal that.' It drove me nuts how many stories Gran told us kids."

"She was an amazing woman."

"No doubt about that."

"So, how do you feel now?"

A pause. "After seeing what I saw, I wish I could apologize to the old girl. You're everything she described and more."

What an idiot.

"Don't be too impressed, kid," I huffed. "Most of the time I just get lucky."

"Luck is a useful skill, too."

True.

I craned my head around. "You said your name was K. Harcourt ... the 'K' wouldn't happen to stand for 'Kal,' would it?"

His teeth shone very white in the dark. "No, sir. Not at all. It stands for Kenneth." He turned and clomped away in those ridiculous boots. "I had it legally changed five years ago."

I had to laugh.

"What's so funny?" came a familiar voice.

"Hiya, BB. What took you so long?"

"Traffic." The Director of the BSI sat down next to me on the dock, a briefcase on his lap.

I looked at the woman with the big, big eyes. "Jeanie, do you mind?"

She smiled and kissed me tenderly. It was everything I'd hoped it would be. I watched her sway as she walked away. She had a very nice ... sway.

Back to business. "How long have you known, BB?"

"That you were alive? Or that you traveled back into the past to 1943?"

"Both."

He scratched his graying head. What remained of his hair stuck out at odd angles, a testament to his lack of sleep. "To the first, I always knew. The second, well ... when I became Director."

My eyes opened wide. "How and how?" I blurted.

His laugh irritated the hell out of me. "You remember your yearly physicals?"

"Of course."

"Four years ago we developed a device so small it can't be seen with the naked eye. A nano-locater. You've been lojacked for the past few years."

Interesting.

Still, something nagged at me. "How long has Ghost been reporting on me?" A shot in the dark.

That shot hit home. BB smiled and said, "The whole time you were gone."

Hmph. Figured, the sneaky spook. "How come you never stopped me? You could've at any time."

"Of course, but if I stopped you, you couldn't have beaten that monster of yours."

I almost snarled that it wasn't my monster, but wisely kept my trap shut.

"You see, Kal, we are the BSI, we kill the Supernaturals that prey on the people we're sworn to protect. Iku-Turso had been a thorn in our side for some time, but we couldn't take direct action because of our close ties to Finland."

"So you 'pushed' me into faking my own death?"

He shook his head. "No, you did that all on your own. Hell, I thought you would just cut-and-run."

"So you used me."

BB stared hard into my eyes. "What would you have done in my position?"

Good question. I considered it a few moments and sighed. "Exactly the same thing. Let a 'rogue' agent you could easily disavow kill a monster valuable to Finland's heritage without damaging relations, should the Finns find out."

"Got it in one, Kal."

Hmm ... looked like I wasn't as clever as I thought. A humbling experience, dealing with BB. "And the other?"

Click, click went the catches on the briefcase and a file landed in my waiting hands.

It was an old, pre-'80s folder, olive drab with the words TOP SECRET in bold, faded letters on the front. I opened the file.

And there, in glossy, grainy, black and white, was a photo of yours truly. The camera had caught me full on, my eyes staring at a point to the left of the lens, my face a mask of both consternation and fury. It looked as if my arms were resting on one of those folding poker tables.

I knew exactly when the picture had been taken ... 1943, my interrogation by the MI-7's Colonel and Bureau Agent Oliver. My face flushed at the memory. I hadn't even seen a camera.

Behind the photo were several typewritten pages, all single-spaced. On those pages were everything I'd discussed with the

Colonel, along with an After-Action report from Richard Fleming and one Rebecca McTavish. Detailed records of who I was, where I was from and what I had accomplished.

"Damn," I muttered.

"Thanks to close relations with MI-7, the Bureau has known you your whole life, Kal, and has been watching you."

"The Bureau could've—" I blurted.

"Saved your sister?" BB finished. "Not hardly. We are not in the habit of changing the future, or the past, or whatever."

I recalled Mouth's letter. "Everything I did, the people I killed, didn't accomplish a damn thing, then."

"I don't know, Kal. Maybe there were things that changed, but only minutely, on a scale we cannot measure. Time abhors a paradox and will do what it can to safeguard the Big Picture."

"The Big Picture?"

"Yes, and it's a very Big Picture indeed. One person alone isn't enough to change it." BB once again dug into the briefcase. "As for you not changing anything, well, here's something that was given to me by my Mossad counterpart the first time you went to Israel to cross-train with their agents. Give it a look and tell me you didn't accomplish a damn thing."

A hardback book landed in my hands, the dust cover faded and crinkly. The front depicted a swastika crumbling apart in a pair of strong hands. The title read, *Legends of the Holocaust: God's wrath and the Call Hakola.*

It was enough to make my mind wobble and slide off the rails a bit.

"Seems like you had more of an impact than you thought," BB said dryly.

"The Jews ... the ones released from the Natzweiler caves ..."

"They spread the story, the legend, of a stranger who bore God's Wrath against the Nazis. The stranger was faster than the wind and crushed Germans under his feet. It was further evidence of your travel to the past. We were in some doubt, because the notes

Ms. Fleming had left indicated you had served in the Bureau for ten years." He grinned, a rare event. "Imagine that."

Imagine that, indeed.

A thought occurred to me. "BB, what are you going to do about that other world? The one with the Coliseum?"

He pursed his lips. "Oh, the President, in what I consider to be unprecedented wisdom, has declared it off-limits except for a cadre of select scientists. The Bureau will keep it secret from the rest of the world. Maybe someday mankind will once again step on the soil of a different world. But first we have to use the one we inhabit with a little more wisdom."

"The President said that?"

"Yep."

"Hmm ... maybe I should've voted for him."

That earned me a laugh. "Good job with the coil, by the way," he chuckled.

Oh, Lord. "You've known about that since the beginning, right?"

"Right."

"What are you going to do with it?"

He pursed his lips. "It's potentially a WMD, so we're going to bury it, hide it and the knowledge of how to make it until there comes a time we really need the thing. Like we did with the Unholy Grail and Spear of Longinus. There are some things man shouldn't mess with."

True. I had to give the boss bonus points; he was worried more about people than politics.

"What now, BB?"

"What do you mean, what now?"

Dammit, he was toying with me! "What's going to happen to me now?" I grated.

"Oh, that 'what now.' Well, how about you come on back to the Bureau?"

"What if I don't want to?"

"Forgive me ... I phrased that as a question, but it wasn't at all."

Oh.

"And?"

BB sucked in a deep breath. "We're still rebuilding the Bureau after that Whitcombe fiasco. We've recruited several people, but we've had to take some … shortcuts. I want you to help us remedy those shortcuts."

"Remedy, how?"

"You are going to assume a brand new position in the Bureau as its one-hundred-first asset. Fifty agents, fifty support personnel, including Special Branch and Secretaries, and one kickass Recruit Trainer."

"You have got to be fu—"

"No, I'm not," he shot back, steely eyes colder than winter. "Your mission is to do your damndest to keep those Green Peas alive, to show them how to kill Supernaturals. Consider yourself Green Pea Leader One."

Oh, lovely. What was next, sodomy and mutilation? "And?"

"What?"

I sighed. "There's always an 'And,' BB."

"And you will do whatever I tell you to do. As always."

My mind raced furiously, trying to find an out, but I couldn't come up with a single one. I had technically violated my contract, which meant I broke the law, and when Bureau people broke the law, they tended to disappear with abrupt finality. It wasn't hard to figure out which way I'd jump.

Crap.

I squinted at the boss. "Couple things, BB."

He squinted right back. "What would they be?"

My hand came up, fingers spread in a V. "One: repeal, at least temporarily, the ban on relationships in the Bureau. You can recruit from ex-agents who haven't adjusted fully to civilian life. It will fill a lot of gaps for you. Besides, the Brits never had a policy against it; only the Russians and ourselves made it taboo."

BB scratched his head and considered this for a minute. "Granted. That's a good idea. At least until we fill the ranks for a couple years running. But I thought for you that way led to madness."

A few months ago I would have been vehemently against the idea of an agent forming a relationship while in the Bureau. What had changed? I thought of Mouth and Richard, Edith and the Colonel and of my own barren life, of my first love that I had kicked to curb in my near-insane quest for revenge. All those years of loneliness, trying to fill the void in my guts with a series of one-night stands with women I didn't even find interesting. A life devoid of intimacy because to be intimate was to admit weakness, a vulnerability that could get you killed. But I realized something in my hiatus from the Bureau, realized that all my carefully constructed adamantine walls against personal attachments …

I realized I had been full of crap.

It wasn't intimacy that made you weak; it wasn't love, or friendship. Those things made you strong, kept you fighting against all odds. No, the real weakness was being alone because that kind of solitude could leave you wide open for spiritual poison, the kind that turns a person into an uncaring automaton.

"Things change, boss," was my only reply.

BB never missed a trick. His watery eyes bored into mine and he snorted. "What's the second thing, Kal?" he asked softly.

I lowered one finger, leaving only the middle one. "Don't leave me at the Warehouse wiping the noses of those Green Peas all of the time, boss. I need to get out and see some action once in a while. Have my own team."

Watery eyes half-hidden behind glasses stared at my middle finger and then his lips twitched in a smile that disappeared so fast I was afraid it had never been. "Okay, Kal, you got it. See you Monday."

Monday? "This Monday, Boss?"

BB nodded and stood, pulling one last item out of the briefcase. "Yes."

"That's tomorrow!"

"Then you better get some rest." Something dark flew through the air and landed in my lap. My fingers tightened on leather before it could fall into the Bay. "Here, a present long overdue. Been in a safe at Warehouse for the past sixty-eight years. Waiting for you." With that he walked off into the night.

In my hands was a book. Old, leather bound with gold inlay. I whistled … a first edition of *The Hobbit*. On the inside cover was faded, cramped writing in an impeccable hand:

> *To Kalevi Hakala,*
>
> *Thank you for all you have done for King and Country. We will always remember what you have achieved even though the world of the mundane will never know your sacrifices.*
>
> *We recalled, after you left our company, your request for an autographed copy of this book and are more than happy to oblige. We hope, in time, that the volume reaches your hands.*
>
> *With our sincere thanks and fond wishes,*
>
> *Yours,*
> *Edith and Colonel John Ronald Reuel Tolkien*
> *His Majesty's MI-7*

Interesting-er.

COMING SOON, BOOK THREE

FROM THE FILES OF THE BSI

I LEFT MY HAUNT IN SAN FRANCISCO

Born in Helsinki, Finland, **Mark Everett Stone** arrived in the U.S. at a young age and promptly dove into the world of the fantastic. Starting at age seven with the Iliad and the Odyssey, he went on to consume every scrap of Norse Mythology he could get his grubby little paws on. At age thirteen he graduated to Tolkien and Heinlein, building up a book collection that soon rivaled the local public library's. In college Mark majored in Journalism and minored in English. Mark's first book, *Things to Do in Denver When You're Un-Dead*, was published by Camel Press in July of 2011. *The Judas Line* will be released in 2012.

Mark lives in Denver with his amazingly patient wife, Brandie, and their two sons, Aeden and Gabriel. You can find Mark on the Web at www.markeverettstone.com.